Lacey Goes to Tokyo

by C.H. Lyn

Miss Belle's Travel
Guides Book 1

COPYRIGHT

Copyright © 2019 by C.H. Lyn

Third edition.

Cover Art by Tracey Barski

Edited by Lucy Felthouse

Proofread by Sharon Pickrel and Tracey Barski

Content Warning

Violence
Language
Homophobia
Loss of a Parent
Mention of Child Abuse
Mention of Sexual Assault
Attempted Sexual Assault

Hey there, readers. This content warning page is a little tricky, and I want to be as clear as possible. This book, and series, covers a lot of hard topics. Child abuse, forced sex work, sexual assault, etc. At NO point in this book will there be a description of rape. At NO point in this book is there a sex scene between a sex worker and client. Later books contain romantic scenes, purely between loving, consenting adults.

Chapter 9 contains a dream during which sexual assault is mentioned. Chapter 16 contains an attempted rape—the scene is short and not from the perspective of the victim.

It is the opinion of this author that, while these are real life problems that must be addressed, they are portrayed in television and books often enough. None of the books in this series will detail the sexual abuse of any person because that is not something I want to write.

DEDICATION

For my girls, my friends, and all the women in my life.

I love you.

Preparing the Journey

Don't leave clothes in the wash or dishes in the sink. The smell is gross, but you also don't want a bunch of chores to do when you get home.

Put clean sheets on your bed before you leave. This will make collapsing at the end of your trip much more enjoyable.

Make sure plants are watered and general clutter is cleaned up.

If someone is watching your house and/or pet, leave a list of instructions. Even if you've already told them everything, a list will help make sure they remember the little things each day.

Store weapons, equipment, anything that can be called probable cause in a secure place. Having your house sitter find your ammo cache probably won't end well.

Set lights on a timer. It will look like someone is home at different times of the day. This helps limit the potential for break-ins and frustrates police surveillance.

If no one is watching your house, let a trusted neighbor know you'll be out of town. Ask if they can collect your mail. A full mailbox several days in a row is a dead giveaway that no one is home.

Suspend newspaper delivery for the time you are gone. A stack of papers on the curb is another sign that your home is vacant.

Make sure someone you trust has an itinerary of where you will be. Try to check in periodically. Always use a burner; tracing a call is almost instantaneous, no matter what Hollywood says.

Have a secure home base waiting for you.

CHAPTER ONE

MISS BELLE

THE COLOR RED

There's a gentle pop as I open my silver and black compact and use the reflection to check the street behind me. I've stopped three times already: to check my phone, search for a missing item, and to unstick my not-actually-stuck heel.

The footsteps paused each time, but none of my false excuses gave me the chance to look behind. You can never just glance back. Once someone knows you've seen them, their need to be discreet goes right out the window.

I pull a small black cylinder from the clutch and roll up the brilliant stick of red. I am a firm believer that red lipstick should be applied only on special occasions. Red is a significant color and deserving of respect. My father gave my mother red tulips on the day of my birth and that of my sister. My brother proposed to his husband with a bouquet of red roses. And before Nana died, she requested to be buried in her stunning red dress.

Tonight has been a night for red. And continues to be as the figure behind me takes a silent step forward. I apply a thin coat to my bottom lip and push it to the top, running my lips together the way Nana taught me years ago when we played Shirley Temple.

The shadows passing through my tiny makeup mirror tell me the man on my tail is closer than anticipated, and I have a few blocks left to go. I close the compact with a satisfying snap and continue on, my heels clicking against the dirty cement.

You would expect a shadow to be rather uninformative, but from his height, girth, and the way he sticks to the middle of the sidewalk rather than skulking along the wall, he must be one of three possible men, all of whom share the same profession. I exhale, releasing the tension I'd been holding. Whichever of the men he turns out to be, the threat is minimal. Annoyance, rather than fear, creeps into the beginnings of a headache.

I pull my phone out again, for a real reason this time. My girls keep nagging me about an upgrade. I flip the sturdy plastic up and click through the contacts.

To Marissa, I send:

Headed home. Make sure the girls did their chores and kept the Manor clean ;)

A wicked grin curls my lips at the smiley face. I can picture it now: some district attorney up in front of the judge with a whiny, indignant voice. "See, Your Honor. She used a wink in this text message. What do you think *that* means?"

And the judge gives him the highest of eyebrow raises before dismissing the case entirely.

I glance back now—discretion on my part is no longer necessary. The last few blocks pass uneventfully, and when I arrive at the steps to the Manor, I turn back around and smile as the man steps under a streetlight.

"Officer McKinley." I grin. "How lovely to see you. You didn't follow me all the way from the gala, did you? Seems like an awful waste of taxpayer money."

McKinley glares. "It's *Detective*."

I can't help but chuckle, which only makes him more frustrated.

"Oh, do come in, Detective."

He doesn't like my tone, but of course, he follows me up the steps. Any offer of access to my home is one that this particular thorn in my side just can't resist.

He waits patiently as I knock rather than dig through the clutch for my keys. Marissa—Missa, as I've called her since childhood—opens the door, a knowing smile playing across her lips.

"Miss Belle, you're home early." She steps aside and gives me a peck on the cheek as I cross the threshold. "And Officer McKinley, lovely to see you again." A surprised smile lights up her face, eyes widening to sell the effect. She, of course, is anything but surprised by our malevolent visitor; good communication pays off.

"It's Detective." He glares again but follows me through the door and into the grand foyer. His gaze catches on the spiral patterns along the ceiling, in decorative contrast to the eggshell blue walls.

I love the Manor. From the stone steps leading to the massive, intricately carved wooden door, to the high ceilings and the gazebo in the backyard, everything about this house is perfect to me. It has always been perfect. From the moment the realtor walked Missa and I up those same steps almost eight years ago.

Sure, the stairs winding up to the second story, and then the third, needed sanding to avoid splinters on bare feet. And we gutted one of the many bedrooms on the second floor to replace it with an expansive library. But aside from a few cosmetic changes, the Manor was everything I'd ever wanted in a home. Its soul was exactly what we'd been looking for. Finding it, only a week after arriving in New York, seemed like it was meant to be.

Since outright buying the place—cash—Missa and I have gathered a collection of antique tables, chairs, and paintings. They now line the hallways of all three floors. I'm not a fan of carpet, but we do have a few beautiful Turkish rugs thrown over the hardwood. My favorite is on the third floor—an embroidered tiger lurking in the jungle.

The foyer leads into the living room, a community space for all my girls to relax and a nice big area for game night. I'm still suspended from Monopoly—what with Missa needing to get new dice after *someone* chucked them out the window. I don't like to lose.

We have a flat-screen TV, the new Xbox One, PS 4, and Nintendo, lined against the far wall. The inaccurate sounds from a first-person shooter game filter in through the hallway.

On either side of the TV are shelves and shelves full of books—placed there once we'd filled the library upstairs. A massive coffee table sits in the center of the room on one of my rugs and is surrounded by dark brown couches, loveseats, and two recliners.

The kitchen sits beyond. My stomach rumbles at the scent of a late dinner wafting into the foyer. I can't wait to try Sarah's newest recipe.

I set my clutch and phone on the long cherrywood table to the right of the front door and turn to my guest. "What can I help you with this evening, Detective?"

"You can tell me what you were doing at that gala."

Sad. I thought he'd have more to justify following me home. Not that I'm disappointed. I'd rather contend with a bored cop chasing his tail than someone who actually knows what they're doing.

"Is it a crime to attend the New York Gala?" A hint of malevolence in my voice turns the joke at his expense.

"I don't see how a travel writer merits an invitation."

"I'm pretty sure that's on the list of things that are my business." Without my say so, the patience I've been clinging to slips from my grasp. "Is there anything I can actually help you with?"

Missa's gaze narrows; I'm usually a little more polite when dealing with the police. But it's been a long night, I have bookings to confirm, and the dull seed of a headache has blossomed into a throbbing behind my right temple.

"You can cut the crap and admit what's going on here." He takes a step forward, trying to intimidate. But a middle-aged, overweight, underpaid, balding man in a suit made ten years ago, is hard to be intimidated by. And he's not the first to request I 'cut the crap.'

It's all I can do to keep from rolling my eyes. "Whatever you think is happening, isn't. I run a legal, respectable, lucrative business. And frankly, I'm tired of you and your pals skulking around and disturbing my girls."

Missa gives me a look, and I sigh. I've been playing nice with assholes all evening and don't have the patience for this.

"Can I get you a few cookies for the road, Detective?" Missa smiles.

McKinley's hard look softens. A flash of lust glints in his eye and his lips tilt up in a reluctant effort to return the smile.

This is why we work so well together. I may be sharp, but damn, she's got the looks. Long, golden hair, brilliant blue eyes, sometimes partially obscured by her wide-framed glasses, and the kind of legs models wish they had. It helps that she's already in her pajamas, and it's a warm spring night.

Missa and I got everyone matching pajamas for Christmas last year, which didn't really work since we all share a washing machine. But Missa kept hers, and the violet silk booty shorts and flowery tank top are working wonders on my policeman problem.

He nods helplessly, and I can't suppress my grin. Missa turns and bounces through the living room into the kitchen. A few of the girls ask some questions, but she tells them to hush and wait.

With the beautiful woman out of the room, McKinley returns to his usual self. He looks me up and down, taking in the black, strappy heels, and striped black and silver dress. Like most women, I'm much more comfortable in jeans and a graphic tee, but I do dress up for business.

"This is getting old, Belle. You know we're on this house like rats on the subway. Eventually, you're gonna slip up, and I'll be there when you do."

Part of me wants to tell him he'd make better headway getting rid of the rats.

"*I* think eventually you're going to get tired of this. You have no proof of any wrongdoing, just a head full of suspicions, a few phony complaints, and a captain riding your ass to be done with this." I purse my lips and cross my arms over my chest. I want him to make the next move, to fold, or give me something to work with.

He shakes his head and rubs his temple. He takes a couple steps and glances into the living room, but there's nothing to see. A few girls are playing Modern Warfare, one or two are reading, and the rest are helping finish up dinner. We know how to keep a clean house.

He comes back and leans against the staircase. I can tell he's not done, even though it's almost two in the morning and he surely has other places to be. But I'm not bending, so he goes for the Hail Mary. "You've got a house full of whores here. And I'm going to prove it. This place is a fucking disgrace, and you're gonna rot in jail for as long as possible."

Now, I'm already frustrated because it's late, I've got an early morning, and I had to shake hands with a bunch of dicks-for-brains politicians tonight. Oh, and the headache.

I only have a few things that truly set me off. I don't like animal cruelty, I hate child abuse, I can't stand homophobia, texting while driving irritates the shit out of me, and when I haven't eaten for three or four hours I become a real bitch. But nothing, *nothing* sets me off, like someone calling my girls whores.

And that's when I make a mistake.

I stride forward, heels bringing me nose to nose with this prick, and tell him to get the fuck out of my house. My cheeks and the tips of my ears burn. My heart pounds, jaw clenches, and hands curl into fists.

Excellent timing, as that's when Missa comes back in with a Tupperware container full of chocolate chip cookies. "Here you go." She flashes him a bright grin. "Some for the rest of the precinct."

But she stops a few feet away, her eyes on me now as I am way too close to an officer of the law and clearly about to do something stupid. Her head tilts just a smidgeon to the left, and her eyes widen in a warning look that pierces through the red haze to reach me. A talent only she has.

I step back, take the Tupperware from her, and pass it into McKinley's hands. "It's been a long night, Detective. If you have any more questions, maybe we can talk in the morning." It sounds like a question... It's not a question.

"Yeah, all right."

He opens the door, and Missa gives a cute little wave. As usual, he can't help one last jab before he goes. "Don't *work* too hard."

I slam the door behind him; the glass rattles in the window.

Missa's smile disappears faster than those cookies will. "What the fuck, Belle?"

At her tone, the fire in me dissipates as quickly as it came, and I'm left with a drained, sore body, and a stupid headache. "I know, I know. I'm sorry. It was a long night, Missa."

"So, you antagonize the police?"

"I was as polite as can be up until the end."

She gives me 'the look.' "Well, that's just some bullshit."

"All right, fine—I was as polite as *I* could be."

"And what exactly happened when I left the room?" Missa puts a hand on her silky, pajama-clad hip and raises an eyebrow.

I sigh again and lower my voice. "He said we have a house full of whores."

She rolls her eyes and glares at me. "Well, yeah, we do."

I can't do this right now. The tight dress is pinching my skin, my ankles ache in these high heels, my hair is pulled back, and a very uncomfortable bra is suffocating my boobs. "Missa, can we drop it, at least for now?"

It doesn't take more than that because she knows. She sees right through me. She flashes another one of her smiles, this one sincere and loving, and nods. "Turn around." Her soft yet firm voice could compel armies to return home.

I obey, and she takes the pins out of my hair and unzips my dress.

"Now, go upstairs," she loves to do lists, "get changed," they make her feel centered, "and then come down, have some dinner, and relax with the family." Tick off one task, then the next; she's quite methodical.

"I've got so much booking to do." I try to keep the whine out of my voice. "There were a lot more clients at the gala than we expected."

"And you've got them all memorized, you don't let people book less than seventy-two hours in advance, and you can work on it tomorrow. For now, put on some pajamas and come hang out."

"This is why I love you, Missa."

"I know."

She prances into the living room, and I hurry upstairs to my bedroom. Ten minutes later I'm back with my hair in a ponytail. Gray sweats and a giant yellow sweatshirt have replaced the dress, and a pair of super fuzzy socks have replaced the heels.

As I step into the living room, everything decompresses. Alex and Anita are playing video games. Anita is winning, but Alex will catch on soon enough. Anita is a pro. Her jet-black hair is pulled into a braid, her eyes intense, focused on the screen.

Lacey is reading Tracey Barski's latest suspense novel, a pale pink cardigan draped over her shoulders, her knees pulled up to her chest.

Jeanette is working on a puzzle on the coffee table, and laughter echoes in from the kitchen.

I follow the sound and find Sarah and Missa dishing out platefuls of pasta. When Sarah sees me, she lets out a yelp and gives me a hug. This girl is the huggiest person I've ever met. When we found her in Detroit, she really didn't seem like the kind of person who would hug that often. At work, she's a badass. A dominatrix, actually; it's her specialty.

Josie is perched up on the counter, running a hand through her newest hairdo, a bright pink pixie cut. Josie has a unique skill; she looks like she's twelve. It helps to have a girl who looks like she's twelve and is actually twenty-two because it means the girls who *are* twelve can go to school rather than do the things she does.

You don't like me right now, I can tell. People don't usually like me when they find out what I do. Then again, people don't often find out what I do.

I don't have some horrible back story. I had a nice dad, a caring mom, a fun nana, and a decent education. My reasons for this business are my own, though if you get far enough along, you'll find out what I'm doing here. A girl born and raised in a quiet town in Northern California, living in New York City, and playing pimp to a bunch of hookers.

Though, as I said before, nothing pisses me off more than people calling my girls whores. They're so much more than that.

Missa calls that food is ready. Josie hops from the counter and sets the table that consumes the center of the space. After a moment, soft jazz replaces the sound of gunfire from the video game. Alex and Anita, still talking about their rivalry, fetch glasses for everyone as they enter the kitchen. Lacey follows them, her nose still in the book, and Jeanette trudges behind after a few minutes, disappointed she had to leave her puzzle.

I sit at the head of the table and watch my girls. They're not really girls; they're women. Strong, independent, beautiful, and incredibly intelligent women. Warmth fills me, chasing away the cold detachment I form when dealing with cops and clients.

We eat and, as usual, the food is delicious. Sarah started out not knowing how to make cereal, but following a course on cuisine, she can do anything in the kitchen.

"How'd it go, Miss Belle?" The hint of an Austrian accent dances across Jeanette's voice.

"It went really well. We got a few new contacts. Some in France." I eye Anita. She takes every opportunity to get over there for the shopping. "And some regulars updated their information."

Sarah's pasta is amazing, and I tell her so. Homemade shell noodles, sautéed chunks of garlic, a hint of spice that tingles my tongue but probably doesn't even register with Alex or Anita. I close my eyes and savor the crunch of roasted asparagus sprinkled with parmesan cheese. We eat in a comfortable silence, broken by munching and the soothing tones of Ellington filtering in from the living room.

"Who did you see this time?" Alex leans forward, her black braids falling in front of her shoulders.

I swallow my bite and grin at the eager look on her face. "Well, George Clooney wasn't at this one, but I did see someone from your favorite movie."

Her dark eyes go wide; her favorite movie is *The Devil Wears Prada.* And there's a specific actress she's utterly obsessed with.

"I also saw our favorite VP." I turn to Missa, sarcasm lacing my voice.

She rolls her eyes; I hate our Vice President.

"What time did Damen go to bed?" I ask. I need to schedule *another* assignment with him and the VP. Poor kid.

"A few hours ago," Missa shakes her head. "Prentice set another appointment with him?"

"Yup."

She growls. "There's nothing worse than a fucking hypocrite."

"My dear," I stand and stretch, "there's nothing better than a rich hypocrite."

She gives an eyeroll, but I know she agrees. Putting powerful men in compromising situations gives us a lot more to work with than putting powerful men in normal situations.

I kiss the top of Missa's head, grab hers and my dishes, and set them in the sink. "I'm off to bed. It's been a long night. Lacey? When's your flight in the morning?"

"JFK to Heathrow 9 a.m., Heathrow to Haneda 5:30 p.m. I should be in Tokyo a few hours before the appointment, plenty of time for setup." She doesn't look up, her mousey nose still stuck in her book.

My heartbeat quickens. The way it always does when one of the Guides is about to go on a mission. I step behind her chair, wrap an arm around her shoulders, and kiss her temple.

My steady voice does not betray my anxiety. "Good. Message me when you get to the airport. I plan on sleeping in."

I trudge up to the second floor and press an ear against Damen's door. The kid has nightmares sometimes. All is quiet, and I groan as I climb the last set of stairs. The temptation to collapse is strong, but I've got garlic tomato sauce in my teeth and I don't fancy the taste of that in the morning so I move on to the bathroom and pluck my toothbrush from its jar on the counter. My zombie eyes glare at me from my reflection as minty bubbles drip down my chin.

Winter sheets are still on my bed. Silky powder blue ones are folded at the foot of the bed, but there is no motivation to change them right now. So, I crawl between brown cotton flannel and succumb to my dreams.

CHAPTER TWO

MISS BELLE

A HEALTHY BREAKFAST

I wake up in a heavy sweat. I had the dream again. That, plus flannel on a seventy-degree night, is too much. The covers have already been kicked to the floor. I sit up and plant my feet firmly on the cold wood. It's been two weeks and three days since I dreamt of that night.

I always thought it would be the eyes. Whenever I watched a movie, and someone died... I always thought if I saw a dead body, the eyes would catch me. Lifeless. Soulless. But it's not the eyes that get me. It's the red. The blood flowing from their bodies, through the cracks in the wood, dripping down into the water. The weight of the cold metal presses into my hand. I can't unclench my fingers, even as I wake and find that I'm holding my sheets, not the forty-five caliber.

I take several deep breaths, willing my muscles to relax. Eventually, my fingers are mine again. I rub my temples.

Missa's scream still echoes in my head as I stand and stretch. It's 8 a.m.; so much for sleeping in. I can never go back to bed after one of my nightmares. But they come less often now. They shouldn't still come at all. It's been almost eight years.

I check my phone. Lacey will be at the airport by now. That girl is early to everything. It's because she doesn't mind waiting. She's got more patience in her pinky than I do in my whole body. Sure enough, a polite, to the point—*At the airport, boarding in 30 minutes*—winks up at me from the screen.

A crash sounds from downstairs and my gaze snaps straight to the monitor sitting on my desk. A bird moves on the upper right corner of the screen—one of the exterior cameras—but nothing is out of place.

"Damen dropped a dish!" Missa yells up the stairs at me.

An unexpected sigh of relief makes me grumpy. There's no reason to be so paranoid. And yet, as a woman in my line of work... shouldn't I always be paranoid?

I didn't always want to run an elite escort service. When I was young, I wanted to be an actress, then a cop, a career woman, and later a philanthropist. Missa and I grew up together. She went off to school in LA, and I stayed at my community college, working on a history degree and living with my then-fiancé. But one thing led to another, and here we are.

I gaze out the massive bay window. It's got a light coat of tint—not for any nefarious reason, but because I sleep in a pair of undies and don't feel like flashing the whole street in the morning. My bedroom is on the third floor, so that helps. So does the magnificent Norway Maple in the front yard.

I can make out a gray pedo-van across the street between the branches. A plumber sticker is pasted to the side. I can tell you one thing: we are *not* buying tickets to the policemen's ball this year. This is getting ridiculous. They're probably in there stuffing their faces with Sarah's cookies.

I pull on a dark green tank top and settle cross-legged on the squishy armchair in front of my desk. Last night was busy. I met with almost a dozen guys, and one very excited lady, and have calls scheduled throughout the next few days. The first one isn't until this afternoon, so I've got time to set up some spreadsheets and study my calendar.

My cell buzzes and I frown at the name on the screen. It's 7 a.m. in New Orleans. My little brother should be sleeping in and enjoying Sunday brunch with his husband. I flip it open. "Hey, Nicky, what's new?"

"What the fuck, Ana?"

I haven't had my coffee yet. The confusion is pretty intense.

"What?" I snap. I squinty-glare at my computer screen since Nicky isn't there to glare at.

"Are you next to a computer?"

"Yes."

"Check your email. And get a new damn phone so you can check it while talking on the phone."

"That's exactly what I'm doing," I grumble. "Talking on the phone and checking my email. Jesus, Nicky, you sure know how to say good morning."

"Just click the link in the fucking email."

"I'm going!" I yell into the phone. Nicky is pissed, and I'm racking my brain to figure out why. But then I see his email and the URL of the link he attached. And I get it.

I double-click. There I am, on some stupid celebrity news website. *Vice President Chats With Locals at New York Gala.* I'm wearing that silver and black dress. A glass of champagne is in one hand; my head is thrown back in a laugh. I'm flashing my most convincing fake smile, and I'm shaking hands with the most homophobic politician our nation has had in a long time.

A stone plummets into my empty stomach.

I get it.

"Nicky…"

"Don't," he spits into the phone. I hear the hurt, and my heart breaks. "Just don't, Ana. I can't believe you."

"Nicky." I need him to listen.

"Do you know what he's doing next week? Your new friend? He's trying to make my marriage illegal! He's trying to pass the bill *next week*, and you're at a party with him?"

"Nicky, please listen to me." Shit. My hairs stand on end, the muscles in my neck and back tightening with stress. How am I going to get out of this one?

I hear mumbling on his end, followed by, "I'm coming, sweetie, go back to bed."

Nicky focuses back on me, his horrible eldest sister. "I just don't get it, Ana. How dare you." His voice cracks.

"Nicky, come on. You know I'm not like that."

"I don't know anything about you. Not anymore." There's a click and then the dial tone.

My eyes burn, and I chuck my phone at the wall. It thunks and drops to the floor completely unharmed.

"Damn."

I turn around. Missa stands by the door, my Serenity mug in her hand, the scent of coffee rising with the steam. "Nicky?"

"Yeah." I sniff. "I haven't seen him since the wedding, and I had to run pretty quick after the reception."

"Fucking Russians."

"Yeah." I rub my neck with one hand and reach for the coffee with the other. Missa walks over, hands me the mug, and leans against my chair to read the computer screen.

"Shit… No wonder he's pissed."

"I know. And I can't *tell* him anything." Tears burn at my eyes again.

"It'll be fine, Belle. That bill isn't making it to the floor, much less passing."

"But Nicky won't know why. He'll still think I'm some homophobic asshole."

"We'll take care of it. We always do." She turns and heads to the door. "Come down soon, okay? Sarah made breakfast, and you've got to eat before you start working."

I nod, and she shuts the door.

The coffee is hot and strong. Just how I like it. What's the damn point of sweetener anyway? Drink a fucking hot chocolate if you don't like the taste of the bean.

A sigh escapes my lips. Last time I saw Nicky was almost two years ago. He and Ray had a beautiful wedding on a beach in Florida. My sister and I were in the wedding party, and our parents were overjoyed. So were Ray's. He's a sweet guy. They met in college in New Orleans, and now they both work in the music industry down there.

I wouldn't blame Nicky if he thought I didn't agree with his lifestyle... I hate that word. Being gay isn't a lifestyle.

Anyway, I had to leave the wedding early. Literally right after the first dance. I didn't have a choice. Jeanette had called; trouble in St. Petersburg. Someone stole a flash drive with a timeline for troop advancement into Ukraine. All flights in and out of the country had been suspended for seventy-two hours, and the poor girl was stuck in Russia.

That was the last time I saw Nicky. After an urgent goodbye, I ran from my baby brother's wedding. And sure, I call him. I send Christmas gifts and birthday cards, but it's been far too long since I've seen him.

I see my sister a lot more often. She's in Brooklyn, painting and going to school. I buy some of her work now and then, usually through Damen. She'd never let her big sister spend the money I spend on her. I don't let her come by the Manor, but if she did, she'd see a lot of familiar wall art.

I slip into a pair of jeans, grab two stacks of almost identical paperwork, and head downstairs.

A plate of French toast waits for me in the kitchen.

"Ya know," I give Sarah a pointed look, "if you ever want to give up the life, I'd pay you to cook for the Guides. You'd make as much as you do now."

"More," Damen says with his mouth full. "I'd donate five percent of my bonuses."

"Me too." Josie grins from the countertop. She licks the syrup and powdered sugar off her plate.

Sarah laughs.

"You think it's funny," I point my fork at her, "but last time you went on assignment, we ate pizza and frozen burritos for a week."

"I'm honored." Sarah grins. "But I can't stay at home while you guys do all the work."

We all laugh, and I lay out my spreadsheets, one right above the other so the dates line up.

"Okay... Damen."

He looks over at me. The dead-eyed, "What, Mom?" look a teenager gives when told to do chores. "Don't tell me..." His Peruvian accent dances through his words.

"Yep." I put a blue check mark on Thursday's slot on my bottom spread. "He says he wants to relieve a little tension before the bill is voted on."

"Does he understand the irony of this?"

I don't answer right away. I just popped a massive forkful of syrup-coated French toast into my mouth. I swallow my bite and chug a bit of coffee. "I didn't ask."

"I'm getting tired of this, Miss Belle. I want to go back to Peru. I need to see my family."

This gets my attention. We've had this conversation before, several times in the last six months.

"Damen." My warning tone sends the girls from the room. "We've discussed this. You can't go back, not yet. It's too soon after the election."

"There is a good man in office now. It is a much safer place."

"Yeah, because you're good at your job. Which is what makes it so dangerous for you. Buccero may be locked away, but he has plenty of allies who aren't happy about the loss of position and influence. I do a good job covering tracks, but I still want you to wait a little longer."

His fork hits the plate hard. He's frustrated with me. I understand. His mother and sisters are in Peru. I sympathize, but he knew what he was getting into. Letting him visit before an extensive process of security checks would only put his family in danger.

"I want to see my family, Miss Belle." He leans on the table, sharp jaw set. His dark, mocha-colored hair hangs in his face. He's not happy. I'd feel worse about it if I hadn't warned him about this from the beginning.

"Dammit, Damen. I know. I want you to see them too. But you know how dangerous it is. Give me a few more months to put together a detail, make sure we do this right." I put a hand on his arm. "This is the last time with the VP. We're gonna have to burn this bridge to get things done. After Thursday, you'll take a break, and then we'll see."

He glares at me. But sighs. He rakes a hand through his thick, wavy hair, and leans back in his chair. "I know you're only looking out for me, Miss Belle. And I appreciate it."

He stands up, rinses off his plate, and puts it in the dishwasher.

"You've been patient with me." I bite my lip. I planned on telling him in a couple weeks, but he deserves it. Kid's been working really hard lately. "So, I've got something for you." I write the number down on the corner of one of my sheets, rip it from the rest, and pass it across the table. "It's your mom's new number. She's farther south, in a little town outside Arequipa."

His eyes light up. He grabs the paper and cradles it against his chest.

"You need to be careful. Two-minute conversation, tops."

"Thank you, Miss Belle. I just want to let her know I'm okay."

I nod and smile. Damen runs from the room and back upstairs to call his mom.

She already knows he's okay. I've spoken to her four times in the last six months. Twice while getting her settled into their new town. Once more to let her know an old, retired cop friend would be dropping by since he decided on a change of scenery. And again just a few days ago to tell her Damen would be calling sometime soon, and to remind her to keep the conversations short.

I turn to my spreads. If I focus, I can finish the escort half by noon. Which is good, because it means I'll have the numbers ready for my calls later today.

My eyes pop open. A blurred set of letters is gray in my vision. Something is beeping at me.

My head snaps up. The way it does when you wake up and know in your bones that you're super late—heart hammering, forehead immediately sweating. I fell asleep at my desk. A line of mascara is smeared across the keys, and the left side of my face is sticky with hairspray.

I've been making calls and scheduling appointments for the next six months. I've spoken to fourteen people in the last six hours, in three different languages, no less. It's after eight o'clock at night. Exhaustion scratches at my bones.

For me, making calls isn't just pulling out my phone and giving someone a ring. I set up my backdrop, lay out two or three of my cutest tops (to highlight whichever assets the client is likely to respond to), style my hair, and do my best makeup job. The calls are always video; I don't allow my Guides to see someone if I haven't seen them first.

The beeping hasn't stopped. It's my computer. My Skype is going off. It's Lacey, who should currently be several thousand feet in the air somewhere over Eastern Europe. I grumble and double click her picture.

She appears, and I sit straighter. She's got me up on her phone. As usual, the girl looks like a classy, Korean, 1970's version of Audrey Hepburn. To clarify, her makeup is impeccable, from the perfectly framed eyebrows to the small, brown, painted freckles speckled across her nose and cheeks.

Her "sea after a storm," monolid eyes are wide, her lashes what most girls only dream about. Full lips are painted a deep maroon.

Her long, dark hair is pulled back into a high ponytail. A gray Beatles shirt with massive arm holes hangs loosely on her body. A bit of skin is just visible between the bottom of the word *Love* and her high-waisted, bell-bottom jeans.

She's walking, which is why I can see the whole outfit. Her screen swings up and back down with each step. Her voice is calm, though the smallest of wrinkles between her eyebrows tells me she's aggravated. She steadies her phone as the call connects.

"Hey, Lacey. I didn't realize they allowed video calls 30,000 feet up."

She raises an eyebrow. "Of course not. The flight's delayed. It looks like I'm going to be in London for the next four hours."

I lean forward in my chair, elbows going onto the desk as concern rises in me. "Will that give you enough time?"

She shrugs a bare shoulder. "I'll be fine. It gives me about two hours from arrival to the appointment. I was hoping for the planned four, but Chang can take care of things until I get there."

"Excellent." I nod, relaxing slightly. I should have known Lacey'd have it covered. She always does. "Did you already contact him?"

"No, but don't worry about it. I'll give him a call. It's not like I'm all that busy at the moment." A grin breaks across her serene face. "Besides, it looks like Miss Belle needs to get some rest."

I sigh, and my eyelids droop without my permission.

"How did today go?"

I love this girl. Even when she's stuck for four-plus hours at Heathrow, she still takes the time to ask about me.

"It was fine. We've got a busy year ahead of us. Anita's been booked for a full two months in the fall, and I've got a big project to work on with Josie this summer." I stretch back in my chair and reach my fingertips as high as they can go as a yawn escapes me.

"I'll let you get some sleep." Lacey does a crappy job hiding the laughter in her voice.

"Message me when you get there. And be safe."

She nods once, and the screen goes dark.

Delays often happen while traveling. The important thing to remember is to enjoy the journey and not get hung up on when you make it to your destination. So, if you're stuck somewhere, take a minute, relax, get something to eat, and enjoy some good, old-fashioned people watching.

Chapter Three

Lacey

Layovers are a Hassle

I hurry through the massive food court, focusing on the coffee shop ahead of me rather than the dozen or so different scents forcing their way into my nose. The sweetness of sugary glaze you can almost taste on the back of your tongue; the thick, salty, warmth in the air from the multitude of fryers; the weird, cold smell that accompanies cheap sandwich meat... I march through them all to order my drink and then sink into a plush armchair in the far corner.

My fingers curl automatically around the small blue and green orb dangling from a silver chain around my neck. I lean back, take a deep breath, cross my short legs, and sigh. Four hours. There are now four hours to burn in Heathrow, one of England's largest airports.

Miss Belle is a mess. The poor woman's been working for weeks with no break. She set up my assignment in record time. When the congresswoman called, we only had a week to get things together. Quite a time crunch for one of the more important assignments I've done lately, but I get to see Nathan again. It's been a long time.

I haven't seen him since my old life.

The barista brings me a small Americano. I flash her a smile and take a sip before pulling out my little black book.

I need to call Chang and have him set up the room. The Park Hyatt isn't my favorite hotel in Tokyo (it's a little far from any of the national gardens for my taste), but the Auto Manufacturing Leaders conference takes place there this week. It makes sense that the CFO of the second most productive car manufacturing company in the United States is staying in the same hotel.

The phone rings once, twice, three times. I glance at the round silver watch on my wrist and realize it's three in the morning in Tokyo. I wince and go to hang up when a sleepy voice barks, "Who is this?" in Japanese.

"I'm so sorry, Chang," I respond in the same language. "I didn't realize what time it is there. It's Lacey."

His tone immediately changes, and it's clear he's woken up at hearing my name.

"Lacey!" Heavily accented English this time. "How wonderful to hear from you. What can I do for you?"

"I'm headed out your way for some business. I planned on getting there four hours before my appointment, but I got stuck with a delay and won't be leaving London for a while."

"Oh, no."

I hear the grin in his voice. He didn't know I was heading to Tokyo. Miss Belle must have been serious about cutting him out after the last Japan trip.

"What can I do to help? You know I'd do anything for one of Miss Belle's girls."

I let out a silent chuckle. Miss Belle is the only one allowed to call us "girls." I'm fairly sure it's one of the reasons for the cutting out. "I need you to set up my staging room. I'll email you the details. It's a normal set up, but no video this time.

Just audio and emergency equipment. Do you still have my bag?"

"Of course!" There is a shuffle on the other end of the phone. "I'll have it all taken care of before you arrive. I'll be waiting for your email."

"Thanks, Chang. I owe you one."

"Yes." His tone goes dry. "Perhaps you will speak to Miss Belle on my behalf? I notice I do not get a call from her as often as I used to."

This time my chuckle is loud. "I'll see what I can do. And I'll call you when I fly in."

"Thank you, Lacey. It is always wonderful to hear from you."

I hang up and set down my phone. I sip my Americano and gaze around the bustling airport. A row of fluffy teddy bears with Britain's flag line the edge of the coffee counter. Twin little boys keep pulling one down while their mother (I assume) exasperatedly tries to order a drink.

Men in suits, women in heels, and tourists with their camera phones clicking away pass me in a sea of faces.

Miss Belle always says I sit too still. She says I have too much patience. She and I were in line at Starbucks, and the people in front of us took about five minutes ordering. By our turn, she was cursing under her breath and stamping her foot hard enough to break a heel.

My gran always said we need to have patience and understanding for those around us. She taught my foster siblings and me the meaning of a deep breath and the value of a calm mind. Those lessons helped a lot after she died. I learned to be still, at peace when fire raged around me.

It's not a lesson any sixteen-year-old should have to learn. But it was Amanda or me, and she was only ten. I told Miss Belle when she found me that I knew what I was doing. I'd have done it again.

I shake my head and focus on something else. Gran passed a long time ago, but it still burns to remember she's gone.

I buy a *New York Times* from the barista, offering a smile to the twins as I sit back down. Their mother glares.

It's probably the shirt. Or the pants. Or the whole outfit. I used to mind when people looked at me that way. Now it barely grabs my attention.

I settle back into my chair and flip open the paper. I should do some research on Nathan's security team and on the other guests at this week's event, but I'll have time for that on the flight. Now, to catch up on current events. Another chuckle escapes my lips. If the paper knew half the current events I know about, a lot more people would be reading it.

*There are a few helpful rules for the traveling portion of a
vacation. If it's a short flight, save money on cheap seats. If
the plane is in the air for more than five hours, splurge on
something comfortable.*
*Always bring snacks, but be smart about it. Don't pack your
world-famous egg salad sandwich—I promise no one will
thank you for sharing that smell.*

Chapter Four

Lacey

A Vision in Lavender

I pull out my tablet on the flight. The gentleman next to me fell asleep in the first fifteen minutes after take-off, offering me some much-appreciated privacy.

I stretch out in my chair and prop up the screen in my lap. I love to fly. I'd never been on a plane before I met Miss Belle. I almost threw up when I boarded the flight out of Houston. And again when the plane took off.

First class is the only way to fly.

Orange juice is placed on my table. I smile up at the handsome man passing out drinks. There is something about a strong jawline that I find unbearably attractive.

He offers to bring me a mimosa, but I politely decline. Miss Belle trusts us all to keep our wits while working, but I don't drink if I can help it. I can't, not after seeing what alcohol can do to some people. A few of the girls I knew, years ago, tried to drown out the pain, the shame, with liquor. It never seemed to really help. It served them like a band-aid would a broken arm. Useless and painful to remove.

I flick my screen and files pop up. Marissa puts together our information packets on these short notice assignments. I usually prefer to do my own research, but she does a beautiful job.

Nathan Blake. His picture is new. He is older now, of course; gray hairs are fluffy behind his ears, and he seems to have gained some weight. It's expected. I haven't seen him in four years.

He didn't work as a CFO back then. But as a top lawyer for a major car manufacturing business, he could afford my company. It helped that my company didn't cost nearly as much as it does now.

Nathan isn't a handsome man. His jawline is not strong, nor his nose pointed, nor his eyes entirely bright. He has a round face, broad ears, and a thicker neck than you'd expect for a man with such a slim body—well, it was slim, back then.

He confided in me. And I in him. His secrets gave me something to hold onto. His promises gave me something to yearn for. I still suspect he is the one who contacted Miss Belle a little over four years ago. That he may be the reason I got out.

I close out his folder. I don't need information about Nathan. I need information about his security and co-workers.

I actually laugh aloud as I pull up the security team hired by Nathan's corporate office. Marcus Fernand and Kong Erailis, or as Miss Belle calls them, Tall and Quiet.

They work private security when they aren't taking hit orders. One could say our paths have crossed a few times. It will be good to see them again, even if it is during a working visit.

Nathan's co-workers are precisely what I expected. Rich, mostly white, old men bent on making a profit at any cost. I suspect this week will see many women in my profession. I make quick work of memorizing their details. Family members, previous employment, scandals, anything I may need to know to keep the conversation flowing.

When the plane lands in Tokyo, I'm ready. It's 7:30 p.m. Monday evening, local time. Which makes it 6:30 a.m. in New York. I send Miss Belle a text anyway. She'll be relieved when she wakes up.

Haneda, known as Tokyo International to the non-locals, is one of the nicer airports I've ever flown through. And, though it's my sixth time doing so, I'm still taken by the beauty of the sculptures, paintings, and architecture.

My checked luggage is a small duffle. That's it. The whole point of arriving early was having time to get to my storage locker and remove the plethora of items I keep in Tokyo for such occasions. I'm lucky Chang was ready and willing to help.

He sits in a red Mini Cooper right outside the airport building. A bright, white smile crosses his brown face when he sees me. I offer a small wave as I walk over.

The sun is setting over the skyscrapers. Orange, red, and purple burst across the sky, casting the clouds in a hazy array of colors. Life blossoms around me. Haneda sits on the edge of Tokyo Bay. The actual city snakes up the shoreline, flourishing across a series of bridges and little islands, similar to New York.

Chang jumps from the driver's side, runs around the car, and opens my door. My smile and thanks are genuine. As we pull away from the curb and into the city, I marvel—yet again—at the beauty of the capital of Japan.

Tokyo and New York may share some similarities, both near large bodies of water, both with bridges, skyscrapers, parks, and gardens, but the two cities could not be more different culturally. Even at 7:30 p.m., which is almost rush hour here, traffic is minimal. Those seldom places where we are stopped for more than a few minutes lack the shouting, honking, and show of middle fingers I've grown accustomed to back home. There's also the unsettling chunk of time it takes to get used to the car being on the left side of the road.

I enjoy the serenity of the city as we cross a couple bridges and cruise alongside a beautiful river, but as we get closer to our destination, Chang takes it upon himself to fill the silence.

I stare out the window, barely listening to his words. I speak Japanese fluently. It's not the language that's the problem. Nerves bound through me. For the first time in... probably at least a year. I don't get nervous.

But now, I'm about to see Nathan again. About to spend five nights with him. My chest tightens, and I have to rub at the word *ALL* scrawled on the top of my shirt to release the tension.

The city flashes by. After about thirty minutes, we arrive at the Park Hyatt hotel. I lean across the car and give Chang a kiss on the cheek. "Thank you for the ride and the help. I'll make sure Miss Belle knows how valuable you have been to the Guides."

Chang's dark cheeks turn a rosy red. "You are welcome, Lacey. Please, let me know if I can do anything else to help these next few days."

I smile. "I will."

The grinning, golden face of Bacchus, the god of wine, gazes down at me from above the ground floor entrance. I sling my bag over my shoulder and pull the door open.

The Hyatt is made of three high towers, stacked together like Lego pieces. I take the elevator up to the main lobby, politely declining a guide and letting them know I've already checked in. Chang gave me my keys (the Park Hyatt uses real keys, not the plastic cards found in other hotels) and room number. I skirt around the massive huddle of people in the lobby. A few faces stick out, men and women I recognize from past assignments, but none of them notice me.

The elevator is empty. I pull out a wipe from my purse and start removing my makeup as I go up, up, up, to the thirty-ninth floor. My room is at the farthest end of the hallway. Right next to the stairs.

I slip through the door, toss my bag on the bed, and sort through my things.

The closet is full. Every color dress imaginable, from ballgown to cocktail, black to white, is hung along the wall. Six pairs of heels, two pairs of boots, and three elegant choices of flats are lined up next to the door. I brought jewelry and makeup in my bag, along with all the undergarments a woman in my business is expected to have.

I glance out the window; the view is spectacular. The room is on the side facing the park. Marissa is thorough—no one can peek through this window.

Still, I close the blinds before I reach under the bed where a duffle bag waits for me. I dump the contents on the off-white quilt and line everything up.

Three handguns in different sizes, several blades both serrated and not, a paracord rope, a lock-picking set, and a few poisons in both lipstick containers and mascara bottles. Not bad for such a short notice assignment.

A laptop is already set up on the desk. A purple tulip brooch sits next to it.

I check my watch. Just past eight. I have less than an hour to be ready for the opening night of festivities.

I start with the corset. The pale lavender lace matches my thong. I do up the middle hooks facing front before spinning it around and clasping the last couple on the very top and bottom.

I fix up my hair, twisting a third into a knot on the right side of my head. A dozen bobby pins hold it firmly in place, and the rest hangs down in a cascade of loose curls. Makeup next.

A brush of dark eyeshadow at the edges makes my eyes appear brighter. I know Nathan likes simplicity when it comes to makeup. I press a light gloss to my lips and rub a thin layer of coverup across my skin.

Now the dress. A vision in purple, the hue of lavender sprigs. The color accents the olive skin I got from my mother. The fabric clings to my body, one side dropping past my knee, the other stopping midway down my thigh. The corset is hidden by the halter top that buttons into place behind my neck.

I remove my necklace and press it to my lips for a moment before tucking it into the little clutch that matches my dress.

A short pair of dazzling earrings match the bracelet, which has replaced my watch. Always wear long earrings with your hair up and short earrings with your hair down. Another lesson from my gran. Though she always intended us to dress up for an outing to the theater, not for this.

I take the brooch from the desk. It pins nicely just above my left breast. A final glance in the mirror assures me that this mission will not fail. And, though I've done this several dozen times before, there are butterflies in my stomach, a fluttering flowing through my nerves.

Last time Nathan saw me, I was twenty. Young, afraid, with no control over the events of my own life.

Miss Belle told him of my request four years ago. To avoid, at all costs, the people from my previous life. Nathan was on that list.

But this is important. More important than me and my comfort. And it will be nice, even for a moment, to see him again.

Nervous eyes stare back at me from the mirror. My usual calm demeanor is cracked, and it shows. I'm heavier than I was four years ago. More muscular, more built. Stronger. I flex my arms, and the feeling of that strength runs through me.

I close my eyes, breathe the way Miss Belle taught us. I clear my mind the way Gran taught us. I become still.

When I open my eyes, thick, mascaraed lashes flicker at the top of my vision. A serene smile greets me. I lick my lips, to make sure the gloss won't come off later. The worry is still in my eyes.

I sigh. It's time.

I tuck my room key into the little wrap around my right thigh. A small blade goes in next to it. My phone goes in the clutch with my necklace and a tube of gloss. I step into my heels, black stilettos, which curl up and around my ankles.

The door clicks closed behind me.

Chapter Five

Lacey

Hit Men and Spies

The ballroom is beautiful, all dark wood and clean lines like the rest of the tower. Six dazzling chandeliers hang from the high ceiling. Rows of buffet tables line two of the walls. Impeccably clean windows give a stunning view of the city. Above everyone, a live band plays an instrumental version of what sounds like *The Piña Colada Song* from a balcony along the far wall.

A rainbow of color adorns the women. Some, like me, are here to earn their dinner. I know a few of the consorts. When we make eye contact, I smile and wiggle my fingers in a small wave.

The men are all dressed in black and white tuxedos. Picking out employees of different companies is easy. Tonight is the first night of the convention, and most of the people who work for the four largest American car companies are still uncomfortable mingling with each other.

A dozen members of the hotel security stand in awkward spots around the room. The private security isn't hard to pick out either. Tuxedo jackets have an unfortunate tendency of bulging around holsters.

Heads turn as I walk across the floor. I only recognize a few of the men. Sarah usually works these corporate events.

My heels click on the rose-colored hardwood floor; this really is a marvelous room. I spot Nathan and do a double take.

He has aged more than his picture showed. When we met, he was in his early forties, dutifully climbing the corporate ladder. Now, he looks so much like the other men. The other old CEOs and CFOs and corporate leaders. They all stand together. The top brass from each of the four companies. Unlike their employees, these men know each other and have no problem talking to the competition.

Nathan's back is turned. He's discussing something important and not being entirely truthful about it. He's scratching behind his right ear—always his tell. His other hand holds a glass of champagne, and it looks like it's about to spill as he waves it around to emphasize his point.

His security, or rather his boss's security, remains a little way away. Tall (Marcus) and Quiet (Kong) hold their hands folded in front of them and stand straight and professional.

Marcus's usual mess of brown hair is cut short for this fancier event. He keeps it untamed during their dirtier missions. A shadow of a beard ages his face. The tuxedo is a bit tight on his tall frame. His Nordic ancestry is blatantly apparent in such a crowded room. The man is built like a tree. Marcus excels in his career path; his violent streak is only matched by his wonderful sense of humor.

His partner in literal crime, Kong, fits his tuxedo perfectly. Green eyes—contacts—watch me as I walk over. Diamonds glint from his ears, a gift from a Saudi prince. Cropped black hair is gelled perfectly into place, fitting nicely with his trimmed goatee and mustache. He reaches out a coffee-with-cream colored hand, and I take it.

"Lacey." He nods. The faintest trace of his Hmong heritage is present in his voice.

"Kong." I smile at him and his taller friend. "Marcus. Lovely to see you both."

"You too, Lacey." Marcus flashes a giant grin. "It's been a while."

"Yes, almost a year now. Though I think I read something about the two of you more recently. Car accident in Venezuela? It was clean work."

Marcus chuckles, and Kong glares at him.

"Yeah, that was us."

Kong grunts and punches Marcus's arm. "We haven't been in South America for quite some time. It must have been someone else," he purrs.

I put a hand over my smile. "Of course." I wink at Marcus as I excuse myself and turn toward Nathan.

He sees me. A flood of memories collides against my heart when I finally glimpse his face up close.

The darkness of that room. The stiff blanket and cold floor. Amanda's tears. My own. A thick, hairy arm shoving me against the wall, pinning my throat as a rough voice explained exactly what my new life would be.

Sixteen-year-olds are supposed to think about driving tests.

I blink. Nathan walks toward me. I give him my warm, genuine smile, and I know it reaches my eyes. Because a part of me, a small part I can almost ignore, actually is happy to see him again.

He takes my hand; his palm is sweaty.

"Lacey, I'm so glad to see you."

He sweeps me into a bear hug, and I hold him, gently stroking the back of his jacket. His hairline is receding, and more of it has gone gray than in the picture.

I pull away, my arms still held in his hands. "I'm so happy we could get together, Nathan. It has been too long."

His hands twitch around mine when I mention time. Dull eyes widen with concern, and he takes a step back, putting space between us. I raise an eyebrow.

"I didn't know Miss Belle would send you..." Concern fills his voice. Like a little boy who thinks he may have done something wrong.

I put a hand on his cheek. "I asked to come. I'm more than happy to be here and to see you."

He relaxes and spends the next few minutes explaining the penthouse suite he booked for the week. His need to make me feel comfortable and safe reminds me how much I've changed since we last saw each other.

The night passes quickly. We dance, eat, and chat with people who make six, seven, and eight figures a year. It's 2 a.m. when we make our way to the penthouse. The companies have several meetings tomorrow, so there is no afterparty.

By around four Nathan has passed out on the bed. I set the alarm on his phone. He needs to be up by nine for the corporate breakfast.

The dim light of morning seeps through the curtains. I pull a lavender silk robe from the closet, one of the many items of clothes I had brought to Nathan's rooms after the event last night, and walk through the suite, enjoying the luxurious design.

The bathroom has a double bath and walk-in rain shower.

A small kitchenette is nestled into a corner next to a fully stocked bar. Both face the main seating area, which contains several beige chairs, a few black couches, and a standing light that looks like an elongated paper lamp. A large glass table rests upon a yellow and blue splotched rug. A sheet of thick paper with the week's itinerary of "fun" events lies atop it. Bright green plants sit in large ceramic planters in the corners of the rooms.

The best feature, in my mind, is a half-grand piano nestled a bit to the side of the living room area. A set of bookshelves stand on either side; small, amber lights emit a glow that brightens the dark spines of the books.

To the left of the main door is a petite study space/office room. This is where my walk is taking me.

The door is closed and, upon inspection, locked. I pull a bobby pin from my rumpled hair; a curl tumbles down to my shoulder. The lockpicking set would come in handy here, but a bobby pin is much easier to explain away. I feel for the tumblers, pushing each pin in the lock up and easing it down until it clicks into place. My fingers move with the smooth rhythm of muscle memory.

Two minutes pass. I reach up as the last pin settles and turn the knob. The door screeches at the six-inch mark. I freeze.

The suite is quiet. Thirty seconds pass without a sound. No rustling of blankets, no thud of feet on the floor, no voice questioning my whereabouts.

I turn from the door and go quietly rummage through the kitchen cabinets. There is a small bottle of extra virgin olive oil sitting in the back of a shelf of spices. I grab it.

The hinges are just visible, with six inches between the door and the jam. I dip my clip into the bottle and carefully ooze oil onto the hinges. After all three are appropriately greased, I press a finger to the door and slide it open. There is a small whine, followed by silence.

A smile crosses my face. This is the part of the job I truly enjoy.

I flip a switch next to the door, and a lamp in the corner lights up. A row of carved masks, teeth bared, eyebrows furrowed, and eyes narrowed, on the far wall catch my glance for a moment before I blink and look away. In the center of the room a small desk is covered in folders and papers. A laptop sits on the right side.

I walk around the desk and plop onto the brown, squishy office chair. Here we go. I dig through each piece of paper, leaving them exactly where they were when I started.

Though I find a few interesting financial statements, it's not what I need. An hour and a half has gone by. I open the laptop and quickly place a sticky note from the desk drawer over the camera. None of Nathan's old passwords work. After the sixth attempt, the computer locks me out.

I pull out my phone and check the time. It's 4:30 p.m., yesterday, in New York. Confusing, I know. I get up and shut the office door before returning to the desk chair.

I click on contacts, hit favorites, and Marissa's picture is there at the top, right next to Miss Belle.

The phone rings once, and Missa picks up. "Lacey? What's wrong?"

She is familiar with the time zones too. Getting a call from me at 5:30 in the morning (my time) must be unsettling.

"Nothing; sorry to worry you. I just need some help with a laptop."

"Show me."

I switch to the camera and show her the lockout screen. Missa laughs, her white teeth filling up the screen. "It's an easy fix. Prop me up in front of the laptop, and I'll give you a step by step."

I follow her instructions, and five minutes later, his files fill the screen. "Thanks, Missa."

"Of course." Missa's smile lights up her alert blue eyes. "How are you doing over there?"

I sigh. "I'm all right. One night down, four to go."

"How was it? Seeing him again?" Her eyebrows draw together in concern.

My throat goes dry. "It was strange. A lot of memories surfaced."

"Not many of them good, I'm guessing."

"No." My heart pangs and a buzzing heat goes through my cheeks to my eyes.

"You've been busy since you got there."

A tremor runs through my hand.

"And the mission was really last minute."

I nod. A metallic taste runs across my tongue.

"You probably haven't had time to process all those memories."

I grit my teeth as a tear slides down my cheek.

Missa tilts her head and smiles sadly. "If you get time, do a meditation session. Try to let the feels wash over you, not through you. Don't let them overpower you."

"Thanks, Missa. Can I call you, if..."

"You can call me no matter what." Her smile fades. "I've been there, Lacey. Don't go through it alone if it becomes too much."

I nod and wipe away the tear. It feels silly to be affected by things that happened so long ago.

"Be safe." Missa hangs up, and the screen goes black.

I open the office door a crack, listen for a moment, and go back to the laptop. I dive through the files. Pages and pages of memos, emails, payroll, income, yearly sales, quarterly sales, equipment costs, legal notes—everything I could possibly find on a corporate computer, I find.

Everything except the evidence of slave labor I'm looking for.

Chapter Six

Lacey

Strangers at Breakfast

The clock in the corner of the screen shows 7:30 a.m. I need to be done for today, and not just because time is running out. I've been awake for a long while.

I close out every window on the laptop and use one of Missa's tricks to change the dates where it says "last viewed." When I'm done, the desk looks the same as it did hours ago. I lock the door from the inside and close it behind me.

When Nathan's alarm goes off, he rolls over and strokes my hair back to see my face. I blink sleepy eyes and smile. An hour is not much, but it will hold me over.

"Morning," I mumble.

"Good morning." He sits up and looks up and down my body. The thin white sheet doesn't hide much.

"Will I get to spend the day with you?" Innocence bleeds from my voice. I already know the answer.

"Not today. We can do breakfast together, but I'm in meetings all afternoon. We're trying to get all the important work done today and tomorrow so everyone can enjoy the rest of the trip."

I nod. "Let me throw on something, and we can eat together before you have to go." I brush my hand against his chest as he pulls the covers away and stands up.

I follow him into the bathroom and leave him brushing his teeth at the sink as I move into the walk-in closet. A small row of dresses hangs along one wall, suits along another. In the back, several different pairs of shoes, jewelry, and a few lingerie items nestle in the shelves.

I am, again, thankful Chang was able to help get things sorted before I arrived. It was he who chose items from my private room and had them brought up to Nathan's suite yesterday.

I pluck two dresses from the closet, a pink one and a green one, and hold them up for Nathan's approval. He smiles as he chooses a dark blue suit, pulls on the pants, and gestures at the pink.

I slip it over my head. The thin straps caress my bare shoulders. I turn around and let him zip up the back. A sash just below my breasts tightens. The dress flares out around my waist. Cherry blossoms accent the pale pink. They grow from the bottom of the dress up and around the back, leaving the chest blank.

Nathan has finished dressing and turns to watch me pin up my hair. I smile at him through the bathroom mirror. I brush a bit of blush across both cheeks. When I go to do the eyeshadow, he takes my wrist.

"Don't do the eyes. I love your eyes the way they are."

I let go of the brush, and it bounces on the countertop. He releases my arm and leaves the bathroom. I rub my wrist. It didn't hurt. But it feels like a stone was dropped in my stomach.

I take a deep breath and force myself to relax. I step into a pair of rosy two-inch pumps, pull a matching purse from the shelf, and head to the sitting area.

My clutch from last night is on the coffee table. I transfer my little wallet, tuck my personal room key in a small pocket between the inner lining, and swing the strap over my shoulder. I put my phone in an outer pocket. I'm ready to go when Nathan steps out of the office with his laptop bag. There goes the plan to search it during his meetings.

"Were you in here after I went to bed?" he asks.

The muscles in my face tense even as I consciously force them to remain neutral. "No. Sweetie, you wore me out last night. I don't think I woke up once." I wink, and the crease in his forehead melts away.

"Sorry." He comes to me and puts his hands on my upper arms. "The door sounded different this morning." He shakes his head. "I'm getting paranoid in my old age."

My forced chuckle sounds real. I take his arm, and we step into the hallway.

Breakfast is a significant event. Two long tables are stretched out in a different, slightly smaller room than the night before. Plates of American and Japanese breakfasts and lunches are scattered down the center of the tables. Men and women in red-collared shirts with black ties scuttle around, pouring drinks, clearing plates, and bringing out more food.

Businessmen are done up in their day-to-day suits. It's easy to spot the women here on business versus the women brought as guests, most of whom are paid to be here. A particularly tall woman in a dark-blue pencil skirt and jacket glares at me as Nathan leads me to a seat. A red-collared man with a round face and small hands quickly places empty plates in front of us and gets our drink orders.

Nathan's boss, Daniel Jacobson, sits across the table. His wife couldn't make it this week; she's in Colorado with their three children. Instead, a petite Latina woman caresses his arm as he chatters away about different types of diesel engines.

Daniel is a large man, a good thirty pounds heavier than Nathan. Gray hair has taken over his head, and tufts peek out from his flat ears and protruding nose. His 'date' is young. Younger than me, though I can't tell by how much. She wears the plastered-on smile of a girl who is new to the business. A blue cocktail dress hangs off one shoulder.

Miss Belle has never done business with Daniel Jacobson, though she has been referred to him many times. She is meticulous when it comes to picking our clients, which is one of the reasons we love her so much.

Nathan, not knowing I have been briefed on his work associates, introduces me to his boss. Daniel stands up to shake my hand, forcing me to rise as well. His eyes go straight to my chest as I reach across the table and politely grasp his oversized palm. As we sit again, he introduces his date, Delilah, with the voice of someone who has smoked consistently since middle school.

"It was a bit last minute." He gives an inappropriately large grin to Nathan. "I convinced the wife to cancel, but then I couldn't get ahold of my regular. You got lucky, though!" He nods pointedly at me. "I've never been able to get a girl from Miss Belle."

Nathan clears his throat uncomfortably. This is not usual breakfast talk. Daniel takes a sip of his mimosa and leers at me.

Delilah's face is frozen in an embarrassed smile. I meet her eye, take a breath, and let out a burst of giggles. Her brows come together in confusion, but she laughs as well.

"Oh, Mr. Jacobson." I toss a hand in the air. I am carefree, enjoyable, relaxed. "Nathan said you had a sense of humor, but my goodness. And at breakfast!" I ease out the laugh and heave a pleasant sigh, stroking Nathan's arm before reaching for the plate of finger sandwiches in front of me.

The confusion on Daniel's face is rapidly replaced with a prideful smile. He is a big man; he made the women laugh.

"How did you know I'm one of Miss Belle's girls?" I ask with a coy smile. I plunk two cucumber cream cheese sandwiches on my plate.

Daniel chuckles. It's not a grandfatherly, Santa-type of chuckle. It's dark. The sound sends a chill through my veins.

"He," Daniel gestures at Nathan, "has been bragging about it for a damn week." Jealousy glints across his eyes for a moment. His smile goes tight as his gaze flicks to the girl at his side.

I lean my head on Nathan's shoulder. "You're so sweet."

He sits a little straighter, his chest protruding a bit more than usual.

"Well, I'm starving." I pull a bowl of steamed rice toward my plate. A healthy spoonful of the sticky grains land on the white and gold porcelain. I dump a strip of fish (mackerel, maybe?) and a chunk of veggies on top of the rice. A small bowl sits next to my plate. I pour miso soup into it and, rather than use a spoon, lift the whole thing to my lips as I sip up the delicious Japanese staple.

Nathan digs into a plate of waffles and eggs, everything coated with syrup. Daniel chugs his mimosa, pausing only to snap at a waiter to bring more butter for his pancakes. Delilah nibbles on her wheat toast, though seeing me eat gives her the courage to put some rice on her plate as well.

"So, today is a tour of the National Museum." I nudge Nathan. "That should be fun."

"Sorry, little lady," Jacobson interrupts as Nathan opens his mouth. "We have meetings all day today and tomorrow."

I look at Nathan. I've known since before I landed that he wouldn't have time for me today. But the more it looks like I am desperate for time with him, the better my cover is.

He nods. "I wish I could come, but like I said before, we've got to get through the business stuff. Once it's done, I'll be able to focus on you."

I stick out my bottom lip just a bit. Nathan grins, happy that I'm sad I don't get to spend time with him.

"Well, I'll just stay here, then. It won't be as much fun without you."

"No, no, you go, have a good time. I'll want to hear about your day when I get done. Besides, everyone else is going."

I was hoping for a nap. But spending time with the company employees who aren't required for meetings is good too. Things get said at outings. Things that wouldn't commonly be mentioned in the confines of a conference room.

I spot Marcus walking along the edge of the room. He looks much more comfortable in a regular suit jacket. His white shirt is unbuttoned a few too many, likely because of all the beautiful women in the room. A couple of the hired ladies keep glancing his way; clearly, the chest hair is working.

I catch his eye and give him a little wave.

"Do you know our security team?" Nathan's tone holds an edge.

I flash my teeth. "A bit. I met them a few years ago. Their security work sometimes crosses paths with my profession."

Nathan frowns, and I lean into his arm, putting one hand on his thigh and tickling his inner leg. "Miss Belle knows them more than I do. But it's polite for me to say hi."

He relaxes and smiles down at me.

Daniel grunts as he stands up. "We'd better finish up here, Nathan. I want to get this work shit out of the way." He grins at Delilah. "Then we can really have some fun."

Nathan kisses my temple, then stands. "I'll see you when we're done today." He grabs the laptop bag from under his chair, and the two men walk away, pausing in the middle of the room to chat with a few people.

A young man catches my eye as he comes in the main door. Unlike the staff or guests, he wears torn jeans and a pale blue T-shirt with the Captain America shield. I recognize his face, but I can't place it. The stubble on his jawline and his baggy eyes don't help. Maybe a former co-worker of Nathan? Though he seems too young. I'm sure I've seen his picture somewhere.

Trying to figure out how I know him takes second place in my mind when he walks straight up to Daniel and Nathan and starts talking.

Nathan's face twists in anger. Within a moment, Marcus and Kong appear and each grab one of the newcomer's arms. He yanks from their grip and walks with them to the exit. I wipe the curious frown from my face even as an alarm in the back of my mind tells me I know him somehow. Kong and Marcus step back in and have quick words with Daniel.

The conference room empties. The shuttles don't leave for the museum until 11 a.m. so that everyone has a little bit of time between breakfast and a thirty-minute drive.

I tell Delilah I'll meet her in the lobby at 10:55 and head to my room. Not the suite, my room. I take a few minutes to run through my computer. The audio from Nathan's suite is clear; Chang knows how to set up a microphone. I pick through yesterday's recording. There isn't much from before I arrived in Tokyo. And absolutely no mention of a slave factory in Thailand.

Oh well, there's always today. I grab a larger purse, transfer my wallet and phone, then add some snacks from the minibar, my Canon EOS Rebel (a birthday gift from Missa), and a decent-sized knife (a birthday gift from Miss Belle). I change out of my dress into a pair of high-waisted shorts, a tank-top, and a set of powder blue flats. I fix a nonchalant smile on my face and ride down to the lobby.

Marcus and Kong are there, keeping an eye on the door while chatting with each other.

"I'm telling you, that's not at all how you prep a lure," Kong says in exasperation.

"I watch The Discovery Channel. I know how to fish."

"Binge-watching shark week does not make you a fisher-man." Kong's eyes roll skyward.

"I'll bring my gun. Problem solved." Marcus gives a sharp nod to his shorter friend, his arms crossed over his chest.

Kong doesn't respond, but the pained look on his face makes me wish I could join their upcoming fishing trip.

I stifle my chortle and go outside to chat up some lawyers from Nathan's company while we all wait for the buses.

By the time we return to the hotel, I am struggling. Yawns punctuate every sentence, and my eyelids are like lead.

Kathy, a blonde Brit who shares my profession (sort of), suggests that a group of us girls go for coffee.

"I'd love to," I mumble through another yawn. "But I've got to catch up on some sleep. Maybe tomorrow."

They chorus me away with goodbyes, and I head up to my room. I slide the key into the lock and lean against the door to push it open.

I slip out of my clothes and collapse on the bed. My alarm is set for 3:30 p.m. That will give me a full hour and a half before Nathan is supposed to be done with his meetings. And they usually run long.

My toes curl at the comfort of the silky sheets. I do a full body stretch. My neck pops, my ears ring for a second, and a massively long yawn squishes my eyes closed. I fade into sleep, my exhaustion too much for my thoughts to keep me awake.

The National Museum of Tokyo is a definite "must visit" when you stay in the city. The entrance, with its gorgeous water feature, makes you want to whip that camera right out. The inside is stunning, too. A grand staircase takes you up before branching to the left and right. Take your time viewing all the historical sights in this amazing building. And don't forget to stop by the bookstore to pick up a read for the flight home!

Be realistic when you plan a museum trip. People often think they can see everything in a matter of hours, or that they will have the patience to stay until they do see everything. Neither of these is a likely outcome. To prioritize your time efficiently, do some research ahead of time. Find out what exhibitions are on display, decide what sounds the most interesting, and have that be the centerpiece of your tour. Make sure you have time to check out some of the constant pieces, but don't let yourself get drained!

CHAPTER SEVEN

MISS BELLE

ROASTED GARLIC NUTS DON'T SMELL THAT BAD

I am flying through the air. It's nice. Until I slam against the bright red mat and my ponytail jams into the back of my head. The oxygen leaves my lungs with an "oomph." Above my head, the ceiling fan spins around and around and around.

"So, to avoid that," Dee stares down at me, one hand on her hip, "you stick out your right leg and leverage yourself against my weight."

I grunt in response and push myself off the floor. "Or," I glare at her through the hair falling out of my ponytail, "I stop paying you to beat the shit out of me."

Dee flashes her giant, white smile, even whiter against her dark umber skin. She brushes a hand through her short, curly purple hair. "You don't pay me to beat the shit out of you. You pay me to *train* you to beat the shit out of other people."

"So true." I walk to the side of the mat, grab my water, and chug down several mouthfuls.

"Let's do one more round and call it a day, yes?"

I nod, my mouth still full of water, then swallow. I've known Dee for almost eleven years. She was an exchange student from Haiti and went to school with Missa and me during our senior year. After a stint in the Marines, she spent the last four years winning bodybuilding tournaments, and now owns a private gym in New York. She trains all the Guides.

I come at her with a right hook. She blocks and sweeps her leg. I dance backward but dart up again before she plants her foot. I feint with my left hand while my right swings in to connect with her stomach.

My grin vanishes as she grabs my arm and moves to hurl me over her hip and into the ground again. I do as she said, stick out my right leg and trap it between her legs. In a fluid motion, I turn and yank up hard. I lift with my legs, push against her with my shoulders, and successfully swing her over my body. She lands and then jumps back up in a matter of seconds with a wide grin.

"Much better."

I pour another swig of water into my mouth and swish it around before thanking her. I lift my shirt off my belly and use the fabric to wipe the sweat from my forehead.

Dee walks over, holding a can of roasted peanuts. She pops a handful in her mouth. "Are you and Missa going to the reunion?"

I raise an eyebrow and sigh. "What makes you think I'd do that?"

She laughs and slaps my shoulder. "It'll be fun. Seeing everyone again. It has been a while."

An incredulous chuckle/snort makes her glare at me.

"It will be." She sits on the mat in front of me and extends her left leg in a long stretch.

"Who goes to their high school reunion anyway?" I shake my head. "I don't need to see anyone I don't already keep in contact with." I bend down and unlace my sneakers.

"Ha." Dee points at me. "I think you just do not want to visit your parents."

I straighten and glare. "That's not it. I just think it's unnecessary."

"Well." She stands up and puts the lid on the peanuts. "You've got a few months to change your mind. I hope you and Missa come. I'm going."

I take a deep breath and nod. "I'll ask her."

Dee grins. She is fully aware that if Missa wants to go, I'll go. And Missa is much more likely to want to fly across the country to visit people we don't give two shits about. Don't ask me why. I think it's ridiculous.

I head back to the Manor. The family Prius hums along the cement. The leaves are all green; New York is gorgeous in the spring.

I left late today, so I hit the entire five o'clock traffic cycle. By the time I get to the Manor I'm cursing like a sailor and wearing out the horn in the car.

A beige van parked across from our garage gets my attention. A growl escapes my lips, and I grit my teeth. My frustration with the NYPD simmers in my chest as I pull into one of the garage spots. I honestly don't know what to do about this incessant stalking. Which I suppose could be called surveillance as they *are* the police.

I collect my bag and water bottle, then do a double check to see if I left anything in the car. Levi, the oldest of the Guides, and the only man besides Damen, is anal about people forgetting "personal items." Leave a bag of roasted garlic nuts under a seat *one time*, and suddenly the world ends.

Missa is waiting for me at the front door. "Did you get everything out of the car?"

I roll my eyes and heave a sigh worthy of a fifteen year old. "It was one time!"

She chuckles. "It smelled like garlic for two weeks."

I give her a squinty glare. She opens the door, and we go inside.

"What's wrong?" I sling my workout bag onto the floor. "You don't usually wait for me by the door. I feel special."

"Lacey called."

I glance at the clock in the hall and do some quick math. "What happened?" My phone is out, my heart thundering when Missa puts her hands up.

"Nothing. She's fine. Just needed a hand with a laptop password."

"Jesus, Missa. Don't scare me like that."

"She knows what she's doing, Ana."

"I'm aware." I put a hand on my hip and frown at Missa. "You field calls from the girls all the time to help with stuff. Why does this one require you giving me a heart attack to let me know?"

Missa sighs. She brushes a hand through her long, golden hair. A wrinkle in her forehead and a grimace tell me she's more than a little concerned about something. Intense sapphire eyes give me a hard look. "She's struggling."

I furrow my brow in an unspoken question.

Missa pulls me into the kitchen and pours a cup of her strawberry, banana, and mango smoothie straight from the blender. "Lacey is having trouble with this one. Being with

Nathan... It's bringing up all the old memories. I think it's getting to her more than she thought it would."

I nod. Worry rises up in my stomach. "She's got a while left on this one. Think she'll be all right?"

"Yeah." Missa sits across from me and leans over the long, wooden table. "You know how it is. Little things can bring... bring stuff up. This is a *big* thing."

"I'll call the doc, set up a few hours for Lacey when she gets back."

Missa nods. The doc is our house psychiatrist. She's helped us quite a bit in the past. She is one of only a handful of people outside of the Manor who knows the whole scope of what we do.

"What about Amanda?" I take a sip of my blended fruit and wince. There is something very tart in this batch.

"She didn't say anything about Amanda. But we should try to get her talking about that when she gets back."

I nod and bite my lip. "Do you think she'll manage the next five days?"

"Four."

I raise an eyebrow at Missa.

"Today is Monday here, but it's Tuesday for Lacey."

A low groan escapes me. "Time changes are a bitch." I close my eyes and rub the bridge of my nose. "What are we gonna do, Missa?"

She hears the frustrated sadness in my voice and comes around the table. "What do you mean?" She wraps slender arms around my shoulders and rests her chin on the top of my sweaty head.

"We've got cops right outside the door, Lacey's in for a damn rough week, Damen... my brother..." My throat does that closing up thing that eventually leads to crying. "I don't know. I sometimes wonder if this is all worth it."

"You wonder what would have happened if you never came to LA."

It's not a question. But I can feel the fear in her voice. The terror that she is responsible for how my life turned out.

"No." I grip her arm and squeeze it. "Sometimes I wonder what would have happened if I never went to the doctor. What it would be like to still be with Dan. To be married now, with..." I swallow. "But I have no regrets when it comes to you, Missa. You're my best friend."

She lets me go and sits in the chair next to me. "And you're mine. We do good work here, Ana." She grins. Her voice takes on a mocking tone. "Miss *Belle*."

"Shut up." I shove her lightly, and we both laugh.

"Oh, I almost forgot... your parents called."

My stomach drops, and my eyes go anime-wide. "*What?*"

"Yeah. They want to talk to you about something. I'm gonna assume it's about Nicky."

"Fuck," I breathe out the word with a heavy sigh. "Okay. I'll call them."

"You should give them your cell number."

I glare at her again. "I don't need my mother calling me in the middle of a gala. Or my dad while I'm waist deep in the Amazon."

She laughs, her head thrown back, eyes squinted shut, and whole body shaking. A true guffaw at my expense. I can't help but chuckle along with her.

I organize my thoughts while I shower.

Only a few more days until Damen goes to see the VP. It will be his last visit and his last assignment for a while.

Nicky's marriage will be secure for the next four years. I'll call him over the weekend and patch things up.

I scrub shampoo into my hair.

Lacey will be fine. She can handle herself for a few more nights, and it's a pretty simple assignment. The hard part comes from her past with Nathan Blake. I'll have to talk to her about Amanda when she gets back.

My neck aches as I tilt my head back to rinse out the bubbles. I pour a quarter-sized pool of conditioner into my palm and massage it into my scalp. I pull my long hair forward and rub it between my hands.

The police are a more complicated problem. As much as I *love* a constant police escort, having the cops stationed outside the house around the clock is a bit much. If they somehow got the resources to follow my girls, it could lead to some interesting conversations. Unless they made a significant upgrade to their cyber division, I'm not worried about any arrests. We have a pretty foolproof system of getting paid.

I stand under the water. Steam rises from my skin. I close my eyes and let the water soak my face.

I'll take a break after this one. The rest of my girls are working on their own projects. Lacey and Damen are the only two with significant assignments this week. Maybe next

Monday I'll sleep in, eat cake, binge-watch *Firefly* or *Lord of the Rings.*

I shut off the water, wrap a fluffy purple towel around my torso, and return to the bedroom. With a sigh, I collapse onto my bed. It's going to be a complicated week.

*Do some research on the country you'll be visiting. Find out
how to deal with any legal trouble you might encounter.
For example, most places have pretty similar rules when it
comes to driving, but in Japan, the legal driving age is eighteen. If you're bringing someone younger along, you'd better
be prepared to be their chauffeur.
As a side note, the major cities in Japan have amazing public
transport systems, so you'll really only need a car if you plan
on venturing into rural areas. Research your city destinations
ahead of time. Know when the buses, trains, and metros are
running.*

Chapter Eight
Lacey
Dreaming Sucks

I'm standing to the side. I'm always to the side. Never in my own body or watching from above. In my dreams, I'm always standing a bit to the side of myself. Everything is just a little off.

Eight-year-old me floats down the stairs, cheeks flushed. She's wearing pale blue pajamas, a Christmas present from a few weeks earlier. The babysitter did her long black hair into two braids with bows on the ends.

I watch her run to the front door. She's worried she might get in trouble for still being up. It's late, almost midnight. The babysitter comes up behind her, a concerned look on her face. The door fades into nothing.

It's not Mom and Dad standing there. It's supposed to be Mom and Dad. A policeman takes off his hat when he sees little Lacey. He kneels.

I don't hear what he says; I didn't that day either. I remember the sound of the door opening. I remember the babysitter's breath catching. I remember her sobbing behind me, but I don't remember his words.

I fall. Sink through inky black space. When I land, I stand before a small wooden house. A rocking chair sits on the porch. The mailbox is painted purple with green leaves.

A van pulls up, and a social worker opens the back door. Little Lacey steps out. She is older now. Her face is red, her eyes puffy. Her hair has been chopped off. It sits flat and unflattering, just below her ears.

A small, pink bag is on her back as she stares at the house. I remember thinking this might not be so bad.

The front door opens, and a wrinkled form steps out. The woman is small. Old. White hair is puffy on the top of her head. Little Lacey frowns, and I remember thinking she looked like she was wearing a cloud.

Little Lacey steps back as the woman comes down the steps. She walks like a younger woman. Powerful strides exude purpose and confidence. She opens her mouth to speak. Instead of words, horrific creatures pour from her lips.

Long, thin, shadows form with clawed hands. They come, racing, screaming toward me.

Little Lacey and Gran fade into nothing, and I can't move, can't breathe, can't close my eyes as the creatures tear at my clothes, my hair, grabbing and pulling at my body.

They strip me to nothing. But my hands won't move. I can't lift them to cover myself. Shame fills me as faceless strangers surround me. They watch, wondering aloud why I don't stop this from happening.

"She must like it."

"Whore."

"Slut."

Someone spits in my face.

The ground opens underneath me. The grasping demons release me as I fall, fall, fall...

I snap upright. My breath comes too quick. I can't get enough oxygen. The sheet claws at my legs, and I kick it off with furious desperation.

Beads of sweat run down my forehead. My hair sticks to my face; I taste salt on my lips. The little hairs on my legs stick straight up; goosebumps cover my limbs.

The alarm is still beeping. I grab my phone and click 'dismiss.' Tears fill my eyes as I press my palms to my forehead.

I need to get it together.

I don't want fear clouding my memories of that house. I loved Gran. I still remember what she said to me that day, the day I was placed with her.

She told me hello. She said she was sorry about my parents; she said she could never replace them and didn't want to. And she told me that as long as I was with her, I would be safe, I would be fed and clothed, and I would be loved.

There was another girl at the house for a little while, Stephanie. But when she turned eighteen, she left for college and Gran brought home Amanda. Little, three-year-old, big-eyed Amanda. She looked so scared. I gave her my doll, the only one I had left from my mother. She smiled at me, and from that moment on, she was my sister.

It was good for six years, six of the best years of my life. But Gran got sick. I was fifteen, Amanda was only nine. I cried every night after Gran told me. Amanda would crawl into bed and cry with me. She didn't know why we were crying, but she curled up against me until I stopped.

The social worker was kind. She found us a home together. Gran always insisted I focus on school or I might have had a job. I might have been able to take care of Amanda by myself.

Instead, they placed us in *his* home.

A chill goes through my veins, and I gag.

I crawl out of bed, leaving sweat stains behind on the sheets. I sit on the carpet and run my hands across the fabric until it numbs my palms. I cross my legs and rest my hands, palms up, on my knees.

My breath regulates as my heart rate decreases. I close my eyes and let waves of calm pass over me. I become like a stone. A stone on the shore is still and silent. Waves pound upon it, the wind roars around it, but it does not make a sound.

The obvious flaw in this analogy is that with each wave, a small piece of the stone is broken down.

My muscles relax. I stand and stretch my arms above my head. I press my palms together between my breasts, take one leg off the ground, and place my foot just above my knee. After a moment, I switch feet. My breathing is steady.

I ease myself back down and place one leg in front of my body, knee bent and flat on the floor. I slowly lift my back leg up behind me, reach my torso around and stretch my arms into a crescent shape, taking my foot and holding the position for a count of ten. After switching sides, it is time to get ready.

My phone says it's 4 p.m. I organize my room a bit, switch out my nice camera for a disposable one, slip the 'do not disturb' sign on the doorknob, and head upstairs.

Nathan isn't back yet. I set up some music and start with my hair.

Tonight is just Nathan and myself. After tomorrow we will spend most of our time with his coworkers. He wants tonight to be just us.

I straighten my already straight hair, curling the ends out, so there is a bit of a flare. Then I lean forward and stare hard into the mirror.

I love turning my skin into a canvas, mixing different colors to create a blend that matches my skin tone. Making my eyes bigger or smaller with mascara, liner, and shadows of the rainbow brushed across my lids. Lipstick is my favorite. I own an extensive assortment of colors.

Nathan doesn't like heavy makeup.

I do the foundation and contouring. My cheeks light up. A few extra freckles dance across my nose and cheekbones.

He used to have me wipe off my makeup during our appointments.

I drag the tip of my liquid liner against the edge of my eyelid. Little wings form on either side of my eyes. Small, but perfectly even. A brush of my mascara wand adds layers to my lashes.

My hand quivers as I move to put on lipstick. I set down the darker red and go with a lighter shade.

When I was young, Gran would do my makeup. She taught me how to mix the colors and match them with my outfit. She always referred to makeup as a type of shield. A coat of armor. For when you have a bad day, feel sad, angry, insecure. A brush of lipstick can give you the confidence to go into battle.

After, when she was gone, makeup became a different kind of shield. A way to cover the truth. A way for me to hide behind myself.

I close my eyes and exhale.

My dress for tonight is black, a small thing, one strap across my right shoulder. The fabric pulls across my breasts and tightens under my chest before flaring out just enough that I can twirl and the skirt catches the wind. A single flower, a white iris, is stitched into the strap, just between my shoulder and collarbone.

I pull on pantyhose. Strappy black heels with small white gems increase my height by about four and a half inches.

The main door opens. "Lacey?"

"In here, Nathan," I call back.

"Ugh." He groans as he walks into the bedroom. He throws his jacket on the bed and then sits beside it before bending down to untie his dress shoes.

"How was your day? Is everything okay?" I mean it. I am interested in his day, his emotions. And he always did like when I asked the kinds of questions a wife would ask.

"Yeah. It could have been better. Then again, it could have been worse." He rubs the bridge of his nose and lies back on the bed.

I sit next to him and lie down. I prop my head up with one hand. With the other, I unbutton his shirt under the tie. "What happened?"

"Ehh." He takes my hand and kisses my plain fingernails. "Just some numbers issues. We have a couple factories—"

Factories.

"—that aren't adding up on some government forms. I didn't think I'd have to deal with this during the trip. I was hoping to spend a relaxing week with you. Especially..." Nathan pauses and glances sideways at me. "Especially after hearing from Miss Belle that you were finally ready to see me again."

I break into my warmest smile. "I missed you, Nathan. It's been too long. Thank you for being patient with me."

I finish with his buttons and loosen his tie, taking it apart with one hand. I keep the concerned wife act going. "What's wrong with the numbers? Are the employees not getting things done quickly enough?"

He helps me with the tie. "It's nothing like that. Our production has skyrocketed this last quarter." There is a pause. "Don't worry about it, Lacey. I'll have it all sorted out before Thursday."

I stand up, take his hand, and pull him to his feet. "I'm just happy to be here with you." I wink. "Even if you have to work."

"Well," he turns away, pulling out a fresh suit and getting dressed, "I'm done with work for tonight. I've got reservations for us at RyuGin." His chest puffs out a bit.

"That sounds lovely." I help adjust his pocket square and get my black and silver clutch.

We walk to the door. Nathan stops in the living room and checks the lock on the office door.

"Important secret documents?" I give him a sly grin, and he returns the smile.

"The answers to life's biggest questions."

I squeeze his arm as we step into the hallway and walk to the elevator. "Here I thought you were a spy, and it was information your enemies need to bring you down."

He looks down at me before pressing the button for the lobby. "No one can bring me down."

The warm smile I give him creates little crinkles around my eyes. We sink through the building. A serenade of soft jazz fills the brown and gold box.

The elevator opens up on the ground floor, and Nathan guides me toward the door. Marcus and Kong stand beside a sculpture of spikes stemming from the ground and curving into hooks, talking to Daniel Jacobson.

"Give me just a second." Nathan pulls away, but I keep his arm.

"Are you bringing security to dinner?"

"No, I just need to check on something."

I pout. "I thought you were done working."

He pats my arm and chuckles. "It'll just be a quick sec."

I cling to his arm and follow him to the men. It's a trick Miss Belle taught us. Stay with the mark. Let them think you can't be without them for a minute. And men are more likely to continue their conversation if you are staring up at one of them rather than facing the group.

"… to make sure he was taken care of," Daniel says.

"We tossed him out and alerted the front desk and hotel security." Marcus flexes his crossed arms.

"Do more." Daniel glares at Marcus. "I don't want problems this week."

"There is a *limit* to what we can do, legally." Kong's deep voice holds an edge.

Nathan steps into the circle. "Everything all right here?"

"Yes." Marcus tilts his head at me.

"All they did was send him from the building," Daniel grumbles.

"You paid us to do security." Kong glances at Nathan. "If you'd like more than that, you know our fees."

"The situation is taken care of, yes?" Nathan asks.

"Yes." Marcus nods curtly. "If he returns, we will discuss other ways of dealing with him."

"Enjoy tonight." Nathan pats Daniel's shoulder. "Don't worry about the kid. Work is almost done; let's have a good time while we're here."

Daniel looks at me and gives Nathan a tight smile. "Good reminder. Have a fun night, you two."

Nathan nods and leads me away.

"What was that about?"

"Nothing important."

"Hmm," I grumble. "It sounded important." I squeeze his arm as we walk through the door. "It sounded like you're going to have to do a lot of work this week." I pull him around and stick out my bottom lip in a pout.

He grins at me. I clearly want to spend all my time with him. I don't want to share him with work. "I have a little more to do tomorrow, but tonight is about you. I promise."

He leans down and kisses my forehead. His lips are dry.

We walk a ways, enjoying the dwindling sunlight. Nathan holds my hand, chatting about the last few years.

A limo pulls up to the curb; Chang is the driver. His presence doesn't surprise me. It's likely Marissa asked him to wiggle his way into the evening, especially after our talk last night. She likes for us to know we have someone on our team. Even half a world away from home.

The drive is only about fifteen minutes.

RyuGin is one of those restaurants most people only dream of dining at. There is an extensive waitlist and an even more extensive set of conditions for the diners.

Nathan takes my hand and helps me out of the limo. He says something to Chang, and the vehicle pulls away from the curb. The building is gorgeous. It has staggered levels—one tall and shimmering, set with strips of black panels and sections of gold and white light wrapping around it, the other shorter, but no less beautiful with matching gold slatted windows. The corners are rounded, giving the structure a softer look.

I turn, admiring the park just across the street. There's an idea... if Nathan doesn't feel chatty enough during dinner.

We have a reservation (as one must in a place like this) for the regular dining area. Nathan tries to bribe our way into a private room, and grows increasingly agitated as he fails, until I caress his arm, pointing out how beautiful the main room is. My gushing compliments, assuring him of how pleased I am with the restaurant, calm him down.

The place smells delicious and looks spectacular. We are seated. The waiter pours the drinks. There is no need to order in a place like this, the chef knows what he wants to make. You eat it, or you don't. The first three courses arrive without interruption. Nathan chats about the conference, who came, who didn't; we gossip about wives who declined invitations, opening the way for women of my expertise. I tell him about a juicy bit of gossip I overheard at the Museum regarding a Christmas party and a blowjob. He laughs a bit too loud; the waiter gives us a look.

Each time my water reaches the half-way mark, a well-dressed man rushes to my side and fills it to the brim. Each plate is brought out at just the right time. The scent of warm spices greets me with the soup. The clean, cold, fresh taste of fish accompanies the tiny bites I take of the sushi course. When the meat comes, I stick to the veggies.

Nathan pesters me about the wild duck. I politely refuse, and he isn't upset about my not eating meat—not this time.

"So," I say as we reach the dessert course.

Nathan reaches his spoon across the table and—without asking—takes a bite of my strawberry-topped cheesecake.

"I heard you guys have been looking to cut costs on the new factories."

He swallows the cheesecake without chewing and gives me a sharp look. "Where did you hear that?"

"I don't know." I shrug it off nonchalantly. "Someone on the trip today was talking about cheaper labor. I know that kind of thing interests you." I slide my hand across the table, warmth seeping through my movements. "I like talking about things that interest you."

He relaxes at my smile and we discuss the pros and cons of labor outside the States for a few minutes. Well, he discusses. I smile along and pretend I don't already know most of what he tells me.

None of it helps narrow down my search.

Once the meal is complete and Nathan has paid, we ride the elevator to the ground floor and step out into the night. The cold surprises me. It's warm for Japan this time of year, but I still shiver in the sixty-degree weather. Nathan offers me his jacket. We cross the street at my suggestion and begin a stroll through Hibiya Park. The movement, and the sweet smell of the cherry blossoms warms me as much as the coat.

A gaggle of children race by us as their family leaves the park. Nathan pulls me closer to his side and gives the couple a polite nod. They don't stare the way many would in the States. Japanese culture is a little different, more accepting of couples with such an age difference.

It's a bit early in the season—and definitely still too cold—for the cicadas to start their songs; the insects are strictly summer creatures in Japan. But I catch sight of a few lightning bugs in the trees and bushes. I point them out to Nathan and enjoy his excitement.

He says they remind him of Texas.

I change the subject. "I'm impressed with your progress." We sit on a bench and I wrap myself in his arms. "CFO in only four years? Not everyone would be able to get that far so quickly."

"Well, I've been with the company longer than that. You remember, I worked in the legal department back in Houston for a few years."

I nod. A fountain to the left of us creates a steady backdrop of sound, akin to a small waterfall, for our conversation.

I push a bit more. "Didn't you get that promotion pretty recently? I thought I heard Mr. Jacobson talking about it."

"Yeah," he relents. "I suppose it was a pretty big jump from where I was."

"What made them *finally* realize your potential?" I exaggerate my words, making it sound like I knew all along he'd be helping run the company someday.

"I found a hole in our labor division. Money being spent that didn't need to be. With Jacobson's help, I cut down costs by almost forty percent."

My pulse quickens. This is the right track... we just have to stay on it. "Wow, that's a lot, huh?"

He chuckles and gives me a condescending smile. "Yes, Lacey. That's a lot. Imagine if you were forty percent cheaper. It saved the company quite a bit of money."

I swallow down the heat that rises up with his words. Taking a moment to hide my face, I pretend to examine the fountain; I close my eyes and breathe in the crisp air. The pounding of water on water numbs my mind for a moment, allowing me to release my anger.

"How did you do it?" My voice is innocent, curious, awed. I glance back up at him with wide eyes.

He falls for it. "It was just some maneuvering of labor, setting up factories in new places, hiring different people to run them."

Okay, he kind of falls for it. This vague information is about as helpful as a paddle in the desert.

"Where are the new places?" I lean into the question with a hint of neediness and longing. "Maybe they're close enough to the east coast that I can see you more often?"

There it is. That look in his eye, the one that tells me he believes he is the most important thing in my life. The one that says he believes I would do anything for him. Me. The woman he is currently *paying* to be with him.

"Sorry, darling, the new factories are in our Asian markets. Even if they were in the States, my dealings with them are purely numbers related. I don't actually visit the factories."

Ego—it does great things for my business.

I give a smile and a disappointed sigh, then curl tighter into his chest. We sit in comfortable silence for a few minutes, watching other couples wander the park in the evening chill.

Asian markets. That's the most helpful clue I've gotten since arriving. It doesn't narrow the options by a lot, but hopefully, it will be enough to get what I need later tonight.

I can't keep pushing Nathan. Too many questions will lead to the kind of answers he can't give me. And when people find themselves unable to answer questions, they start asking them instead.

We stand and walk on, rounding the far side of the park and heading back to where we began. We pass a little tree with a sealed plastic box holding books. Little clay statues, trees, bushes, and benches line a clean concrete walkway. A second fountain, with a base of water large enough that the surrounding city lights reflect off its surface, looms before us.

I lose myself, just for a moment, in the beauty around me. I forget who I'm with, why I'm here, all of it. I gaze, transfixed, at the glittering surface until Nathan gently tugs my arm, and we continue on.

He pulls his phone from his pocket and clicks a few buttons, and by the time we reach the road, Chang has arrived with the limo. He rushes around to open the door for us, and his hand brushes my arm as I step inside. A small sign that he is there if I need him.

Nathan doesn't see.

Tomorrow is the last day of meetings. So tonight will be quiet, just Nathan and me in his suite.

I change into my white lacy booty shorts and a white tank top and head into the living area. Nathan comes out of the bedroom in a pair of sweats and a Marlins T-shirt. He gapes at me, sitting on the couch, white fabric pulled across my chest.

My arms twitch. An old urge to cover myself is blocked by my mission here. Instead, I shift my body, pulling my knees up, and tucking my feet into the crevice of the couch.

Nathan tears his gaze away from my chest and goes into the kitchen. A few minutes later, the microwave dings. The scent of melted butter and burnt kernels fill the air. Nathan brings the bowl over and taps my knee. I lift my legs, he sits, and I drape my legs across his lap. The bowl goes on my thighs, and we munch on the salty popcorn as *Bloodsport* boots up on the massive flat-screen.

Jean-Claude Van Damme is Nathan's favorite actor, and *Bloodsport* is the film with which he finds the most connection.

I've seen it over a dozen times. But not once in the last four years.

I focus on the popcorn, studying each kernel before placing it on my tongue. I find pictures in the puffy part. A horse, the Eiffel Tower, hearts, and stars. Faces.

Blood splatters across the screen.

Nathan gives me a foot rub, then we cuddle for the rest of the film. We head to bed early. Nathan has something planned for tomorrow evening; he says we will need to get an extra bit of sleep tonight.

He will get it. I won't.

I stare up at the ceiling, watching the fan spin round and round above me. The clock on the wall ticks. The hotel designer messed up, putting a hand clock on the wall. I hear each second as it passes.

Finally, Nathan's breathing becomes heavy and long. Soft snores interrupt every few seconds. I slide out of the covers, tiptoe across the floor, grabbing my purse along the way, and return to my search.

I pick the lock again, and his office door opens with ease. Pulling it closed behind me, I flick on the light and settle into the chair. This time I *will* find what I was sent here for. The possible locations for this information shrank with last night's search. They shrank more with the conversations I overheard throughout the day.

Within twenty minutes, I find the file. A factory in Thailand has all the correct information for product output, materials, electricity, and square footage. But their labor details are severely lacking. A few people in management positions, and a description of how much money they're spending on food—zero information about the people actually on the assembly line.

After a few more minutes of digging, I find details of the weapons bought for use at this factory, along with the coordinates of both the factory itself and the small village from which the people were taken. My jaw clenches as I think of the men, women, and children stolen from their homes. People made into slaves, so a multi-million-dollar company can save a few hundred thousand a year. My stomach churns.

I snap away with my disposable camera, twist through a full roll of film and pull another from my purse. I capture every shred of evidence three times over.

I get out my phone and call Miss Belle. "I've got it," I murmur.

"All of it?" A chair scrapes across the ground on her end of the phone. Footsteps click along a wooden floor.

"Yes." I push out my chair and lean forward, tilting the laptop up for a better angle. "I've got the financial records, the location of the village, and the location of the factory. It's in the Bueng Kan province, right on the border."

A door opens and closes—silence over the line for a minute.

Then, "Is the village in Thailand or Laos?"

"I think Laos, but I have the coordinates. I've got the pictures. I'll send them tomorrow morning."

"All right. So not much else to do on this trip." A sigh expresses her relief.

My chest heaves as I inhale. "Nope. Just getting the film to Chang in the morning. It won't be any trouble. There are a few meetings Nathan will be busy with."

I take another breath and it shakes through my lungs on the way out. My lips quiver.

Miss Belle is quiet.

"Then I'll be headed home." Unlike me to break a silence.

"You could come home tomorrow." Miss Belle's voice is monotone. She is neither encouraging me to leave my assignment early nor is she urging me to stay. To my knowledge, she has never once suggested a girl leave a mission early.

"That would seem a bit suspicious, wouldn't it?"

"We could take you out of the field for a while." Again, she is problem solving, not putting her own emotion or opinion into the mix.

It is tempting. So tempting to leave. I know when I sleep tonight, I will dream again. I know each moment I spend with Nathan will chip away more and more from my stone self.

I lick my top lip and pull the bottom one between my teeth, biting before I respond. "If I left, it would be the end of the assignment. It could break my cover. And it would ruin our reputation with more than a dozen clients."

Her steady breath is all I hear for a full ten seconds, then, "The decision is yours. If you can finish it out, do so. If you think this mission will break *you*, come home."

My eyes burn and my nose itches. "It's only a few more days."

I almost hear her nodding. Almost see her crack a half-grin. The one she wears when something is wrong, but she doesn't want to admit it.

"Call me, Lacey. With anything. Me or Missa, anytime."

"I know." I smile at her concern. At the love she has for me, for each of us.

I close out everything on the laptop, change the 'last viewed' times on the documents, and swing the door closed behind me.

My eyes adjust to the darkness. A hint of blue light filters in from the large windows.

I return my purse to the living room table. I slip the camera back into it and put both rolls of film in the little zippered section on the side.

I stand.

The light turns on.

My breath catches as I hear the floor settle under Nathan's weight.

"What are you doing out here?"

I turn, facing him with a sad smile on my lips. His gaze is locked on me.

"I couldn't sleep."

His eyes dart to the office door. My heart skips a beat—I left the desk lamp on.

"You know I always had trouble sleeping." I squint as I force my smile to grow.

"I'd hoped you'd be able to sleep with me beside you." There is pain in his voice. As though I've offended him with my insomnia.

I release a soft chuckle and step away from my purse, toward Nathan. "I slept better last night than I have in ages."

A lie.

"Being next to you helps more than you know."

I take another step and run my hand up his chest.

"But sometimes I need to walk around a bit, breathe some fresh air, stretch out." I go on my toes and kiss his cheek. "You understand."

He takes my wrist in his hand and puts his other on my shoulder. "I do. His gaze flicks to the office door. "But do your walking, stretching and breathing in the bedroom. I don't want to be apart from you even for a second."

I nod. Widen my eyes and flutter my lashes. I'm a good little girl. I'll stay where he wants me.

LACEY

THANK HEAVENS FOR QUICK ROOM SERVICE

I stand to the side again. I watch little Lacey hold Amanda's hand as they walk through the front door. I want, with everything in me, to warn her. But it's a dream. And I can't talk.

Instead, I watch it happen with a dense weight in my stomach. Watch little Lacey—not so little now—get pushed up against the wall. She struggles. The Beatles poster behind her head swirls with psychedelic colors.

I can't move. I can't do anything to stop him as he pins her to the wall. His arm against her throat. Her head jammed into the poster. His body is pressed up against hers. She feels him, his excitement at this display of violent power. He whispers in her ear.

Other voices whisper in my ears as shame spirals within my heart. They repeat the words, "whore," "slut," "skank," over and over. Tendrils reach out from the poster and grab at me.

I can move now. I stumble backward. I glance back at little Lacey, tears running silently down her cheeks as his hand moves lower. But I don't help her. I just run.

I race through the house. Walls dissolve around me, melting into a thousand arms that grab at my clothes. The whispers around me turn into screams. I panic. I reach the front door. It's wrong. Red. Dripping. Melting away. I run through it and sink once more into sheer, cold darkness.

I wake up screaming. My body shakes; sweat drips from my forehead. The sheets are tied up around my legs, and I kick them off in frantic, quick motions.

That was when I learned to be still. To be silent. I kept Amanda with me always. Unless *he* had a job for me. I walked with her to school. I made her wait to walk home with me. I slipped into her room after... every night to make sure no one else did. The only time I slept was when she was cuddled up in my arms.

We made a deal that day. When he came into my room and changed the course of my life forever. I wouldn't fight him as he sold me to anyone he wanted. I wouldn't call for help. I would be good. And he wouldn't touch Amanda. Little, ten-year-old Amanda.

I press my fist against my forehead, pushing the images out of my mind.

I could have left at eighteen. But they wouldn't give me Amanda, and she was growing up. He kept his word if I stayed. He didn't use her.

I crawl from the bed, landing on the floor and leaning back against the mattress. The sound of water spraying against tile echoes out from the bathroom. Nathan must not have heard me. Hopefully, I have a few minutes before he gets out.

My face is cold, clammy, likely incredibly pale. The lines in my palms are damp and dirty. My fingers shake. Each breath I take only fills a quarter of my lungs.

The water shuts off. I snap up and run out of the room. I stop in the kitchen and stick my head in the fridge. After a moment, I close the door, pulling out a little boxed cranberry juice.

By the time Nathan comes looking for me, I'm perched happily on a stool, sucking my juice through the small straw. He is still in his boxers, his hair damp and pressed against his round head. I peer up at him, innocent, bleary-eyed, and tired, and he smiles.

"I thought I heard you yelling while I was in the shower. Is everything all right?"

"Yes." I sheepishly bow my head. "I thought I saw a spider. Just some lint."

He raises an eyebrow. "Okay."

"I ordered room service." My voice quavers just a little. I strengthen it. "Go get dressed, and we can eat together before you start your meetings."

His head tilts to the side. He enjoys the wife-like questions a lot more than the wife-like directions.

"I want to spend some time with just you." I stand and go to him. "You said we're spending time with everyone else tonight. *And* I won't get to see you for most of the day."

He sighs. "All right. I'll be right out."

I grin and bounce away. As soon as Nathan leaves the room, I pick up the living room phone and quietly order breakfast. Today I make it as American as possible. Eggs, pancakes, French toast, bacon, sausage, and coffee with loads of cream and sugar. I ask them to put a rush on it. It's a woman on the phone, and I tell her I was supposed to order it half an hour ago, and my husband will be quite frustrated with me if it doesn't arrive soon.

She sympathizes, and the food arrives twenty minutes later.

Nathan wants to talk during breakfast. "So, what exactly happened?" Bacon grease drips from the left corner of his mouth. "When you left?"

I freeze, a speared pancake coated with syrup dangling a few inches from my lips. I swallow down my fear and pop the sugary breakfast into my mouth. I tilt my head in a "what do you mean?" gesture. I chew slowly.

"I haven't seen you in four years, Lacey. I know you went to work for Miss Belle. But... I never heard from her, apart from letting me know you wouldn't be available to anyone from your time with—"

Before he can say the name, I choke and cough and sputter. I make a mountain of noise. After making a show of getting some water, relaxing my cough and being able to breathe again, I smile at him. "I was... trained by Miss Belle for a bit."

"I thought you'd picked up some new tricks."

If only he knew.

"Yes." I delicately tear apart a piece of pancake. "Then it was business as usual. I kept working, but with new clients. Miss Belle's clients."

"She was good for you then?"

I raise an eyebrow. "Yes. I'd say she was the best thing that could have ever happened to me."

A smug smile crosses his thick, greasy lips. "Well, then you should know... *I'm* the best thing that happened to you. I'm the one who called her. After I saw you that last time..." He shakes his head in disgust, though the smile remains in place. "I had to get you help."

I watch him for a moment, waiting for a sign, any tell that he is lying. But there is nothing.

I've had my suspicions about this for a long time. But I always hoped it wasn't because of Nathan. I can't stand the thought of owing him.

I gush, thanking him, telling him how wonderful my life is now. Telling him he saved me. Telling him I practically owe him my life. Telling him he is my knight. My prince. My hero.

I don't tell him that I was sixteen when he first came to me, not eighteen as he thought. I don't tell him that during the four years he paid for me, I wore makeup to hide the extent of my bruises.

I don't tell him how, after a while, some men get tired of paying for the basics. I don't tell him the room was dark on purpose. I don't tell him the last time he saw me wasn't even a bad night. A dislocated finger, sprained wrist, cut lip, and sunset-colored bruise across my cheekbone was nothing but a standard Friday.

I don't mention that if he hadn't demanded I remove my makeup, he wouldn't have even known.

Finally, he has to leave. "Just a few hours of meetings, then I'll be back for you."

The phrasing sends a shudder through me. I splash a smile across my lips. "I can't wait."

I lose my breakfast when he leaves. Tears press from my eyes as I heave over the white porcelain.

I call Missa. The moment the phone clicks, I say, "I can't do this."

Those words haven't left my lips in a long time.

"What?" Missa shushes someone in the background.

It's 8 p.m. in New York. The family, those at home anyway, will be sitting down to dinner. I should have called Miss Belle.

But I told her just this morning that I'd be fine. And now I'm letting her down.

"I can't finish this. I… I need to come home tomorrow."

"Okay." No silence, no hesitation. She and Miss Belle must have discussed this already. "I'll book you a flight. Are you sure you want to wait until tomorrow?"

I sigh. "Yeah. Nathan has an evening planned. A show and something with his boss. It will already look horrible for me to leave early, but leaving today would set off too many red flags."

"I'll email you as soon as the flight is confirmed. And I'll call Chang to take you to the airport."

"What should I do with the film? I can still send it today."

"It'll get here the same time as you, if not later. Stow one roll in your carry-on, and the other in your purse."

I nod, remember I'm on the phone, and say, "Okay."

"Stay safe today, Lacey. You've done the hardest part of this mission. Just focus on getting home now."

It's time for goodbye. To hang up and get to work. I clench the phone between my fingers. "Missa…"

"Yeah?"

"I'm sorry. I'm sorry I couldn't…"

Her sigh is heavy. "We'll talk when you get back. You have *nothing* to apologize for. You shouldn't have been sent on this assignment in the first place. But that's between Miss Belle and me. You take care of yourself. We'll see you soon."

I shower and dress; I have a trip to an art exhibit that I desperately don't want to go on. But it must be business as usual until tomorrow. My stomach churns as I make my way down to the lobby.

The Do Not Disturb sign is still dangling from the door to my own room when I return from the exhibit. I slip inside and pack up my carry-on, tucking one of the film rolls into an outer pocket. The other remains in my purse. My mind flashes through several excuses. Reasons I can give to Nathan to explain my early disappearance.

I have almost two hours left until I need to get ready for the evening. So I sit. My miniature metronome ticks steadily in front of me. The carpet provides a comforting cushion. I cross my legs under me, and I breathe. Really breathe. Silence fills me. The oxygen I take in consumes every ounce of space in my lungs.

I push through the thoughts of the mission, past worry for letting down my family, fear of getting caught, doubt as to my abilities. I thrust deeper down into my mind. I see Amanda. Beautiful, perfectly innocent Amanda. I kept her safe for so many years.

I dig deeper still, plunging past my bitter sadness over the loss of Gran.

They stand in front of me when I reach the bottom of my mind. They wear the same outfits. A sleek black dress with a pearl necklace. A handsome pinstriped suit with a triple fold pocket square.

I used to think I could be Batman. My parents died coming home from the theater after all. There were a few issues with my fantasy. The first was that our family was not wealthy beyond comfort. The second was the difficulty in finding revenge against a drunk driver serving a thirty-year sentence.

They smile at me. I smile back. Mom steps forward and puts her hand on my cheek; I helped with her nails for that night. The white polish is perfect on her left hand, a little shaky on her right. It accents her skin, just a shade darker than mine.

"You be good now, while we're gone." Her words are like a whisper. Soft, tender, and gentle as they caress me. I never want her to stop talking.

"She's always good." Dad walks over. One hand in his pocket, the other pulls a toothpick out of his mouth and tosses it aside. He bends down in front of me and winks. He does a little eyebrow wiggle, the one that used to make me laugh until I couldn't breathe. "Little Lacey is the best gosh darn girl in Texas."

"Of course she is." My mother smiles at me. Her eyes tilt up at the edges, just like mine. "Stay well, my little love," she says in Korean, offering me the tiniest wave before turning to go.

And that's it. That is all they say.

No matter how hard I try, how much hypnosis I practice upon myself, meditation, therapy, even in my dreams, my parents are never able to say more than their last words to me.

When what I want, what I need, more than anything, is to have a conversation with them one more time. Even if it's just in my head, I need them to say more. To tell me I did the right thing with Amanda. To tell me I didn't make a mistake by staying in that house.

They turn and walk away. My father opens a nonexistent door. My mother pats his arm as she walks through the invisible doorway. They fade from view. The last thing to go is my mother's hair. Dark, like mine. But with a tinge of red at the edges.

Now it's just me. Standing alone in the blackness of my mind.

One of the bad things about traveling is how lonely it can be. Depending on your trip, you can be surrounded by loved ones, or alone in a foreign place. Sure, maybe you've made a few friends, but they are all new, and none of them know you the way family does.

It is important to note here that I don't necessarily mean biological family. I mean the family you have when you are home. Be it friends, neighbors, siblings, parents, work buddies, etc.

The point I'm trying to make is that you must ensure a connection with the people who love you. Don't find yourself two weeks into an adventure, smacked in the face with a bout of depression and severe homesickness. Call your mom. Call your friends. Tell them about your experience, or just say hi. But keep that connection. Don't let the isolation of the world drag you down.

CHAPTER TEN

LACEY

NEVER MESS WITH A WOMAN'S CURLS

My carry-on is ready to go, but I pack up my other things and get my luggage set up on the bed, ready for Chang to pick up when he comes for me tomorrow. He will store most of it until my next mission in Tokyo.

I sway in the elevator as it takes me back to Nathan's suite. There's an hour left before he returns. I'm going to make the most of it.

The curling iron provided by the hotel is high quality. I twist small chunks of my hair around the rod and come away with perfect little ringlets. It only takes thirty minutes to curl my mass of dark hair. I get through half of *Abbey Road* before I start on the makeup. My outfit for tonight is a two piece. The black top hovers just above my waist, leaving room for dangling diamonds to drape down my stomach, hanging from my pierced belly button. I slip into a pair of flared black linen pants with silver stitched swirls climbing up the right leg. Boots with a two-inch heel complete my ensemble.

I wouldn't usually wear so much black. But I have an idea of what kind of party this will be, and it's better for me to blend into the shadows rather than stand out in a bright top.

My makeup is simple. Nathan already won't like my outfit as much as the others I've worn so far. It's too edgy, too strong.

I need it tonight.

He comes in as I put the finishing touches on my lipstick. Sweat beads down his forehead and he wipes it away with his pocket square. The bedroom door closes, and he walks over and collapses on the bed.

I take a breath.

My smile lights up the room when I walk to him. So happy to see him, missing him after all day apart. "Hey, you."

He unbuttons his shirt and gestures for me to join him.

I crawl up and lean down over his chest, careful not to press on my curls.

"Hey." He groans and loosens his tie.

"How was work?" I stick out my tongue on the last word.

He laughs. "It was a pain. Still dealing with that stupid factory. How hard is it to fix some paperwork?"

"No idea." I push myself up, sit next to him on the bed, and help tug at his tie. "That's why you're the business one, and I'm the cute one."

I move to stand once his tie is loosened, but he grabs my wrist. "Stay here with me. Just for a bit."

I grin at him. "I spent thirty minutes on these curls. I don't want them to flatten before the party tonight."

"No one will notice."

I give him an exasperated giggle. "The other women will notice."

"You're worried about a bunch of whores judging you?"

I freeze. A cold rush goes through me, just under my skin.

He hasn't noticed that something is wrong. Instead, he sits up, kisses my cheek, and finishes getting undressed.

I stand and leave the room.

I fiddle with my phone while I wait for him. The temptation to call Miss Belle flitters around in my head. But a pang of burning guilt in my gut tells me not to. I've let her down. Talking to her right now will only make me feel worse.

Nathan comes out. His perfectly tailored, two-thousand-dollar suit is actually quite handsome on him. The salt and pepper in his hair accent the gray and black striped tie. He holds out his arm, and I take it. He kisses my forehead, and I smile up at him as though everything is all right. As though I am not one of the whores he spoke of earlier.

I grab my purse and his arm, and we are off.

The restaurant is in the third and tallest of the Hyatt buildings. The food is fantastic, though Nathan pushes a bit harder today for me to put aside the seafood and try his steak. I politely decline, reminding him of my desire to stay away from eating meat.

Dessert is delicious, if a bit tense. Nathan is frustrated with me. My lack of bending to his will.

When we leave, I am happy to go to the theater. He won't be able to talk to me during the show, and I won't be able to see his dirty looks in the dark.

The senior staff and partners of Nathan's firm are attending a show tonight. We are meeting them at the Kabuki-za Theatre, a good twenty minutes closer to Tokyo Bay than the hotel. Normally I know Nathan would have wanted to book another limo, but by the time he realized the show wasn't at the hotel, they were all booked. I tell him I don't mind; it's a chance to experience the real side of Tokyo. The subway system runs until midnight, but Nathan vehemently demands we take a cab. Apparently, during his first encounter with Japanese subways, uniformed men with white gloves pushed him onto an already full train, leading to a severe lack of personal space.

I barely stifle my laugh as he tells me how terrible it was. A cab pulls to the curb and the driver clicks a button on the dash. The back door opens. Nathan gestures for me to climb in, grumbling about overcrowded subways and cabbies who don't open doors for you.

I pat his arm sympathetically. At least he's stopped glowering about my eating habits.

The Kabuki-za Theatre is about as classically Japanese as it gets. From the clean white walls, red trim and lanterns, and gold accents, to the kirizuma roof (one of many Japanese roofing styles, but definitely the one American tourists most associate with ancient Japan). Twin purple banners, marked with what looks like a white bird in a circle, hang above the entryway.

Though the theater is by no means small, the skyscrapers of present-day Japan tower behind the shorter building. In the dark evening, their light, and the lights from the traffic, seem to diminish the beauty before us.

Nathan takes my arm. We join the throng of excited theater goers and make our way into the ornate building.

I'm thankful that we ate before coming. The smells coming from the food service stations are intoxicating. Spices seep into the air, spiraling up from the steam rising from pots of fresh soup and noodles. A shorter, elderly woman passes in front of us, and I am struck with a heart-wrenching memory of Gran, sitting up late into the night, keeping my nightmares away with steaming mugs of jasmine tea.

I turn away, unlatching from Nathan's arm and trying to focus on anything else. A red table covered in Kabuki figurines catches my eye. I fiddle with one of the little pieces of porcelain.

"Do you want one?" Nathan murmurs from behind me, his warm breath brushing against my ear.

"Not right now." I move away from the table, smiling.

Concern causes a crease in his forehead and a distance in his gaze. He rests a hand on my shoulder. "Everything okay?"

"Everything is wonderful. Tonight has been lovely." I caress his arm. "I want to wait and see the show before I decide if I want one of these."

He nods and his hand slides down my shoulder and rests at the small of my back. We make our way through the crowd of tourists and locals, all vying for a better view of the products on display.

Once through the doorway into the actual theater, we climb a set of red and gold carpeted stairs to our seats in the balcony. A loud, obnoxious laugh bounds through the air. Daniel is in the seat next to ours. Delilah sits next to him, a loose smile on her face; they both smell of vodka and weed.

Daniel is in a pair of swimming trunks and a button up Hawaiian shirt. Delilah catches each man's eye in her low-cut, stunning, red cocktail dress. My outfit is a bit low class for this event, but next to them, I feel perfectly attired.

The show is hilarious. Men in vibrant outfits with sheet white faces and every style of wig imaginable, dance, argue, fight, and fly across the stage. There are acrobatic tricks, adult jokes, and even a few dangerous stunts. It defines the word spectacular.

I laugh with Nathan, holding his leg as I double over in fits of giggles. His chest expands each time I toss a happy grin in his direction.

Intermission means snacks. Daniel makes for the food, snapping at Delilah to stay put while he finds them something to drink. Nathan asks if I'm hungry; I tell him dinner was too fabulous for me to be hungry, but I'd love some tea.

He leaves to get drinks as well.

I jump over a seat and give Delilah a friendly nudge with my shoulder. "What do you think so far?"

"It's not what they said it would be."

I frown. That's not the response I was expecting. "I think it's pretty good. I wasn't expecting anything really different."

"Well no." She faces me. Her eye makeup is heavy. "You're with Mr. Blake, and you've done this before."

Oh. The gut punch of realization almost makes me flinch.

She turns back toward the stage. "It's just not what they said."

I want to respond. I want to pull her into a hug and tell her it never is. I want to reassure her that it's not easy for me either.

Daniel returns and watches me until I move over. They didn't have his preferred alcohol. He grumbles that the second half better be shorter than the first.

Nathan rejoins us a few minutes later. He hands me a steaming cup of green tea, which I sip gratefully. We hold hands during the rest of the play.

Nathan asks me if I enjoyed the show. I tell him it was splendid. I thank him for including me and ask what is next.

We make our way to Daniel's penthouse. In the cab, Nathan pulls out a little Kabuki figurine, one of the ones I'd been eyeing. My insides knot up.

I hate how good it feels when he is kind to me.

Chapter Eleven

Lacey

Now What?

It takes Daniel and Delilah almost a full five minutes longer to arrive. We step into the elevator and ride it all the way. At the top floor, we walk down a narrow hallway and board a separate elevator. With the scan of a keycard, this one takes us right to his suite.

Daniel's penthouse is almost an exact replica of Nathan's. It's larger, with a second bedroom and bathroom down a little hallway. The kitchenette is sticky, empty bottles and food wrappers scattered across the counters. The air in the living room is stale and smells of smoke. The office door to the left is closed.

Marcus and Kong arrive. Marcus settles himself at the piano. As people join us in Daniel's room, he launches into a beautiful piece. It's Chopin, *Nocturne in C-Sharp Minor*, if I'm not mistaken. His face changes as his fingers caress the keys, sad notes dangling in the air. Hard hands melt as they do a slow waltz across the ebony and ivory. His eyes close, the rough features softening into an expression emoting pain, even despair.

Kong finds a corner with a good view of the door.

Delilah wanders to the piano and leans against it, her eyes closed as she listens to the music.

Daniel's face pinches in a twisted frown, and he stomps over to her. His hand closes around her wrist as his gaze lands on Marcus. "I'm paying you to work security, not play this crap," he spits.

Marcus freezes with his large fingers dangling over the keys. A forced smile parts his lips, and he stands up with a nod. The elevator dings and a group of men from Daniel's company arrive. Marcus closes the piano. He places himself across the room from Kong, still with a good view of the door, and takes a Zippo lighter out of his pocket. He rolls it between his fingers, playing with the shiny silver metal.

We sprawl across the living room area. Delilah has replaced her dress with a see-through pink top, a white lace bra underneath, and a petite, black mini-skirt. Several more women pour into the room, also wearing sheer, tight, short clothing. Laughter abounds. Someone turns on the TV. Old episodes of *Friends* play across the screen. English subtitles accompany Japanese audio.

Nathan sits in the lounge chair, and I plop down in his lap. He runs a hand through my hair, tugging the curls.

"See." He pinches my thigh. "No one cares if your curls are flat."

I stick out my tongue, and a flash of lust shoots through his eyes. A colleague shouts his name, and Nathan's attention turns.

Daniel tears apart the bar and pours everyone a shot. Delilah hands them around, tripping on her six-inch stilettos as she goes. Daniel cackles and tells her to take off her shoes. She kicks them into the corner as he pulls a small bag of white powder from his pocket.

The coffee table becomes a set up for cocaine and ecstasy. Daniel rolls a hundred-dollar bill and recreates a scene from a bad gangster movie as he bends over with a razor blade.

Delilah continues passing around drinks, taking plenty herself. Smoke fills the room, turning the girls giggly and the men hungry. Someone orders room service. They bring food and more liquor.

I hold a glass of wine and chuckle away offers to drink. The other girls fill their belly buttons with whiskey. Fat, old men feel young and strong as they drink from youthful skin. Nathan runs his hands over my bare stomach, playing with the diamonds hanging from my belly button. Each drink has him pulling me tighter into his lap.

One of the men disappears into the bedroom with two of the girls. Daniel shouts after him to keep the charges down and guffaws.

Another of the girls gets up and stumbles into us. "Sorry!" She giggles. Bright purple pigtails stick out on either side of her head. She opted for a more childish look tonight. Her short forest green skirt and the matching top which is twisted into a knot below her breasts reminds me of thin mints.

"Hey." She slurs just a bit, but her smile is genuine. "You're one of Miss Belle's girls."

The edges of my lips tug upwards in a smile I can't stop. Not that I want to. Being referred to as one of Miss Belle's girls is something I love. It may sound possessive to some, but it reminds me I have a home. And a family.

My jaw clenches. I think about the email I received before we came upstairs. My flight leaves tomorrow at 3:30 p.m. A heaviness presses the space between my breasts.

I shake it off, my smile snapping back up as I nod to the purple haired girl. "She's the best."

"I've heard." She leans in and murmurs near my ear, "I'd give anything to be one of hers. Please tell her for me?" She stands and says, louder, "I'm Shimmer. It's wonderful to meet you."

Her gaze turns to Nathan. "I'm so jealous." She winks at me. "I don't have a date tonight. Mr. Jacobson got a bunch of us to come for the last few days of the event. But there aren't enough men to go around." Her bottom lip turns out in a plump pout.

Nathan erupts with laughter and grabs her wrist. "Lacey's always been one to share. Trust me, I've known her longer than anyone."

The heaviness in my chest drops to my stomach.

Shimmer lets out a high squeal and bats his hand away. "Maybe later." The laughter in her face doesn't quite reach her eyes. "It's too quiet in here."

I reach out, with as much discretion as possible, and squeeze her arm before she walks away. Nathan extends his free hand, and smacks her ass, hard, once she's turned around. She stumbles forward but throws back a giggle and another wink.

I watch her walk away and pick up some of the little blue pills on her way to the stereo. Music fills the room.

Shimmer dances alone in the corner for a few minutes. Eventually, she makes her way over to Marcus and tumbles into his lap. Her eyes are glazed over. She says something, and he whispers in her ear. He plays with one of her ponytails. Kong smirks from his side of the room.

"So!" Daniel grins over at Nathan from his seat on the floor. "Did you get those numbers fixed for the Thailand branch?"

I swirl my full glass of wine and pretend to be absorbed with the television.

"Not just yet." Nathan takes a swig of his drink. Ice clinks in the glass. "But it won't be difficult. I've worked out a way to spread the production values to our shops in the States."

"Excellent. That's why I hired you, Nathan." He raises a glass, and everyone joins him. "To free labor!" he shouts. Liquor splashes, spilling down his arm. "Saves us money for hookers and blow!"

Everyone lets out a chorus of laughter.

"Hear, hear!" Nathan grins at his boss. "To a creative man with great ideas, to not getting caught, and to lawyers just in case."

I let out the expected laugh at his cleverness. The lawyers in the room puff up their chests and try to catch the boss's eye.

But Daniel is distracted; he grabs Delilah's arm and pulls her down. She falls onto him, eyes wide, a forced laugh erupting from her lips. He paws at her for a few moments before turning his attention back to his drink.

"Thailand?" I raise an eyebrow at Nathan.

His grin shrinks at the edges.

"That can't be all his idea." I wink at Nathan, jerking my head at his boss.

Daniel's head twitches as he rubs the loose coke off his large nose.

Nathan frowns up at me. "I didn't think you'd want to hear about business."

"Anything to do with *you* is interesting to *me*." I tap his nose and get up off his lap. "Come dance."

The eyes of every man are on me as I spin around Nathan. It's one thing to hire a hooker, escort, prostitute, whichever she'd rather be called. It's another thing to be with one of Miss Belle's girls. And every man here knows that. Most of the women too.

There are a few other madams with a reputation as intense as Miss Belle's. But most of them stick to a specific hemisphere. And none of them have the more complicated side of the business.

An elevator ding cuts through the indie rock music Shimmer put on. The doors open and a tall, white bellboy in an ill-fitting uniform pushes a cart into the room. Kong stands and moves closer.

A couple three-tier cake stands piled high with mini cupcakes, a silver jug of coffee, and a set of sugar and creamer rest atop a black cloth. One of the lawyers and two of the girls dive for the cupcakes.

Daniel cackles and shouts something about money for room service. He flips one of the rolled-up hundreds in the direction of the bellboy.

He picks it up and mumbles something that is lost in the noise of the room. Daniel turns his attention back to Delilah.

"Hey." Nathan gently nudges my chin up so my eyes meet his. "You all right? You seem distracted tonight."

"I'm fine." I smile at him and stroke his chest. "Just thinking of how sad I am to only have a few days left with you."

"Well, now that you're comfortable seeing me again, I'll be calling Miss Belle quite often."

I turn and fold his arms around me as I sway against him.

After a few minutes, Nathan sits down again, and I stand behind him, massaging his neck as he decides if tonight is a good night to do a couple of lines. Almost five minutes pass before I realize something is wrong. Something is missing.

There was no ding.

My fingers freeze. I could have missed it, my mind tries to rationalize. I probably didn't hear it. I probably forgot I did hear it.

But Miss Belle's training takes over. I don't doubt myself anymore. It's not who I am. And I didn't hear that elevator. I didn't hear the doors open to take the bellboy back down, away from this drug, smoke, and hooker infested penthouse.

I glance around the room until I spot the office door. And the light coming from the crack between the door and the hardwood. My stomach sinks.

I squint around the room, hoping no one else has noticed. I catch sight of Kong as he stands, his focus locked on the office door. His hand slips behind his back, under his shirt. He catches Marcus's eye. The taller man picks up Shimmer and sets her to the side.

Marcus joins Kong, and the two of them approach the office. The large man's movement across the room has attracted more eyes. Nathan turns to watch them, along with a few other men and most of the women. Daniel doesn't notice. His face is buried in Delilah's cleavage.

Marcus puts his hand on the doorknob and flings the door open. It slams into the wall. There is a scuffle. A pinched shout, a fist slams into flesh, the thick bodies of the two security guards block everyone's view. Barely ten seconds pass.

Kong drags the bellboy out by the back of his shirt and tosses him to the floor. Everyone is watching now. Daniel stands and takes a shaky step forward.

The hat has fallen off, the young man's face revealed. Blood drips from his left nostril. Bright, green eyes stare defiantly at the crowd.

He is the same man who interrupted brunch on the first day. As I make the connection, I also realize how I know his face. His name is Ryan Morris, Tennessee royalty in the form of a congresswoman's son, a reporter for *The New York Times*, and the reason I am here.

"What the hell is going on?" Daniel glares, not at the bleeding reporter in the bellboy outfit, but at his highly paid security team.

"He was in your office. Snuck in as the bellboy." Marcus shuffles a bit and glances at Shimmer.

"How in the fuck did you let that happen?" Daniel wipes at a spot under his nose. A guttery growl escapes his throat as his gaze darts around at all the people.

"Get out." He gestures to the door.

Nobody moves.

"*Get the fuck out!*" A few of the girls flinch at his shout. They grab clothes scattered around the room and flee into the elevator. Some of the men follow—the lawyers and lower level management. This is too big for them.

I gently tug Nathan's arm. Maybe we should leave. It's what I'm supposed to want, to get out before anything happens. Fortunately, Nathan must stay. This is his mess too.

He pats my arm. "It's okay. Just sit over there for a minute."

I sink into a recliner and watch the men surrounding Ryan. Delilah shrinks into the corner of the couch, fear in her eyes as she glances back and forth from the men to me.

Daniel glares down at Ryan, who is now on his knees.

"I'm going to see what he got into." Nathan puts a hand on Daniel's shoulder to get his attention. The older man nods.

"Get him a chair," Daniel snaps.

Marcus lifts Ryan by his arm, deposits him into a dining room chair, then goes around the rest of the penthouse, kicking people out of the rooms and sending them to the elevator.

Kong reaches into one of his many pockets and pulls out a yard of paracord. He yanks Ryan's arms behind the chair and ties them together in a swift, efficient manner.

Ryan doesn't speak. His chest rises and falls in ragged breaths. His head hangs, blood still steadily dripping from his nose. Kong shuts off the music and TV. Delilah shivers as she stands up and walks to Daniel. She whispers something in his ear.

He turns. The lines of his face are pinched together in a mask of fury. He raises his arm.

I rise from my cushions.

Delilah falls to the floor as the back of his hand slams across her cheek.

"You'll stay here and shut up," he shouts at her.

My eyes are too narrowed, my breath coming too fast. I force my fists to unclench. I remember what I should look like right now. Doe eyed, scared, fearful of the big man and his bodyguards, worried for my Nathan, and angry with this intruder. I should not have murder in my eyes as I stare at Daniel.

He turns and paces back and forth in front of the chair.

I go to Delilah and lift her from the floor. Tears stream down her cheeks. Her right eye is puffy and red, the swelling just starting up. I take her to the kitchen, keeping the men in my view until we turn the corner.

There is no ice in the freezer, just a pint-sized bottle of vodka. I take it out and wrap a towel around it before pressing the cold glass to her cheek.

"Stay in here," I murmur.

"Wait. Please don't go." Panic laces her voice.

"How many times has he hit you?" I catch her eye and don't look away.

She shudders and glances down.

I remember what that's like, being too ashamed to look into people's eyes.

"Don't go to him again." I clutch her hand, squeezing her fingers. "Don't let him hire you again after this weekend."

Delilah's gaze darts up, and for a moment, I catch a glimpse of the fire under her fear. "That's not up to me."

I nod. "Write down a way for me to contact you. Hug me when you come out and slip it in my hand in case we don't see each other later."

"You're going back out there."

"I have to."

"They're going to kill that man. You know that, right?" She shivers. "Daniel kept talking about it. If-if he came back."

I turn and leave her in the kitchen. I don't need a description of Daniel's cruelty. And I already know what Marcus and Kong are capable of.

A thud greets me as Marcus's fist collides with the reporter's sternum. Ryan groans and spits blood onto the beige carpet.

Marcus takes a step back, and removes a silver Zippo lighter from the fist he used to hit Ryan. I can't quite make out the engraved initials on the side of the metal. He shakes out his fingers and then flicks the lighter lid open and closed, open and closed.

Daniel shouts in the reporter's face, spittle flying from his lips. "What did you find?"

"Nothing." Ryan coughs. "I didn't have time to find anything."

Nathan walks out of the office. I curl up in the recliner again. He slaps a file folder down on the coffee table. A cloud of white puffs out where it lands before floating to the floor. "He knows it all."

"No." Ryan shakes his head and swallows hard. His gaze darts to Marcus's lighter. "I don't. I swear. I was only there for a minute. I didn't have time to see anything. I—"

Kong cuts him off with a backhand across the face. "Silence."

"What do you mean?" Daniel glares at Nathan.

"I warned you, sir. I told you not to print out any of this information." Nathan sinks onto the couch, a hopeless, defeated look on his face.

"You mean, he got everything I printed?"

Nathan nods. "I assume so. The folders were open and scattered across the office. If I had to guess, I'd say he knows everything."

"You do not have to guess." Kong's deep voice sends a shudder down my spine. His hands clench and unclench. "We can make him tell you what he knows."

"And anyone he's shared the information with." Marcus cuts in, his lighter flipping closed with a snap.

"I didn't." Ryan blinks rapidly; sweat beads down his temples. "I swear. I didn't tell anyone."

"An email account had just been closed out on the computer." Nathan shakes his head.

"See…" Marcus takes a step toward Ryan. "To me, that sounds like you lied." He flicks the lighter open and produces a flame, then watches the light flicker and dance.

"Please." Ryan looks from Daniel to Nathan to me. He blinks rapidly, fear etched across his face.

"Tell us." Daniel clenches his fists. His beady pinprick eyes are barely visible behind his red, swollen, saggy skin.

Ryan takes a breath and shakes his head no.

Marcus lets the flame on his lighter die. He reaches out a thick, calloused hand, and holds the metal to Ryan's neck.

I stand as the scream cuts through the air. Nathan looks over at me, and guilt washes across his face. I face him and give my bottom lip a small quiver; the violence is scaring me. I'm a delicate flower who should not experience such behavior. I see in his eyes that he falls for it.

Ryan is nodding; tears stream from his eyes as he gulps in air. "I sent it." A bright red welt forms on his neck as he flinches away from Marcus.

The bigger man sits down. His lighter goes into a jacket pocket. He pulls a knife from his belt and proceeds to practice balancing tricks with his fingertips.

"What?" Daniel demands.

"Everything I saw."

I close my eyes. Faint buzzing echoes at the edges of my mind. I sigh through my gritted teeth.

Focus.

I move toward Nathan and put a shaking hand on his shoulder; I can't handle this anymore. I am fragile and scared.

"I told my editor about all of it," Ryan continues. "I just wanted to follow the story. I needed evidence."

"That's enough." Nathan pats my hand and stands up. "We need to discuss this." He looks to Daniel, who nods.

"Where do you want him?" Kong asks.

"In the bathroom." Daniel's hand shakes as he gestures to the bathroom off the hall. "Cuff him to the toilet."

Kong grabs Ryan's upper arm, and Marcus cuts the rope holding him to the chair. The two escort him to the bathroom. I watch them walk away. Thoughts, plans, ideas, and prayers buzz through my mind. All the while my face remains the same: passive, frightened, a perfect mask of innocence.

Daniel looks at Nathan. "Now what?"

CHAPTER TWELVE

MISS BELLE

BLACKMAIL IS HARD AND CONGRESSPEOPLE ARE STUPID

A—heavy—sigh escapes me. This guy...

I flip through the stack of pictures on the table in front of me: a blackmail packet for Mr. Mark Prentice, the Vice President of the United States of America.

I know, that was a bit blunt. It's going to be an intense couple of days.

A plate of celery, carrots, and spicy peanut dip sits to the side of my packet. I hum as I spoon a thick glob of peanut goop into the groove of my celery. A satisfying crunch fills the air, and I turn the page in my folder, chewing my veggie goodness.

I've got information on this barely human sack of crap dating back over a year. Since before he became VP, but not before he started his anti-gay campaign. Hypocrisy—it pays the rent.

Damen has been his favorite since the beginning. He and Levi had an appointment, but Levi was too old. Damen is almost twenty-one, but can still pass as a seventeen-year-old. Now, a year and a half later, I have a full envelope containing pictures, emails, texts, and a tape with several desperate and pornographic voicemails.

All it comes down to is my big decision. My business won't stay out of it this time. Mr. Prentice will know Damen was a part of it—Damen doesn't mind at all. My problem right now is keeping the rest of my clients in public office (of which there are a ridiculous amount) in the dark about this blackmail thing.

There is also the choice of whom to send this delicious envelope. Mr. Prentice, his wife, his secretary... his mother? A grin slides across my face; that would be almost too mean.

It's the VP or his wife. I think we will go with the man. I can save his wife for next time I need something done.

He'll pull his support for the bill, and no one will know why. The slimy man who recommended my services to him, a stout lover of leather boots who runs the Defense Department, assumed Mr. Prentice wanted work from one of my girls. He said as much at the gala, asking if he had spent any time with Sarah.

This is good news for me. Mr. Prentice isn't likely to spill my beans if there is any threat of his beans being spilled as well. Human behavior tells us as much. Mr. Prentice is one of those who will do anything to protect his reputation.

You'd think men like that would've learned not to fuck anyone but their wives.

Missa walks into the kitchen and plops down across from me. She grabs a carrot stick and crunches on one end while she talks. "How's the blackmail going?"

I give her a squinty look. "How'd you know that's what I'm working on?"

"You were singing 'blackmail folder' to the *Blues Clues* tune, again."

I smile. "Not terribly. Just have to wait till tomorrow for the cherry on top."

"Excellent." She leans back in her chair and tightens her ponytail. "Did you decide on him or his wife?"

"I'm going to go with him. We'll be able to use his wife later."

Missa chuckles. "You can be so evil."

I grin over at her. We've both seen enough evil to know what this really is.

"Any word from Nicky?" She picks up a stack of pictures and lays them out in front of her.

"No, he's not returning my calls. Doesn't surprise me, but hopefully, he'll talk to me after the bill falls through."

She nods as she rearranges the photos. Missa has a better eye for what should come first. She's always been the more artistic one.

My cell buzzes, and I pick it up hopefully. Not Nicky. It's Lacey, which is odd because in Tokyo it's 4:30 tomorrow morning. My brow creases into a frown. The flight Missa booked for her doesn't leave until the afternoon.

I flip up my phone and turn on the speaker. "Lacey, what's wrong?"

"We've got a big fucking problem, Miss Belle."

Missa stares at me across the table; between the two of us, we've probably heard Lacey curse three or four times in the last four years. She says there's a problem, it's something serious.

"What's going on?"

There's a muffled sound on the other side of the phone—the click of boots on hardwood and a door shutting.

"The kid showed up tonight. Ryan, the congresswoman's boy."

"Fuck." Missa puts a hand to her forehead.

"What happened?"

"I have all the information ready to go. It's in my bags ready to fly out tomorrow. Or, today, I guess. We're up in the penthouse, the guys are having some drinks, snorting some coke, and this kid comes in dressed like a fuckin bellboy. Damn it. I should have—he showed up at the first breakfast, but they booted him fast and I thought..."

She's talking fast, her words sharp and angry. She sighs, and there are more footsteps before she speaks again. "Miss Belle, the short of it is, the kid is handcuffed in the bathroom, the men here know he's a reporter, and they're going to burn it all."

I look up at Missa. Her eyebrows are pinched together, her gaze fixed on the phone with an unwavering intensity.

"What do you mean, burn it all?" she asks.

"I mean, he sent it all. He emailed his editor, from Jacobson's laptop. He sent the coordinates, the financial trail, everything he could get his hands on. But, none of it was official documents for the company. So, if they clean up their loose ends in time... they're off the hook."

A shiver goes through me, and I lean forward. "The factory?"

Her shaky sigh gives away the panic hidden from her voice. "In seventy-two hours, there will be no factory, no village, and no workers. They're giving management time to complete their current batch, and then they're going to shut the whole thing down. Jacobson and Nathan want confirmation the job is done before the weekend is over."

Her voice cracks. "They're going to kill everyone, Miss Belle. No witnesses. That's over 120 people. Men, women, and children."

It feels as though I've been plunged into an icy bath. I meet Missa's eye. The horror on her face matches my own.

"The kid?" I ask.

"They know how much he knows. And when there isn't any tangible evidence, he is still a source who's seen the operation. I doubt he'll last till dawn."

I lean back in my chair and close my eyes. Why can these things never go easy? "Where is everyone now?"

"Daniel took his girl to... let off some steam. Nathan is in the office deciding how best to handle this and trying to figure out if they should call in a lawyer. The hitmen are watching the kid." There is a pause. "Listen, Miss Belle..."

I cut her off. "We'll talk when you get back."

"I'm not coming back today." There is no waver in her voice. The steadfast determination that makes Lacey one of my best assets comes in loud and clear through the phone.

I bite my lip and remain silent for a moment. "Okay."

Missa's gaze snaps to me. I shake my head at her.

"What about Ryan?" Lacey interrupts the silence. All business.

"Don't let him die. Try to get him out if you can. But don't compromise your cover with Nathan."

I'm out of my chair now; the phone is in my hand as I race through the hallway and up the stairs.

"Missa!" I call behind me. "Get me on the next flight to Thailand."

A chair scrapes in the kitchen.

I focus back on Lacey. "If you need to, stall them. I'll get his dumb ass when I'm done at the factory. You said I have seventy-two hours?"

I fling the door to my room open, go to my closet, and grab my go-bag. I toss it and my phone on the bed, and then strip off my sweats.

"You did at two o'clock this morning," she grumbles.

"All right. I'll call the congresswoman on my way. Be careful, Lacey."

"You too, Miss Belle."

The line goes dead. I hike up my jeans, pull on my boots, and yank a jacket off a hanger. My go-bag—well, go-back-pack—has everything else I need; passport, underwear, tooth-brush, etc.

We've all got one.

I run back downstairs.

Missa is fast; my ticket is printing as I walk in. "Do you need me to call Thomas?" she asks.

Thomas is our guy in Thailand, kind of like Chang in Tokyo.

"Yeah, get together the usual kit. And see if he can hire some muscle."

"You know I can print another ticket in about two min-utes." She hands me mine and gives me an expectant look.

I shake my head as I fold up the paper and stick it in my backpack. "I need you to stay here, Missa. This thing with the VP *can't* go wrong."

She frowns, but nods and pulls out her phone. "Your flight leaves in an hour and a half. I've already got you checked in. Better get to the airport. I'll make sure Thomas has everything ready when you land." She pauses, and the expression on her face makes me stop as well. I stare at her. "We need to talk about Lacey."

My teeth grind together as my jaw clenches. "I know. When I get back."

She nods and hands me my keys.

I give her a quick hug and head out.

The garage door clickety-clacks as it rolls up. I put on my backpack, grab the keys to my bike—a cherry-red Ducati 996—take my helmet off the workbench, and hook up my cellphone to my headphones. I pull on the helmet, throw my leg over the motorcycle, and tap my visor down.

I type a few numbers into my cell and put it in my jacket pocket. The ringing starts as my bike vibrates to life.

The phone clicks. "Congresswoman Morris's office," a bubbly, sweet, southern voice answers.

"Get me the congresswoman, please."

"I'm sorry, the congresswoman is in a meeting. Can I take a message?"

I roll my eyes as I back out of the driveway. The cop van isn't across the street right now. They must be out to lunch. My beautiful baby rumbles beneath me as I rev the engine and speed down our quiet road.

"No. You can go *to* the meeting and tell her Miss Belle is on the phone. I need to speak to her immediately."

"I'm really sorry." The sweetness has left her voice. She's the agitated secretary now. "I can't do that. It's an important meeting."

"This is more important than whatever meeting she's in. Get her on the phone. Now."

An impatient sigh comes over the line. I should be the one sighing. A minivan honks at me as I make a sharp left and escape the stop-sign-filled side streets.

"Listen to me right now. I'm not playing around here. Get her on the phone, or I guarantee you'll be printing up new resumes this time tomorrow."

There is silence for a moment. I squeeze between two SUVs going fifteen in a twenty-five.

"Goddammit! This is about her son. Get her on the *fucking* phone," I shout.

"Please hold."

Annoying tinkling music comes on the line as I slow to a stop at an intersection. I shake my head and sit up, taking a moment to stretch while I wait for the light to turn. It goes green and no one has picked up the phone. I roar across the street and weave my way to the onramp.

There is a click. "Why are you using this line? You can't just call me like this. I'm in the middle of a meeting with the Attorney General."

The hair on my neck stands up. An angry growl escapes my lips before I clamp them shut. I inhale. Breathe deep.

You'd think I'm mad because of how she's speaking to me. Me—the woman who supplies her with a steady fix of orgasmic medication in the form of Levi's gentle Cajun accent and easy smile. But I'm not. I'm mad because she didn't listen and now Lacey is in danger. Well, more danger than usual.

"What the fuck, Morris?"

"Excuse me? You do *not* speak to me that way." Her entitled, wealthy Tennessee drawl comes across the line. I can picture her sitting at her mahogany desk, bleached hair just a little too loose, mascara just a little too thick. Clothes, nails, and accessories screaming of old family money.

"I'll speak to you however I want. Your son is handcuffed to a toilet in a Tokyo penthouse because you didn't listen to me."

She gasps, and my chest tightens. I'm being harsh. But, Jesus—I told her to keep him in the States until I got confirmation the job was done.

"What happened?"

I sigh. "Ryan is in Tokyo. He went to the conference and started asking questions. He got kicked out. So, he showed up at a penthouse dressed as a bellboy. I told you to keep him in the States. I *told* you to let me get the details for the story before he went for broke!"

"Is he okay?" Her voice cracks. "What's going to happen to him?"

I don't answer right away. A guy in a Hummer doesn't check his side mirror, and I slam on the brake and swerve into oncoming traffic to avoid being another cross on the roadside. "I'm taking care of it. Dammit, Harriet, why didn't you listen to me?"

"I tried telling him, I did. He told me he was just going to check out some private investors at the conference. He's a grown man, what was I supposed to do?"

"Anything to keep him in the country. That's what."

"I... I'm sorry, Miss Belle."

I shake my head as brake lights pile up in front of me.

"We can discuss this more when I get done. I'll be unreachable for a few days. Contact Marissa if you have any questions, but keep it to a minimum. We'll reach out when this is taken care of."

"Please, Miss Belle."

I grit my teeth. The pain in her voice, the fear for her son, it's too much.

"He's my only son."

"You should have listened to me."

I reach into my jacket pocket and end the call. Congresswoman Morris's fear for her child is understandable. But she put Lacey's life, and over a hundred others, in danger by not doing what I said. I only have so much pity for people who can't follow instructions.

JFK is slammed with people. What else should I expect on a Thursday at four in the afternoon?

I grab the slip from long-term parking and jog to the correct terminal. My passport, ID, and ticket are clutched between tense fingers before I even reach the security line.

My go-bag is airport-ready. I'll pick up my actual gear from Thomas when I reach Thailand. Skipping the check-in line, and having my ticket ready cuts down about twenty minutes on a day like today. Online check-in really has revolutionized air travel.

There are four security lines today rather than the usual two. Sometimes things do work out.

The balding elderly woman ahead of me offers a toothy smile and gestures for me to go ahead. "You look like you're in a hurry, dear. My flight doesn't leave for four more hours."

I thank her and brush past. I fling my bag, jacket, and boots onto the conveyor belt before stepping into the peeling yellow footprints. A tall black woman gestures me through. She gives me a curt nod as I grab my things and go.

I've got fifteen minutes before the plane is supposed to take off. They are boarding the last few people when I get there. I make it on and settle into an aisle seat in coach. There is no more room in the bins, so I tuck my bag under the seat in front of me.

A young middle eastern couple shares the row with me. The woman is thin, and flowing coal black hair peeks out from beneath a stylish yellow scarf. Her husband, I assume, fiddles with her rings as they chat together in an Arabic dialect. It's not the Iraqi Arabic I'm familiar with, but a few words and phrases jump out. The accent sounds Gulf, which is logical, as we are headed to Qatar.

I turn off my phone and tuck it into my bag. Missa has all the calls for the Guides now. Hopefully, things go smoothly with Damen. Hopefully, Lacey doesn't run into trouble getting Ryan out of Tokyo. Hopefully, the cops don't pick the next few days to up their game at the Manor...

Hopefully, I get to that factory in time.

Hopefully a lot of things. All of which are currently outside of my control. Which I hate. I stopped biting my nails a long time ago, but times like this, the urge resurfaces. When the plane reaches height, I can turn my phone back on. But even if Lacey gets Ryan out, she won't risk calling to update me. Not now that everything has gone to shit.

I lean back in my seat and press my fingers to my temples. My foot bounces against the floor at a fast, jittery pace. Unwind. Relax. Accept the lack of control. Plan the next step. I've got a layover in Doha, one in Bangkok, and then I'll meet Thomas in Chiang Rai (a province in Northern Thailand). By the time I arrive, I'll have less than forty hours.

I've had worse time crunches. But failure doesn't often mean the slaughter of an entire village of people. Except maybe Damen's thing in Peru. But we had more resources with that one. And more time.

The plane starts moving, and the captain's voice comes over the speakers. It's 83 degrees outside. And it's 95 degrees in Qatar. Fahrenheit, of course. He gives the usual rundown of when we are supposed to land, reminding everyone to keep their seatbelts fastened, be careful when opening overhead compartments, and always remember to tip your stewardess. The stewardess at the front of the aisle rolls her eyes.

The safety briefing is quick. As we take to the sky, I put my newest book in the seat-back pocket in front of me.

Qatar is a Muslim majority country, and while I'm not religious in any form of the word, I do believe in respecting people's cultures. I pull a thin, green scarf from my bag and drape it over my hair. Then, I turn with a smile and greet my neighbors.

The woman's face breaks into a surprised smile at my flimsy Arabic, but she responds with a happy hello, and her husband politely shakes my hand. We chat for a while. The wife speaks English and, through some translations, we can hold a simple conversation in Arabic. It's never too late to add a chapter to my vocabulary.

Besides, it's a twelve-hour flight. I might as well make the most of it.

Chapter Thirteen

Lacey

Coffee Makes Me Sleepy

My hand falls to the side, and Delilah whimpers. She is pressed against me on the couch. I put my arm back around her and give a gentle squeeze.

Tonight has been never-ending.

Nathan called the factory in Thailand. I slipped into the office during this conversation to check on him. I massaged his neck while he spoke to them. While he discussed the financial cost of killing 120 people. While he made sure they knew to burn the village as well as the factory.

I stepped outside for a "cigarette." It's not far from plausible. Nathan is well aware of how much I used to smoke.

I called Miss Belle. Then I called Chang. I lit up just enough to get the scent of smoke on my clothes and between my fingers.

I got two hours of sleep. The men went off to discuss things with their top lawyer. Delilah came out when Daniel was done with her and laid down beside me, tucked against me like a little spoon. I didn't have any nightmares this time.

It's almost 6 a.m. Nathan is sleeping in the guest bedroom. He didn't wake me when he finally went to sleep. Daniel is in his own room. I get up slowly, letting Delilah stir for a moment before sinking into the couch and falling back asleep.

I pull a leopard print throw blanket off the recliner and drape it over her fragile form.

The wood chills the balls of my bare feet as I silently cross the floor. On the other side of the kitchen, a hallway leads to a bathroom and the guest bedroom Nathan occupies. I stop in the kitchen and fiddle with the coffeemaker. It's a high-tech one, very quiet.

After a few moments, the scent of dark roast coffee fills the air. I take two mugs from the cabinet, one red, one blue. I fill both with the hot, black coffee. I pull a mascara tube from my clutch, upend it, and watch as clear liquid flows from the small bottle into the blue mug.

A spoonful of sugar goes in each as well. The fridge is bare, but a little thing of milk sits in the back. It expires in a week. I pour a pinch in the mugs.

I hold mine by the handle, the other by the bottom. The ceramic heats my cold fingers. I make no sound as I tiptoe to the corridor. Plush carpet meets my bare feet once I step into the hallway. Random paintings, just shadows in the dim light, line the walls. A thin hall table is pressed up against the wall opposite the bathroom.

Marcus lounges in a chair brought from the dining room. His shirt is ruined. Specks of dried blood spatter the front. Stained handprints, from where he wiped the blood off his fingers, cover his pants. A half-empty plastic water bottle sits on the floor next to him.

His eyes are barely open. But he is awake. His knife is out again; it dances between the fingers on his left hand.

The suite is dark, and the hallway is darker still. He looks up with a wary gaze as I come over. He stands and positions himself in front of the bathroom door. A relaxed smile plays across his lips even as he looks me up and down, visually scanning my clothes for weapons. He gives the knife one last twirl, then slides it into his pants pocket. "Lacey."

"Hey, Marc. Long night." I stop a few feet away.

"You should be sleeping." He glances at the door down the hall. "Are you going to Mr. Blake's room?"

I purse my lips. "No."

He tilts his head. "What can I do for you, then?"

"I can't sleep anymore. Coffee?" I extend my arm.

He takes the mug, then looks at me. I take a sip of mine, and an easy smile crosses my lips.

"I put in milk and sugar, I hope that's okay."

"Yeah." He raises the mug to his lips. "I can't drink it black."

"Will Kong be back soon? I can make him a mug."

"No." Marcus shakes his head. "I've got watch for another hour."

I nod, and we stand together for a while, both drinking the steaming liquid. The roasted beans are of high quality. A rich, smoky flavor flows across my tongue, the sugar masking a hint of bitterness.

The silence is nice, calm compared to the last several hours. Tension eases from my shoulders in the darkness. We don't need words. Not to stand and drink and wait for the sun.

I've always liked Marcus. His chipper personality is too much for some. But if you are patient, another side of him comes out. It's that way with most people, I think. No one is only one way.

After about ten minutes, I turn to him. "I was wondering." I lean against the wall and set my mug down on the long table next to me. "Would I be able to speak to the reporter?"

He lowers his mug to the side. His shoulders go back, hands forward. The muscles in his arms flex, the ripple visible even through his shirt. The easygoing smile on his face is gone, replaced with a thin frown and serious eyes. "I can't let that happen. You know that." His eyebrows draw together. He is frustrated I asked. Marcus and Kong know Miss Belle; they've met several of the Guides on various missions. In their eyes, we are escorts, nothing more. No one has needed to break their cover around the hitmen before. Hopefully, I won't either. But it depends on how the conversation goes before the coffee kicks in. I need to get this done quickly.

I lean forward and take a small step. A flick of my neck sends a cascade of curls over my shoulder. A twitch of my shoulder sends the edge of my shirt to rest on my upper arm.

"I just want to ask him a few questions. I need to protect Miss Belle's interests." I take another step forward and reach my fingers up toward Marcus's chest. "I have to make sure he isn't going to say anything when he gets back home."

Marcus grabs my wrist. Thick callouses rub my skin. "I'm sorry, Lacey. That's not going to happen." He releases me and takes a step back. "But don't worry, he won't be telling anyone about you or Miss Belle."

Blood thunders in my ears. I take a deep breath; I need to calm my heartbeat. I inch toward Marcus, a mischievous smile on my face. "Come on, Marc. You can let *me* talk to him. It'll only take a second."

The bushy caterpillars above his eyes rise. He lets out a short, dry, chuckle and gives an incredulous shake of his head. "Who do you think you're playing here? I'm a professional. Not one of your fat, old, johns. You can't just bat your eyelashes at me."

I lick my lips and sigh. "I didn't think so. Not with your reputation." I shake my head and pick up my mug again, taking a sip before I speak. "The two of you have a very high standard for the jobs you accept. It makes me wonder why you'd take this one. After all, this is a low-level security gig. Not an assassination."

He chuckles. "It's not always assassinations, Lacey. We're expanding our business. Private security pays well."

"Ah." I flash a big grin. "This was supposed to be a big cash babysitting job?"

"No." He gives me a squinty, not really mad, glare. "It's a foot in the door. A stepping stone to getting our own firm up and running. Me and Kong, we did security back in the day. It's time to get back into it."

I nod thoughtfully. "So, it's probably pretty important for this job to go well. To build your reputation as security guys rather than hitmen?"

"Exactly." He nods once and sips at his coffee. The mug is almost empty.

"That's unfortunate," I sigh. I shift my weight.

"Why?" His mouth opens in a long yawn.

I glance at him. My chest is tight. I already feel guilty for messing up their job. "Just that all *this* happened." I wave my hand at the bathroom.

"Yeah." He runs his free hand through his cropped hair. "It shouldn't mess us up too bad, though..." He pauses as another yawn pulls apart his lips. "If anything, it'll show how skilled we are at adapting to different situations."

The edges of my mouth tilt up. "Good point."

He nods, and his head lolls before he snaps it back up. "Sorry," he groans. "I'm feeling beat."

"It's been a long night," I murmur. I cross the hall and lean against the wall next to his empty chair. The rippled stucco presses against my bare arm.

He inhales and lets out a sigh, slowly, as though the act of breathing is an effort. His eyelids, heavy with thick lashes, droop down and cover the top half of his eyes.

"Come sit." My voice is so soft he can't refuse. My smile is warm, inviting, safe.

He walks over and sinks onto the chair. "I've got to call Kong to take the rest of this shift," he slurs.

I put a hand on his shoulder as he reaches for his phone. "Shhh. I'll call him for you."

There is a clink as I set my mug down on the table.

Marcus stares at the red ceramic. His gaze flicks to his own, then switches to me.

His eyebrows draw together. His mouth opens. The fog filling his mind lets through a single thought. "What'd you do?"

I smile.

He lurches to his feet, and I duck to the side. His mug drops to the carpet with a soft thud. Massive hands reach for me. I lunge forward. I kick between his legs, and he doubles over in pain. He snaps up a second later. The drugs slow him down, but he is still incredibly strong.

I dodge a swinging fist. His other hand grabs the back of my head, fingers lacing into my hair. He tugs, and I fall to the floor. He drags me across the ground like a doll. I grasp at his hand, raking my nails into his skin.

His words are incoherent as anger spikes from his lips. His movements are slow and jerky.

I twist my hip and kick at his legs. The first misses. He stops walking and looks down at me. His arm swings and his open palm slams into my face. The inside of my left cheek splits open. Blood erupts in my mouth.

Pain spasms through my shoulder as the force of the blow knocks my upper body into the floor. But he let go of my hair. I roll onto my back and kick again.

My foot connects with the back of his knee. He buckles. His right knee hits the carpet.

I don't hesitate.

I push hard with my arms, and I'm on my feet. I fling out my right leg. His head is at waist level. Circling my leg around his neck, I then move my weight forward. I lean on him as my left leg hooks into place above my right foot, locking my leg around his throat.

I shift again, and as I lean back, we go down. I grit my teeth as I hit the deck. Blood spurts from my mouth and oozes down my chin.

Marcus's leg is twisted underneath his massive form. He groans. He reaches for me, but his struggles diminish as I flex my leg. Pressure closes off his windpipe. He stops breathing.

I release my legs, and his body thumps to the floor. I crawl around, lean my head close to his chest, and wait for the rise and fall.

He is alive. Shallow breaths pump in and out through his open mouth. I roll his body to the wall.

He is huge. In a fair fight, he would likely kill me. Unless I got very, very lucky. Miss Belle and Missa don't encourage fair fights; they encourage survival. This thought makes me feel slightly better about shoving him out of the way.

I wipe the blood from my jaw and take a few deep breaths. My left cheekbone is bruised. Blood still seeps from my cheek, filling my mouth with the taste of metal.

The bathroom is to my left. I pull a bobby-pin from my mass of ruined curls and try the door. It's unlocked.

I open the bathroom door and turn on the light.

Ryan gasps and blinks against the brightness. He huddles against the toilet bowl. His hands are fastened around the u-bend. Blood is caked down his face, from his nostrils to his chin. A purple bruise has swollen his left eye almost shut.

He mumbles something as I walk in.

I stop at the sink and spit. Red splatters against the white porcelain. I run the water for a moment and splash some into my mouth. The cold stings my cut. I swish and spit, then turn to the man on the floor.

He shivers and mumbles something again.

"Shh." I twirl the bobby-pin around my fingers.

"Please..." His southern drawl seeps from the word as he scrambles away from me. He can't go far. But his knees are pulled up to his chest, fear splashed across his face.

"I'm not going to hurt you." I sigh. "I'm trying to get you out of here."

He swallows and squints at me.

I keep eye contact as I work to release his wrists. "I'm going to uncuff you. Then we need to move. Fast. I have to get you out of this building before they know you're gone."

He nods. I pull him to his feet.

"Stay behind me. Be silent."

He nods again.

Marcus is still on the ground. His breathing is shallow but steady. I pull Ryan past him and move toward the elevator. I scoop up my boots as we pass through the living room.

The suite is silent. Early morning light coming through the windows only adds to the stillness around us. I jam the button on the wall and wait, barely breathing.

The elevator dings. And something moves.

I push Ryan behind me and turn. Delilah's head is up, sticking out from the leopard print. Her eyes meet mine. The elevator doors open, and I reach behind me, pushing Ryan until he moves through them.

Delilah bites her lip, her eyebrows pressed together. Dried clumps of mascara are stuck on the space between her eyes and cheekbones. A pale blue bruise lights up a palm-sized portion of her face. I stare at her, my face a blank mask.

Her eyes close. Her head slumps back onto the pillow.

I exhale in relief and join Ryan in the elevator. I hit the floor button, then repeatedly press 'close doors' until they slide shut.

"Who are you?" His gaze is locked on me.

I am silent as I lace up my boots.

"Where are you taking me?"

I don't speak. Soft jazz music tinkles in the air around us. Ryan's breath catches.

I glance his way. Fear is etched across his face. He must be older than me. Maybe twenty-six or twenty-seven. But pain, panic, and terror shine through those green eyes. I doubt he's ever been hit. I doubt his blood has ever been purposefully spilled by another person.

He is weak. I pity him.

"Please. Tell me something."

"I am taking you somewhere to hide until my friend can come get you."

"But who *are* you?"

I face him. The little numbers on the display are counting down. We are almost at the upper lobby. "I'm the one who was sent to retrieve the information you were after. No more questions. My friend can fill you in on the way to the airport."

The elevator dings open to reveal a jungle. The upper lobby is windowed with massive glass panels. Plants hang from the ceiling, line the walls, and fill most of the interior. Hand carved hardwood benches sit evenly spaced among the beautiful green creatures.

I step out and make my way to the stairs. I turn after three yards. Ryan is still standing in the elevator. I go back, reach in, and grab him by the wrist.

I drag him through the vegetation and to the stairwell. We race down the stairs until we reach the bottom.

Never take the elevator to the floor you're actually trying to go to. Use it part way, then take the stairs. If anyone is following you, they won't know what floor you're really on.

I move us slowly now, watching for anyone who may be up this early.

The front desk is quiet. The main lobby is empty of guests. We walk through to a set of glass doors inlaid with silver.

The last building of the Hyatt is mostly food and shopping. None of the shops are open yet, but a few employees make their way to the breakfast restaurants.

I pull Ryan to the stairs. In most hotels and office buildings, staircases have a small cubby at the bottom. Amanda and I made a fort in one when Gran took us to Disneyland.

Ryan stares at me as I pull him into the cramped, cob-webbed, cubby. He grabs my hand when I turn to leave. "Where are you going?"

"I need to get back."

"They'll kill you if you go back there."

I shake my head. "I am very good at my job, Ryan. You need to stay here until my friend comes to get you. His name is Chang. He'll tell you he knows a guy with a boat. Go with him. Go home."

"I can't just let you—"

I rip my hand away and glare at him. "You put your life, my life, and over a hundred innocent people's lives in danger because you didn't follow a simple set of instructions. Do as I say. Get on the first flight back to America and *stay there.*"

He swallows and nods.

I take a deep breath. I've been trained not to do that. Not to snap and let my emotions take over. I shut the stairwell door behind me and take a few calming breaths before I make my way to the elevator.

Chang will arrive within the hour. My next task is dealing with Marcus.

My mind buzzes in the elevator. Things I can say to him, excuses I can make to the others, a last resort if things don't go my way. I run the tip of my tongue across the slice in my cheek. The blood has stopped flowing, but the metallic taste is still in my mouth.

I stop at my personal room on the way back to Daniel's suite. My favorite gun, a Remington RM380, named Frida, fits comfortably in my right boot. I hum as the elevator takes me back down.

I'm striding across the upper lobby when someone catches my eye near the elevator. Kong remains unmoving as I approach. His arms are crossed over his chest, and he watches me as my boots click on the tile. We are both silent, waiting for the ding. At last, we board, and face each other. I can see myself in the mirror behind him. I don't look great.

I hold my breath. Frida presses into my calf.

"You look unsettled, Lacey."

"Not at all."

"If I were you, I would be unsettled."

A nerve, pinched when I hit the floor, spasms in my back. I wince.

"I got an interesting call a few minutes ago."

I stare.

"From Marc."

I don't speak.

"He wanted me to see if I could find you. He is very angry. Something about his manhood... and coffee."

I watch Kong. He doesn't appear threatening in any way. If anything, he seems amused.

"I saw your face when Jacobson hit his whore," he says. "You are not a *normal* prostitute, are you?"

"What are you going to do?"

Kong smiles. It is a rare sight, and unnerving. "I'm going to find out where you hid the reporter. Then I am going to take you to Mr. Jacobson and let him decide what to do with you."

I swallow. Panic rises inside me. I put tremendous effort into breathing normally.

"Maybe he will be kind to you. Such a beautiful woman." Kong turns and faces the door.

Something in his voice, the way he says 'beautiful,' his accent, lights an idea inside me. "What do you know about the information the reporter was trying to get?"

He turns to face me again.

I continue: "The information I got, long before he showed up?"

His eyebrows rise at this revelation. "I am not paid to know."

"I found evidence of a factory, being operated by slaves, in Thailand."

Kong doesn't move. "And?"

I lick my lips. "It's in the Nan province. Right along the forest."

His nose twitches. His right eyebrow raises. I lock my eyes on his.

"The village, where they got the slaves. It's on the other side of the border... In Laos."

He inhales, and fury blooms in his eyes. "You know this?"

"Yes."

His gaze darts around the elevator. He breathes out through his teeth. "Why do I care?"

I let out a half sigh, half chuckle. "Don't *pretend* you don't. I see your anger. Hmong people are working in that factory. They're the ones who will be slaughtered when Jacobson and Blake are done using them."

He shifts his weight. "That has nothing to do with my job here."

"You'll let them get away with murdering your people?"

"Even if I wanted to stop them," he shakes his head, "it's too late. There's nothing I can do."

I take half a step toward him. "That might not be true."

He frowns and tilts his head at me. "What do you have in mind?"

A half grin slides across my face.

CHAPTER FOURTEEN

LACEY

DAMSEL IN DISTRESS

Kong carries me through the door. I let out a convincing whimper as he sets me on the recliner.

Nathan rushes to me, fear etched across his face. He runs his hands over me, taking in each bruise and drop of blood. I've added a few injuries: a slice on my right arm, a black eye to complement my cheek. It sells the story.

Daniel strides back and forth along the hallway. Each time he passes the bathroom, he pauses to glare at the open door. Delilah watches his movements from the kitchen where she slowly nibbles on a leftover cupcake.

Marcus sits on the floor, leaning against the couch and pressing a frosted bottle of vodka to his crotch. A line of red, swollen skin rings his neck. He glares at me.

A gentle hand strokes my hair. Nathan murmurs in my ear, apologizing for getting me into this, asking what happened. I tell him, through thick, terrified breaths.

Ryan had a handcuff key on him. He got free in the bathroom and bided his time. I had stopped to say hello to Marcus on my way to Nathan's room. I couldn't sleep. I wanted to be with him. Ryan burst from the bathroom and attacked us. Marcus fought him off, but he was also trying to defend me. Ryan was able to knock him unconscious.

He took me, dragged me into the elevator and used me as insurance to get out of the hotel. Kong stopped us in the empty lobby. He managed to rescue me, but Ryan escaped in the process.

Fortunately for me, Kong was able to make a call to Marcus before the others woke up. It only took a few minutes of convincing, but judging by how he keeps looking at me, Marcus isn't pleased with the arrangement so far.

"So, he's gone then?" Daniel stares at his security team.

"It would seem that way." Marcus winces as he stands. He limps to the kitchen and switches out vodka bottles. He returns, pressing the new one against his leg.

"Why the fuck would you prioritize protecting a *whore* over keeping him here?" Daniel roars.

Delilah flinches and takes a step back. Kong's nostrils flare, and Nathan's grip on my shoulder tightens. I keep my mouth closed, but the pressure sends pain shooting through my back.

I quiver my bottom lip and bite my tongue hard enough to draw tears. "He... he said he was going to kill me."

Nathan glares at Daniel. Then he looks Marcus in the eye and says, "You did the right thing trying to keep her safe. Thank you."

Daniel looks like he might explode. His fists shake at his sides. There is tense silence for a moment.

Nathan finally breaks it, looking at Kong. "What do we do now?"

"It will take him a while to get back to the States." Kong pulls out his phone and taps at the screen. "The next flight, assuming he leaves from Tokyo, doesn't board until 4:30 p.m. It's a thirty-hour trip to New York if he leaves today."

"That's assuming," Marcus grunts from the kitchen, "that he has all his documentation ready to go. It's more likely he'll hunker down somewhere in the city and fly out in a few days."

Daniel nods. His eyes have a faraway look as he gazes out the window at the city below. "How much would it cost me to have you two find him?"

Kong glances at his partner. "That is something we would need to discuss."

"Discuss it. Let me know. Soon." He shoots them a dangerous look and glares at me. "It better not be much, since you're the ones who fucking lost him in the first place."

He turns and goes to the coffee table. A dusting of cocaine sits next to a mound of ecstasy pills. "In the meantime, no one is to say a word about this to anyone. As far as the rest of the conference knows, the kid was a practical joker. He's been dealt with, and everything is on track for the rest of the weekend."

Nathan nods. "We have a few more events today and tomorrow. Then the final brunch on Saturday. By the time we get home on Sunday, everything in Thailand will be taken care of. Even if the boy calls anyone, it will be too late."

Kong's eyes meet mine for a split second. "Marc and I will discuss finding the reporter. We will be in the conference room by breakfast with an answer for you."

Marcus shakes his head; his nostrils flare as he limps by me. I sigh and sink back into the cushions on the recliner.

Daniel and Nathan discuss the payment to the men in Thailand. They run through some quick numbers. How much money they would lose if they shut everything down right away. Fortunately, greed holds out, and they keep their original plan. Miss Belle still has some time.

Nathan takes my arm, lifts me from the recliner, and steers me toward the elevator. "Let's get you cleaned up before breakfast."

I follow him willingly.

He talks to me in the elevator, down the hall, and into his room. I let him, one ear listening in case I have to respond.

I have two and a half more days. My original flight leaves Saturday at 3:30 p.m. Between now and then I must get through two organized brunches, another museum trip, a shopping trip, and a dinner and dance. Not to mention anything Nathan wants to do with just the two of us.

A smile sneaks across my face before I turn my lips down again. Chang will be picking up Ryan now. He changed the name on my ticket; the Tennessee boy will be home by the middle of the day tomorrow.

The Language Barrier
If you are going somewhere you don't speak the language, learn at least a few words. I've found it helpful to know how to say "please," "thank you," and "sorry." Even if you have zero interest in learning a new language, knowing those three phrases will make your interactions with the locals much more pleasant.
It's also nice to learn the word "bathroom."

Chapter Fifteen

Miss Belle

Old Friends

The Gulfstream lands in Chiang Rai. I've been traveling for twenty-eight hours. Eleven of which were layovers. I've gotten ten hours of sleep. I could kill the next person who rolls their eyes at my horrible pronunciation.

Though, to be fair, my Thai isn't as good as my Russian, Mandarin, or Spanish.

Chiang Rai International Airport is small but clean and cute. I, however, am the opposite of clean and cute at the moment. I stop in the bathroom before leaving the building. A raccoon face stares back at me from the mirror. The raccoon needs a shower.

I pull soap from my go-bag, along with a toothbrush, hair-brush, clean underwear, and a fresh shirt. No pants—everyone knows jeans last at least five days if you don't spill anything sticky on them. Once my mouth is minty fresh, my hair is up in a loose ponytail, and a light sweatshirt covers my clean *Guardians of the Galaxy* T-shirt, I head out to meet Thomas.

Ah, good old Thomas. I've known him almost six years now. Missa and I met him early on in our career before we painted the Manor and had more than two girls in our care. He was a bit of a rebound for me—if you can call a two-and-a-half-year gap between men a rebound.

We were working a case near Zambia. It was a small matter, but Missa and I handled it ourselves. A favor for a friend going through a rough time.

Thomas was working the same case, though his reasons were far purer than ours. Once the ex-warlord was dealt with, we had a couple of extra days before we had to be back in New York. I spent my time with Thomas. Pretty sure Missa taught an elementary school full of children how to play guitar. Priorities.

I tug my phone from my bag and send off a quick "here and alive" text to Missa. Then I push open the glass doors. Dim light casts a gray shadow over the buildings and street. If my math is correct, and also my digital watch, it's 7:30 a.m. on Friday. The sun is still hiding behind the mountains to the east. It's only about seventy degrees right now, but the temperature will rise with the morning light.

A horn beeps to my left. My face breaks into a grin as Thomas hops out of his Jeep and comes to meet me. It's work from here on out, so I take a few seconds to appreciate his—well, himness.

His dark eyes glint; every time light hits them, tiny specks of gray sparkle. Small creases on the edges of his eyelids show how often he smiles. His black shirt is almost invisible against his skin; the man is darker than the far side of the moon. Chocolate is not the correct word to describe him; coffee would be closer.

Tan cargo pants are tucked into a pair of boots at the bottom of his insanely long legs. At 5'7", my height is average. At 6'4", he makes me look like I'm perpetually standing in a hole. A paracord bracelet is wrapped around his wrist. A jade necklace, a gift from his little sister, hangs tight around his neck.

"Miss Belle." He smiles and pulls me into a tight embrace.

I inhale his scent. We aren't in love, never were, but it's not often you can trust someone with your life. He is one on a very short list of people. Plus, he always did smell delicious. "It's great to see you, Thomas."

"You as well. It has been too long." His Tanzanian accent is thick. Each word he speaks sounds like honey dripping from his lips.

"Everything ready?" I pull away, back in work mode.

He chuckles. "The Jeep is fully stocked. I will show you when we get out of the city."

I walk with him to the Jeep, and raise my eyebrow. "What is this?" I drop my backpack on the curb and put a hand on my hip.

He glances down at me. "What do you mean?"

"I mean—" I kick a tire on the rusted heap of junk in front of me, a frown on my face. "What am I looking at here? This thing is older than I am."

His eyes narrow and he puts a hand on the vehicle. "This is a 1987 Jeep Wrangler. A very reliable vehicle. And one I restored myself last year."

I raise my hands in a defensive shrug. "I'm just saying, it looks like junk to me. Are you sure it'll get us there?"

He picks up my go-bag and tosses it into the back. It lands on two full, brown duffels. "Just get in the car."

I can feel the eye-roll as he walks around to the driver's side.

"You have not changed a bit, Miss Belle."

I wink at him and then hoist myself up and jump into the passenger seat. "Neither have you, and stop calling me Miss. You aren't a john or a girl. It's just Belle with you."

A good luck charm hangs down from the rearview mirror. Two pictures stick out from a crease in the dashboard. One is his family. They stare up with loving smiles from in front of their small wooden home. The other picture is a red-headed, freckly man with bright blue eyes and a sheepish grin. I lean closer when I see this stranger. Of course, it's been five and a half years. Why wouldn't there be a stranger in Thomas's life?

The engine comes to life, and I have to admit, it's purring.

"Who's this?" I point to the blue-eyed man.

Thomas's face lights up like I've never seen. He sits up straighter and grins over at me. "His name is Ben. He's from Australia."

"I see." I give him a sly grin. "How long have you and Ben been together?"

"Two years this November."

"That's great. You'll have to tell me all about him."

Thomas bobs a little in his seat. I don't think I've ever seen him this excited. "We met at a construction site, building houses in Myanmar. He came with his brother, and we just... we just clicked, Belle. Is that the word? Clicked?"

"Yeah." I laugh. "That's the word."

"Yes, we clicked. Everything about him is incredible. He is so kind, smart, sweet; he can cook. He got me a dog for our anniversary."

His happiness is infectious. I smile. "That's wonderful. I'm so glad you're happy."

He chats to me about Ben. About his family: his brother, who punched a man in the street for calling Ben a slur, his mother, who cried when he brought Thomas home, then baked them both a peach cobbler.

He tells me about their dog, a mutt with a broken tail that twists to the left. The love flowing from his voice sends pangs of longing through me. Not longing for him—Thomas is wonderful, but he was never mine. No, I miss that feeling of belonging, of having someone there when I fall asleep.

We rumble along quiet streets. Chiang Rai is a calm city. Relatively small, not quite as big as the town I grew up in.

I've been many places in my life. My family traveled when I was young and—well—now I obviously travel quite a bit. But I've only been to Thailand twice, and never this far north. It's stunning.

A hundred lush shades of green surround us. Hills start small on the edges of the city, then grow and grow into thundering mountains in the distance. The sky is so clear I can see for miles. Rays of red, gold, and orange match the progression of the sun peeking from behind the trees.

The homes, shops, and schools lining the street are humble but clearly well cared-for and valued. The main road we are on, and the ones branching out on either side, are paved, clean, and smooth. Well-dressed teachers walk to their schools; early morning business owners fling open their doors and sweep off the curbs out front. A pang of homesickness goes through my stomach.

I reach back and tighten my ponytail. Thomas glances over at me, and I catch the concerned look in his eyes.

"What?" I'm louder than usual because this... vehicle... doesn't have a roof or windows.

"You look different."

"Well, it's been a few years since we've seen each other in person."

"No, you are still more beautiful than words can describe."

I roll my eyes, though the blush in my cheeks betrays how pleased I am.

"You look tired, sad maybe. Like something is troubling you."

"You've seen me for ten minutes. How'd you get all that?"

He gives a cocky, half grin—which I love—and tilts his head. "I can read you very well, Belle."

"Ha!" I throw my head back and slump down into the seat. I pop my right foot up on the dash and tuck my left under my butt. "Or so you think." I raise an eyebrow and look over at him. "Maybe everything is fine; maybe I'm having the time of my life, maybe..."

He glares at me.

"Okay." I tug on the end of my sweatshirt and nod. "Maybe things have been a bit tricky lately. Trickier than usual, that is."

"What's going on?" His voice carries so much emotion I feel safe in this exposed cab.

I am quiet for a moment. Unlike me, but there is *so much* going on I don't honestly know where to start. The Jeep clickity-clacks along a bridge over the Kok river, and I sit up a bit to see the water better.

"It's a lot right now. I've got the police breathing down my neck back in New York. My little brother thinks I hate him because he's gay. One of my Guides is having a hard time being so far from home. But it's too dangerous to send him back right now. Missa has to deal with a blackmail thing we've got going because I'm *here*. And—I'm here. The Tokyo job got fucked up, Lacey's in danger, and there are over a hundred more lives that depend on me, and you, right now."

I take a deep breath and keep going. "Plus, I'm the one who gave Lacey this assignment, and it's killing her. Not, you know, literally. But it's the hardest job she's had with me. Part of *my* job is to protect my girls from what she's going through right now."

He is still and silent as I rant the list of things stressing me out. I miss talking to him. It's not like some huge weight lifts from my shoulders, but there is less tension in my neck.

We roll along and pass the last few buildings that make up Chiang Rai. Thomas finds a small dirt road, and we pull off. I hop out of the Jeep and come around to the back. Thomas unzips the first of the duffle bags. I can't help but smile up at him.

"This is perfect." I caress a sniper rifle. "Any back-up available?"

He shakes his head. "No one I trust."

I nod and sigh. I was hoping we'd have better numbers, but you get what you get.

"There are also a couple of good machetes, two vests, and some smaller guns. We should be ready to take down an army."

"Let's hope it doesn't come to that." I dig through the other bag a bit and pull out the sack of apples I knew would be there. My hand brushes against a black box about eight inches across. "What's this?"

His mischievous grin makes me raise an eyebrow. "That is a new toy. A present from Ben."

It's clear he isn't going to fill me in at the moment, so I move on. "I'm hoping there won't be a crazy amount of security."

"That is also my hope. But what is it your scout boys say? Always be ready?"

"Close enough." I laugh and zip the duffle closed. The bag of apples joins me in the passenger seat. A dull, yellowish red one catches my eye; I rub it on my shirt before locking my teeth into the skin.

"So," Thomas says. He starts up the engine and steers us back onto the road. "It sounds like you are very underwhelmed right now."

"Overwhelmed. And yeah. It's..." I exhale and tug on my ponytail. "It's all a bit much."

"Is there anything I can do to help?"

I smile over at him. "No, but you're a doll for asking." I take another bite of the apple and crunch on it between words. "Anyway, I've got a game plan for everything. I just need to do this first."

"What is your plan for the police?"

My mouth is bursting with apple juice. I chew and swallow before answering. "I'm going to talk to the precinct captain. There's no way the surveillance is sanctioned. They don't have enough evidence for that."

"You know what they have?"

"I've got a good idea." I roll my eyes and toss the apple core into the vegetation on the side of the road. "A neighbor complained about girls coming and going at all hours in 'risqué' clothing. And supposedly they got an anonymous call straight out saying hookers live there."

"That is all?"

I frown. "I think so. That's the only reason I can think of for them to be suspicious."

His fingers tap against the steering wheel. "That seems like not enough for surveillance."

I bite the nail of my pinky finger and slowly bob my head up and down. "You're right. Maybe I need to look into this more."

The Jeep bounces over a chunk of bumpy road. We are getting farther into the farmlands and away from the city.

He glances over at me. "And your brother?"

My cheeks puff out with the amount of air in my sigh. "It was a miscommunication type thing. And—of course—it was because of the job, so I can't really explain myself to him properly."

"He thinks you are a homophobe?"

"Ugh. Yes. Someone took a picture of me with the Vice President."

He sneers, looking like someone shoved an old sock under his nose.

I sigh again. "It's other stuff too. I had to leave his wedding early because of an issue in Russia. I don't know the best way to explain to him that I'm not what he thinks. Well, not without telling him what I actually do for a living."

"What would be so wrong with that?"

I raise an eyebrow and purse my lips. "I can't tell my little brother that I work as a madam for a house full of escorts." Unintentional scorn laces my words.

He pulls sharply to the side of the road and shuts off the car. Dust and gravel spin through the air around us.

"What?" I glance around.

He stares at me, an angry glint in his dark eyes. "You are not just that. You are not *just* a madam. You are a powerful woman. With many connections around the world and a network of information that could cripple nations."

I twist my jaw to the side in a grimace. "My network isn't *that* extensive."

He puts a calloused hand on my arm. "You are more than you say. It is unfair of you to sell yourself small."

"Short." I put a hand on his and take a deep breath. "Thank you, Thomas. I appreciate it."

I gaze out on the horizon. The sun has risen rapidly. It shines down on us, lighting up the countryside. "Lately, I've been drifting. I feel like my life is lacking meaning."

"Lacking?"

"Missing. Like what I'm doing with my life isn't worth anything."

I feel his eyes on me, but I avoid his gaze. My eyes burn, and my throat itches with anger. There is no reason to be crying right now. I grit my teeth and hold in the stupid saltwater trying to leak from my face.

He starts the Jeep and quietly pulls back onto the road. I shouldn't be, but I'm disappointed that he didn't try to fix it. That he didn't reassure me that I'm worth something, that my life matters.

The only sounds are the wind and the birds. We pass rice paddies for miles. Thailand and India are neck and neck as top exporters in the world.

One of Alex's regulars is in the agricultural division in New Delhi. She comes back after each appointment with some random fact about Indian agriculture. And for some stupid reason, I remember all of them.

The mountains in the distance inch closer as the sun passes overhead. By about 10 a.m., we have reached the halfway mark. To our right, a burst of trees, bushes, and tall grass cover the landscape. The Doi Phu Nang National Park runs along either side of our route. I'd love to stop and hike to one of their gorgeous waterfalls, go for an illegal swim, have fun.

But that's not in the cards. We don't have time for fun. I'm not some tourist here; I have a job to do. I lean my head back and gaze blankly at the telephone poles shooting past.

Another hour goes by. Thomas pulls the Jeep over in a small town and fills up with gas. I leave him at the pump and buy some snacks. I grab some prawn crackers and a little container of flower-shaped cookies. The young woman behind the counter stretches out her neck to get a better look at me. I smile and thank her in Thai. Her eyes widen a bit, but she smiles and waves me out of the store.

I toss my sweatshirt into the back. The day has warmed up nicely. I munch on my goodies in the passenger seat and squint at the picture of Ben. His shy grin makes me smile. Thomas deserves someone who smiles like that.

Thomas hops back in the Jeep, and we chug along down the road.

"What's the plan when we reach Nan?"

"Ehh." I fold up my cracker bag and stick it under my seat. "The plan is a bit complicated." I lick my fingers. "We have the coordinates of the factory, but we need to do some recon before we go in guns blazing."

"To check out their numbers?"

"Yeah, and to see what kind of security they are working with. I've got a vague number of the people employed there, but I don't know if they are all security guys. And I don't know what kind of equipment they are working with."

"How much time do we have?"

I glance at my watch. "About forty hours. If we're lucky."

He raises a thick eyebrow at me. "That is not a lot of time, Belle. You said they plan on destroying the factory after this time?"

I breathe out slowly. "Yes. From what Lacey heard, they are shutting down everything, and killing everyone when they finish their last lineup of product."

He shakes his head; angry eyes glare at the road.

I brainstorm as we drive. We have limited options for this operation. I don't know what kind of weapons we are dealing with, how many men they have, or the location of the village.

Lacey has all of it on her film, but there's no way she's been able to overnight it with everything going on. It's lucky she gave me what she could, including the coordinates, when we talked the first time, or I'd have nothing to go on.

I eat another apple and the rest of my flower cookies on the way to Nan. Thomas pulls the Jeep over at a—haha—Thai food place. We grab a table, and I take a map of the area out of my bag.

"Okay." I point a black polished fingernail at the paper. "We are here. The factory is here." My finger moves about an inch north. "The village is supposed to be just on the other side of the border. But I don't have an exact location."

The waitress walks over, and I fold up the map. A green apron is tied low around her slim waist. Black pants, shirt, and sturdy shoes clash with her bright makeup and the pigtails just above her ears. Her smile is sincere.

We both order—Thomas with fluidity and beauty, me with a lot of stumbling around pronunciation and pointing to the menu. The waitress is nice about it, chuckling along when I do, and accepting my apologies with a heavily accented, "Is okay, is okay."

They must get enough tourism that my horrible Thai isn't that unusual.

Thomas grins at me from across the table when she leaves, and I stick my tongue out at him.

When he steps away to use the restroom I pull out my phone and call Missa.

There is a click and then silence.

"Hey?" I say.

"Hey, yourself. What's going on?"

Someone's grumpy. "We're in Nan. Grabbing a bite to eat."

"You called to tell me that?"

"Yeesh, what's up with you?"

"It's 12:30 in the freaking morning!"

"Oh yeah, crap. My bad."

She groans, and I hear shuffling on the other end of the phone. "It's fine. I needed to talk to you anyway."

"What's up?"

"Lacey called. She's fine. She got Ryan out, but we're going to have to deal with Kong and Marcus sometime soon."

"We'll get to them when this is done. Did she happen to give you any info on the village?"

"Yeah, actually, I emailed you the location. Not much beyond that, though I do have the name of the weapons supplier. It's Korskofsky."

I chuckle and lean back in the booth. "That's fantastic to hear."

"Why?" Her groggy voice tells me now is not the time to be laughing into the phone.

"He owes me a favor. From that thing in Poland."

"I don't remember." She yawns. "I'm too tired to remember."

I grin down at the table. "Go back to sleep; sorry I woke you up. Thanks for the info."

"No problem," she yawns.

The phone clicks off as Thomas sits back down.

"Everything is okay?" he asks.

"Yeah, just getting some extra help from Missa. We've got the location of the village now. Or, as soon as I get somewhere with Wi-Fi."

The waitress returns with our food. The smells have the salivary glands in my mouth going nuts. It all looks delicious. Say what you will about fancy restaurants, there's nothing better than chowing down at a little diner in a small town. No matter what country you're in.

We load up on carbs and protein. We've got snacks with us, but it's not like we know when we'll have time to eat a proper meal again.

A steaming plate of white rice sits next to my two main dishes. I have to shovel the plain grains into my mouth as soon as I swallow my previous bite. I can't handle spicy food. I love spicy food, but without something to cut the heat, I'm pretty sure I'd die. Or at least my face would catch fire. Or melt off. Does skin melt?

In between huge bites, we agree to check out the village first. It will be a great place to set up camp and keep an eye on the factory. With all the people in the factory, it should be nice and quiet. We can hunker down, get our bearings, and set up a full-on tactical op.

A big part of traveling is experiencing different cuisine. It's important to remember some essential tips when trying out new foods.

First, street meat is street meat no matter what country you're in. The source is suspicious, the safety is questionable, and the sanitation is nonexistent. That being said, if you're up for eating meat cooked in a cart, it can be some of the most delicious food you'll find.

Second, don't order salad unless you are 100% sure you know how they wash the greens.

Third, it's really easy to buy a tiny pack of stool hardeners and another of stool softeners. If you get a chance to explore the different levels of cooking, there's a good possibility you will want to have these. Fingers crossed you won't need them, but better safe than sorry.

Chapter Sixteen
Miss Belle
Nonlethal Force

"Because you owe me," I say into the phone.

"That is a lie. I owe you nothing."

"Poland, Korskofsky! Freaking Poland. Where your douche of a nephew almost got you *and* half a dozen of your guys blown up. Pretty sure me and Alex saving your *entire* Central Europe operation means you owe me."

I hear a very grumpy, very Russian, sigh on the other end of the phone. "Fine. But you will tell no one. It is not good business to give away such information."

"Cross my heart, K. Whaddya got for me?"

Thomas loads up our packs while my Russian contact fills me in. All is going according to plan until he names the mercenary supplier.

"Wait—they're using McKinnan's guys?"

"Yes."

"Shit." I heave a sigh, and Thomas looks up at me, concern in his dark eyes. "All right, thanks, K. Let's catch up next time you visit the States."

"Won't be for a while, Miss Belle. Things are getting sticky over here."

I frown. Something in Korskofsky's voice is off. His line of work is always sticky, so what's different this time? Curiosity floods my brain, but I don't have time to discuss it with him now. I make a mental note to call him when this specific operation is over. Though, with McKinnan's mercs on the board, that could take longer than I'd prefer. "I'll want to hear all about it over coffee. Take care."

"And you, Miss Belle."

I flip the phone closed and head down a shallow embankment to where Thomas's Jeep is resting. We're maybe a mile from the village, having crossed into Laos not too long ago. If the jungle weren't so dense, we'd have needed to park farther away, but sound doesn't travel far out here.

Thomas flings a thick, leafy branch across the exposed metal and steps away. He did a good job. From the road, no one will be able to distinguish his rust-bucket.

We load up, he tosses me a pack, and we make our way toward the village. I fill him in as we go. "They've got the usual weapons for this kind of operation. A few semi-autos and a handful of bigger toys. It's the mercs themselves that will be a problem."

"We figured they would be a problem, didn't we?" Thomas gives me a half grin and lifts the edge of his shirt. A beautiful 1911—solid metal, standard army issue back in the day—rests happily at his waist.

I shake my head. "Different kind of problem. These guys aren't the top, but they have a unique setup. We've got to try and be as... nonlethal... as possible with them."

Thomas stops on the road and gives me an incredulous look. "Why?"

"They run a different operation than we're used to. If we permanently dispose of a bunch of their guys, they'll send a new group *and* set up a revenge team." My mind is spinning already with how I can deal with McKinnan. Money will need to change hands. But he's a real professional; he won't let a job go unfinished. And a chunk of change won't be enough to convince him to do something that might ruin his reputation.

Thomas rolls his massive shoulders in a frustrated shrug. "Nonlethal. How do we manage that when the goal is to ruin their contract and stop them from murdering innocents?"

I grunt. A pure, frustrated, guttery grunt. "If I knew that, I'd be telling you the plan instead of the problem. Let's get to the village, scope everything out, and make our move from there."

We walk in silence. About half a mile down the road, a tree with a trunk about the size of Thomas's waist blocks the way. The end isn't cut; chunks of root are torn from the ground. It should have been cleared away immediately, but with the villagers at the factory, there's no one to do so.

Or there is...

There are people. Movement. The village isn't empty. We crouch for a few minutes, scanning the area. It appears that the only people left here are women and children, and the elderly.

The village is small. Three winding paths lead around an array of raised homes and connect along the edge of a stream before turning and becoming the main road. We stick to the side, stopping before the stream and crouching in the vegetation.

A bent, elderly woman hurries along a path toward a wooden, tin-roofed house at the edge of the road. She tugs on the arm of a little boy, maybe five or six years old. He stumbles along behind her, barely keeping up. I frown; there's no need to drag the child.

Then I see why.

A middle-aged Thai man follows behind them—I know from the Thai police uniform he is wearing. He drags a young woman by the hair. She's maybe sixteen or seventeen, and the terror on her face is unmistakable. A machine gun hangs from his shoulder.

A furious shiver runs across my skin. Next to me, Thomas's body is stiff. A low growl comes from his lips—a bird in the bush nearby squawks and flies into the sky.

The man pauses. Thomas rises an inch. I grab his bicep and squeeze. He sinks back down but turns to look at me. Fire glints in his eyes. His lips are straight, nostrils curled in a furious snarl. "We cannot let this happen," he murmurs.

I nod. "We also cannot go in guns blazing. Follow me."

We leave our duffle bags in the vegetation near the creek. Thomas brings a shotgun, and I carry a small handgun.

We skirt around the path and slide up next to the house, just around the corner from the door. There is crying inside. A little boy is saying something. I can't understand him, but the tone is familiar. He is begging.

The door slams shut, and I take a glance around the area. This house is pretty secluded.

I tap on Thomas's shoulder, and he moves around the side of the house. He stands in front of the door; I stand to the side. I pull a blade from my boot. Six inches of steel rests in my hand. I flex my fingers around the rubber grip.

I nod.

He pulls the door open; I burst into the room. The old woman and boy huddle in the corner. The woman's hand blocks the boy's eyes.

The girl is on her back. She struggles against the man. Moans and quiet sobs tell me she has learned not to scream. She kicks out, and he grunts. He kneels on top of her, trying to position himself.

His gun lies to the side, forgotten.

The sound of the door opening gets his attention. I step up behind him as he turns. I grab his hair with one hand and yank. With the other, I bring my knife across his neck. An ear to ear smile under his jaw sends a spray of red onto the girl.

She screams and crawls backward, stopping at the wall. She clutches her knees to her chest, ragged sobs shaking her body. A long tear runs up the side of her dress. She scrambles to cover her legs with what remains of the fabric.

The man slumps. I release his hair, and he falls to the side. His bowels release and a toxic smell fills the house. The old woman stares at me, still covering the boy's eyes.

Thomas taps my shoulder. I turn to him.

He gives me a curt nod and shuts the door.

Some may think me harsh. But if Thomas and I agree upon anything, it's the fitting punishment for rapists.

He kneels next to the old woman, who I assume is their grandmother, and I go to the girl. He speaks quietly. I recognize the language; it's Hmong.

I don't speak. Couldn't if I wanted to. I drop the knife, then sit next to the young woman, close but not touching her.

She shivers but glances up at me. I spread my arms, just a little. Just enough.

She falls into them, clinging to me as wracking sobs go through her. I stroke this strange woman's hair. Just enough pressure in my grasp to make her feel safe, but not trapped.

Her tears soak into my shirt. The blood on her chest stains my arms.

While Thomas talks to the old woman, the boy joins us, clutching the girl and burying his head in her side. We all sit for several moments.

This is the time in movies and books that always drives me crazy. Because you think we got here just in the nick of time. You think we saved her. You think we stopped the unthinkable.

We did not.

As the grandmother explains, her eldest granddaughter has been raped six times since the factory opened. By the dead man on the floor. Her mother is dead. Killed for fighting back when they tried to get to her. Her father is at the factory. Though whether he still lives, they don't know. The grandmother has been trying to keep her grandchildren safe. But the boy has been beaten. Bruises crawl across his torso. And the girl...

Thomas gets our equipment from the stream. We stay in the house for a few minutes. Just long enough to get some answers.

The man was a Thai policeman. Bribed by Jacobson's company to assist a mercenary force with keeping everyone in line. A rotation of two mercs and six amateurs watch the village. They switch out every three days. Today is day two.

Good. We have a full day before someone new comes to check on the village. As long as we don't raise the alarm, this should be a smooth portion of the job.

Of course, we will have to move fast today. Someone is going to notice a missing buddy, especially with so few people running security here.

The mercs and amateurs are staying in the village leader's home. During the day, they wander around, taking what they want from the people here and making sure no tourists come up the road.

Thomas and I load up. I strap two extra clips to my belt and tuck another knife in the small of my back under my shirt. A half-inch thick, ten-foot-long, strip of rope hangs from my hip. A handkerchief is tied around my neck.

Thomas slings an assault rifle across his back. The hilt of a large blade protrudes from his boot. A small machete hangs from his belt, and he is still holding his shotgun.

We move the man's body before we go. The dead weight is heavy, but the grandmother helps us carry him a few yards away from the road. We cover his body with brush and toss his gun on the ground next to him.

A handful of dirt covers each drop of blood between the body and the house. Inside, the girl and boy scrub at the floor. The girl has changed clothes. She stashes the bloody garments behind her bed. Thomas stops both of them for a moment and speaks to the family.

They gaze at him intently, following every word.

We leave. Once the door is closed behind us, I glance up at him. "What did you say?"

"I told them to stay inside. To tell no one they saw us. And to leave the man and his gun where we put them." He turns to me, his eyes sunken deep within their sockets. "If they tried to seek revenge, they would die."

I nod and move out.

We stick to the edges of the buildings. Buckets of water, rope, tarps, wood scraps, and slabs of aluminum lie scattered around the outer edge of the village.

Thomas finds another Thai man pissing on the side of someone's house. He approaches silently, stepping around sticks and leaves, small clouds of dirt puffing out where his feet land. His left hand covers the man's mouth. His right swings around the front of the stranger's body. Metal pierces flesh.

The man's pants are still down when he dies, Thomas's blade deep in his chest.

I grab a tarp and we drape it over his bloody body.

We move on.

In the center of the village, a small marketplace attempts to survive. Two men, both white, tall, and muscular, walk back and forth along the main road. They each carry automatic weapons. Unlike the two Thai men, they are equipped with professional-grade gear.

Thomas and I crouch behind a shed, watching the men walk away. When they reach the last house, they turn and walk back. They move slowly, eyes scanning the area, fingers to the side of their triggers.

As they grow nearer, I squint. There it is, a small symbol sewn into their matching black T-shirts, just above the right pectoral. I roll my head back and utter a silent sigh as frustration fills me.

Thomas stares at me. His eyebrow twitches. "How do you propose we deal with this situation, save these people, if we can't attack the men paid to kill them?"

"I didn't say we couldn't attack them. We just need to try not to kill them. Did you bring any tranquilizers?"

His mouth is slightly open, eyebrows raised, eyes squinting, an incredulous exasperation glinting through them as he tilts his head at me. "You want us to take on a highly trained group of mercenaries... and try to knock them all out? How about you tie one arm behind my back too, this doesn't sound hard enough."

"We've each taken on harder missions."

He lets out a massive sigh. "I brought two tranq guns and a couple of rubber bullet guns; they are in the Jeep."

"You brought poisons as well, right?"

"Of course."

"Good. Let's get back to the Jeep and reload."

On our way back to the Jeep, we 'subdue' another amateur. We roll his corpse down a small ditch on the side of the road and scatter a few fallen branches on top.

"See." I nudge Thomas as we scurry away from the village. "Three down, five to go. This'll be a cakewalk."

"Why would you want to walk on cake?"

I blink and hurry to the Jeep. In a small compartment beneath the trunk area, a little box sits, wrapped in a white towel. I unwrap it and run a hand over the violet case. Then I open it and grin at the contents.

This box used to be mine. I gave it to Thomas years ago as a gift. A reminder of the good we accomplished together. The lives we saved. Six small bottles nestle in lavender satin cushions. Three small syringes lie next to them.

I pull out two of the bottles; identical fluid swishes around in each. I fill all three syringes and cap them before tucking them into an outside pocket of my left boot.

Thomas loads up the two tranq guns and hands me one. It feels different. I don't like it. I've only used a tranq once, during training.

We walk back toward the village.

"What is the plan?"

I grimace. "I was hoping we'd have more time. We can't exactly do recon of the village after taking out three guys. I think our best bet is to get the rest of them in as small a window as possible. We can't let them radio for help. We'll tie up the mercs and leave them here. Tonight, we can slip down to the factory and figure out a plan for that."

"So, the plan is to defeat the bad guys?"

I glare at his tone. "To put it simply, yes."

"I am just saying, you don't actually have a plan for the village."

I clench my jaw. "I did... We just, sort of, launched into it early."

He nods.

We get to the grandmother's house and knock quietly on the door. The boy lets us in, and we sit for a moment, go over things before we act.

Our primary goal is to disable the mercs. We need to try not to kill them. Like, really try.

This group, they're professionals, and they're like brothers. If we kill them, they'll send other guys to finish the job, and then dispatch an army to kill us. So, for now, we do everything we can to get them out of the way. And I'll come up with a way to *keep* them out of the way, as soon as we save these people. I groan internally.

Thomas will approach the village square from the main road; I'll come around the side. We will take out the mercs, then deal with the remaining amateurs.

The Thai police spend most of their time by the market.

When they aren't raping people.

The mercenaries patrol along the main road, up and back, all day. When we are both in place, one will cause a distraction, and the other will hit them, either with the tranqs or the methohexital in the syringes.

I take out my ponytail and re-set it higher on my head. I position my handkerchief over my mouth and nose and tuck it under my ears before tying it at the back of my head. I pull eight bobby pins from a pocket, then stick four on each side to stop the handkerchief from sliding down.

Thomas leaves first, and I follow.

Chapter Seventeen

Miss Belle

It's Called Manners

I skirt along the outer edge of the town, following the stream until it arcs right and leaves me to the dirt. The sun is bright overhead. Soon it will begin its slow descent.

A large house sits a few yards away. Glass windows give the dwellers a beautiful view of sunsets over the mountains. This is the village leader's home. From the grandmother's intel, I stand at the far end of the village, just a few houses from the village square and the main road. A woman cries softly somewhere nearby. I follow her voice.

A window on the right side of the house is cracked open. The home sits a meter off the ground, just tall enough for my eyes to be level with the opening. A woman, possibly in her forties, sits on a twin bed in the corner of the room. Her thick black hair covers her face. Tinges of gray line her cheekbones. She holds a baby in her arms. The child is silent, and my heart freezes, but then a tiny hand wiggles between blankets.

I pause under the window, ready to inch toward the front of the house. A gasp makes me bite my lip. I turn to the woman. Her tired eyes are wide as she openly stares at me. I smile, then remember the handkerchief.

Her eyes meet mine. She tilts her head in a silent question. I nod, hoping I am reading her correctly. She holds up two fingers and points to the front of the house.

I nod again and move forward in a crouch. Whatever she thinks of me, clearly I'm a better choice of stranger than the men out front. A glimpse around the corner shows her truth.

The scent of tobacco wafts from the two men. Smoke billows from their mouths as they laugh in between puffs. Their guns hang, useless, from their shoulders. One says something in Thai and the other repeats it in Hmong in a mocking, high pitched tone. They both cackle again and one slaps the other's shoulder. It's a good joke.

They face away from me. Little gaps between houses give them an obstructed view of the market. Shadows flicker by, but there is no one in the immediate area. Just empty homes.

I straighten and step forward—plant my foot softly on the hard ground. I clutch the handle of the machete on my hip. A gentle movement silently releases it from its sheath.

It's not a little machete. It's not a toy. It's a full length, foot and a half-long blade. Gerber steel. Sharp enough to cut through a piece of paper on contact, thick enough to sustain blows with hard metals. A row of teeth lines the top. Good for sawing. Wood. Bone. Whichever.

I can't use a gun. The sound would devastate all element of surprise.

Both men could turn at any moment. Their chatter dies down to a low rumble in my ears. My peripheral vision guides my feet around noisy objects on the ground. I am right behind them.

A third Thai man steps out of the house next door. All three of us look at him. His gaze lingers on me. His mouth opens.

I lunge forward as he shouts and bring my blade down between the neck and shoulder of the first man. He never had a chance to turn around. I yank the metal free from the bone as his body drops.

I half turn. A kick hits me square in the side, and I fly to the left. I land on my left knee, my right leg still planted under me. I suck air through my nose.

As I stand, I switch my machete to my left hand and pull a smaller blade from a sheath on the right side of my belt. The third man has reached for his gun. He raises it as I hurl my arm back and fling my knife with as much wrist flick as possible.

The blade lodges in his right shoulder, and he drops the front of his gun.

The second man comes at me again. His left foot kicks forward. I dance to the side. He swings a fist. I duck, but the tip of his hand grazes my jawline. A bloom of blood erupts in my mouth.

I use the force of the blow to move me sideways. I crouch, closing the distance between us—the tip of my machete slices across the back of his thigh.

His knee hits the ground. A loud grunt escapes him as he raises his no longer forgotten gun. I kick the hard metal into his shoulder, and he falls to the side. I swiftly kneel and drag my blade across his neck.

As I stand, piercing pain shoots through my left shoulder blade. Warmth seeps down my arm, trickling along my elbow to my fingertips.

I spin. The third man stares at me. Intense hatred flashes through his eyes. The two dead men were not rapists and thieves in his eyes. They were likely friends. The pain of losing them fuels him.

The blade I planted in his shoulder is clenched in his left hand. Fresh blood—my blood—coats the metal. His right arm hangs, useless, at his side.

He snarls at me with yellow teeth. He lunges forward again. The blade swings toward me, and I parry with my machete. The effort sends a burst of pain down my arm and into the left side of my back.

He swings again, and I step to the side, leaning my upper body to the right. We dance now. Circling each other. My left arm will not land a functional blow. Not with blood still dripping down from my shoulder. His right arm continues to swing. More blood pours from him than me.

I tug down my handkerchief and breathe deep, easing the pain in my shoulder and preparing myself for the next attack. I switch my machete back to the right hand.

He shouts something. My grasp of the language is bad—at best—but I know what a cry for help sounds like.

"No one can hear you." I spit blood at him, laughing.

Laughing during a fight knocks people off their guard, especially if blood is leaking from between your teeth at the same time.

His eyes widen. He says a few words, and his gaze darts around in frantic movements. It lands on me. I catch his eyes with mine and don't blink.

"The rest of your friends? They're dead."

He doesn't understand me. I know this. But the tone of my voice, the vicious smile playing across my swollen lips, they're enough.

He lunges at me with a furious scream. I sidestep and kick, using the same move his friend did. My foot connects with the right side of his ribs. The momentum sends him several feet to the left and his body hits the ground.

I walk toward him. He is on his knees. I kick again. The blow lands squarely on his right shoulder, and he rolls backward.

He cannot use his right arm to help him stand. He drops the knife. His left hand clutches at the gash on his shoulder. Pain splashes across his face.

I stare down in disdain. I wonder how much money he took for this job. I wonder how many women he raped. I wonder if he has a family.

My breath comes quick and sharp.

I kneel and grip the handle of my machete. I tighten my hand. Sweat sticks my skin to the rubber.

The sensation of slicing through skin, through muscle, through veins, is not one that's easy to forget. My bones know how it feels. My muscles remember the movements.

His blood spills onto my boots. The red takes me to another time. Another pair of shoes splattered with death.

A door slams behind me, and I jump then wheel around, spreading my legs into a fighting stance. The woman from before stands on the porch outside the house, baby in her arms. She looks older in the light, laugh-lines spread across her cheeks. But worry fills a deep crease in her forehead, just between her eyes. A wrinkled hand gestures to me.

My boots squelch on the wet ground as I walk toward her. Her gaze is on my shoulder, and I glance down. My shirt is torn. Blood no longer drips down my arm. I bend my elbow and raise my arm.

"Fuck." Pain spasms across my back. A wince I can't control flashes across my face.

I can only see the edge of the cut. He didn't slice through my bra, thank God. I take the steps up to the door slowly. The woman puts a hand on my other arm and gently tugs me inside. She's shorter than me, maybe 5'1". Her grip is rough; the callouses on her skin scratch against my freckly complexion.

Crossing the threshold, I'm hit with the scents of hundreds of meals over years of home cooking. Seasoned meat, steamed rice, sautéed veggies; the air is thick with spices. A simple wooden table with half a dozen stools around it sits in the middle of the room. Wilted flowers in purple, pink, and blue stick out of a tall wooden vase in the center.

The home is clean. Nothing is out of place. I immediately notice the trail of blood I am leaving on the wooden floor. My face flushes. Three women, all shorter than the one with the baby, hover in a far corner. They shrink away from me as I come in. I raise my right hand in a hello gesture, but it doesn't translate with the machete in my fist. The women flinch. I sigh.

All three of them wear traditional Lao outfits. Coins dangle from their hips, the edges of their skirts, and their headwear. The heads of several children poke out from a room farther in the house. One of the women snaps something, and they disappear.

I offer up a small smile, hoping to alleviate some of the fear. The woman closest to me gasps and another bursts out, "*Daa!*"

I hope it means something nice. But I'm not putting money on it. The woman who brought me in, the one with the baby, waves her hand at the others and speaks in rapid Hmong. She drags me to a wooden stool and gently pushes my right shoulder until I sit.

I set the machete on the table. I immediately regret doing so as a pool of blood collects at the tip and drips onto the wood. I inhale and lift my left arm. Pain slices through my shoulder blade and down my back. I grit my teeth and rest my forearm on the table.

My breath comes in quick shudders.

Pain is manageable in a fight. It's manageable once the injury is patched up. Right after a fight? When your blood isn't pumping with fury, when you aren't tensed up, ready for another blow? It's less manageable. In fact, it hurts like a bitch.

Especially something like this. He sliced through my shirt and curved the blade at the end. I can feel my flesh where it's fluttering away from the bone and muscle. Each breath of air sends a sharp burst through my exposed nerves.

The kind woman pushes the baby into another's arms. She comes to me, clean cloth in one hand, a bottle of something in the other.

I lean away, roll off the stool, and stand with a shuddering wince. She raises her hands. I watch them, gaze wary.

It's an overreaction, maybe. But this woman doesn't know me, and I don't know her. That bottle could have anything in it.

She speaks to me in Hmong. I shake my head and tell her, "I don't know what you're saying. I'm sorry. I don't speak Hmong."

"Help," she says in English.

I furrow my eyebrows.

She gestures with her hand, the one carrying the bottle toward me. "Help."

I have to get to Thomas. I need to be in position by now.

I also have to get my cut patched up. A wound, at least one this open, is going to hinder my movement more than a little. I swallow, close my eyes, and grimace. I peek one eye open and sigh.

She gestures again, and I sit. I leave my shirt on. She pulls back the fabric, ripping the cloth a bit.

She says something in Hmong. I assume it's the equivalent of "get ready." I inhale through my mouth. At the top of my breath, she pours.

Acid stings through my flesh. Fire burns apart my skin. Tiny, sadistic men with hot pokers dance along the inside of my cut and stab me repeatedly. You can have as much self-control as you want, but when something hurts this much, you make some fucking noise. I pinch my lips together, but muffled groans still echo around the room.

My vision spots. I grasp the edge of the table, breathing rapidly as my muscles clench and my jaw tightens. A moment passes, and the pain has eased. I release the table and breathe through my mouth.

The woman pats my shoulder and presses the cloth to the wound. I pull a roll of gauze from a pocket on my pants. I pass it to her. She says something—thank you, maybe.

She lifts my left arm and unrolls the gauze around me. It pins the cloth in place, wraps around my neck, down my chest, and under my left arm. She does this a few times, ties it off, and gives me a satisfied nod.

I grin at her, and she raises an eyebrow. She shakes her head. The exasperated look of a tired woman is universal. I frown, confused.

She walks to the kitchen, pours water from a jug on the counter, and brings it back to me. She points to her teeth, then to mine, then to the blood on the table.

Right. I lick my gums. Yep, the metallic warmth of fresh blood greets my tongue. No wonder the women are afraid of me. I swish out my mouth, look for a good place to spit, find none, and swallow the red water. I smile at her again, and she nods approvingly.

I stand up. The other women shuffle farther into the corner away from me. The woman who helped me waves her hand and snaps something in Hmong.

"Listen," I sigh. I know full well that she doesn't understand me, but I have to thank her anyway. It's called manners. "Thanks for patching me up. I have to go. But I'll be back. Probably. Maybe. Anyway, I've got to go."

I take my machete from the table and sheath it. I don't know why, but I give her a small wave before I shut the front door behind me. The little woven curtain shakes against the glass.

I shuffle down the steps. Guilt pits in my stomach. Thomas has been in position—probably—for a while now. Waiting for me. I step over one of the bodies and make my way toward the market.

Two children scurry past, maybe six or seven years old. Their terrified gazes dart between me and the bodies. One trips before the other yanks his arm toward the house I just stepped out of.

I follow the curved dirt road past a few more houses. The marketplace opens before me. At one time, it was probably a bustling hub of activity. Many stalls run along the edges of the road. The scent of cooked meat, fresh fish, and tasty herbs cling to the walls and overhangs.

Bright flags dangle from the walls. Blankets, clothes, and knickknacks are sorted on a few of the stands. Something tells me this village brought in tourists now and then. It's highly likely the fallen tree we passed on the road had more to do with the mercs than the weather.

Only a few people trickle in and out of the market. A withered old woman, her dark hair wrapped up and stacked on her head, buys fruit from a small child sitting on a short wooden stool. Two elderly men talk as they hobble down the street. A few other people pick up meat, fish, and vegetables from the three open stalls. The people of this place, trying to continue as normal a life as possible with everything they're going through.

Anger rolls through my belly.

I tug my handkerchief up above my nose again. I'm tall, white, and covered in blood splatter. They stare but are silent.

I reach my position. I crouch down behind a handcrafted wooden canoe at the end of the market. The main road stretches out before me. In the distance, two men walk toward me. The glint from their guns sparkles across the sky.

Thomas is a little farther. I know where he is supposed to be, but I can't see him. Not yet. The mercs draw closer; both wear matching uniforms. One is tall, with brown hair and a slouch. The other is short, slightly darker skinned, and walks with purposeful steps.

When they reach the halfway mark, a strip of cloth waves through the air where I know Thomas should be.

I wait.

The men come to the edge of the market, chatting amongst themselves and ignoring the locals. They turn, and as they make their way back down the road, I stick my hand out and signal.

Thomas emerges. The mercs freeze and stare at the giant black man walking toward them. His hands are loose by his sides, a smile on his face. His gun isn't visible, likely tucked into the back of his pants.

I step out from behind the canoe and move forward. They are closer to me than Thomas, but he walks confidently toward them.

"Hello!" he calls, offering a friendly wave. "Do you speak English?"

One of the mercs moves his gun, pointing it at Thomas's chest.

"Yes." The other merc steps forward. "You shouldn't be here."

"Well, my truck broke down a ways back."

The one with the gun up glances around. I freeze. His gaze settles on Thomas, and I continue to inch forward.

I'm about ten feet away, crouched under the edge of one of the raised houses. I retrieve the two syringes from my boot pocket. With my thumb, I flick the cap off each.

I need to cross the distance between the men and me. I need to inject them with the methohexital. And, most importantly,

I need to make sure neither of them fires a shot or radios for help.

I inhale through my nose and take a step. Then another. Then three in a full sprint.

One of them hears me. As his head turns, I skid, like pulling into home plate.

I throw my right foot in front of me and slide on my hip, a needle clenched in each fist. I pass through the gap between the men and jam—with all my strength—the needles into both men's thighs. As I push down hard on the plungers with my thumbs, liquid disappears into their flesh.

"One... two..." I whisper. And all is panic.

One man shouts. I see a blur and am flung sideways as his boot connects with my face. Blood spurts from my nose and immediately soaks into my handkerchief. Painful but not broken.

I roll, arms tucked into my chest. After one rotation, I come up to my knees and then my feet. I slide the machete loose of its sheath and face the man before me, blade in hand.

Ten, eleven, twelve...

Thomas lands a blow on the taller man. He staggers back and comes up swinging.

The man before me, the darker of the two, lifts his gun with one hand—the other reaches toward the walkie-talkie on his belt. I lunge with a shout. My blade slices across his arm, just enough to sting, but not remove a limb.

He drops the walkie-talkie on the ground and spins away. His left hand goes to support the head of his gun. I dance forward and dip to the right. I make contact again and a second slice opens up his other arm.

Twenty, twenty-one...

Thomas is somewhere behind me. Out of my sight, but I hear him fighting.

A quick jab to the merc's throat causes him to block me, dropping the gun altogether. I lunge and kick it aside. He puts up his fists. A smile crosses his face.

Twenty-eight, twenty-nine, thirty...

I swallow.

He swings, and I duck. But now he's next to me and his elbow jams into my sternum. All the air leaves my chest.

Thirty-five, thirty-six...

I drop and kick out my left leg. It connects with the outside of his knee, and he yelps.

He comes at me again. This time slower. He lands a blow in my ribs, but not hard enough to crack any.

My turn to grin.

Forty-three, forty-four, forty-five...

I step around him. Taunt him.

I'll stay in one place too long, a fraction of a second too long. He'll swing. I'll duck. Or sidestep, or dance back. Over and over, round and round we go.

He's slower now. Slower than at the start of this fight. Slower than me. His blows—the ones that connect—are mild, at best.

Sixty-seven...

He gazes down at me, fear in his stare. The fear fades as a glassy sheen coats his eyes. He leans back, then forward, then back again. I tug my handkerchief down and tilt my head to the side.

He lands with a thud. Dirt floats up in little spirals around his body.

I turn to help Thomas.

The massive man sits, quite contentedly, on the back of a passed-out mercenary. "That took you a long time."

I lean to the side, hand on my hip, and glare at him. "I couldn't exactly throw my arm around his neck and hold him till he passed out."

He chuckles, stands, and says, "I meant to get to position. But you were slower taking him down also."

I sigh and jut out my jaw. "Shadup."

He laughs aloud this time. "I take it you met some trouble?" He gestures to my left shoulder.

"Yeah. But we don't have to worry about the Thai police anymore. If the grandmother's intel is right, we're out of bad guys for a little bit."

"Pity." The edges of his eyes wrinkle in a dangerous expression. "I was hoping to help avenge these people."

I rest a hand on his arm. "You'll get another chance. We've got a whole factory of guys left to dismantle."

He nods and looks around. I follow his gaze and swallow. The villagers have surrounded us.

Women, in a variety of colors and outfits, both traditional and not, hold the hands of small children. Elders stand behind them, their hands, wrinkled and cracked, held forward. The girl, brother, and grandmother from before approach us from behind.

The woman who patched me up steps through the crowd. The baby is back in her arms. She speaks, gesturing with her free hand.

I glance at Thomas.

He moves toward her, towers over her. She is small, but there is a fierceness in her voice when she speaks to him.

"This is the village leader, Daone," Thomas says, having translated her words.

I give her a nod. She returns it quickly, then looks back at Thomas and speaks again.

"She thanks us. Tells the people to offer us food, shelter, anything we need." He responds to her in Hmong.

I fidget uselessly, mentally kicking myself for not listening to Hmong audiobooks on the plane ride. "Ask her about the factory. The fastest way to get there. Any side roads in."

He nods and continues speaking to her. A few others join in the conversation. Then more. After a few minutes, most of the village is talking at him.

Thomas's brow furrows. He puts his hands up, and the chatter dies down. He leans closer to her, listening intently, then turns to me. "There is the main road. But also an old goat trail that leads around the back of the factory."

"How do we reach it?"

He says something in Hmong.

The woman responds.

"We follow the stream... cross a blanket... and then another few kilometers and we are there."

"We cross a *blanket*?"

He asks her to repeat, and she does. Annoyance—clear no matter what the language—fills her voice. She adds something else, throwing her free hand in the air and rolling her dark eyes.

He nods. His eyes are wide. He is bent in half, trying to be as close as possible to the tiny woman. A sheepish look crosses his face, and he says something that sounds like an apology.

"What?" I ask.

"They speak green Hmong. I speak white. *Some* words get confusing."

I raise my eyebrows. "Did you get in trouble?" The grin forming on my face won't go away.

He glares at me. "It's the same language, just a different dialect. Some words are..." His words fade into a twisted frown as he takes in my amusement.

I can't help it. He looks so indignant. I burst out laughing, clutching my side and wincing as my back shrieks in pain.

There comes a point, on any trip of more than a couple days, when you just don't want to do it. You don't want to take the tour, ride the bus up the mountain, leave the hotel/hostel/campsite, etc.

So don't. We are all mildly brainwashed into thinking something has to be done at every minute of every day of a journey. But that's just not true. If you are feeling drained and need to recharge your batteries, take a day and recharge them. Whatever you wanted to do will likely be there tomorrow.

Chapter Eighteen

Lacey

Retail Therapy in Ginza

I have to go shopping. I don't want to go shopping. I don't want to do anything. I want to lie here in this bed with the sheet pulled up over my bruised face.

No.

I want to find out what is going on with Miss Belle. The mission isn't done, that much I know. Once it's finished, I'll get a call, probably from Missa. Maybe then I'll be able to breathe again.

It's Friday morning. With all that happened at the party, Nathan and I spent yesterday in his suite. Me recovering from my "ordeal," and Nathan working out of the private office, trying to accomplish some kind of damage control.

Something rustles around outside my safe sheet-cocoon. It shouldn't be Nathan. He's been gone since 7:30 this morning—thank goodness.

"Lacey?" Delilah's timid voice breaks through my sleepy haze. "You said to come get you up in time for the brunch."

I sit up and pull the blanket from my head. She winces at my bruises, but says nothing.

She's ready for the day in a cute green dress with just a little flare at the bottom, black flats with tiny bows on the top, and an adorable matching green bow tied into her dark hair. She's getting better at dressing for specific events. Makeup is caked on, a bit more than I would have gone for, but I assume she's covering the bruise left by Jacobson.

"Hey." I roll from the bed. My shoulder aches, the cut on my arm burns, and my face is swollen. Makeup might not properly cover the extent of the damage this time.

"You look horrible."

I glance at her from beneath my tangled, unwashed curls. Her golden-brown eyes are full, concern spilling from them in unmasked emotion.

"I feel horrible." I stumble to the bathroom and splash water on my face. A glance in the mirror makes me shudder. There's a lot of work to do before I'm actually presentable, especially for a day full of social events. "I'll be out in a bit."

The steaming heat and powerful water pressure take away some of the pain in my back. I massage shampoo into my hair. The scent of mint and raspberry alleviates some tension; I almost feel normal again.

After I soak, blow-dry, and moisturize, I'm back to feeling human. Delilah sits on the bed; her hands folded delicately in her lap. She waits, ever patient, for me to slip into the blue top and skirt I've saved for this outing. The makeup takes a long time. I apply coat after coat to disguise the extent of the bruising. Even then, my black eye is impossible to hide altogether.

Fortunately, I have a pair of matching blue, bug-eyed sunglasses to go with the outfit. I brush on a last bit of mascara and slip into my white flats. Delilah stands up and follows me out of the bedroom and out of Nathan's suite.

"You didn't have to wait for me." I glance at her as we board the elevator.

"I didn't want to go down alone."

I frown. Today is brunch and shopping with the women, then dinner and a dance in the main conference room. We won't have to see Nathan or his sweaty boss until nightfall.

I want to drop off the remaining film roll in my room—my private room. It's been sitting in my purse since the day I packed my carry-on, ready and waiting for me to board a plane that has long left without me. I don't want to be carrying it around in my purse for the rest of this weekend. I glance to my right, watching Delilah in the elevator mirror. Weighing my chances of her asking questions, I reach out and press the button for floor thirty-nine just as we pass forty-one.

She blinks and her gaze shifts over to me.

"I'm feeling nauseous," I explain. "I need to stop for a second."

She nods, eyes still wide and innocent.

I step out when the doors open. "I'm just going to walk around for a minute. I can meet you downstairs..."

"I'll wait for you here," she murmurs. Her arm moves, I assume to hit the 'hold' button on the elevator.

"Okay."

It's not okay. It's annoying. But I swallow my irritation as I move down the hallway. Delilah has had a very stressful several days. I ought to be understanding.

I let myself into my room. A big black duffle is on the bed. In it, I have already packed the less subtle items. My weapons, surveillance gear, extra cell phone, paper maps, and clothes that a typical escort wouldn't be needing. Combat boots, for example.

Chang is coming to pick it up tonight. There is too much suspicion going on right now and this bag doesn't exactly scream normal escort. He will hold it for me, sending the film via express post, then restocking and changing things out as needed until my next mission in this part of the world. He has a couple of similar bags. But this one is mine.

I stick the film roll into an outer pocket. The other is already in a pair of rolled-up socks at the bottom of my carry-on bag. I pull the socks out and stuff them into the duffle, then store my carry-on back in the closet. I lock the door, double check that the "do not disturb" sign is still in place, and dash to the elevator.

Delilah is still there, waiting with the doors open. An elderly couple stands behind her in the elevator. The man seems entirely distracted by his hands, but the woman wears a glare that I usually reserve for people who talk in the theater. Why they didn't just take the second elevator, I couldn't tell you.

The wife mutters something to her husband, and I catch the last few words. She is speaking Korean. I react to the sound the same way I would react to smelling my mother's cooking again. Inside, at least. On the surface, I must remain smooth. I take a deep, calming breath and barely maintain my composure.

I face them, bend slightly in a bow and say, in Korean, "It was kind of you to wait, thank you."

The woman's expression softens. She nods as Delilah hits the button for the lobby. I face the doors, not trusting myself to continue a conversation.

The elevator dings. We disembark. As Delilah and I step out and face the lobby door, I have a better understanding of her nerves. For someone like her, someone new to this life, the sight of all these women can be intimidating. There are about a dozen of us—the high-end escorts who serve as "wife" to their men. These aren't the whores from the other night. These are specialty women, capable of changing every aspect of their behavior to suit their clients. Most are incredibly wealthy, several are "managed" by the same Mister, and all are essentially *owned* by a man.

They stare as we approach. I've met several of these ladies in the past, and the ones I don't know personally, I know by reputation. The same can be said for me. All of these women know of Miss Belle. And by now, they've all heard that I work for her.

Delilah is an oddity herself. It became apparent in the first few events that she's not only new to the game but also new to the life. As a companion to one of the most prominent people at the conference, no one would expect her to be an amateur.

Alicia, a tall brunette from France with an unwaveringly thick accent saunters over, a dazzling grin on her face. She and I have worked several of the same events in the past.

"Lacey," she purrs. The other women follow her over to us as her long arms embrace me. I reciprocate her affectionate squeeze. "I did not know that you would be here. I haven't seen you since the first brunch. I was worried we would not get to spend any time."

My smile is genuine as I rest a hand on her arm. "I'd never pass up a chance to go shopping with you, Alicia." My wink sends a chorus of laughter around the group.

"Where shall we go for food?" a heavy-set, dark woman, Ruby, asks. The bracelets on her wrist jangle as she fiddles with her expensive purse.

"I know a place in the Ginza district," a petite blonde, Giselle, pipes up.

Alicia bounces on the balls of her feet in excitement. Ginza is on the higher end of the shopping areas in Tokyo. Precisely the kind of place Alicia loves to spend her money.

We make our way out the revolving door where a large, navy-blue van waits for us. My eyes widen under the thick sunglasses as Chang strolls around the side, whistling something from a cartoon.

"Ladies. Where to?" He gives an overdone bow and opens the van door.

Giggles erupt throughout the group. Alicia takes charge and tells him where we're going and then climbs into the front row of the van. The rest of us follow her, chatting amongst ourselves, wondering which man ordered the ride.

I stifle my knowing grin and plan on buying Missa a nice bottle of wine when I get back to New York.

Soon enough, Chang has us rumbling along the highway toward a day of coffee, food, and ridiculously priced shoes. I let the other women talk, occasionally offering an "mhm" or "yeah" but not concerning myself with the meat of the conversation.

My breath is even and steady. I slowly clear my mind. We go over a nasty bump, and someone grabs my arm. I glance to the left. Delilah is sheet white, her fingers clenching my bare skin hard enough to bruise.

Why is she so terrified? Why was she so scared to get to the lobby before me? I stroke her fingers until she releases the vice-like grip on my arm. Giselle, sitting on her other side, gives us a confused look. I raise one shoulder in a shrug.

Once Delilah's skin returns to its regular color, I lean over to her. "What's wrong?"

She shudders. "He was so mad. So mad when that man got away." A sidelong glance tells me she fully remembers waking up in the early hours of the morning and seeing me sneak Ryan out of the suite.

The little hairs on the back of my neck raise, and I nod. "Did he hurt you?"

Delilah swallows. She ignores the question, shooting a glance at Giselle, who is flat out staring now. The back row of the van isn't large, and the girls up front aren't talking loudly enough to drown out my conversation. "Will they find him?"

I don't have to ask who she means. There is no reason to tell her that Marcus and Kong did me a favor. For all she knows, they are hunting Ryan down as we giggle about shopping. "I don't know."

Her eyebrows draw together. Her breath picks up again. It looks like she might hyperventilate.

I glance at Giselle. Her alert gaze meets mine, and she flashes me a small smile before turning away. Girls like us are good at hearing things.

"Listen," I mutter to Delilah, "you don't need to worry about any of that anymore. Focus on having a good time today. Focus on getting through the rest of the weekend."

Delilah's eyes are wide. The whites around her amber irises have a reddish tinge.

The van stops and Chang hops out. I turn away from Delilah and follow the other women out of the van. I don't have the time or energy to do any more babysitting on this trip. As far as Delilah is concerned, the drama is over. She needs to toughen up and get through the rest of this weekend.

She's right behind me getting out and almost falls on me in her hurry. We join the group as Kathy, the Brit, thanks

Chang and hands him a generous tip. He gives it a dirty look before pocketing it. The Japanese do not tip. He tells her he will be waiting for us to get done with our day and points to a parking garage across the street.

Alicia, our unofficial leader, charges forward, and we all fall in behind her like a cluster of ducklings.

The restaurant is in a building called Okura House. Bills is the name of it, and it's beautiful. It has light wood, white marble table tops that match the bar, soft lighting, and fresh sprigs of some kind planted in large clear containers every few feet along the back of a row of booths. I'd like to sit at the bar alone with food and caffeine and my thoughts. Maybe next time.

Alicia gestures to the hostess and speaks some bad Japanese. They push a few tables together and seat us in three groups of four on one side of the booths. I'm with Ruby, Kathy, and Iva. Iva is new to me, though I know that Miss Belle, Alex, and Jeanette have all met her before. She's Polish, and they have intersected at several Eastern and Central European events. I take off my sunglasses and receive a quiet round of gasps from my table.

"Ladies." I grin. "Let's not make a big deal out of an embarrassing moment. Suffice to say I should not mix wine, tequila shots, and stairs."

They laugh. I laugh. They probably know I'm lying.

Delilah is diagonal to me at her table. She keeps trying to catch my eye, but I twist just a little, looking like I'm focusing on the conversation with my group. Alicia and Giselle join her, along with a light-skinned African woman speaking with a magnificent accent.

Chatter picks up, the women gossip happily, and I order a triple espresso with an extra shot, a stack of banana pancakes, a breakfast plate—sans the sausage, and two tiny squares of blueberry coffee cake. Kathy's eyes go wide when my food comes. Ruby bursts out laughing, and Iva snickers before picking lightly at her slice of toast.

"Did you have a busy night?" Ruby asks loudly, shooting me an exaggerated wink.

Kathy turns pink trying to keep in her giggles.

I spear a potato, take a big bite out of the end, chew, and swallow. "You could say that."

Kathy snorts.

Iva sucks on the side of her bottom lip and raises an eyebrow. "I heard the Jacobson party got cut short. And that you were in your room all day yesterday. That's why you missed the art exhibit."

"Just because the party ends early doesn't mean I stop working. And just because I'm in a hotel room, doesn't mean my night isn't busy." I meet her eye for a second. She looks down. Something in her attitude grates against my already fragile nerves.

"I hear that!" Ruby laughs again, raising her mimosa. "Hell, we're working now. Nothing like shopping on the job!"

Kathy laughs along with her, but Iva remains silent. She sips her tea.

The last of the food arrives, and our table is quiet for a few moments as Kathy and Ruby dig into their breakfasts. Everything is delicious, especially now that I've slowed the ravenous shoveling of food into my face.

The pancakes are light, buttery, and sweetened with banana and powdered sugar. The potatoes have been cooked with mushrooms and tomatoes and offset the sweetness of my pancakes. My triple espresso is Instagram worthy in its tiny red mug with the foam shaped in a perfect heart, and I take a picture for the travel guide page Missa runs. Then I sip my drink and pick at my melt-in-your-mouth coffee cake. Conversation from the tables around us reaches my ears in bits and pieces.

"— pretty good for a new girl," Giselle says from beside me.

"I agree." Alicia's accent is unmistakable.

Delilah mumbles something too quietly for me to hear. I shift a bit to the right. Giselle reaches out a hand and rests it on Delilah's forearm. "But you've got to be more careful with your movements."

"Sorry?" Delilah's unsure, confused.

I sip on my coffee, fingers pressed around the mug.

"Well," Alicia's voice has taken on an air of disciplining a small child. "The way you got out of the van this morning... you have to get better at hiding such injuries."

My jaw locks.

From the edge of my vision, I watch as Giselle pinches Delilah's elbow. An audible intake of air and a visible flinch follow, making the other girls laugh.

I clench my mug and press my feet into the floor. I manage to keep my face passive.

"Exactly," Giselle chitters. She pats Delilah's wrist. "That sort of thing gives it away. If you want to get good gigs like this, you need to get better at hiding it when it hurts."

Her matter-of-fact tone sends a shard of ice through my heart. A chill goes down my spine. I focus back on my plate of food, pushing out the voices of Delilah's table, giving her advice on how to cover up injuries.

Ruby and Kathy are talking again. To my dismay, the conversation is still about the party. I can't catch a break this morning. Or yesterday. Or the whole trip.

I clench my toes and gently set my mug back on the table. I pick up my fork. As much as I'd like to go throw up at the moment, I need to eat. The lack of sleep I'm dealing with needs to be counteracted with something. Caffeine will only help so much.

Ruby waves her hand dismissively. "Well, I heard the whole thing was a prank. Some kid who got fired last year wanted to mess with one of the lawyers."

"No, my guy told me it was a bit more serious than that. He had a gun or something."

They both look at Iva.

"What about you?" Ruby asks.

"I wasn't there either. But I'm not surprised something went wrong." Iva busies herself with a very precise bite of her bacon.

"Why not?" Kathy frowns at her.

Iva finishes chewing. She looks up at Kathy. "Because... when one of Miss Belle's girls is there, something always goes wrong."

A numb sensation runs across my skin. My fork dangles an inch from my open mouth. I recover in a split second, popping the food in my mouth and chewing. I give Iva a "go on" look as Ruby and Kathy stare at me with wide eyes.

She gives a noncommittal shrug. "Every time I've had an event scheduled and one of Miss Belle's has been there, something has gone wrong."

I swallow and let out a convincing laugh. "So, every time those girls have had an event with you something has gone wrong? It sounds like the same could be said about your work."

Kathy chuckles. Ruby continues to gaze at Iva and me.

"I don't... that's not..." Iva bites her tongue.

"I'm just saying," I continue. "Correlation doesn't always equal causation."

Iva sighs through clenched teeth. "I wasn't—"

I interrupt her, a condescending smile on my lips. "Yes, you were. But that's okay. I'm used to people being a little envious of Miss Belle. She is quite a woman."

Ruby's eyes are about the size of silver dollars, and Kathy is once again trying to hold in giggles. Iva's eyebrows are drawn together so hard that little lines crease her forehead. Her pursed lips are white, her nostrils flaring with each breath.

I turn back to my food, steadfastly ignoring her anger.

After an awkward moment, Ruby and Kathy launch into a loud conversation about the World Series. Kathy is surprisingly into baseball, especially for a Brit. I pitch in a few comments. I knew a guy who was into the Oakland A's back in the day. But for the most part, I keep quiet and finish my meal.

My calm demeanor, finding mild humor at the situation, laughing off someone's jealousy... is very much a mask.

I'm furious. Someone claiming Miss Belle's jobs led to things going wrong—that's bad. And dangerous. I need to tell Missa as soon as possible.

Unfortunately, I'm stuck with a group of women who are very good at eavesdropping for at least another two or three hours. I wait until my check comes, toss some yen onto the table, and excuse myself to the bathroom.

I send off a rapid text message to Missa.

Ran into an old acquaintance of Miss Belle's while checking out a local restaurant for the book. She made a comment about some issues with the boss's work. Kind of rude. Should I say something to her? Or just fill you guys in when I get back? xo, thanks.

I return to the group as everyone finishes up paying. Alicia clasps my arm and pulls me through the door.

Her conversation with Delilah thunders to the front of my mind as I cover up my own pain from her touch. I adjust my sunglasses, making sure they cover my face. Our merry band of women splits into smaller groups after breakfast. Several ladies are only looking for shoes, and the rest of us are on the hunt for literally anything. Alicia and I lead one pack into a cute little stationery boutique, Itoya. We separate only when she sees a stunning leather purse on the far wall.

My phone beeps.

From Missa, *Is it a time sensitive thing?*

I shoot back with, *No. Just a little annoying. Comments about her other books.*

I wander over to look at a display case full of ornate pens. I wasn't planning on spending a lot during this trip, but the beautiful things in this store are calling my name. After a moment my alert goes off again. *Understood. Fill us in when you get home... Miss you.*

I tuck my phone back into my purse. I feel someone behind me and turn. Delilah is standing awkwardly at a shelf of globes. Her gaze flicks to me, down to my purse, and back to the shelf. She wants to ask about Ryan. This girl is surprisingly committed to finding out if he made it or not.

But she doesn't speak. Or make eye contact with me. I walk over to her. Above us, over a dozen globes cover a small alcove in the ceiling. I clutch my necklace, rolling my own small globe between my fingers. I stand next to Delilah and slowly spin one of the blue and green balls.

"He won't get caught," I mutter under my breath.

She swallows. "I just..." She turns to meet my gaze. Her eyes are magnified by the presence of tears yet to flow. "They were going to kill him. I haven't... it's never..." She swallows again, clenches a fist and blinks away her tears. When she meets my eye again, there is something different about her stare. "It's been bad. It's always been bad. But it's never been 'murder in a hotel room' bad."

We stand in silence for a moment. I study her face, her young, bronze, innocent looking features. The coldness in her voice makes me think I may have judged her innocence too early. A few of the other women walk by. Delilah turns from the globes. We move deeper into the store, and stop at a table of intricate notebooks.

"They won't catch him," I say again. I grip her hand and give it a small squeeze. I want to ask about her arm... when it was that he had time to hurt her even more. But there are people around us.

She turns away, and wanders deeper into the little boutique. I don't follow.

I'm fishing around the wall of purses when the bell on the door tinkles. The unmistakably vast bulk of Marcus enters the shop; Kong follows him. A glance shows me that the other girls haven't noticed. I slip over to them, pretending to be absorbed with a finely embroidered scarf.

I give Kong a sidelong glance with an unspoken question.

"We aren't going to find him."

I nod and open my mouth to thank them.

"You and Miss Belle, you owe us pretty big," Marcus mutters. A look at his face tells me his pride—and probably his balls—are still wounded.

"I know. And believe me, she knows. The amount you and Marissa agreed upon yesterday will be in your account once I board the plane back to the States on Saturday, and I've been told that Miss Belle will be calling you personally once she finishes up in Thailand."

Kong's gaze bores into me. This mission, this discovery that we are not what we seem to be, is likely a significant shock to both men. They've known Miss Belle for some time now. While they've probably guessed there was something beyond prostitution going on, knowing it's something as big as stealing secrets and missions to Thailand is a whole other ball game.

I meet his stare with an unapologetic one. After a moment, he turns, grabs Marcus's arm, and the two of them leave the store. My gaze follows them out.

It's foolish to hope our paths won't cross again. Miss Belle is going to have her work cut out for her next time the world of private security crosses ours.

I stretch my neck from side to side, enjoying the sensation in my muscles. My body is bruised, tight, strained. A long, slow inhale through my nose brings a wave of calm. Another one relaxes my tense shoulders. One of the other girls calls me over to an incense display in the corner. I fix a neutral smile on my face and go to her. Only got two more days. I can do this.

Chapter Nineteen

Lacey

Cause for Concern

We are back. The van pulled up right on time. I pay more attention to getting out this time. I offer Delilah my hand. Since I'm looking for it, I can see the pain on her face as she manipulates her left arm. We all fish through the shopping bags until we find our own. The women bought so much, Alicia and Ruby volunteered to get a taxi so everything could fit. The two of them bought more than anyone else, so the cab may have been their way of making sure nothing got mixed up.

I run up to Nathan's suite, eager for a quick nap. I leave my bags on my side of the walk-in closet. There is already a limited amount of space in my section from all the varieties of clothes I had sent up from my room on that first day.

I collapse on the bed and immediately succumb to the darkness.

My phone's alarm wakes me up thirty minutes later. I stumble from the bedroom and into the living area. Upon drawing the curtains, I find that the sun is beginning its descent into the skyline. It is midafternoon; the meetings should be ending soon. I have time for a swim before I need to get ready.

I slip into my swimsuit, a black two-piece that emphasizes what it's supposed to. A white overshirt covers my bare skin. I will have to rebandage my arm, but the cut I made isn't deep enough to worry about getting it wet. And hopefully, moving around in the water will help my aching muscles.

I slip a pair of sandals onto my feet. My clutch holds my phone, the key to Nathan's suite, and the key to my room.

I pinch my cheeks a smidgen to wake myself up, grab a fluffy white towel, and get on the elevator. It makes a stop in the upper lobby. When the doors open, Daniel and Nathan are standing in front of me. Daniel is wearing a look of fury. Nathan is wearing one of confusion, shame even.

Damn.

Maybe I *can't* do this.

Daniel grabs my bandaged arm, and rips me from the elevator. I wait until Nathan is facing me to let the pain and emotion show on my face. I accompany it with a terrified gasp that is only half exaggerated.

"Calm down," he says to Daniel. "You're scaring her."

His lack of reaction, and the way he isn't meeting my eye, makes my heart thud harder in concern. My mind races through the events of the other night.

Three people know about what really happened with Ryan. Two of them assured me, only a couple hours ago, that everything was in order. Given the amount of money Missa is going to pay them, I don't think Marcus and Kong would have sold me out.

But how could Delilah have? If she'd told Daniel about what she saw yesterday, he and Nathan wouldn't have let me leave the room, much less go on a shopping spree.

If she told Daniel later, he would have hurt her for keeping it to herself. Of this, I am sure. My mind flashes to Delilah's arm. No. That doesn't fit the timeframe.

I clear my mind of these thoughts and focus on the situation at hand.

Daniel still has my arm, though his grip loosened slightly at Nathan's words. He pulls me to the library. It's a small room, four or five rows of shelves on each side. Panels of light shine a golden glow along the top and bottom of the walkways, but beyond that, the room is dim.

The two men move me to the farthest end of the farthest aisle. Nathan's eyes are downcast, still not meeting mine. His lips, too, are turned down, his face drawn and weary. Daniel... Daniel looks sober for the first time that I've seen.

That alone is cause for concern.

"What's going on?" I demand of Nathan. My voice is pitched, angled up in a "desperate damsel in need of protecting" kind of way.

"That's what I'd like to know," Daniel growls. "What do you know about what happened the other night?"

"Which night?"

"Wednesday night, or Thursday morning, whichever. You know what I mean. What happened with that reporter?"

I look at Nathan. My eyes are wide. I pour as much wounded disbelief into my expression as I can. "How can you think I'd know anything about that?"

He still doesn't meet my eye.

"You were the last person with him." Daniel crosses his arms, the right side of his upper lip pulled up in a sneer.

I let out half a breath in something resembling a chuckle. "Because he kidnapped me. I certainly didn't *want* to be the last person with him." I glance at Nathan again. "This is ridiculous. The only reason I'm here is because you wanted to see me."

His gaze darts to mine. I take advantage of the eye contact. I grasp his bicep, clinging to him like a life-raft.

"And... and because I wanted to see you." I change the tone, more innocence, and less insolence.

"You're here to earn a check," Daniel says scornfully.

"Hey, now," Nathan interjects.

I honestly can't tell if it's because Daniel just called me a whore, or if it's because of the implication that I'm not here just because I missed Nathan. Either way, at least he's speaking now.

I face Daniel. I square my shoulders, shake my head a little bit, rub my fingers against my palms, and take a deep breath. I make a show of building up the courage to confront the big man. "I don't know what happened with the reporter, but I'd never be dishonest with Nathan. I'd never do anything to hurt him."

For some reason, Daniel is still smiling that scornful smile. "Then explain your room."

"My room?"

"The extra room you have at the hotel. The private one nobody knew about. The room where you're hiding that goddamn reporter!"

The silence is stretching and (very unlike me) I feel incredibly compelled to break it. But with what? It's true. I have a room. A secret room that I never once mentioned to Nathan. It is not hiding a reporter. But it is hiding a load of surveillance equipment, a few very nice weapons, and a decent number of evening gowns, shoes, and general feminine articles.

Hmm. Feminine articles. Clothes. Shoes…

"Of course I have a room," I exclaim. "I work for Miss Belle. This isn't an amateur operation. I need a place to store all my things." Again, I turn to Nathan and hold onto him. My hand is on his chest this time. "I'm not going to dump all of my outfits, bags, shoes, and… extras in your room. There wouldn't be space for any of your things."

Nathan frowns. "I got the suite for you." He sounds like a wounded animal.

"Oh, sweetie—"

"That's bullshit," Daniel interrupts. "No whore is going to waste money on something like that."

The hair on the back of my neck stands on end. This act of playing the good girl, the fragile little flower, the innocent, delicate damsel, is beginning to fray. Having to behave this way, as though I'm still the girl I was four years ago, it's too much. Fury bubbles up within me, threatening to undo me in a way I haven't felt in a long time.

Stone. I must be a stone.

Too long has passed. Full seconds while I attempt to calm myself. My face hasn't changed; I force my eyes to stay wide, my lower lip to tremble ever so slightly, in an effort to maintain my mask of meekness. "Miss Belle runs a very organized operation. Nothing is too good for her clients."

Nathan looks convinced.

Daniel glares. "Humph. I've never *been* one of her clients. That's not something I'm familiar with."

The realization that a good portion of this accusation stems from jealousy hits me like a truck. It doesn't help with my fury.

"Well," I inhale deeply, "it is standard practice for an assignment of this caliber. I'm here to make Nathan look good. I'm here to make an impression on your competitors. To do so, I need to have a plethora of options when it comes to my clothes, makeup, and jewelry. I will never wear the same outfit twice. I can change clothes multiple times during the day, and I won't be caught wearing the same thing as another woman."

My tone is firm, defiant, secure. This is real. This story of the clothes. This excuse.

This is something I learned in the year of training before I received my first assignment from Miss Belle. As such, it is something I take pride in. And my pride is showing.

Nathan looks down at me, his lips pinched together, the skin around his eyes wrinkled into little lines as he squints at me. I assume he is wondering where this strength came from. I immediately switch gears and offer another meek smile.

"I only want to do the best for you, Nathan. Especially after all this time."

Nathan glances at Daniel. His hard look is melting.

Daniel, however, looks as furious as ever. "Then you won't mind if we check."

I do believe my heart has stopped beating. It at least pauses for a few beats. When it starts up again, I throw on a happy grin. "You want to go poke through a bunch of clothes?" I turn to Nathan again. "If you want to see all the lingerie options, I can bring them to our suite to show you."

"I want to see if you're lying. Which I'm pretty damn sure you are. Just because you've got Blake wrapped around your little finger—"

Nathan bristles at this, glaring at his boss.

"—doesn't mean you have the rest of us fooled."

"We need to see the room, Lacey." Nathan rests a gentle hand on my shoulder.

My tired mind works overtime; these two men cannot check my room, but I can't think of an excuse. I can't think of a reason for them not to. I can't think.

Daniel takes my arm again. My left one this time, so at least avoiding the cut. He steers me to the elevator and his sausage finger jams the "up" button.

Nathan stands behind me and to the right. His arm rests around my back, holding me in a supportive way. I don't think he suspects me, not really. That will change once they see the duffle bag.

Daniel stands two steps to my left, arms folded over his chest. His breathing is heavy. He radiates a dangerous level of anger.

I contemplate my options. It wouldn't be hard to take down both of these men. They are unhealthy, unfit, and likely have zero notion of self-defense. Not to mention the surprise factor when tiny little me manages a throat kick.

As that thought reaches the forefront of my mind, the nerve in my back spasms again. I glance down at the black flip-flops on my feet; those won't help either. Taking these two down will add to an already uncomfortable amount of pain. Not to mention the bridges it will burn. The danger it would pose to Miss Belle, Missa, the Guides...

I close my eyes for a moment as the elevator rises up, up, up. When I open them, I watch little glowing numbers count their way to an increasingly limited number of choices. We hit 37 by the time I decide. When we get to the room, I'll take them down. Incapacitate, then drug. I have a little something that should inhibit short term memory. Stuff like that isn't consistent, to say the least, but it's better than nothing. I'll figure out what to do with them from there, once they are unconscious.

The elevator dings. The doors open.

My plan is ruined.

Marcus and Kong wait by the elevator door. Daniel gives them a curt nod. Marcus has a nasty grin, accompanying the nasty bruise on his neck. Kong's face is expressionless as usual. I probably imagine the concern I see playing through his eyes.

Daniel and Nathan turn right. I trudge along between them, my arm still in Daniel's grip. Marcus and Kong bring up the rear, blocking my exit and increasing my anxiety. At the end of the hallway, a flash of green rounds a corner, walking quickly away, leaving the hall to the door empty and silent. My senses, already heightened by the events of the last two days, are going haywire at being surrounded by four men... four dangerous men, more than capable of many things I don't currently wish to think about.

"Key," Kong says as he steps around Nathan. Apparently, he and Marcus will be entering first.

I pop my clutch and hand him the key.

I'll take all the blame. There's nothing else to do. I can't let this moment, this mistake on my part, take down Miss Belle. I won't.

Kong pushes the key into the lock.

I'll say I was working alone. I figured the information from this weekend would be worth something. I was trying to make a quick buck. The equipment... the equipment is stuff I'm selling. Again, stolen. Again, trying to make some extra money on top of what I make working for Miss Belle.

He turns the doorknob.

Stone. I am stone.

With a small push from Marcus, the door opens, and Marcus and Kong hurry into the room.

I step forward, but Daniel pulls me back, his grip still tight on my arm. "You wait out here with me. I want to see your face when they find him."

Nathan slips past Daniel and into the room. The blood in my veins is like ice.

As soon as one of the men sees the duffle on the bed... it's over. I swallow, attempting to keep my breathing even and calm.

"I've got a bag here. Hang on."

I hear rummaging. I hear Marcus's voice.

It's disturbingly victorious.

"We've got something."

It's fun to branch out when you're on a trip. Check out something new. Scared of heights? Go ziplining. Afraid of the ocean? Start small with snorkeling, then maybe even a scuba trip. Don't like bugs? Eat a chocolate covered cricket! Broaden those horizons, explore and conquer your fears. There's nothing quite like the feeling of victory when you've done something you were afraid of.

Chapter Twenty

Miss Belle

Fucking Spiders, Man

A dense wall of green follows us along the left side of the trail. Vines covered in giant leaves weave in and out, back and forth, along the tree-line. Massive trunks, with roots shooting out like wide stars into the ground, rise up, up, up into the sky.

One glance upward, and it feels like I'm falling. The sky is emerald—little bursts of blue peek through the openings. Blue fades into purple and then red as the sun sets somewhere beyond our vision.

The stream to our right creates a backdrop of sound. Babbles, drips, and rushing water balance the cries of different animals, shrieks of birds overhead, slithering snakes in the brush.

Our footsteps are heavy here. The goat path hasn't been used in the month since the mercenaries took over. The jungle creeps in on the dirt, wishing to reclaim its land.

Each time my boot touches the ground, I can feel the groaning of the earth. Leaves and twigs snap under us. No matter how careful we are.

I lose balance at a steep downhill. Flinging out my hand, I grab a tree trunk for support. Something soft grazes my pinky. My eyes go wide as I bite down on my tongue and the urge to scream. Every nerve in my body tenses as I fight two decades of fear instilled in my bones.

I have trained to suppress fear. To turn it, use it for my own purposes. But the spider as big as my face leaning up against my hand distracts from that training. It's a Thai Black Tarantula, also known as an "earth tiger"—because giant spiders need a scarier name.

"What is this little guy doing in a tree?" Thomas's hand, only slightly bigger than the tarantula, though about the same color, reaches toward the "little guy."

"Hunting for delicious California girl meat?" The wavering of my voice undoes my joke.

Thomas lets out a small chuckle. "They are not poison to you."

He slips his fingers under the front of the tarantula, and the eight-legged demon gracefully leaves his perch in favor of Thomas's calloused hand. "They only live in dead trees. This one's home is in the ground."

"Lucky me—he just happened to be taking a day trip." I release a breath and force myself to stop shaking. I roll my shoulders back and inhale. My heartbeat slows a bit.

"In my home, the large spiders are a sign of health."

"Tarantulas."

"Yes. Tar-ant-tulas."

I shake my head and watch in silence as Thomas sets his new friend at the roots of the tree. I hitch up my bag, and we walk on. The trail slowly shifts upward, climbing the base of a set of massive mountains.

After about twenty more minutes, we arrive at a roughly thrown together wood and rope bridge—tall posts on either side pin rope handholds into place. The slats of wood bounce in the wind. It dangles, thirty some odd feet above the water.

The jungle climbs up the edge of a mountain behind us. The stream has grown into a rapidly flowing ravine below. Across the bridge, the trail disappears into the thick vegetation. To our right, the goat path continues, winding away from the bridge and the water.

"Bridge," Thomas mutters.

"What?" I glance at the wood, scanning it for rotted pieces.

"The word for blanket in white Hmong is the word for bridge in green Hmong. We cross here."

"Great." It's not actually great. Spiders and heights. Today's just been fucking fantastic.

Thomas goes first. I think about insisting on crossing before him. It's my mission; I *should* go first. But truthfully, I'm grateful to him for taking the first step. He knows my fear.

He was there when I dangled from my fingertips on the roof of a twenty-story building. He was the one who pulled me up. I never minded heights before that.

His weight makes the wood squeak, and I grit my teeth. The man is 6'4" and weighs at least 220 pounds. *At least.* Not to mention the pack on his back. We couldn't bring the Jeep through here; both our bags are stuffed with supplies.

Once his foot hits dirt, I take a breath. My exhale lines up with my first step onto this godforsaken, crumbling, rotted, wooden death bridge.

I reach out a shaky hand and grasp the rope. It is damp and sticky. I don't think about all the birds who have crapped on this thing. I don't think about how high up I am. I don't think about the fall. I loosen my grip, sliding my hand along the rope as I take another step. My heart pounds.

Wind rushes down the ravine; I hear the whistle before the bridge moves. I don't breathe for a moment. My gaze is still stuck on my hand. I watch my arm move back and forth as the colors behind it stay still. When the breeze is gone, I continue across.

I focus on my fingers, clenching and unclenching. I don't look down. The texture of the boards under my feet brings me no relief. My boots slide a bit with each step on the mossy wood. Something crunches and I freeze. I let out a terrified breath, force my eyes away from my hands, and look down.

I stepped on a leaf. A leaf with solid, beautiful, loving dirt underneath it. I glance back. I made it across the bridge. I take the last step, lunging away from the swaying beast.

I bend over and rest my hands on my knees. I take deep, steady breaths with my head down. I swallow several times.

"You can take on three men alone in less than five minutes, but you cannot cross a bridge." Thomas doesn't say it as an insult. Merely an observation. He understands; we all have fear.

"Correction." I straighten up and glance at him. "I *did* cross the bridge. And it took less than four minutes."

He chuckles and pats my shoulder. "We are losing light."

A few kilometers later, we emerge from the jungle. A rocky ledge puts us above the factory. I take off my pack and pull out my binoculars. It's time to see what we're up against.

A wide dirt road stretches across the small valley in front of us. Running parallel to the road is a chain-link fence a couple of football fields long. The fence surrounds an encampment carved out of the jungle. From our perch on the mountain above, the entire layout of the factory is visible.

The sun is gone, disappeared beyond the horizon. But two dozen blisteringly bright lights, evenly spaced along the fence, give us a clear view of the interior.

"There." I point to the far side of the fence. Nestled against an armored truck is a large black generator. "We shut that down, sneak the Hmong out, and torch the place."

Thomas squints at me.

"Kind of torch the place." I grind my teeth. "You know what I mean."

He rolls his eyes and puts up his binoculars. "There are two generators."

I hold up my spy-goggles and scan along the fence. Sure enough, on the side closest to us another generator hums in the night. "Hmm."

My mind flutters through options. Thomas nudges my arm, and I look down.

A line of men trudges out of the only real building in the encampment. I assume it's the factory based on the smoking chimneys, the transport trucks parked on the side, and the overall size.

The men are Hmong. Their clothes are ragged, their faces weary, and their shoulders slumped.

You can tell which ones have broken, which have given up hope of leaving, of seeing their families again. And you can tell which are still ready to fight. It's usually the young men, though a few older ones still carry steel in their gaze. They have black eyes, bruised arms, and blood stains on their shirts.

These are the ones who make trouble. These are the ones who haven't accepted their fate. I recognize the look.

Men—mercenaries—stand on either side of the factory doors. Two more stand farther down the line, and two more walk with the men in front.

The line makes its way to a large, white tent near the fence closest to us. They file in one at a time and come out carrying bowls of brown sludge.

"Delicious," I mutter.

Thomas chuckles.

I frown as I return to looking at the line. One man grabs my attention. He is young with smooth skin and anger in his eyes. He has something up his sleeve. Literally.

I pinch my lips together in frustration. A metal pipe slides from his shirt sleeve as he passes one of the mercs. With a hard swing, he cracks the merc across the head. The man crumples.

It was a good hit. But a foolish attempt. The boy is on the ground in seconds, three mercs on top of him. My muscles contract each time a fist or foot collides with his body.

Thomas rubs my shoulder. "We can do nothing right now."

"I know," I speak through gritted teeth. The mercenaries are standing now, taking turns beating the boy bloody.

When they are finished, the rest of the Hmong workers have eaten their food. Old and young, they stand to the side, watching their fellow worker struggle to stand.

He pushes himself up, and two other men go to him. They help him stumble into a long, narrow building. It's roughly thrown together, no windows and slatted metal serving as the roof. As far as I can see, there is only one door.

"Well, we know where the Hmong are being kept."

Thomas nods. "And where the mercenaries are sleeping." He guides my binoculars to a line of tents on the far side of the Hmong quarters. The factory and the Hmong sleeping area make an L shape. The mercs are in the middle, between each building and the fence.

It's an interesting layout choice. I'd have put some tents behind the Hmong barracks and the factory. Surround them. Maybe they figure a nightly patrol is enough to keep an eye on everyone.

A large man, beefy with long, blond hair and a thick beard, lounges outside the largest of the tents. He sits on an up-turned bucket; his feet stretched out in front of a fire. A few others sit around with him. Two shorter men, both South American, judging by their facial structures, polish knives across the fire from Blondie. A tall, thin man with jet black hair and a waspish mustache munches on what looks like an MRE packet—those gross three-course dinners in a plastic bag the army gives to its soldiers on deployment.

Other men around them appear to be packing up. They load everything except the sleeping gear onto a big truck next to the factory door.

"They are packing up already," Thomas says.

"That seems premature."

"Maybe they plan on executing the men tomorrow morning."

I squint across the factory. Six massive trucks line the dirt road, just on the other side of an immense, rolling gate. Their tires are plump and rest lightly on the ground.

"I don't think they loaded up the product yet." I frown.

"It's likely they are done with everything except loading and will kill the men once that is finished tomorrow."

I grind my teeth and shake my head. "We need to get these men out tonight."

The last of the Hmong workers enter the bunker. A merc slams the door shut and bolts it.

"Lights out!" shouts Blondie.

One of his men jogs over to the generator closest to us and shuts it down. Small pools of light remain, flickering over the open space near the tents and at the gate entrance. The rest of the encampment is dark. The mercs are concentrated on keeping the prisoners in, not keeping anyone else out.

I glance at Thomas. "They just made that a whole lot easier."

"Indeed."

"Priority one needs to be getting the workers out."

"Agreed."

I put the binoculars back up and do one more sweep to fix a map of the encampment in my head. "All right, let's—"

But I don't finish. Something moves to the left, just outside my peripheral vision. I shift, scanning with the binoculars to pinpoint the disturbance. Down the hill, about 120 yards from us, a lone figure shuffles through the vegetation toward the main road, barely visible in the darkness.

"What the fuck?" I lean forward, which doesn't help me see better, but I do it anyway.

Vaguely, I hear Thomas ask me what I see. I don't answer, my gaze locked on this stranger.

I watch the person—man, I guess from his walk—get closer to the fence. A dark hoodie covers his face, and shadows hide his body. Something bounces up and down on his chest.

I take the binoculars away and blink for a second. When I look through them again, a ray of light bounces off his camera, and I realize who he is. "Son of a—*son of a*—*sonofabitch...*"

I'm up. Running across the flat slope we are on. When I hit the jungle, I slow down. I swear under my breath as I make my way through the brush. I try for silence, but silence won't matter if this fucking idiot gets to the mercs before I get to him. I stagger my footsteps to at least *attempt* to sound like something other than a human.

Thomas crunches through the trees behind me. He is bigger, has to go slower to avoid making more noise.

I reach a steep downhill, covered in thick bushes and tall grass. I'm doing a half-jog down it, gravity speeding me up a bit, when my ankle catches on a tree trunk. I lean into the fall and spiral, landing on my side. Unfortunately, this doesn't stop me. The momentum carries me down, now precariously balanced on my hip, thigh, and forearm.

I squint through the darkness while trying not to slice up my arm on the foliage. Closer... closer...

I hit him with my extended leg. He goes down with a yelp. Someone in the camp shouts something. We are very close now. Only a few yards from the fence.

I jump on him and sit on his stomach with both hands over his mouth. I duck my head just as a beam of light passes over us. Someone watches the green behind me closely. After a moment, they move the light along. A few seconds later, it shuts off completely, and someone laughs. After a moment of darkness, my eyes adjust to dim light from the moon streaming down through the trees.

I keep one hand on his mouth and raise the other to form the universal "shush" sign. He nods.

I roll off him. He sits up, and his hood slips down. Green-eyed, dirty-blonde, Tennessee royalty, Ryan Morris rolls his neck. He checks his camera for damage.

My hands shake; I fight the urge to beat him senseless. The urge is winning. "Follow me," I murmur.

He looks at me. I give him my "do what I say, or I'll kick your ass" scowl. He stands up.

We walk a little ways back into the jungle. Not up the mountain again, but parallel to the road away from the factory. By the time we've reached a safe distance, my patience has run out.

I turn around, grab him by the front of his hoodie, and slam him against a tree. "What the *fuck* do you think you're doing here?"

He pushes back, and I slam him again, harder this time. His head bounces off the bark. He's a couple of inches taller than me, but I've got fury on my side: fury and training.

"I-I came to get the story." He swallows.

I lock my jaw to keep from screaming. My nostrils flare as I inhale. Muscles tremble as anger floods my bones. I glare at his pale, fragile face and curl my fingers around his sweatshirt, ready to kill.

"Belle." Thomas's warm, soft voice brings logic to my emotional rampage.

I loosen my grip a bit.

"*The story?*" My face is inches from his. "The story is that you almost got one of my girls killed. You almost got a village full of innocent *people* killed. You may *still* get sixty or so men killed just by being here." I speak too quickly. My words flow together in a jumbled mess that barely comes out audible.

"I know. I just—" Ryan stops, his eyes wide. "Are you... do you work with Lacey?"

I resist the urge to slam him into the tree again. "Yes. I'm the one your mother hired to get you the evidence of this operation. Lacey works for me. And you almost got her killed, you…" I can't find a word bad enough to explain how stupid this man-child has been.

Thomas puts his hand on my arm. I exhale and release Ryan. He stands in front of me, green eyes staring down like a beaten puppy. This close, I notice half of his face is badly bruised and swollen.

"I know I put Lacey in a tough spot. And I know I'm responsible for what they're going to do to the factory. But I need to get the story out."

I sigh in disgust, and he backs up.

"It's the only way I can help," he says in a low voice.

"You can help by doing no such goddamn thing."

He tenses and his eyes narrow.

"Listen," I scowl, "the whole point of this place getting burned to the ground is that Jacobson doesn't go to prison for life. The whole reason he is ready to murder an entire village is so the story doesn't get out. If you do publish this… if you publish pictures of these people… it doesn't matter what we do here right now, because they will send an army of men to kill them all later."

"Not if the story is already viral."

"It doesn't fucking matter if it's *viral*!" I want to punch him in the face. I still might. "If you put this out, there will be an investigation. If Jacobson is caught using slave labor, his entire empire crumbles and he goes to prison for a very long time." I fight to keep my voice down.

He shakes his head, and I clench my hand.

"No. If I put the story out, they won't be able to touch these people."

I roll my eyes and flail my arms. "Jesus. Are you really that dumb?"

"Belle." Thomas has a warning tone in his voice.

I ignore him.

"Right now, Jacobson thinks you are on the way to the U.S. *specifically* to publish this story. He is trying to clean up his mess. And that means killing all these witnesses. If—by some miracle—we manage to save everyone and convince the mercenaries to say the job is done, we don't need anyone else poking around here. Because if it's discovered that the job isn't done... well, he'll send someone to finish it. And that's exactly what publishing the story would do. It would send him a neon fucking sign that the job didn't get done."

There is silence. Human silence. The jungle is still alive and making all the normal scary nighttime noises.

Thomas stands next to us, facing Ryan. "Do you understand what Miss Belle is saying? If you publish the story you are *trying* to publish, many people will die."

There is something shady in his voice. I tilt my head at him.

"But if you publish a different story," Thomas glances at me before looking back at Ryan, "you may be able to bring down Jacobson, without hurting these people."

Thoughts tumble around in my head. He's right. If Ryan frames the story the right way...

"You can take pictures when we're done." I jerk my head at Thomas. "He's right; you can still make a story out of this. It just won't be entirely accurate."

Ryan looks from me to Thomas and back again. He purses his lips and sighs. "Okay."

Chapter Twenty-One

Lacey

No Shame in a Sex Toy

Fear floods me as the footsteps coming from my room grow closer. My breathing picks up, nerves tingle, hands shake.

Daniel turns to me, a grin of unwavering superiority spreading across his thick face. "I knew it." He sneers.

"What..." Nathan utters from just inside the room.

Someone chuckles.

I frown.

Marcus walks out first, followed by a red-faced Nathan, and Kong, clearly attempting to maintain a professionally somber expression.

One glance at Marcus's oversized Nordic hands is plenty of explanation. He is carrying a large black... item... that I borrowed from Sarah for this particular mission.

Daniel frowns at Marcus's hands. He squints. He leans in.

He practically leaps back at the moment of recognition.

Nathan's tomato-red face is quickly switching from embarrassment to anger. He glares daggers at Jacobson.

"What... what else was in the room?" Daniel stutters, avoiding looking at the... thing.

"Nothing of importance," Kong says. "Clothes, jewelry, shoes. And a little bag full of..." he gestures, "...more of this kind of thing."

"Handcuffs," Marcus nearly giggles.

"You see." Nathan grabs hold of my arm and jerks me away from Jacobson. I wince as his hand closes over my cut. "I told you, she had nothing to do with it."

"Okay, well... how did that get there?" Daniel gestures at the item, grasping at the last possible straw.

"I uh..." I glance at Nathan, still the unsure, sweet little thing. I keep my voice low, but loud enough for the rest of the men to hear. "I put it back after last time. I didn't think you'd want it lying around your room."

Marcus has to turn around at this point. He walks back into the room and the unmistakable sound of poorly contained laughter filters through the open door.

"All due respect, sir." Nathan struggles to get the words through his tightly clenched teeth. "This is done. She didn't have any part in what happened the other night. We have bigger things to worry about."

Daniel's mouth opens and closes a few times. Finally, he nods, gives me another glare, and leads the security team to the elevator.

As Marcus walks by, he shoots me a wink. Fortunately, Nathan doesn't see.

"Let's go," he says to me.

"Just a minute, if that's okay. I want to make sure they didn't mess anything up."

Where is it?

I do a quick search of the room, disguised as a check of my jewelry and delicates. The duffle is gone. I even check under the bed while Nathan's back is turned.

Nothing.

Dread builds in the pit of my stomach. I take a deep breath, force myself to calm down, and try to think.

Nathan insists on walking me to the pool.

My duffle is gone. Whoever took it has several deadly weapons, some costly equipment, and the film rolls—the entire purpose of my being here.

I need to call Chang. I need to contact the maid service at the hotel. I need to call Missa.

I can't do any of that because Nathan is walking me down to the pool.

"I'm so sorry." He clutches my hand as the elevator travels back down.

I put on my young girl's voice. "I just... I don't understand how you could suspect me. After everything we've been through. And finally getting to see you again."

I sniff. I widen my eyes. They start to burn. I keep them open, forcing the tears to grow.

He looks as ashamed as a man like him can be. "I didn't... I didn't really suspect you. I knew you could never do something like that."

I nod but cast my gaze down. Nathan puts a hand on my cheek and turns my head to face him. I let him.

"Please, tell me you forgive me." He runs his fingers over my bare shoulder and down my arm before resting his hand around my waist.

I fight the shudder building up in my body. "Of course. Of course I forgive you."

He pulls me close. We stand like that, half hugging, until the elevator dings and the doors open. He keeps a hand on my lower back as we pass the doors leading to the fitness center.

The pool is beautiful, and surprisingly empty on a Friday afternoon. That same elderly Korean couple sits in a pair of lounge chairs at the far end. The woman is reading. The man is staring at the water, his book face-down on his lap.

A solitary figure swims the length, creating a gentle little lapping sound as waves hit the edge of the pool. I love that sound.

This room has a familiar scent as well, not the smell of chlorine, but the smell of water indoors. It's a soft smell, a heaviness in the air that seems to caress me, to cradle me where I stand. I can tell, when the air is like this, how warm the pool will be. My skin tingles. I'm eager to be enveloped by the water.

All of this would normally be enough to calm my nerves, reset my mind, get me back to my starting point. But not now. Not with my duffle in the wind, unable to make any calls, and Nathan breathing down my neck.

His hand is still on my back. How long is he going to stay? I need to make those phone calls.

He guides me over to a lounge chair. "Here."

I give him a wide smile. "Thank you, that's sweet. Do you want to run and grab your suit? I'd love to get wet with you."

A flash of lust goes through his eyes, quickly followed by a frustrated frown. "I can't. Jacobson pulled me out of a meeting for his little stunt. We have to go back and get a few things cleared up."

"How long will that take?" I ask. I fail at my attempt to force my lips into a pout.

"A few hours. I should be done when we originally planned. We can get ready for dinner and dancing together."

My chuckle is real. "Sweetie, it takes me a lot longer to get ready than it takes you. I'll be in the suite when you get done with your meetings. Hopefully, I'll at least have my hair done." I flash that smile again.

I glance toward the door.

"Maybe we can come back tonight, after the dance," Nathan suggests.

I nod and get up on my toes to give him a peck goodbye. My lips press against his oily nose. He smiles. He leaves. I breathe.

With Nathan gone, my focus returns to the panic in my chest. I don't fumble. Fumbling is a waste of time. I deliberately open the snap on my clutch, pull out my phone, and poke at the screen as I sink onto the chair.

Chang picks up on the second ring. "Lacey? What is wrong? I thought we were," he pauses a moment, likely thinking of the correct phrase, "*radio silence* until Sunday morning."

"Do you have my bag?"

"Your bag?"

"Yes. My black duffle. The one you store for me."

"No?" There is a curiosity in his tone. "I thought I was getting that from your room tonight, while everyone is at the party. I was to remove the film rolls, send them to the two separate P.O. boxes? Is that not the plan?"

"That's the plan. Never mind." I lower my voice as the swimmer takes a break at the deep end. "What time are you coming tonight?"

"Nine."

"Make it ten."

"Is everything all right, Lacey?"

"Yeah. Everything's fine. I'll see you Sunday morning."

I hang up.

Crap.

My next call is to the hotel front desk. It would be simpler to check in person, but the risk of someone seeing me is too high.

I ask about a duffle that I lost. They have nothing. I ask if my room has received maid service while I've been out. They do a quick check and come back to tell me that the "do not disturb" sign has been on the door since check-in.

I thank them.

I hang up.

Crap.

I close my eyes and slump forward until my elbows rest on my knees. A metallic taste slides across my tongue. There is a burning in my eyes, and I have to clench my shaking hands.

I can't stop the angry, panicky, terrified tears.

Before they can fall, I slip off my overshirt, rise from my chair, and dive into the water. I sink. Down, down, down, until my butt thuds against the bottom.

I'll stay down here, thanks.

My hair springs up around my face in the way that makes everyone with long hair feel like a mermaid. My tears are invisible down here. The saltwater blends indistinguishably with the chlorinated.

I want to. Stay here, that is. But my body betrays me. The oxygen in my lungs, and the fat in my curves, pull me to the surface like unwanted life vests.

Don't they know I am stone?

Stones sink.

But I'm floating. Face-down in the water like some lifeless form. These life vests in my body are flawed. So much is flawed.

Focus.

Someone has my duffle.

Someone took it between the time that I left for the girls' outing and the time I stepped off the elevator with Jacobson.

I flip over and breathe. The oxygen helps me think.

I flip back over and kick my legs, propelling myself toward the far end of the pool. I didn't know how to swim when I met Miss Belle. I'd been in a pool a few times but had never taken classes.

Now, I can surf, snorkel, scuba-dive, and hold my own against a heavy current. The still water around me barely provides enough resistance.

Someone has my duffle.

My mind surges with the physical activity. I do an under-water somersault at the wall, plant my feet firmly against the tiles, and kick off.

A thought forms in the edges of my brain. I swim. Back and forth, back and forth, letting the thought grow through the muddled mess that has been my mind lately.

Someone has my duffle.

And I think I know who.

She is sitting at the bar. Black glass countertop, white lights above, her copper-skinned fingers dancing around the edges of a coffee mug. The soft green polish on her nails matches the outfit she hasn't yet changed out of. I'm glad to find her here. I don't think trying to sneak up to Daniel's suite would have looked very good.

Delilah turns as I slip into the chair beside her. I've changed out of the swimsuit and into a black pair of slacks, white shirt, and black silk vest. My shoes are black as well. Fashionable, but without a heel. I can run in a heel, but (as with every other person on Earth) I am significantly faster in flats.

Her brown eyes widen as she sees me. She quickly turns back to her drink, gazing down at the bar.

"Hey." I turn to face her.

"Hey."

"I need to ask you something. I need you to be honest with me. And I need you not to tell anyone."

Her head twitches, just a smidgen, to the side. I watch her profile. She swallows. After a moment, she nods.

"Did you know about my room?"

She nods again.

"Did you tell Jacobson about it?"

Her lip curls up in a sneer. That's a no.

"How did you know about it?"

"I saw your closet when you were getting ready for brunch." Her voice is quiet, but not soft. There is a grated edge. One I may have missed before, given how natural it sounds on her. "Your outfit from the first night wasn't there."

I frown. I don't even remember seeing her that first night. "That doesn't mean I have a separate room. I could have had the dress cleaned."

"We stopped on your floor. I heard the door open."

I am quiet for a moment. When I speak again, it's in a mutter, "Do you have my duffle?"

The little hairs on her arm stand up, and her fingers clench the mug. "I... I'm sorry. I just..."

She takes a breath, cracks her neck, and turns to me. "Listen, I knew you'd have some good stuff. I just thought it would be like, diamonds and shit." Her tone surprises me. There is a sureness in her voice that certainly wasn't there before. "I knew Jacobson was gonna search your room. I heard him talking at the front desk, verifying the room number. I figured if I got there first, you'd be too busy with him to notice if some stuff went missing. But..."

Her gaze darts my way, features reverting to the naïve damsel I recognize. She doesn't continue. Or meet my eye.

Finally, I break the silence. "How did you get into my room?"

"I picked the lock."

I raise an eyebrow and give her an appreciative nod. "You saw what was in my duffle. You knew, or guessed at least, what would happen if Jacobson saw all that stuff."

She nods, her dark hair bouncing across her shoulders.

"So you took it."

She nods again.

"Which means you have it. Somewhere."

She meets my eye this time. Her lips are in a straight, steady line. Her forehead is wrinkled just between her eyebrows, a determined look fixed on her face.

"What do you want?" I ask.

"I want you to take me with you. I want you to get me away from Julio."

"He's the one who booked you with Jacobson?"

She swallows. "Yeah, that and other stuff."

I run a hand across my forehead and pinch the edge of my eyebrow in frustration. "Does he have anything on you? Anyone he will hurt if you don't go back?"

Her fingers go white with how hard she clenches her coffee mug. The line of her jaw tightens, the veins in her neck visible for a brief moment. "No. Not anymore."

I lean forward, resting my forearms on the bar. "I can't give you a guarantee, Delilah. I can't promise Miss Belle will want to work with you. And I definitely can't promise to get you out this weekend."

Her face darkens. I bite my upper lip and heave a sigh.

I glance up and down the empty bar. "What I can say... is that I'll try. I'll talk to my people, and I will try my hardest to get you out."

Delilah is silent, staring at her mug with that darkness on her face. Disappointment? Anger?

"Delilah, I don't have a lot of time right now."

She sighs. "You'll try? You'll really actually try to get me out?"

I meet her eye and don't look away. "Yes."

"Right." She takes a deep breath. "What do I need to do?"

"For now, just tell me where the duffle is. I have to get it back to the room before dinner tonight."

She shakes her head. "Someone's watching your room."

I frown. "How do you know?"

"He was mad. Mad you didn't have Ryan in there. But he still suspects you. I don't... I really don't know why." A fearful look flutters across her face. "I promise, I didn't tell him anything."

"I know."

There is a pause as she considers my words. How few people trust this girl for her to be so honestly surprised by my faith in her?

"He paid one of the hotel staff to watch the room. They'll tell him if they see you or anyone else going in. He'll know about the duffle."

"Where is it?"

"At the bottom of the east stairwell in the small tower."

"How do you know no one will find it?"

"People don't use the stairs. Plus, there's always a little hiding spot at the bottom. This one was extra dirty. No one goes there."

I stifle a smile and bob my head in a shallow nod. I stare at the countertop, working through my thoughts. It will be simple enough to have Chang collect the duffle from the stairwell rather than the room. Assuming no one finds it beforehand. That concern should be an easy fix as well, though.

I pull out my phone and shoot Chang a quick text. *Change of plan. Pick up ASAP. Call when you arrive.*

We sit in silence for a while. Delilah sips her coffee, glancing at me now and then with a combination of facial expressions. First, she looks hopeful, then scared, then worried, back to hopeful, and back to worried again.

I order a coffee for myself when the bartender stops by for a refill. But I can't drink it when it comes. I let my fingers dance around the handle. Little bees buzz around in my head. I almost want to swat at my ears, hoping they will quiet down. But they won't. Not until the problem is solved.

Light floods across my phone screen, breaking the stillness around us. Three little black letters make up the message from Chang. *OMW.*

In a change of pace for my luck lately, I still have almost an hour before I need to start getting ready. I sip on my drink. It's not great coffee. The intense bitterness of the bean suggests it has been sitting, ground, for a while. I get a little cup of cream and another of honey. The combination helps calm the flavor... and the bees in my brain.

I should be getting ready.

I turn my head, letting the opposite side of my face rest against the comforter. This stretches my neck in a lovely way that also helps my pinched nerve.

Just a few more minutes.

My eyes close. I breathe in deep.

The beginning of a peaceful moment is shut down as the scent of Nathan's pillow filters through my nose. I can taste his aftershave in the back of my throat.

I shouldn't have turned my head.

A guttural groan escapes me as I push up and off the bed. A dress, ballgown really, hangs from the door to the bathroom.

I brought it from my private room, along with the silver shoes next to it. Eat that, Jacobson.

I unloop my belt and tug the black pants down past my waist. I kick them into a corner. The vest and shirt follow.

I walk, barefoot, into the bathroom and stand in front of the floor-length mirror. I've never had a real problem with my body. Only with the things it has done.

Evidence of the week is visible on my soft skin. Not so soft now. Not like before.

I used to be so pale.

They liked the pale girls. Pale but with ethnic accents. My half-moon shaped eyes, my dark hair, the full bottom lip. I didn't go outside before Miss Belle.

Now, when I'm home, if the sun is out, I am out. I lie in the hammock in our backyard for hours. I let the rays melt into my skin, enhancing the color given to me by my mother.

I unwrap the bandage around my arm. The cut is scabbing over; not even two full days have passed since I borrowed Kong's knife. The bruise on my face will take longer to fade away. The nerve in my back will last the longest. I lick the cut on the inside of my cheek. The metallic taste is nearly gone.

I run a finger over a scar on my hip, just above my underwear line. Another knife, another mission. That one wasn't on purpose.

Under my right breast, just barely visible and only if I stand the right way, a little black shamrock tattoo is half-hidden by my bra. Two weeks in Northern Ireland will do that to you. I smile at the memory. Those boys were so surprised by my willingness to undergo the ink.

I drop my hand to my side. I meet my own gaze staring back at me in the glass. I am proud of this body. The strength on the outside that matches my inner strength. I flex my arms, watching the muscles ripple. I tense my core, and the little pudge under my belly button hardens like steel. I turn to the side, and the faint outline of stretch marks on my hips catches the light.

I smile. At myself. At my transformation. At my success.

Chang has the duffle. One film roll will be sent Express to Missa at the Manor. The other will go to a private P.O. box in Brooklyn. Someone will pick it up in a week or so. The mission, my mission, the one I am here for... is done.

Miss Belle is in Thailand. There's nothing I can do for her. I process this, acknowledge it, and let it go from my mind.

Daniel suspects me. But all evidence of my deceit is gone. Kong and Marcus won't betray me now. It's far too late to tell the truth and retain any shred of their own credibility. Nathan doesn't suspect a thing. I play my part well.

Delilah... Delilah is a problem left to be solved.

I talked to Missa. Miss Belle is unavailable, obviously. The best move right now is to make sure we can stay in contact with Delilah and wait until I can talk to Miss Belle about her. There are limited resources. But I can make a case for her. I hope.

I think over my options as I shower, shave, exfoliate, moisturize, blow out my hair, and put on my undergarments. A ballgown has requirements of its own when it comes to support.

Even if Miss Belle gets done with her mission before we finish up here and says yes, Delilah can't come to the Manor.

No one comes to the Manor. Not until it is decided that they will work for Miss Belle. I didn't walk through those beautiful doors until I'd been in training for almost nine months.

There is a safehouse in upstate New York. But is that too close to home? The one in San Diego might be more secure. For us. I don't know where her home is. I need to find that out.

It's unlikely that I'll get her into a safehouse on this trip. But women like us run into each other frequently. If not me, another of the Guides will see her soon enough.

I need to talk to Delilah. Tonight. There should be time at the dance.

The door to the suite opens and closes. Nathan's thick footsteps clump across the living room. The bedroom door opens, and I hear an assertive, "Lacey?"

I need to get through tonight. Then it's brunch tomorrow and a ride to the airport. So close to being finished.

I glance at myself in the mirror. My hair is blown out, cascading down in gentle waves. A silver lacy corset rests comfortably around my middle, supporting my breasts but not pinching my chest. Matching panty-shorts hug my hips. A half-grin, (which, I notice for the first time, almost mimics Miss Belle's) crosses my lips.

I've got this.

Chapter Twenty-Two

Miss Belle

Seconds Ticking By

The sliver of silver moonlight in the sky brightens the encampment just enough that I don't need night vision goggles. Which is a plus, because Thomas didn't bring any.

We inch our way back up, through the vegetation, to our overlook. It's the perfect place to scout out the mercs. I have Ryan sit on his ass behind us—the better to stay the hell out of our way—and I settle in for a good hour or two of watching people through binoculars.

An essential part of any operation, and one that is often overlooked, is intelligence gathering. I prefer a couple of weeks, maybe just one if I have no choice. A few hours to prepare is a freaking nightmare.

Maybe if I had a twelve-man team, a couple of seasoned vets, a grumpy leader with a backstory, a jerk who's somewhat funny if you like that kind of humor, a young kid with the sparkle still in his eye...

But I don't have that. I have Thomas. And—ugh—Ryan.

The mercs are really lazing about with this operation. I get why they've gotten comfortable. It's been a month, they're shutting things down tomorrow, and the only trouble they've had so far is probably people like that kid trying to stand up to them.

They have a different kind of trouble now.

The merc patrol team consists of four men. They walk the perimeter of the encampment on their side of the fence. Each time they reach the rolling gate, they stop so two guys can slide it open and go out to check the trucks. All in all, it takes them about ten minutes.

That's it. That is the entirety of the patrol. I haven't even seen anyone check on the prisoners. The guy in charge of these mercenaries has a sparkling reputation. His men aren't holding up to the hype.

The Thai police are restless. There are only six guys, but they wander the camp aimlessly. In the middle of the night. For no reason.

It gives me the willies.

It also gives big ol' Blondie the willies. He keeps staring at them when they walk by. I watch him nudge one of the Latinos and mutter something when a few of them pass their fire.

Thomas and I take turns watching while the other eats or tries to snag a cat-nap. I don't know about him, but my nap was not super successful.

Finally, the mercs pour dirt on their fires, Blondie orders the start of a new set of guys to patrol, and the light in the encampment dims. We have several hours before daybreak, but there is a lot to do.

The three of us slowly make our way back down the hill again. We move around the encampment until we are crouching on the far side of the line of trucks.

I give Ryan his orders. He sets his jaw and squares his shoulders. I think he might actually listen to me and not be a total numb-nuts this time. He takes off for a spot maybe fifty feet down the road.

Thomas and I gear up.

I tuck a nightstick into my belt next to the machete. I flex my hands around padded fingerless gloves. The palm side is gripped to allow for easier handholds. A pointed chunk of bronze caps each knuckle. They were a gift from Missa.

Thomas tucks four extra clips into the lower pockets on his pants. His pair of brass knuckles slide into another pocket.

We are only half equipped. I leave a massive black case next to Thomas's duffle bag in the beastly shadow of a tree several yards away from the road.

My fingertips tingle as I clench and unclench my hands. The element of surprise is so important to this mission—if they see us now, I don't know that we'll be able to save these people.

Thomas pulls his little box, the surprise present from Ben, from the duffle bag and we walk to the road. He kneels, opens it up, and reaches in. He pulls out the little drone with the tenderness of a parent putting clothes on a newborn for the first time.

"Damn," I breathe. "That's a beauty."

"I've wanted one for years," he murmurs. "Get those, will you?"

I crouch down and grab four small screens tucked into a space on the side of the box.

"Only two."

I put two back and close the lid. Thomas sets the drone atop the box and powers up one of the screens.

I'm not bad with technology, but Missa is the savvy one. She'd probably be able to follow all the things Thomas does with the drone.

To be fair, I'm also keeping a lookout, so my eyes aren't exactly glued to his screen. But I doubt I'd be able to replicate his work. I'm left feeling pretty impressed as the cute little machine whirrs to life with hardly any sound. With a few clicks on his screen, Thomas sends it up, up, up into the air. After only a few seconds, it's lost from my sight.

Thomas stands, sets the box to the side of one of the truck tires, and turns to face me. "Power up your controls."

I blink and look at him like he's crazy. "I'm not controlling this thing, right?"

"No. But you have to have it *on* to see what I see."

"Heh, right. Duh." I flip the little screen over in my hand, searching in the near darkness for the on button. Seconds pass. I flip it over again. More seconds. Each one ticks off a mark of how dumb I feel.

"Here." He takes it, powers it up, and clicks a couple of buttons until what is on my little screen matches his.

There isn't much to see for a moment. Wait—there—in the bottom corner of the screen is a bright redish-orange figure. It's tiny. But more figures join it as the drone moves over the encampment. A cluster of men, laid out in long rows, shows us no one is moving in the Hmong building.

Movement in the merc tents is also limited. A solitary figure walks from the porta-potty to a tent.

It takes me a moment, while Thomas flies the drone across the encampment a few times, to get the layout in my brain. We are on the opposite side from before, and the thermal camera doesn't show buildings.

"There." Thomas points at his screen. "The patrol is coming around. We need to move."

He grabs the box, and we backtrack a fair distance into the forest.

They stop at the fence, check the trucks, and move on in a matter of a few minutes. I click a little button on my watch. It's time.

We use bolt cutters on the fence, slicing straight up from the ground, around, and over until we have an oval-sized hole. We gently lower the cut part, trying to keep the bottom in place, until it plops onto the soft dirt. Once we step through, we place two zip ties on either side of the top part. We stand the chunk of fence back up and close the hole. It may be a little time consuming, but it's quieter than trying to slide the fence over, and it's obviously much safer than leaving a gaping hole.

Thomas inches forward, and I follow right behind him. We stay low until we reach the Hmong barracks, then stick to the walls while we walk around. He keeps a wary eye on his little control screen while I tug my lock-pick kit out of my belt and get to work.

Seconds tick past.

My forehead sweats.

After an agonizingly long time, I hear the click I was waiting for. Thomas makes sure no mercs are near us, and we open the door.

A pungent smell hits me hard. The scent of fear, sweat, urine, and other gross stuff we won't get into has made the air thick as a humid day in a swamp. I suppress the flash of rage that runs through my veins at the notion of people being forced to sleep like this.

It's pitch black. We make our way inside, moving silently but quickly. I close the door behind us, and swallow down a little bit of vomit as the fresh outside air quickly disappears.

The unmistakable sound of deep breathing surrounds us. I crack a glow stick and hold it up.

The beds line both walls, stacked like bunk-beds, and are incredibly thin. My light only shows so much, and in this long building, the sleeping men seem to go on forever into the darkness. A pair of eyes open on the cot to my left. Hooded and dark, the man sits up, his gaze drifting between myself and Thomas.

I tug Thomas forward. "Time to shine," I whisper.

"I never understood that one," he whispers back. But he steps in front of me and murmurs to the man in Hmong.

Only a few seconds pass, but it is clear the man is not pleased. He shakes his head vigorously, waving a hand and pointing at the men around him, many of whom are also waking up.

I'm impressed at the silence they maintain.

"What's going on?"

"This is Alang, a village elder. He doesn't want to go. He says they will kill the women and children."

"Tell him we've already taken out the mercs in the village."

Thomas nods in the dim green light and speaks to the man. Several others are awake now, and they crowd around Alang and Thomas.

My large friend is gesturing to himself and me. He points at the machete on his hip. He talks and talks for what feels like forever, explaining our plan for getting them out. Then the men talk amongst themselves. I shift my weight from foot to foot and run my fingers over the brass caps on my knuckles. I heave a sigh.

Finally, Thomas straightens up. He turns to me and nods. "They're ready."

I glance at my watch. "We've only got three minutes left before they come around again. We should just wait it out."

He nods and says something to the men.

While we wait, the leader wakes the rest of the men and explains the situation in hushed tones.

I check my watch about a hundred times. Thomas fiddles with his control screen. Three minutes feels like a goddamn year.

"They are almost to the trucks."

"Anyone roaming?"

"No. Just the patrol. Looks like the Thai are finally settling down around their tent."

I glance at Thomas. His jaw is locked, his eyes bright and focused. If we mess this up... we can't mess this up.

My watch goes bright for a moment; my timer is done. I reset and slowly push open the door. The air hits me in the face, and I take a deep breath.

I have a group of three. The hope being that three at a time has less chance of making a bunch of noise. The Hmong men follow me to the fence. I clip the zip ties, gently lower the chain-link, and wave them through. I follow them, then lead them to the trees. I point.

The first man glances behind him.

"We'll get the rest of them," I murmur encouragingly. In English. Gawd, I'm dumb.

But he seems to get the sentiment. He turns and gestures for the others to follow as he creeps down the road. Thomas has already let them know when to stop. When they reach Ryan, they'll wait for us to get everyone else. Once we've gotten everyone, I'll figure out where to put them.

I make my way back through the fence and to the building. My gaze flicks down to the screen in my hand a few times to make sure no one is coming around a corner. My little orange self is the only one in my area.

It's bizarre watching yourself crouch-run on a thermal camera while you are crouch-running in real life.

Now that I've proved to the prisoners that we can actually get them past the fence, things go much faster. I check in with Thomas, then lead another group to the fence. Rather than take them to the tree-line again, I wave them through and wait for the next set.

Thomas sends another three, and we go like this for about two minutes. We get two more groups out, and I get back to the barracks before the patrol gets near.

There are still so many men.

I pull the door shut behind me, and sticky darkness once again engulfs us. I watch the screen in my hands. Four mercs make their way along the fence line.

I freeze.

The fence.

The fucking *fence*!

Shit.

I turn to Thomas, and he reads the situation from the look on my face. I forgot to close up the fence.

I jerk my head at the door. His eyebrows draw together, and he shakes his head.

I ignore him.

If the mercs see a gaping hole in the fence, this whole thing is over. I inch the door open just enough for me to get through. I take a deep breath as I close it behind me.

The mercs are still a little way away. But they are getting closer by the second. We should have put the hole on the other side of the trucks; it may have bought us extra time while they did their checks. Oh well, hindsight's 20-20 and all that.

Running isn't safe. Even in the dark, that kind of movement is too visible. So I crouch and move as fast as I dare across the open space between the building and the fence. I slide along the side of the chain-link. There. A chunk of darkness without any glint of metal.

I pull two zip ties from my pants pocket. I step through the fence and lift the oval-shaped chunk. It isn't heavy, but I sweat from the effort of moving so slowly. Finally, *finally*, I get it in place. The metal gently leans against my shoulder as I reach over and tie off one side.

The zip tie makes that unmistakable *zshoom* sound, and my breath catches.

Please don't hear that.

I bite my tongue.

I can hear the merc footsteps now. The soft rumble of low voices as they get closer and closer.

I tie off the other side.

The fence is closed. Unless the mercs point a flashlight directly at it or run their hands along the metal, they won't see anything amiss.

I tiptoe backward. They might not notice the fence, but they'd probably have trouble missing a me-sized shadow where none has been during their last dozen rounds.

At the three-yard mark, I turn and move my ass until I reach the tree-line. After ducking behind a rather large chunk of vegetation, I pull out my little screen. Thomas has the drone angled to watch me. I stick my hand up and give a little wave—my fire-self waves on the screen.

The drone moves on, expanding the view until we can watch the mercs pass the hole and check out the trucks. After a few minutes, they are beyond earshot. Well, beyond incredibly quiet earshot. Obviously, if I started shouting, they'd be able to hear me.

It takes about twenty more trips, over an hour, and several more close calls—though I don't forget to close up the fence again—until we are finally on our last group. I slip back through the hole and cross the ground to the building. Thomas and the last few men should be outside by now. They are not.

I squeeze through the cracked door. Thomas is blocking the door, his back to me, as he holds a furious, whispered argument with a young Hmong man.

The boy is beaten, bloody, and bruised. In the dim green light from the glow stick, he looks like death. Or at least like he had a violent encounter with a truck. He's the one from before—the one who hit a merc over the head with a metal pipe.

His arms wave in jerky, sharp movements, and he winces each time the left one rises too high. The men on either side of him are also quite young. They nod along fiercely as he points at Thomas.

Behind them, the elderly man we spoke to at first, Alang, shakes his head in a defeated sort of way.

I tap Thomas's shoulder. We don't have time for this.

He turns to me, his features twisted in frustration. "This is Lis; he and his friends want to stay and fight."

I sigh and rub my forehead just above my nose. "Course they do. Tell them they can't."

He looks at me like I've grown a hand out of my ear and the hand flipped him off. "Obviously I have already said that, Belle. They don't want to hide. They want revenge."

My eye twitches. "Well that sucks for them, doesn't it?" I lean around Thomas and point my finger at the boy. "You're gonna go with the rest of your group if I have to drag your ass."

"Belle." Thomas gives me a skeptical look. "They do not speak English."

"Ohh." I glare up at him. "They know what I'm saying."

"I've been trying to talk him into leaving since you took the last group out," Thomas says. "I don't think it's going to be that easy."

I take a beat and try to stifle my grumbling. Of course they want revenge—who wouldn't after what they've been through? But I can't worry about three men, boys really, during the next stage of this little adventure.

I check my watch. We are down to five minutes. "Lie to them. Tell them they can help once we get out of here."

His head does the little shake that I associate with him hating an idea. "Fine."

He speaks a bit of Hmong, selling the lie with encouraging hand gestures and a lot of nodding. Alang, standing behind them, sees right through it. But the boys seem convinced.

"They say, 'okay.'"

"Great," I murmur. "Let's get the hell out of here."

We inch out the door. Once the five men are on their way to the fence, I re-wrap the chain and secure the padlock.

Once we are out, the fence is closed, and our little group is headed toward Ryan, I let out a sigh. It's not done. Not even close to being done. But we got the prisoners out—every one. Most are a little worse for wear, beaten, bruised, malnourished, but none are dead.

To me, it seems like a frigging miracle.

We reach them, a decent distance from the encampment. The Hmong men are visibly relieved when we arrive with the last of their people. I rub my hands together as we all sort of group together.

I glance at Ryan, then at Thomas. "All right. Time for round two."

CHAPTER TWENTY-THREE

MISS BELLE

STROBE LIGHTS DON'T MAKE IT A PARTY

The best time to attack any operation is just before dawn. In those dark, black and gray moments before the sun reaches the edges of our world.

You know when you can't sleep? When you toss and turn into the early hours of the morning? A lot of people have that, especially when something big is about to happen. And when they do fall asleep, it's a deep sleep. And that's why at 3:45 a.m., Thomas and I are back by the trucks, finishing up equipping ourselves.

I sling a massive rectangular black case over my shoulder and latch it onto my back. A pack of half-inch-thick zip ties sits in the lower pocket on my left pant leg.

Thomas hitches a loose bag onto his back, and we head toward the fence.

The goal is still to avoid killing the mercs, but grievous injury was never off the table. Some will probably die. They chose this life. But if I can get to McKinnan and explain how hard we tried not to kill his men... well, that's getting a bit ahead of things.

I've gone over the plan with Thomas and Ryan. The southern boy is going to have to follow instructions this time. I don't want him anywhere near this. But he *and* the Hmong prisoners said if I didn't give them a job to do, they'd find one.

So, I sent him and the boys off with a stack of small black boxes and very specific instructions for where to put them and when to turn them on. Even more of the Hmong men demanded to help once we all grouped up. At first, I flat out refused. But Thomas got to talking to them, listening to them, and found out how many men were killed on the way here and during the first two weeks. It was more than a couple.

If I'm honest, it helps to have the extra hands.

We arrive at the fence. The gentle hum of the generator sings to our right. Ahead of us and to the left, shadow and darker shadow are the only colors we can use to distinguish the factory building.

This is the part where my nerves buzz. Right here, before everything starts.

The village was a fight; I killed three men in a matter of minutes. Rescuing the Hmong was a stealth move. But this—this is more.

Thomas puts a hand on my shoulder. "We have got this," he whispers.

I nod, tight-lipped.

He briefly caresses my cheek. "Good luck."

"*Bahati njema*," I reply. *Good luck* in Swahili.

We lower the chunk of fence down. I walk quickly, knees slightly bent, so my footsteps make less sound. There are few leaves to crunch under us. Thomas's thicker footsteps land behind me. I take deep breaths.

I go left, Thomas goes right. His job is to place two strobes at the far corner. His massive form pauses at the generator for a moment before disappearing into the dark.

I move on, boots landing with firm silence on the dusty ground. I could cut through the camp to reach my goal, but that seems like a pretty unnecessary risk for the time it would save.

I circle the factory, running a hand along the side of the building as I go. It is so dark here behind the building, out of any line of light.

I reach the corner and steal a glance.

The mess tent is about twenty yards away. Next to it sits the other generator. Behind them is the tent for the Thai police and the lavatories. Then, to the right, the mercenary tents spread out and take up most of the remaining fenced-in space. The area is lit up just enough for someone to reach the toilet in the middle of the night without breaking a leg.

I take a chance and dart out from behind the building. I move as low and quickly as possible until I reach the mess tent. I sneak around behind it to the generator.

I dig my fingers into the shin pocket on the right side of my pants and remove a Rubik's cube-sized rectangle of what looks like silly putty. From my left side, I pull out a detonator the size of a matchbox.

Crouched down and breathing quietly, I pull open a panel on the side of the big black box. I settle the C4 into a crevice. The detonator sits next to it. I slowly push the fuse into the putty.

I click a button on my watch and the time jumps up at me in glowing green numbers. I time the detonator to the second and fix the panel back into place. I've got twelve minutes.

Two strobe lights, the small ones you'd see at a party store but more high tech, are clipped onto the back of my belt. I release them one at a time and zip tie them, one at eye level and one at shoulder level, along the fence.

I need to move faster.

The door to the factory is unlocked. We knew as much, not having seen anyone attempt to secure it in any way. Why would they bother? The prisoners are all securely stuck in their sleeping quarters—haha.

It squeaks as I push it open—fucking door hinges. I've been caught no less than six times going somewhere I'm not supposed to be, because of door hinges. Honestly, people, all it takes is a little WD-40, or even olive oil if you're in a pinch. I usually bring some along on a mission, but Thomas did all the prep for this one, as it was so last minute.

I enter the factory. It's... dark. The lights from outside filter in just enough to make it look like I'm knee-deep in a horror movie. With the first step inside, the stench of burning metal and plastic assaults my nose. This place does not prioritize ventilation.

Massive shapes, the machines I assume, loom out of the darkness. I snap a green glow stick and give it a good shake. A set of metal grate stairs climb up to the second floor on my right. I follow them, my boots clunking on the hard surface. About six steps up, I pull a small cylindrical metal tube from yet another pocket, along with about a yard of pre-cut string. After some Boy Scout-worthy knots, I continue upstairs, an early warning system in place.

The second floor is open and shaped like a big U around the edges of the building. A thin railing keeps one from tumbling onto the machinery below. A walled off room—probably an office—sits at the end, a maze of car parts between me and it. I tiptoe through, quietly bumping into things and trying not to cut myself on anything sharp.

At the office, I set up another little surprise, and then, with barely five minutes left, I head to a window. This is the tricky part. Well, one of the tricky parts.

I do a double-check that nothing on me is going to fall off easily, then I peel the window open. It's one of those stupid ones with a hinge in the middle, where you can either have the top open out or the bottom. I elect the top.

The window is high. Too high for little ol' me.

A box of files fixes my problem, and, leaving my bag of toys near the wall, I hoist myself onto the windowsill. There isn't really a ledge of any kind, and my fear of heights politely reminds me that this is fucking stupid.

I breathe deep and squeeze the wall with my left hand. With my back to the ground, I slowly rise until I'm standing on the sill. I curve my body to the side, folding my torso around the top section of glass.

Switching hands, I grip the wall with my right and then send the left up, reaching for the edge of the roof.

These measurements were done ahead of time as well. Thomas and I eyeballed the layout from our perch on the hillside. It was decided I'd be able to reach the roof from the windowsill.

It's hard to judge distance from—well—a distance. I'm about an inch short.

I know this because when I go up on my toes, I can just feel the edge. My mind flutters through options. Nothing on my person is going to help.

I glance to the left. Nothing.

I glance to the right. A drainage pipe. On the opposite side of the open window.

I don't have time for this shit.

A silent sigh escapes me, and I lower myself back onto my butt. I skootch across the sill and stand up again on the right side. The pipe is close to the window. I test it with my weight.

It's not built to hold me, and it's not secured into the wall very well. But it'll work for the few seconds I need.

My left foot is on the sill, my right hand latched around the pipe a little above my head. I grit my teeth; my right foot dangles in the air. I stretch my left arm up, ready to grab. With my left leg I push off, at the same time lifting with all my strength.

My left hand catches on the ledge. I hold on with everything in me. Now using both arms, I pull myself up. I swing my leg over the ledge and straddle the edge of the roof. I lie still for a moment, my face against the metal. The sound of my heartbeat pounds through my ears.

Time is running out. Thomas is very likely already in place. And Ryan goddamn better be. As for the Hmong men, I can only hope they finished what I told them to do and went back to hide in the jungle.

I kneel and pull the thick, boxy case from my back and lay it out before me. The rifle is cold to my touch, but comforting in my arms. I position myself a few yards from where I clambered up. It gives me a better view of the mercenary tents.

Rubber bullets are very efficient at close range. The farther away you get, the less functional they become. However, I'm less than forty yards from Blondie's tent, so these should work pretty damn well.

I set up the bullets, ready to reload. I line up my sight with the entrance to the tent, prepared to shoot. I check my watch. Forty seconds.

A lone figure saunters through the darkness on the ground. Thomas's height is the only thing that gives him away.

He reaches the opening of the main tent, Blondie's tent. Each hand holds a canister. I check my watch. Ten seconds.

As the little numbers click away, Thomas tosses the first canister into the tent. There is a deafening bang, followed by a flash of light. He throws in the second canister and sprints away.

At the same time, two blasts, one second apart, shake the ground. The camp lights die immediately. The generators are down.

In the next few seconds, men pour from the white tent into the night. Some are screaming; I hear crying and the unmistakable sound of someone trying to blow their nose. Curses, angry shouts, and frantic yells fill the darkness.

Ya know... the usual reaction to a MACE grenade.

It takes Ryan and Lis a few seconds, but then it hits. The strobe lights we set up go off all at once. Instead of their eyes adjusting to the night, blinding flashes strike the mercenaries. In the meantime, Thomas isn't out of flash grenades just yet. He tosses more into the other merc tents as he gets to cover.

The noise, lights, and frantic scrambling to find water for burning eyes causes pandemonium. Normally, I'd hate trying to shoot people in this environment. The lights make it impossible to see clearly.

But the mercs are behaving as predicted. The ones with their guns out are shooting into the woods, mistaking the strobe lights for actual enemy targets. I hope the villagers got out of there fast enough.

I line up my sight with the back of a man's neck, squeeze the trigger, and he drops to the ground with a thud.

I shift the nozzle an inch and fire again. I miss, but the next rubber bullet bounces off a thick-set man's thigh, and he goes down, howling. Another shot immobilizes his arm.

I fire and fire, reload, then fire again. Even through the darkness, I can tell their numbers are dropping fast. Thomas is down there. He is only visible by the light of his cattle prod. It's not his favorite weapon, but I insist on having at least a few of them at each operation.

One of those suckers can take down a full-grown man in a fit of spasms. And with not as much permanent nerve damage as you might think.

Those who didn't get MACEd in the face, try to organize. A few turn their guns on the Hmong sleeping quarters. I grit my teeth in anger. The sound of bullets ripping through sheet metal fills the air.

My awareness picks up something off—an out of place sound. A scream that isn't coming from in front of me. I twitch my head to the left and listen.

Beyond the sound of shots, men below barking orders, and the wind is an unmistakable war cry. Furious, hate-filled screams reach me from somewhere beyond the far edge of the factory.

I could waste my time wondering what it is. But I think it's pretty clear.

I get my feet under me and run at a crouch across the roof. I reach the edge and squint through the darkness. The strobe lights aren't set up this far back, but I make out moving figures, coming toward me through the black.

The string of curses that comes out of my mouth would make Samuel L. Jackson blush. And it gets worse—of course. On my right, where I can see them but the Hmong men can't, a group of five mercs heads toward the noise.

I hit the last guy as the rest round the corner. At the same time, Lis and his fellow ex-prisoners reach the fence. So, I've got four armed mercs on one side, and about twelve unarmed men on the other side.

Well, I shouldn't say unarmed. Many of them are carrying blunt metal instruments or large branches, which is basically unarmed when there's a fence between you and a bunch of guns.

I groan.

The Hmong men climb, and the mercs line up to start shooting. I unclip a smoke grenade from my belt. Pull the pin, wait for just a second, and... toss.

It lands between the two groups. Immediately, I bring my rifle back up and hit a merc right above his knee. The men on either side turn as he collapses to the ground. My second chunk of rubber hits him between the shoulder blades. His buddies switch from staring at him to looking for me. They scan the factory wall, and I take advantage of them facing my direction. A bullet strikes one across the jaw. My next shot misses.

But now the first wave of Hmong has cleared the fence. The one mercenary not looking for me gets off two shots before he is clubbed over the head by a smallish figure that looks like it may be Lis. Fortunately, he fired into a cloud of smoke. Fingers crossed he didn't hit anyone.

The mercenaries turn back to the fence just in time for metal to clash with their skulls. I can hear the cracks from where I am. A brief hope that they aren't dead flashes through my mind.

Lis waves his arm around and his little group huddles up. One of them appears to be injured. My hands shake with anger. Thomas is alone right now. I can't get down there to demand they turn back. Even if I could, there's the whole "no speaking Hmong" issue.

I hesitate. Then, from out of the shadows on the other side of the factory, Ryan and Alang emerge. They seem to be talking the group down...

Hoping Alang and Ryan will stop Lis from causing more damage, I sprint back to my post.

Thomas dances through the tattered tents. He bobs and weaves, avoiding coming face to face with anyone. The vice-like grip that had clutched my heart during the time I was away loosens slightly.

I'd have been responsible if they'd killed him while I was gone from my post.

Four men advance on Thomas. In the dark, with his skin and black clothes, he is practically invisible. But space is limited, and they find him.

Thomas blocks a fist, and a boot collides with his stomach. The man connected to the boot receives a rubber bullet to his cheek. He goes down with, what is likely, a broken jaw.

Thomas wields his cattle prod, doing a fair amount of damage to two of the men. I take down the last one with two consecutive shots to his chest.

I've got a grin on my face until a wasp stings my forehead. No.

That's not right.

It's the middle of the night.

Why the hell would there be a wasp?

But the burning is there. Like the searing pain of hot metal pressed against skin.

Then blood drips onto my chest, and it clicks.

I drop to the ground and roll to the side. When I'm a few feet from the edge of the roof, I stop and press my left hand to the space just a bit above my eye. It's a graze, maybe as long as a silver dollar. I don't know how deep.

I fumble with my pocket. I find a patch, pull it out, slap it to my forehead, and roll back around to my crouched position.

It was a lucky shot. They can't see me up here. It's too dark. Though I realize, as another shot whizzes by my ear, the strobe lights are quite possibly lighting me up like a Christmas tree. Between that and my racing back and forth across the roof, I can't be surprised they found me.

I stay low. A metal door slams against a wall below me. They're coming in. Likely to get me from inside the building rather than firing from the ground.

I take a peek below. It's disturbingly quiet. Not actually quiet, but less loud by far. Thomas is fighting two men. But the amount of bodies on the ground is a good sign.

I lean over the ledge just enough to watch the last two mercs enter the factory—time to go.

My escape route sucks. I leave the rifle—plenty of time to fetch it if I don't die. I run, doubled over, back to where I came onto the roof. The window is still open, the top pushed out into the air.

I lower myself over the edge then maneuver my feet into the open space between the window and the wall.

The muscles in my arms burn. When I can't lower myself anymore, I swing my ass forward and let go. My knees buckle when I hit the floor, and the landing isn't as "Buffy" as I'd like it to be. But I'm alive and with no broken bones.

The minute I land, an explosion rocks the building. My flash bang did the trick. It'll slow the mercs down long enough for me to get some cover. I grab the canvas bag next to the window and—as quietly as possible—sprint across the room and duck behind a stack of metal.

The men stumble up the stairs. The air is thick with tension, sweat, smoke... I try to breathe silently. I peel back the edges of my bag and pull out a black rod, maybe a little over a foot long. I carefully avoid the tongs on the end.

I wait. They file past—six of them. When the last boot passes me, I step into the makeshift hallway and press my cattle prod between the last man's shoulder blades.

He goes down fast, but I'm already sprinting away. A yell is followed by a gunshot. Something shatters ahead of me and to the left.

The muck on the windows is muting the strobe lights, and my eyes have adjusted to the darkness. But I still hit my shin against a chunk of metal. I grit my teeth. The men are right behind me. Another shot whizzes by my ear. I duck behind a large wooden crate.

"Really?" I shout at them. "Shoot first and ask questions later, huh?"

"Who the fuck are you?" one of them shouts back. His voice is high, young.

The group advances. I creep around the mercs until I reach the edge of the balcony. The men now face the stairs again.

I glance over the railing at the mass of machinery on the first floor. It's quite a bit of a drop.

The door slams again. Footsteps pound up the stairs and Thai voices speak to the mercs.

"Tell them we've got this. Get back to the damn tent and stay out of the way." A different voice. My guess is the guy's a heavy smoker.

"Yeah," I call to them. I project with my diaphragm, and the echo is fantastic. "I was a bit confused about why you've got a bunch of locals helping out. Doesn't your company usually handle things a bit more professionally?"

Heavy sounds of footsteps. A blast sends a chunk of balcony clattering to the floor. I inch back.

"It's not our call," the first man yells back at me.

"Shut up, Dante."

I laugh and can practically feel the testosterone in the room increase.

"Spread out." The Smoker pushes someone, and I hear a grunt. "Find this bitch and bring her in, alive."

"Jesus," I cackle and slip to the floor. "Can you say 'cliché'?"

I lie flat on my belly and watch a pair of feet rush toward the machine in front of me. The owner of the feet pauses. I ram the tongs of my cattle prod into his thigh, and he goes down with a scream.

The guy behind him sticks his arm out, and I roll. Bullets hit where I had lain seconds before.

Someone's arm goes around my neck, cutting off the oxygen to my brain. I lift my right arm and wrench it up, causing the pressure on my neck to increase. I slam my fist, once, twice, and three times into the jaw of the man holding me.

His arm slackens, and I get my chin under his muscle. My teeth clamp around his Wookie-esque hairy arm. Blood spurts into my mouth. He releases me with a shout, and I twirl around. The shadow of his hand moves toward me. I duck away, come up behind him, grab him by the back of his collar, and slam his head into the wall.

I hit him against it again, and he slumps.

Another hand grabs the end of my tight braid and yanks. I let him pull me, dropping the cattle prod and releasing my knife from its sheath.

"Gotcha now, bitch." A stale smell hits my nose as the man drags my face up to meet his.

"Yep." I sink two inches of steel into his thigh. He roars.

Bullets zing around me.

Both his hands go to pull the blade out, and I spring back. He's got the knife now, and I don't have my special zappy toy.

His arm swishes through the air, and I block with my left arm. I come up short. The knife grazes my skin. I take a step back, almost trip over the guy I just dropped, and my back hits the wall.

He advances. I aim a kick at his stomach, and he doubles over. I slam my elbow into the back of his head, above his neck.

I lunge for the cattle prod. An army regulation combat boot hits my arm, and I duck to the side.

The remaining mercs have arrived. Two of them stand in front of me, guns drawn. Stale Mouth staggers to his feet. He takes a step toward me, but the largest of the mercs grabs the back of his shirt. It's Blondie.

"Hold on." He's the smoker.

He moves closer, his weapon trained on my chest.

My mouth is dry, tongue like sandpaper. I back up, and my shoulders hit the wall. My breathing is deep. I clench my jaw and attempt to force myself to remain calm.

It's not easy with three Glocks aimed at me.

"Let's see what this bitch can tell us."

Making friends with the locals isn't always easy. If you're traveling in touristy areas, the customer service folks will probably greet you with a smile; if you've chosen a more adventurous vibe, you may find yourself in some less than friendly areas.

Double check what personal security items are allowed in the country you're visiting. Also familiarize yourself with the emergency number—it's not 911 everywhere.

Beyond the basics, remember that you're the one visiting someone else's home. Be kind, follow local customs, and ask around before you head to a place that might be unsafe.

Chapter Twenty-Four

Lacey

Rich People Eat Too

I've seen wealth. Real wealth. The kind of dresses that could feed a family for a year. Ballrooms larger than a house, shoes that cost as much as a car.

This isn't that. Of course, many of these men are ridiculously wealthy, but not all. Looking around, you can tell which of these people make six figures a year and which make six figures a month.

Nathan is somewhere in the middle.

Still, it's one of the more elegant events I've been to in the last few months. And I do enjoy dressing up.

Silver cascades in soft ruffles across my body. Tiny sparkling diamonds glitter in my dark hair. A silver necklace, ornate, with an exquisite collection of yet more diamonds, adorns my neck. It was a gift from Nathan.

It weighs heavily on my skin.

Dinner is in the same conference room as that first breakfast. Large round tables, each seating eight people, are spread in even rows across the floor. A small stage has been set up in the corner; a band, possibly the same as the first night, fiddle with their strings. The cellist looks incredibly bored, the violinist perhaps a bit too excited with his performance.

But the music is sweet. I sway just a bit as Nathan guides me to our table. A little white card with gold calligraphy reserves my seat under the name *Lacey Blake.*

My stomach churns.

I throw a big smile up at Nathan as he gestures to the card. "So sweet," I murmur.

He pulls out my chair and then settles himself next to me. His fingers snap in the air, and one of the many members of the waitstaff materializes. Wine is ordered. The rest of our table is yet to arrive. I content myself with asking Nathan about his day. I offer hopes that everything is still going according to plan. I turn the conversation as much as possible (without seeming obvious) to the factory.

I can't decide if I should be thrilled to hear everything is on track, or horrified. I don't know if it means Miss Belle failed, hasn't arrived yet, or succeeded in both the rescue and in keeping things quiet.

The conversation changes as two high-ranking lawyers and their wives arrive. The women offer me politely cold smiles which I return with a warm one. Nathan and his employees discuss the last quarter, economy cars, and a potential resurgence of "Hummer love."

We make our way through the soup and salad. Finely-clad waiters serve the next course. Steak. Fortunately, there are plenty of sides. I load up on rolls, potatoes, and asparagus.

Our table goes through four bottles of wine before the last of the party arrives. The wives have warmed up to me considerably. I blame the merlot.

The waitstaff has already begun clearing plates around the room by the time Daniel and Delilah arrive. He is leading her by the arm and appears to be walking too quickly. She's limping.

I clench my jaw briefly before plastering a neutral look on my face. Nathan puts a hand on my arm and leans across to whisper in my ear. "He was furious at our meetings. I almost thought he was going to try to fire me. Not that he could."

He sighs, but there is a smile on his lips.

"It looks like he calmed down a bit," I comment lightly.

Nathan nods.

Jacobson greets the lawyers, their wives, and Nathan. He meets my eye for the briefest of seconds, wearing a look that says he'd very much like to take out his anger on me.

I'm not worried. He either still suspects me (which doesn't matter anymore because Chang has all the evidence), or he is merely experiencing that common side effect of being embarrassingly wrong—irrational fury.

They only sit for a few minutes, just long enough for Jacobson to shovel a steak down his throat, before the last of the plates are cleared. The tables empty, diners slowly making their way into the ballroom.

It's the one from the first night, but this time the cocktail tables are confined to the edges of a large dance floor. The band is louder, though still sticking to instrumentals. Little towers of desserts and champagne are staggered around the room. Nathan and I make a bee line for a cupcake mountain. I giggle as he feeds me the pale flower-petal pink frosting on his finger.

Daniel's suspicions won't be erased... but Nathan's desire for me, his belief that I genuinely care for him, should be enough to keep any problems for Miss Belle at bay.

We dance. We dance and dance until Nathan has worked up a sweat and my feet grow sore. He sits with yet another lawyer friend, and I make my way across the room to fetch us more champagne.

I'm in the corner by the band, alone, when Delilah catches my eye. I give her a small nod, and she hurries over to me. She is definitely favoring her left leg.

Blue silk butterflies adorn her chest, melting together as they approach her waist until they become a collection of ruffles draping down to the floor. Her black hair flows in ringlets in which flecks of gold appear and disappear as she turns her head.

She grabs my hand. "Did you ask?"

My face gives the answer before I open my mouth. Her eyes, shining with hope only seconds before, go dark.

"Listen..." I begin.

She shakes her head. "No."

I take her arm as she tries to turn away.

She winces, and I release her, guilt warming my cheeks. I speak quickly. "I still have to talk to Miss Belle. It's not a 'no,' it's a 'not yet.' She's radio silent right now. I need a way to contact you once she becomes reachable again. I'm sure I'll be able to convince her. Really." I give her an encouraging smile.

She half-heartedly returns it. "Yeah. Okay. You'll probably be able to reach me with the number I gave you the night of the party."

She shakes her head and turns away. I open my mouth to say something, anything to reassure her. But then I see Daniel. He's standing across the room, holding a champagne flute and staring, furiously, at Delilah and me. She notices him and, giving me a frightened look, rushes away.

"You want to be careful."

I jump and turn quickly at the deep voice behind me. Marcus glares down at me, a drink in one hand, the other resting in his suit pocket.

"With what?"

"Julio isn't someone you want to go up against."

I tilt my head at him, frowning slightly. "You're warning me?"

He nods.

"Does this mean you forgive me?"

He runs his free hand over his throat. The collar of his bright white shirts slips down, and I mentally cringe at the greenish-purple bruise that runs around his neck.

"No." His tone is hard. "It means I don't like men who beat up on their women. If you plan on helping that girl, you'll want to watch your back."

There is a moment of silence between us. I hear Nathan call my name. I incline my head politely at Marcus. "Thank you."

A cloud of uselessness descends upon me. I can't even help this girl. What has this mission done, really? Delilah keeps getting hurt. Ryan nearly got killed. A village of people is under threat of extinction, and Miss Belle is in Thailand, likely in very real danger, possibly dead.

No.

Don't think that.

I return to Nathan's side and spend the rest of the night there. When we go up to the suite, I find Delilah's number. I put it into my phone.

When I get back, when Miss Belle is done with her mission, I *will* get Delilah out. I clench the paper copy in my hand.

I will.

I'll get her out.
I will.

Chapter Twenty-Five

Miss Belle

Mercenaries are Assholes

Blondie swings, and I double over as his thick fist collides with my stomach.

"Why are you here?"

I inhale sharply and straighten up. "Did you not take Interrogation 101? It's ask a question... *then* hit the subject."

He backhands me across the face. The bandage flies away from my forehead, and the thick oozing of blood down my cheek catches my attention for a split second.

"Why are you here?" he repeats.

I clutch my stomach, playing up the pain to delay. I have no problem answering his question. My issue is getting the drop on three men, each pointing a gun at me.

As much as Hollywood would like to convince us otherwise, my chances of succeeding are slim to none.

"Same reason you are." I spit, and blood-tinted saliva smacks the floor. "Jacobson hired us to do a job."

The gaze of the youngest guy flicks toward Blondie. But the big man is a professional. He keeps his eyes on me. "That's a lie."

"Nope." I work to slow my next breath, to maintain a calm appearance. The gunshot wound on my forehead stings in the chilly morning air. The bandage on my back is growing loose, and my ribs sing their displeasure at my acrobatics. "God's honest truth. This whole thing is going down the shitter. He wants to keep things quiet. And that means a small clean-up crew... not two dozen loose ends."

Blondie and Stale Mouth give each other a glance. The larger of the two curls his fingers again, and I tense my core.

Knuckles ram into my ribs. The sound released from my mouth causes the youngling to take half a step back.

A cracked rib isn't like a cut. You can't feel where the bone is separated. You can't feel specifically where, in your chest, you are injured. But you can feel the pain.

The shuddering breath I drag through my teeth sends sharp stabs through my lungs. I force another pull of oxygen and release it. I stop shaking.

"Jacobson wouldn't betray our company. You're lying, bitch." Blondie raises his gun.

I stand just a little straighter. My instincts flare. Kick the gun? Make a break for it? Probably get shot in the back.

"Stop!" a voice shouts from the darkness behind the mercs.

I frown. That's not Thomas's deep, smooth tone.

Blondie goes to turn, but the voice shouts again.

"Don't move! One step and I light the three of you up like the fourth of July."

Tennessee drawl drips through the words. I stifle a groan, but Blondie freezes. He glares at me as his guys look at him, unsure what to do.

"That's right. Now, drop your guns."

Hesitation.

"Now!"

Blondie lets out a furious growl and leans down. Three Glocks click against the ground as their owners reluctantly drop them. I swiftly reach out a foot, pull one closer, and pick it up.

Pain spikes through my chest, and I clench my jaw to keep from groaning. But I have a gun.

"Strip." I spit the word through my gritted teeth.

Stale Mouth sneers.

"I said strip. Now. Down to the skivvies. Ryan," I call to him. He steps forward, hands empty. "Tie up the men on the floor."

He looks confused.

I gesture with my free hand to the felled men. "The ones already knocked out. Two apiece, arms behind their backs." I hand him a stack of zip ties from my pants pocket. Fortunately for me, these idiots went straight to interrogation instead of searching me.

The men undress. I stay a fair distance away. Far enough to shoot them if one lunges at me.

I never understood why people let their enemies remain fully clothed. Weapons can be found literally everywhere. Did no one watch that *Pirates of the Caribbean* movie? The last good one with Orlando Bloom and Keira Knightley? Girl had a couple dozen guns stashed in her clothes.

It's significantly harder to hide a gun in a pair of boxer briefs than in a pair of hammer pants.

They shiver in the chilly air, nipples hard on two overly hairy chests and one oddly smooth one. I pull six more zip ties from my pocket.

"Arms behind your back," I say to Blondie. It's always a good move to take the most powerful piece out of commission before anyone else.

"Tie him up." I toss two zip ties to the kid. He gingerly tiptoes his bare feet over to his commander and uses one of the ties. "Tighter. And double it up, that's why you have two."

He does. I have him tie up Stale Mouth as well. I move the bigger men several yards away and tie up the kid myself. Then I parade them down the stairs and outside. Most of the two dozen mercs are tied up in a similar fashion. The ones standing are lined up against the factory wall. The injured men sit to the side. And, of course, eight unconscious bastards lie face-down in the dirt at their comrades' feet.

Thomas paces a few yards away. His cattle prod is holstered, replaced with his handgun. The time for "light" aggression is over. If we have any complications now, a shot to the arm or leg will quickly take care of it. Hopefully, without anyone bleeding out.

The Hmong remain grouped near their old sleeping quarters. I can't imagine how hard it must be to refrain from attacking the men who terrorized them for so long. But Alang understood our reasoning. He seems to have a good handle on keeping the rest in line with the plan.

Most of the strobe lights surrounding us are gone, shot all to hell during the fighting. A few still flicker feebly, casting random bursts of light on us. The dawning sky is just light enough to illuminate the faces around me.

I walk up to Thomas. "The Thai?"

He gestures to their tent. Four men kneel, stripped to their underwear, hands tied behind their backs.

"I thought we counted six of them?"

"Mercs killed two in the crossfire."

I nod and tell him about the guys upstairs. He tucks his gun into his belt and goes inside to carry out the men one by one.

My chest spasms every time I breathe. The only moment without pain is between breaths. Though, other parts of my body still hurt during that time.

I need to re-bandage my forehead. The bleeding has slowed, but the gash burns with each gentle breeze. The cut on my arm probably needs some attention, along with my back.

Now is not the time. I direct the muzzle of my gun at the knees of the men standing against the wall. Some carry a deadened look in their eyes, beyond caring. Some, like the youngling, hold a shaky fear in the whites of their eyes. And some—most—have a fiery blaze roaring through their features.

They are angry and beaten. But, as anyone with half a brain knows, beaten at the moment doesn't mean beaten permanently.

I stand still, a good twelve feet from the nearest merc. My muscles burn, but I do not lower my arm. Not until Thomas comes back down the stairs, dragging the last mercenary and dropping him to the ground. Ryan stands a few yards from me, staring at the wounded men with wide eyes.

Thomas returns to me, and we stand together, eyes locked on the line of men.

"What's the next step?"

"*Hey!*"

A shout interrupts my answer.

We turn. A mercenary limps into view from behind one of the last standing tents. Blood runs down his leg from a massive slice in his thigh. His right hand holds a handgun.

Shit.

His other arm is snug around Lis' neck. He lifts the gun to the boy's temple. Lis is struggling, but the merc squeezes, and the struggles stop. A shiver runs through my body... we were so close.

"You let them go." He waves his gun at the line-up of mercs. "You let them go, or I end this boy here and now."

I glance over to Thomas. Who is, unfortunately, standing right next to me. Ryan is a few yards away, but also in clear view of our loose mercenary. Even if he wasn't, it's one thing to pretend to be armed; it's another to take down someone physically holding a hostage.

For the second time tonight, I hesitate, unsure of what to do. Obviously, I can't just release the mercenaries. But my instincts are screaming at me to do something, anything, to stop Lis from being killed.

I put my hands up in a "let's all calm down" manner. I open my mouth, with no idea what is going to come out of it.

Bang.

I flinch as the gunshot rings out. My heart freezes for a split second. Until I register the bloody, gaping hole in the mercenary's forehead. Lis slips out of his limp grip and stumbles toward us. The mercenary wavers for just a moment then collapses.

A cry of fury goes up from his comrades along the wall. Thomas turns and commands quiet.

I turn as well.

Alang is a few feet behind me, his arm still raised, gun in hand.

That was a hell of a shot for anyone to make. I tilt my head just a bit. Alang's face, worn and wary, is hard to read. But as the gun falls from his fingers, I can see the regret—the shadows of war—flash across his eyes. The pain of taking a life is visible in his shaking hand, his clenched jaw.

His gaze meets mine before he turns back to his people. Lis follows him, limping along across the muddy, bloodied earth.

I shake it off. One dead—assuming none of the injured men bleed out—not bad, all things considered.

Thomas asks me again, "What next?"

"We get them contained. Loaded up in one of these trucks." I gesture to the massive transport trucks sitting along the road.

"Hogtie?"

"Yep."

"Injured?"

I pause. The men on the ground aren't beyond repair. A few are gushing small amounts of blood. I note a few gunshot wounds, several blisters around their eyes and nose, and severe electrical burn marks from the cattle prods.

"Patch up the ones who need patching. We can bind their arms and legs."

"We should also gag them all."

I nod. The less communication between captives, the better.

"We should clean you up first." Thomas reaches a hand to my forehead.

I brush him away. "Later. I want these guys secure before we take any breaks."

It takes a good forty minutes to get all the mercs loaded up. We start with the able-bodied/conscious men. Hogtying humans isn't as hard as it sounds, especially when using zip ties. I keep Ryan at the edge of the truck, watching the prisoners as Thomas and I take turns tying them and holding the gun.

I don't let the Hmong men help. I don't want them within arm's length of the mercs—the temptation for revenge doesn't go away all that quickly. They rest against the edge of the fence, watching us work.

The injured/unconscious are next. It's fortunate Thomas is so absolutely massive; he lifts most of the men with ease. The bed of the truck fills up quickly, and the men are pretty squished together. But they'll survive the next leg of the journey—without escaping—and that's all that matters.

I don't know what to do with the dead man. I don't want to leave his body here, but putting him with his fellows feels even worse. I decide on hauling him about forty yards down the road. If things go well with McKinnan (the chances of which have gone down quite a bit), they can come to collect his body.

"Stay here." I look at Ryan. "Watch them. I'll come get you when it's time to take pictures."

His eyes haven't shrunk down to their regular size yet; he still looks like a scared little southern Bambi. But he nods, jaw set.

I walk to the tents and Thomas. We move the body.

I plan aloud as we walk back. "We should get the Hmong loaded up. They can ride in a second truck. You can drive them back to the village while I take the mercs."

I plant my hands on my hips and survey the ruined site.

Thomas ignores my words. He pulls a bandage from a pocket and steps close. "You need to take care of yourself, Belle."

He dabs gauze against my forehead, soaking up the wet blood. I wince as he presses the bandage against the bullet wound. He tapes it in place, and I scan his dark skin.

"You're one to talk." I press soft fingers against a deep line where a bullet grazed his right shoulder. It's not easy to see bruises against his skin tone, but dried blood on his chin and a gash across his cheek mark where someone's fist connected with his face.

He bears other signs of a fight; a faint limp in his left leg, several tears in his black shirt, and his bottom lip is a bit larger than usual.

"I am fine." He pushes my fingers away.

"Right. 'Cause you can worry over me, but heaven forbid I help patch up your fucking bullet wound."

He raises his eyebrows at my sharp voice.

I wince again. "Sorry."

"It has been a long night."

I nod. My brain doesn't want to keep doing things. It wants to sleep, maybe eat, and take a hot bath. Possibly get laid. But definitely sleep. I pinch the bridge of my nose and force myself to focus. We aren't done yet.

The sun is rising on a misty valley. Pink and orange tinge the horizon, but where we are is still all gray. In the dim light, the wreckage is clear.

Only the mess tent still stands. The others are in shambles in the mud. Bullet shells litter the ground. The mercs tried hard to take us down. Pride rushes through my chest, followed by piercing pain as I inhale.

The Thai soldiers mutter amongst themselves. I should care. I don't. They can't help themselves now; on their knees in the mud, practically naked, and hands zip tied behind their backs.

What do I do with them?

I run through options in my head. From bribing them to bribing their bosses, to handing them over to the village, to...

Thomas does a count of the mercenaries. We have them all, for sure this time.

Ryan helps get the Hmong men into another of the massive trucks. Only a few of them are severely injured, but *all* are malnourished, exhausted, and beyond stressed.

I search the factory. My rifle is still on the roof, but I can't get it now. Well, I could, but that would probably involve my cracked rib breaking all the way. I collect my bag and the weapons I dropped during the fight. Then, I look for the gas.

This place is run on generators. Generators are generally run on gas.

Beams of light filter through the windows. But my magnum flashlight comes in handy on the ground floor. These machines are massive. It makes me question how long this operation has been running. There's a huge door at the end of the building, sort of like a giant garage door. It appears to roll up against the ceiling. I assume this is to load the car parts into the trucks.

That's where I find what I need—a dozen five-gallon red gas cans. Several are empty, but there is plenty left to serve my purpose.

I start on the other side of the factory, drizzling out a steady stream of toxic-smelling liquid. I empty three cans into the factory, limiting myself to the ground floor. Outside, I pour another five gallons into the barrack beds, across the downed tents, and into the mess tent.

The Hmong men are safely stowed away. Ryan is back to keeping watch on the mercenaries. I chuck the red gas canister into a pile of canvas as Thomas walks up to me.

"What do we do with them?" He gestures to the Thai police on the ground.

The metal of the gun in my waistband is warm; it has been pressed against my skin for so long. At Thomas's words, the weight of it draws my attention as though it only appeared there once he asked.

There aren't a lot of options.

My gaze is stuck on the horizon. I vaguely notice the men on the ground fidget. Numbness spreads through my hands; my fingers twitch against my leg. A long moment passes.

I reach back and grab the gun. I clench and unclench the rubber grip. My pointer finger is straight. I tap it along the edge of the muzzle.

That's how you do it, only touch the trigger if/when you're ready to shoot.

"Check on the mercs. I'll finish this."

Thomas grabs my arm. "What do you mean, finish this?"

It's only then that I turn my eyes away from the sunrise. I step back and jerk my arm out of his grip.

"You *know* what I mean." I gesture at the men on their knees. "We can't just let them leave. I've thought about other options. There aren't any."

"Belle..." There is a warning tone to his voice.

"I'm doing what needs to be done, Thomas. The same way I did in Zambia. It was fine back then. You didn't have a word to say against it. Why now? Because that was *your* family and this isn't?" I lick my bottom lip and sigh. "None of this can get out. No one can find out these people survived.

What happens when they tell someone? The entire village gets wiped out."

Thomas stares at me for several long moments. His lids are heavy. Weary circles under his eyes are heightened in the odd light of the morning. He grits his teeth. Finally, he nods.

I don't wait. Don't think. My feet carry me around, behind the men. I lift my arm, clench the gun, and squeeze off eight shots.

I hope that none of them knew what was coming. That they remained blissfully unaware of their fates.

I moved quickly at least. There is no need to stir fear in a man about to die.

Thomas turns around and walks away. I watch him go. The muscles in his back are tight, his shoulders straight.

I wait a moment for the muzzle to cool, and then I tuck my gun back into my waistband. It's time for Ryan's project.

He is surprisingly calm. He places the bodies carefully, not mentioning the manner in which the Thai men died, nor complaining about handling the dead. After snapping several shots of the ruined tents, a dead man in the doorway of the barracks, blood seeping into muddy puddles, and the vast factory, he tells me it's time.

I take a road flare from my bag and strike it. Red flames spit from the end. With a glance at the truck full of Hmong men, I toss the flare into a patch of gasoline.

Within seconds, flames seep into the factory. They lick up the walls, lighting up the world with a haze of smoke. Among the cracks and pops of the flames, Ryan's camera is click, click, clicking away. He'll get what he needs.

The fire won't spread outside the encampment. Not with the open dirt between it and a very damp jungle.

Thomas is in the cab of the truck holding the freed Hmong. I hop up into the passenger's seat. A painful spasm shoots through my ribs. I ease back slowly, exhaling in short bursts. The slice in my shoulder burns as it presses against the cushion.

Thomas's tree-trunk torso is leaned up against the edge between the seat and door. His long legs stretch across the floor; my left foot brushes against his shin as I struggle into the chair. Soft snores ease from his wide nostrils.

I don't want to wake him. We've been up for—Jesus—thirty-plus hours? Ryan should be done soon. I had planned on letting him and Thomas take the Hmong back to the village while I drive the mercs to McKinnan... but no, I'm not going to make that drive in my state. Plus, there are two mercenaries in the village I still need to pick up.

Ryan taps on my window, and I gingerly hop back out of the cab. I do a check of the mercs. Then we are on the road. Ryan and Thomas ride together. I chug along behind them with my prisoners. The road is bumpy, and the trek back to the village is very round-about. I furrow my brow and concentrate on the wheel beneath my fingers, the gears beneath my feet, the road beneath the tires.

We leave the dead to the flames.

Chapter Twenty-Six

Lacey

Airport Security

I make a show of checking all the bags. There is *so much* that didn't fit in Nathan's room. His flight leaves first, thank goodness. I walk him to his gate, only two letters and three numbers out of my way.

We say goodbye. It's long, drawn out, and just what you'd find at the end (or beginning) of a Hallmark flick.

I'm on autopilot the whole time. I go through the motions—hugs, tears, vocal expressions of the sureness with which I will miss him.

Lies, basically. A thirty-minute show of lies for all the good people headed to Denver.

I lose twenty pounds of stress when his plane finally boards. My walk back to the New York gate is immensely peaceful. At least, until I get to the food court area.

Delilah is there, facing Jacobson and looking scared. Nothing abnormal there—she always looks scared talking to him. No, the problem here is that her gate is in a totally different section of the airport. And leaves much earlier than his.

We are done at the airport. That's the standard rule. Unless the client pays for the flight (which usually means flying together and continuing services on the plane), our duties are complete as soon as we get through security. So why is he still with her?

I perch on a bar stool, wave off the bartender, and watch them.

He takes her arm. She jerks from his grasp and walks away. He follows. I move as well, keeping him in my sight. She enters the family restroom. As the door is closing, Daniel slips his fingers in the crack, pulls it open, and goes in.

I run, but it takes a good thirty seconds to get there. A lot can happen in thirty seconds. I try the door. Unlocked.

The contents of her purse are scattered across the floor. Jacobson has her up against the wall, his fingers wrapped around her throat. Her small feet barely reach the ground. Equally small hands grasp at his thick arm.

"Admit it!" he spits.

"Hey." My shout is loud enough to get his attention, not loud enough for the outside airport-goers to hear.

He turns to me, releasing Delilah. His eyes blaze with a fury all too recognizable—the fury of a weak man beaten by a strong woman.

"She helped you," he snarls. "She helped you and that rat bastard reporter."

He takes a step. An unfortunate move, really, as it puts him the perfect distance from me.

I shift my body weight, pivot on the ball of my left foot, bring my right knee up, and extend with all the built-up rage I've accumulated through the week. The outside edge of my right foot hits him squarely in the sternum. He flies back with harsh force.

Delilah, choking slightly, but aware enough to hurriedly grab her things, shoves them in her purse then moves to stand beside me.

Daniel recovers a bit, and starts forward again, his hands stretched toward me.

For a split second, I see a different man, a different pair of hands.

Then I'm back. A rapid feint to the left is followed by a throat punch with my right fist. He gags. I kick again. This time he slams backward into the porcelain sink.

I grab Delilah's hand, open the door, and drag her from the room. Back outside, in the corridor full of flyers, everyone is business as usual. I pull Delilah along, which doesn't take much once she gains her footing and actively starts walking with me.

I stop at the first security person I see. In fluent Japanese, I quickly tell him all about the strange white man who asked my friend and me to carry something for him on our flight. I explain how he wanted my friend to take a bag for him. And he wanted me to put several small baggies filled with white powder into my purse. When we vehemently told him "no," he angrily went into the bathroom. We heard loud grunting and ran to find the nearest security guard.

As expected, this leads to a rather large group of strapping security persons snatching Jacobson from the bar he scuttled to after our encounter. His beer smashes on the ground. He pulls the stereotypical American tourist attitude, his voice getting louder and slower with each failed attempt to tell them he has no idea what they are saying.

By the time they round the farthest corner and leave our sight, he is angrily demanding to speak to a manager. It's all I can do not to laugh.

Instead, I turn to Delilah. "You're coming with me."

"What?"

"Let's go."

"But what about having to contact Miss Belle?"

"I'm not letting you go back after what just happened. Jacobson will tell him." I shake my head. "It won't end well."

She nods.

"You have your passport? Or did they give it to Jacobson?"

"Yeah. He wasn't taking the same plane as me. I only have it 'cause this one was in Japan. Last time was near L.A. and they didn't even let me have my ID."

"Good. Follow me."

I lead the way, marching us back through security and to the luggage check-in desks. I pick an airline based out of the States.

The man behind the counter has bags under his eyes. His shirt is wrinkled, the watch face on his wrist scratched, and his hair disheveled. Clearly, a man on the end of a long shift. I hurry up to him.

The smile on my face is genuine.

I offer a greeting, and it is returned. I reach back and tug Delilah's passport from her fingers. Sliding it and mine, across the counter, I say, "We need two tickets on the next flight to Chicago. Please."

CHAPTER TWENTY-SEVEN

MISS BELLE

THE GUILT TRIP

The village reunion is one of those moments. The ones where music swells in the movies. The ones that tug on the ol' heartstrings.

The Hmong men are slow to dismount from the truck. Their eyes dart around, looking for the men who were holding their families hostage. But the hesitation disappears when the first little kid sees his dad. Then it's all running (or limping), hugging, crying, and a good amount of falling in the dirt as children pile onto weak limbs.

A rush of relief makes my fingers tremble as I see the girl, boy, and grandmother from yesterday—it feels like a week ago—find their father.

I leave Thomas to speak with the elders. It turns out that Alang is the husband of Daone, the woman who patched me up.

I have a more onerous task. I get Ryan's help. We drive a little way down the road, then open up the semi-truck. As much as these men probably deserve to be hogtied for the duration of a ten-hour drive—that's about how far it is to their compound—I don't think that would help facilitate good relations in the future.

So, I untie them, one at a time, with Ryan holding a gun to their heads. I use rope and chain I took from the village. Semi-trailers have these massive rings attached to the flooring. They are used for strapping down cargo—which is precisely what I plan on doing.

I tie them six to a ring, backs in the middle, forming little circles. They remain gagged.

It's agonizingly slow work. I could go faster, but as with many things, the faster you go, the higher the risk. There's also the matter of cracked ribs, cuts, and some significant bruising. I lay the injured men, well, the severely injured men, along the back. Their arms and legs are bound in different ways depending on their injuries.

It takes long enough that Thomas joins us about halfway through. I send Ryan to get a bucket of water. He goes through the mercs who are already re-tied and offers them water.

The young ones take it.

Blondie and his equally large and grumpy guys, refuse.

I'll try giving them some more when we get halfway there. I worked too damn hard to keep these guys alive to let them die of dehydration on the way to their boss. It's gonna be hard enough to negotiate after bringing a truck full of prisoners to McKinnan. I have a feeling I'd be eating a bullet if I left him with a truck full of bodies.

I still need to think of what to say about the body we left behind. The mercenary Alang killed.

I glance at my watch. 7:30 a.m. Time doesn't feel real. I pinch the bridge of my nose and squeeze my eyes shut for a brief moment. There is a clatter as Thomas pulls down the truck door and a clacking as he winds a heavy chain around the latch, securing it in place with a massive padlock.

I can feel him watching me as I slowly roll my shoulders back and stretch. I wince as pain stabs at my chest and back.

"We have been invited to eat. Daone insists on feeding you before we leave."

"I'm not going to say no to that. I could eat a hippo."

He shakes his head. "A hippo would eat you, Belle, not the other way around."

I look at him for a moment, then nod, take a very slow and painful deep breath, and head to the Jeep. I grab my go-bag, then hurry back into the village. I use Daone's bathroom before we eat. I wipe the dirt (and as much blood as I can) from my skin and put my jeans back on, as well as a fresh shirt.

I don't taste the food. I inhale it. My tongue burns from the steaming veggies and rice, but I don't care. I eat three platefuls, almost as quickly as the men who came back from the factory.

I sit for a while with my hands folded over my stomach, legs splayed out, face numb. Finally, it's time to go.

Daone takes my hand as Thomas gives Alang and Lis one last goodbye. She presses a small bracelet into my palm, and heat floods my face from my cheeks to the roots of my hair. I give her a sharp nod. She returns it.

Thomas hops into the cab of the semi, starts her up, and chugs down the road toward Bangkok. Ryan and I follow him in the Jeep. I've got to admit, it's a smooth drive.

It's nice being able to just follow Thomas. My mind has that buzzing haze you get after studying for too long. Thoughts and emotions are trying to pierce through. But I don't let them. Not yet. I have to deal with McKinnan, then I can think about what happened.

From my best recollection of the rumors about the place, McKinnan's compound is about ten hours from where we are, maybe an hour or two outside of Thailand's capital. Missa will get me some more precise information when I feel up to calling her. I sent her a quick text, *still alive, got the prisoners out*, that kind of thing. But I need a little while before I have an actual conversation with her.

I lean my head back against the seat and tighten my grip on the steering wheel. I breathe deep, flinching even as I enjoy the crisp morning air.

Almost there. Almost done.

Just a little more.

We drop Ryan at an airport around the halfway mark. I walk in with him, catching some stares at the bandage on my forehead.

We wait for the plane to start boarding. It's a small airport, just a few gates and not much in the way of security.

Ryan clutches his camera between those tender, never-worked-a-day-in-his-life hands. You'd think I'd have softened up toward him after helping us and all. But I haven't forgotten who got us into this mess in the first place. Every time I frown at him, my bullet graze stings.

They announce boarding. It's in Thai, but the meaning is pretty clear. He gives me a nod and turns to get in line. I reach out, snatch the back of his shirt, and drag him toward me.

I shove him against a pillar. Pain pierces my ribs, but I move through it, holding him in place for a moment. A tiny woman with two small children utters a gasp and pulls her little ones toward the plane.

"You will *stick* to the plan. Understand? No going off and doing your own thing. No improvising. You do exactly what I've told you to do."

"Of course!" He's indignant. Like he'd never dream of going off script.

I glare at him and lean in. "I shouldn't need to incentivize you, but you've got a bad track record for following instructions. So, let me tell you this... I've got enough on your mom to destroy her career and put a permanent black mark on your family. Don't fuck this up."

Wide, green eyes, lined and bagged from the fear and strain of the last forty-eight hours, stare at me. It occurs to me that he hasn't considered how his mother knows me. That's going to be an uncomfortable conversation.

He boards the plane. I watch him go, hoping I'll never have to see him again. I head back outside. The muscles in my back burn. I roll my shoulders and wince as the slice in my shoulder blade shrieks at me.

Thomas leans against the Jeep, his thick arms folded over his chest. His eyelids are heavy. The lack of sleep is creeping up on him. It'll hit us both hard soon.

But I can stave it off. I can keep myself awake long enough to get through dealing with McKinnan. I lean against the metal next to Thomas.

"Do you feel better?" he asks.

"What?"

"Our talk earlier, you said what you do may not be worth it. Do you feel better after saving all those lives?"

I open my mouth, pause, and close it again. Finally, I nod. "I feel more worthwhile. I know what I do is important. I know I help a lot of people. But at the same time, when I get home, I've got to deal with Lacey. This job took a real toll on her."

"Your guides volunteer for what they do. You do not force them—" He holds up a hand as I open my mouth again. "And you do not *guilt* them into working for you."

I sigh. "It's hard to say no sometimes. After pulling people out of the messes they get trapped in... It's hard to say no to me. I know that."

He puts a hand on my arm. "My sister said no. She felt no guilt when she turned down your offer."

I stare at him for a moment.

When we rescued his little sister from the warlord's complex, she had a fury in her like nothing I'd seen. She could have gone a couple of different ways. My way—aggression, violence, retribution, wasn't right for her. And neither was the common (and understandable) reaction of falling into depression and despair. Instead, the young woman, barely sixteen at the time, created a program for girls who are victims of abuse. With a little funding—from an unnamed source—she now has three schools dedicated to training girls in education and self-defense. She works with local police departments to train recruits to understand the dangers girls face and combat them without bias. They also work to educate the men and boys in the area how to treat women.

If she weren't in Africa, she'd have been *Time's* person of the year at least once.

"Yeah." I nod. "But not everyone is as strong as your sister."

"Do not discount the choices people make for themselves. You do good, Belle. A lot of good."

I give him a little smile and watch as a plane takes off. We stand in silence for a while. I pull an apple out of the Jeep and eat it on the hood.

"It's a long way to McKinnan's complex," he says.

"I know." A yawn steals its way out of my mouth.

"Will you make the drive?"

"Yeah. I can do it."

He shakes his head. "You'd think you would know how to ask for help by now."

I step away from the Jeep and face him. "What's that supposed to mean? I *did* ask for help. And you helped."

"Get in the truck."

"You've got to drive your Jeep home. And I don't want you there when I talk to McKinnan. It needs to be a one on one conversation." I don't say it, but I especially don't want him there if it goes badly.

"I called Ben while you were in the airport. There is a diner an hour away from the complex where you can drop me off. He'll pick me up."

I heave a sigh and nod. "Fine. But I'll drive the first shift. You get some sleep."

"I won't fight you on that." He locks the Jeep—a bit of a silly move in a car with no roof—and hops into the passenger side of the truck.

I climb up, put the monster of a vehicle in gear, and we are on our way. Thomas falls asleep within minutes. I hook up a pair of headphones to my cell and call Nicky. For about the twentieth time his phone rings once and then goes to voicemail. I leave the same message I've left every time I've called.

"Nicky. It's me. Obviously. Listen, I can explain that picture if you'd just give me a chance. Call me back. Love you."

I sigh in frustration and call Missa. She fills me in on the stuff I've missed.

Everything went well with the blackmail; by the end of business Monday, the VP will have pulled support for his bigotry bill. Damen is taking a month or so off of work; apparently, he's headed into Brooklyn for the week. Lacey made her flight. She'll be home soon and has an appointment with Doc scheduled for tomorrow. There's something else, something Missa isn't telling me about Lacey's mission, but I'll get it out of her when I get home.

Missa is dealing with Lacey's security problem. She gets along with those two better than I do. Then again—she gets along with pretty much everyone better than I do.

"Thanks again for dealing with everything, Missa."

"I don't know why you always thank me. It's literally my job. We work together; that's the whole deal."

"It's nice to be appreciated," I grumble.

There is a decent-sized pause, long enough that I take my eyes from the road to see if the call dropped.

"I don't like you going in there alone," Missa finally says.

"I'm not dragging Thomas in with me. The factory was different. This is going to be a matter of my negotiation skills. I don't want to risk his life like that." I throw a chuckle onto the end of my sentence. Like it's a joke.

But it's not.

Missa doesn't laugh. "You are a skilled negotiator."

"I can't bring a gun with me this time."

"That's not funny."

"I'm not joking. This kind of thing is loads easier when I'm the one with a weapon."

There is a huff, almost a laugh, or maybe she's just sighing at me. "I've been asking around about McKinnan. You'll need to bring your A game to the table with him."

"Do you have the account info we need?"

"I will as soon as Lacey lands. Levi is picking her up from the airport."

"Good." I like negotiating. I'm not bad at it. But it's a hell of a lot easier when you're working with a full deck.

"Be careful, Belle. Please. I know you're having a rough time right now, but... be careful."

"Don't worry about me. I feel better."

It's true. Watching families reunite is a good way to make a person feel like what they do has value.

"I'm glad." Her voice carries hesitation like she doesn't quite believe me.

"Can you get Lacey a ticket to California? For the end of the week. I still need to call them and let them know she's coming out."

"Sure. Call me when you drop off Thomas."

"I'll call you when I finish talking to McKinnan."

"Ana—"

"I'll call you after McKinnan. Love ya, Missa."

"Yeah." She sighs. "Love you too."

Going home can be bittersweet after a fun journey. But it can also be a blessed relief. If you've used your time well, done the things you wanted to do, explored new places, met new people, etc., then coming home can feel like the perfect end to your trip.

Try to make sure you have a couple of days back home before you have to return to work, school, or whatever. Once you've settled back in, get in contact with those friends you made while you were gone. Try cooking one of the meals you enjoyed. Print out a couple of your favorite pictures. But most of all, enjoy being home.

Chapter Twenty-Eight

Lacey

Snickerdoodles

The flight to Chicago is uneventful. Delilah is quiet. She tears up the *Sky-Mall* magazine. We have a short layover, lucky with how last minute the flight was purchased. But a quick two hours in JFK gives us enough time to get through customs and grab some food, and gives me time to book a ticket from Chicago back to JFK on my phone.

The taxi driver looks a little confused by the lack of luggage, but he doesn't say anything as we climb in, and I provide him with the address from memory. I stayed at this house for the first three months after leaving Houston. The building is as I remember: red bricks, cloudy windows with graying trim, a vast garden that dies almost entirely in the winter. Right now, however, it is blossoming with the promise of a fruitful spring.

It's chilly in Chicago. Smoke rises from the chimney. The stone pathway leading to the front door is partially concealed by overgrown ivy dangling from a wicker arch.

Erin meets us at the front door. Her smile does little to reassure Delilah, but that will change. I promise a phone call within the day and bid them both goodbye. I climb back into the idling taxi, and we make the return trip to the airport. I watch Chicago pass me by during the forty-five-minute drive.

Some would complain about the size of the city, the amount of traffic, the cold. I don't mind them. I've always enjoyed the cold; heat reminds me of Texas.

Delilah is safe. Safe holed up with Erin. If anyone can take care of her until Miss Belle's return, it's Erin. She's one of the primary educators used by the Guides during our training year. I owe her much.

I owe a lot of people.

I call Chang while I wait for the plane to dock at the gate. I thank him for his help this week. He reminds me to put in a good word with Miss Belle, and this time I actually mean it when I tell him I will.

My head hurts. My heart hurts. My body hurts.

I board the plane. I sink into my chair. A pair of headphones bleed *The Night We Met* by Lord Huron into my head. I reach up and take the bobby pins out of my hair. Dark strands fall around my face. I snuggle into my cardigan.

The flight home is quiet and short. I doze on and off, trying not to fall into a deep sleep. That's where the nightmares are.

At long last, the tires thump against the pavement in New York. It's done. I'm home. First class means the front of the plane, but I don't want to get off. I want to sit a while longer, the noise of the engines dulling my thoughts.

I swing my bag over my shoulder and take my time walking through the baggage claim to the exit.

Levi is sitting in the Prius right next to the door. He gives the horn a little beep-beep when he sees me. The corner of my mouth twitches up. It's hard not to love Levi. He is older than us, older than Miss Belle, but one of her best. Since my first day in the Manor, he's treated me like a little sister. It shouldn't be a surprise that he volunteered to come to pick me up.

"Hey, darlin'," his southern twang sings to me as I open the door and climb in.

"You didn't have to come get me; I know I threw the schedule off."

"I didn't mind the extra few hours. Gave me the opportunity to grab lunch with a cute bartender I met last week."

He winks, and I think he probably grabbed more than lunch.

"Well," I smile over at him, "thanks for coming to get me."

" 'Course." He pulls away from the curb and slides into traffic. "How're you holding up?"

I shrug one shoulder.

"You know Missa scheduled you an appointment with Doc."

I don't say anything, but he must feel the slight shift in air pressure as I grind my teeth in frustration.

"It's standard practice for an assignment like this. You know that."

"Yeah." I stare out the window.

"It doesn't mean she or Miss Belle think any less of you."

"They should."

He hits the brakes a little harder than necessary as we come to a red light. "What do you mean, 'they should'? That's some bullshit."

I shake my head as he stares at me. "I wanted to come back early." I bite down on my tears. "I almost wrecked the mission."

"Don't be ridiculous." He moves us forward as the light goes green. "We've all had one time or another where we wanted to come home early. That's natural. Especially with such a difficult assignment."

I shake my head again. He's just trying to make me feel better. I've *never* heard about anyone else needing to leave early.

"How do you think I felt when I went back to Alabama? Had to spend *three weeks* in the same town as my homophobic, piece-of-shit brother? You remember he gave me this," he points to the gnarled scar behind his right ear, "when I was twelve? And I had to go back there and deal with him. You think Miss Belle didn't schedule an appointment with Doc for me when I got back?"

He gives me a sidelong glance. "It's standard practice, Lacey. They wouldn't be doing you any favors letting you not talk about it."

I nod, but turn away from him. Whatever Levi says, I almost gave up on my mission, and my stomach burns just thinking about it. That, plus taking Delilah to the safehouse without permission... I feel like I'm about to be grounded.

Missa is waiting out front when we pull up to the Manor. Levi parks and takes my bag in the house. I hesitate at the steps.

Missa shakes her head and hurries down to me. She wraps her arms around me tight, and I bury my face in her golden hair. She whispers in my ear, "I'm so glad you're home." There is a pause, then even quieter, "You did the right thing. I'm very proud of you."

I relax, wrap my arms around her slender, tall torso and squeeze, inhaling the comforting scent of her rose oil. The physical contact, the safety of her arms, her words, are enough to relieve what feels like pounds of pressure.

Then a man's deep voice sounds behind me and the muscles in my back clench. "What's wrong with her?"

I freeze. Missa gently releases me and pulls me a little behind her.

I am only slightly relieved to see that the voice comes from a large-waisted man with a badge on his belt. My mind heard someone different.

"Nothing at all, Detective."

He ignores Missa and eyes me. "Getting back from a trip?"

Missa's hand is still on my arm, and she opens her mouth to answer for me, but my training takes over.

I force as genuine a smile as possible across my face. "Yes! I just had a lovely research trip to Tokyo. You know, preparing for Miss Belle's next book." I meet his eye and hold his gaze until he looks away.

"Right. It just looked like something was wrong." He stares at Missa.

She grins at him as well. "Nope. Just welcoming her home. So nice of you to keep an eye on us, though." Her gaze slides away from him and lands on the gray van parked across the street.

My grin grows as the detective's chunky cheeks turn a rosy tomato color. I turn to Missa. "I'm going to go unpack."

She nods. "I'll be in in a minute. I want to have a word with our dear detective."

My smile disappears as I go into the Manor. Cops out front—that's never a good sign. I give Anita a small wave as I pass her in the living room. Sarah waits for me in the kitchen, a big smile on her face and a plate full of snickerdoodles in her hands. My favorite.

She makes them for me after every assignment.

I tell her thanks and kiss her on the cheek. Then I put six of the cookies in a napkin and abandon the rest of the house in favor of my room.

I climb the first set of stairs and enter the second door on the left. Pale pinks and greens drape over and around my double bed. The walls are eggshell blue with different flowers painted on that I add whenever the urge strikes me. Pastel colors everywhere. My bookshelf is full, and a few small stacks of hardcovers in the corner of the room remind me that I need to get another one.

I set the cookies on my bedside table next to a small stack of books, close the curtains on the huge window, and collapse into my sheets. A dreamless sleep engulfs me.

Chapter Twenty-Nine

Miss Belle

The Congo

Remember that feeling you used to get on Christmas or your birthday? That hope before you'd opened your last present that maybe, just maybe, you'd get that bike, or puppy, or kitten, or—hell—pony, for you overachievers. I like to think I have that level of unbridled optimism regarding most things in our world. It comes from a steadfastly middle-class upbringing and being white in America.

Upon approaching the mercenary compound, I feel that optimism dripping away like the oil in my first car (a 1995 Saturn that, judging by the smell, had at one point been stolen by a group of angry, homeless, horny, cats).

The compound is what I expected. Large and fenced in, multiple buildings nestled together, watchtowers along the border, and a massive rolling front gate. A small gatehouse with dusty windows sits just on the other side of the chain-link. Everything is brown. The trees and brush have been cleared away. Logical—makes it hard to sneak up on the compound. Even inside, from what I can see, there isn't much color to speak of.

I pull up to the front gate and let the truck idle for a moment. The sun is getting ready to dip below the tallest of the buildings. I take a few deep breaths. My heart beats at a rapid flutter.

I clench my hand and swallow. I need to calm down. After a mission like the one we just had—guns blazing, fire, pain—it takes more than a few hours to get back into a normal state of mind. Not that I should be entirely back to normal just yet. Paranoia is a vital gift to hold onto when you're dealing with dangerous men. But there's a difference between the kind of paranoia that can save your life and the kind that can get you killed.

There is movement on one of the watchtowers. I reach up, separate the hair in my ponytail, and tug it tighter. Then I roll down the window and place both hands on the steering wheel. A moment passes.

Three large men emerge from the gatehouse. Each looks like they are trying to win the Mr. America pageant. All three carry M16s. The tallest is blond and looks somewhat familiar; a long machete hangs from his waist. Another is maybe Hispanic. It's hard to tell through the *Top Gun* sunglasses he has on.

The most oafish looking of them—which isn't saying much—opens up a smaller, door-sized section of the gate I hadn't noticed before.

He walks to the driver's side door and glares up at me. "This is private property."

The smartass in me wants to say, "No shit." The smart-without-the-ass part of me nods. "I understand. I have a delivery for McKinnan."

The man's eyes widen just a touch. Just enough for me to know McKinnan is here.

"No one here by that name."

I nod again. "I get that you have to say that, but I know he's here and it's really important that I speak to him."

He is silent for a moment. Then he gestures to the back of the truck with the end of his M16. "What's in the truck?"

I blow out a little air. "I need to talk to McKinnan."

"This truck ain't moving another inch 'til I see what's in the back."

I tilt my head to the right just a little. My tone is braver than I actually feel. "I'm not showing you what's in the back until I talk to McKinnan."

He looks at the other two. When his gaze meets mine again, he raises his gun and points it at my forehead. "Step out of the truck."

I do so, slowly. Adrenaline is an excellent pain reliever. But as soon as things calm down, the pain comes back full force. Sunglasses comes over and frisks me. I cringe as he pats my ribcage. He notices and uses a softer touch on the rest of me, which is as appreciated as it is strange.

I'm not a moron, so all he finds are the car keys and my cell. A few more mercenaries have trickled over from the complex. They stand in a little cluster on the other side of the fence.

The blond guy takes the keys from Sunglasses.

"I really should talk to McKinnan before you open that," I interject.

"Is it booby trapped?" The blond's voice is deep, but not the creamy deep that Thomas has. It's more like he's trying to hold in a burp while he's talking.

He's not winning any awards for brains over here, asking me a question like that.

"No. But I'd like to explain the contents before he sees it."

He heads around the truck anyway, until the first man calls him back.

"She could be lying." He shoots me a glance that's half suspicion and half exasperation. "Let's get McKinnan down here. He can decide what to do with her."

He shouts at the group on the other side of the fence. One of them takes off toward the tallest of the buildings.

"I don't like waiting." The blond glares at the first guy. "Plus, you're not the boss of me."

The smartass side of me opens my mouth. I firmly close it and press my lips together.

The blond guy walks to the rear, and I hear the key go into the padlock. Shit. I take a couple of steps away from the truck.

Sunglasses notices this and puts a hand up. "Wait!"

He's too late. Metal grinds against metal as the blond undoes the latch and slides up the door.

There is silence for a moment. I take another half-step toward the front of the truck.

His deep, confused voice is loud enough for the men on the other side of the fence to hear. "What the fuck..."

There's a fear, instilled in all women at a certain age. Sometimes it takes longer; some girls don't recognize the emotion until they're sixteen or seventeen, some are forced to realize their fear at a horrifyingly young age. But most women begin to feel that uncomfortable itch around certain men at about twelve years old.

We force it down. We hide it until it flares up to protect us from that one guy at work, or the trainer at the gym, or the creepy relative. Some women don't force it down. They are constantly wary, and quite often treated like paranoid psychos for it. Some women push it down so far that when something does happen, they don't even recognize it as abuse.

It's hard, nearly impossible to describe. It goes beyond that chill up your spine in a dark alley. It's a subtle sense of dread. The knowledge, however slight, that you're in the presence of someone who will take pleasure in hurting you.

I have that feeling now. That feeling that if this goes wrong, many horrible things will happen to me before I die.

More incentive (I guess) to make sure things go according to plan.

Who am I kidding? Nothing ever goes according to plan.

My back slams into the hot metal grate of the engine block. A yelp escapes my lips as the slice in my back opens under the bandages. Sunglasses has his hand on my chest just below my collar bone.

I swallow and try to get my breathing under control. My palms sweat, my blood pounds, and fear pumps through me.

"Get some fucking bolt cutters!" the blond practically screams from the back of the truck.

You'd think they were all bleeding out or something.

The mercenaries on the other side of the fence scramble to slide open the rolling chain-link. Someone runs forward with the requested cutters.

I take a step forward. Sunglasses shoves me back again. The pain in my ribs sends a sharp ring through my ears. I take a couple of shallow breaths, trying to manage the pain. He pulls a handgun from his hip and points it at my gut. "Don't move."

I clench my jaw. This is going downhill a lot faster than I thought it would.

The men are making quite a commotion in the back. After a few minutes of mutters, grunts, and incoherent words, the blond guy steps around the truck and makes his way toward me.

He is holding up Blondie.

Shit. That's why the man looks so familiar. They must be cousins or something.

"What did you do to my brother?" he shouts.

Not cousins.

"He's fine. Just a little dehydrated. He'd be feeling better if he'd taken the water I offered him."

Sunglasses' mouth twitches at my defensive tone. To be fair, Blondie (older Blondie) is ashen-faced, clammy, and sagging a bit against his brother.

"She..." He licks his lips.

Should have taken my water. Idiot.

He tries again. "She ki—" He breaks down coughing.

I'm suddenly glad he didn't take the water. Something tells me he was about to inform them about the merc who didn't make it.

"Where's Lucas?" someone asks.

Blondie points at me. I swallow. So much for that.

Fingers tighten around gun grips—a few twitch toward triggers. Only Sunglasses keeps a steady hand. A steady hand with a muzzle pointed at me.

"What's going on out here?" A gruff, thick voice reaches us from a figure marching toward the truck.

McKinnan stacks up to his reputation. He is a big man. Tall, but also broad, though not with the same muscular definition many of his men have. He looks like someone pulled him through time from a 1900 expedition into the rainforest. From the bushy, dirty-blond, handlebar mustache to the odd safari get-up complete with butterfly sword and knee-high canvas boots, he is both frightening and laughable.

I'm definitely not laughing.

"This one." Sunglasses steps to the side, gesturing toward me with his free hand. "Our men are in the truck. From the Jacobson job. Lucas is missing."

McKinnan sizes me up. There isn't much to look at. I've got no makeup on, leaving my bruised face complete with a poorly bandaged bullet graze, unhappily exposed, my hair is in a moderately ratty ponytail, my jeans are somewhat clean, and my black T-shirt isn't what you'd call low cut. His eyes linger at my chest a second longer than necessary anyway. He looks over Blondie.

"Dehydrated. Get him and the rest some food and water."

"A few need medical attention," I interject.

He flicks his gaze in my direction before looking back at his men. "Get them cared for. I think Miss Belle and I need to have a little conversation."

I raise an eyebrow.

"You've got quite a reputation, Miss Belle. I know what you look like. Though..." he sweeps his massive hand—roughly the size of a small dinner plate—across the truck and his men. "I can't say this is what I expected for the first time I'd meet you."

"You're going to *talk* to her?" the younger of the blond brothers demands.

"We should be finding out what happened to Lucas. Then she should die," the man who first spoke to me says.

A shiver runs down my back, but I keep my face still.

"I'm going to talk to her." McKinnan's voice has taken on a dangerous tone. "Take care of our men."

There is a general grinding of teeth. But everyone is silent. I can't tell if it's fear keeping them quiet, or the knowledge that nothing they say will change his mind. From what I can see, he isn't packing—apart from the butterfly sword.

He turns toward the compound and gives a lazy wave. A mercenary, the size of your standard WWE fighter gone Hollywood grips my upper arm. He goes to pull me forward, but I'm already walking, essentially dragging him along as he still has my arm.

We follow McKinnan across the open ground. The largest building is also the first in the complex. Only three stories high, it is surprisingly vast. Stepping inside illuminates the reason. A massive courtyard takes up the middle. Benches, trees, bushes, and flowers line the walkways. Several fountains send the sound of dribbling water through the air. No walls block the first floor from the oasis in the center. Clay-red pillars stand at even intervals along the edges where indoors meets outdoors.

The merc tugs at my arm. I'm enamored with the beautiful scene before me, so carefully hidden in this dust-colored building. We go right, through a thick wooden door and up two sets of stairs. Anxiety grasps at my chest. Adrenaline pumps through my veins. Only a near decade of training stops me from a wild, and likely fatal, escape attempt.

I'm here for a reason. I'm here to do a job. This is part of the plan.

The thought is only mildly reassuring.

We reach a set of double doors on the third floor, also made of wood, but much more intricate. McKinnan may have his men bunk in tents on assignment, but he clearly has a specific and expensive style. He pushes the doors open and holds the left side for me. The merc releases my arm, trades a look with McKinnan, and stations himself outside the office.

I catch a glimpse of him pulling out a handgun before the wooden door meets its partner with a gentle thud.

A massive mahogany desk—I assume it's mahogany; to me, any fancy dark wood is mahogany—takes up a quarter of the room. It's neat, organized without looking empty. A black desktop monitor somehow matches the ebony and ivory bookends on the bookcase behind the desk. An antelope head, with full antlers, hangs from the wall on the far side of the room. It rests directly over a large glass and wood display case featuring an assortment of ancient hunting rifles. I am comfortably knowledgeable about guns, but these are way outside my range of expertise.

Old maps, many of them of the Congo, adorn the wall across from the window. Based on Missa's intel—which is almost always spot on—that's where McKinnan got his start in the mercenary sector, working for the highest bidder during the second civil war. There was some nasty stuff going on during that time. A lot of corruption, a lot of civilian death, a lot of opportunities for an ex-Ranger to make his mark as a ruthless killer. McKinnan has spent the last twenty years building his reputation and his company. He comes to the States now and then, collecting contracts from the government.

He hasn't done any of his own jobs in quite a while, but the man still has hands on every mission his company contracts. Well, he used to. I find it hard to believe he had much to do with the security disaster that was the factory compound.

I face McKinnan. The window to my left is tinted on the outside. It limits the light coming in but gives the orange sunset in the distance a subtle dim glow.

"What in the hell are you doing here? And what happened to Lucas?"

McKinnan steps behind his desk, gestures to one of the black and brown leather-cushioned wooden chairs before it, and settles into his own, larger, leather-bound chair.

I take a deep breath, meet his eye, and say, "Lucas is dead. I'm here to come to an arrangement. To ensure no revenge is taken for the life lost and to compensate you for the damage done to men, equipment, and pride over the last twenty-four hours."

He stares at me for a long time. Finally, he strokes his bristly mustache and says, "Sit."

I sit.

"Lucas was one of my best. How did he die?"

"We had the rest of your men captured. He took a hostage."

McKinnan nods. "He told you to let my men go."

"And I told him to release the boy. He did not."

"How did you kill him?"

My foot twitches, and I catch myself just before letting out a sigh. I have to tell him the truth. His men all saw Alang take the shot. "I didn't. One of the Hmong being held prisoner took the shot. His father was a marksman during the war. Taught him how to defend their village."

He nods again. Then stares at me. My anxious tongue wants to chatter away, find a solution, fix this as quickly as possible. But some things need more finesse.

I bite the inside of my lip. Finesse is Missa's forte, not mine. The wait is excruciating, but I manage it.

McKinnan is the one who finally breaks the silence. "Why shouldn't I go kill the man who killed Lucas? Even the scales."

I briefly clench my jaw before forcing my features into a more neutral expression. "The scales are already pretty uneven in *your* favor. Many men from the village died on their way to that factory and during the first week. Not to mention the fatalities *in* the village while the men were gone."

A slight tilt of the head tells me that McKinnan was unaware of this. So, he really *didn't* have hands on this operation.

Interesting.

I lean forward, rest my elbows on my knees and fold my fingers in front of me. I meet his serious gaze with a somber one. "It is something close to a miracle that so many of your men survived."

"Injured."

"How pissed would you be if I brought you a truck full of uninjured men? They did their job. I did mine better."

"I'd like to hear about that. About how a madam, a woman who runs a house of international escorts, managed to pull this off. What are you doing out here?"

I bob my head up and down a little bit. "There are definitely a few things you'll want to know about. But I'd like to come to an arrangement first."

"You're concerned about my operation coming after you."

I shake my head. "I'd prefer for you not to come after me, but my real concern is the village. Jacobson paid you to destroy it. Obviously, that hasn't happened. I need to make sure it doesn't happen."

"You have no concerns for your own wellbeing, Miss Belle?"

I give him a humorless smile. "Oh, I have plenty of concerns for my wellbeing. Your reputation for never leaving a job unfinished is... impressive. I'm asking you to not only leave a mission incomplete, but also to restrain your men from destroying the village for their own reasons."

"Putting aside the death of my man, and the humiliation of the rest, why would I risk my future contracts like that?"

"I've worked out a way to convince Jacobson that the job is done. He and the people he works with will be convinced that you've accomplished what they paid you for."

There is silence for a moment. McKinnan pulls a small wooden box across the table toward him and fiddles with the lid. "How?"

I lick my bottom lip and rub my sweaty palms on my jeans. "I burned the factory to the ground. Its destruction was well documented. The Thai police involved—"

"Thai police?"

I meet his gaze, not letting my surprise at this question register on my face. "Yes. The Thai police Jacobson hired to help your men."

Something dark flashes across his weathered features. His nostrils flare, and the hand on the box tightens quickly before relaxing again. "Go on."

"The Thai police involved did not survive the incursion. They were... strategically placed when everything burned. My photos look very much as though many lives were lost."

"And you think the photos will be enough?"

I bob my head in confirmation. "I think the photos, combined with your word that the job got done, will be enough. In a matter of days, Jacobson will have plenty to deal with. He won't be looking into anything outside his lawyer's office."

McKinnan tilts his head.

I answer the unasked question. "A set of photos, as well as the story of a slaughtered village of people who had previously been used for slave labor by an American company, is going to land on the editor's desk of *The New York Times.*"

"That will point the finger back at me. Jacobson will know where the photos came from."

I shake my head. "When you give Jacobson the pictures, assure him that all other digital copies have been deleted. He'll leave them on his office computer, which will be broken into."

"How do you know they'll be in his office?"

"Because he's a moron."

McKinnan raises his eyebrows and nods in a "yeah, he is" kind of way.

There is another pause—longer this time.

"And when they check the village? When a huddle of reporters go in for confirmation?"

"The exact location of the village is not going to be shared. It's far enough from the factory remains that I don't anticipate problems. Beyond that, the Thai government has been... encouraged to release the discovery of human remains, suggestive of a fire, along the border of Laos."

Thanks to Missa's diplomatic abilities, ties in Bangkok, and skill with storytelling.

"The government's release will confirm the story in *The New York Times*, and they'll be limiting access to the area. Which is another reason Jacobson will be convinced you've handled your end. Though by then, he'll be preoccupied."

There is another bout of silence. McKinnan watches me until I get that itchy feeling that accompanies being stared at. But I'm not about to look away first.

His fingers drum against the desk until he finally speaks. "You've got quite a lot of this all worked out. How did you know I wouldn't just shoot you when I saw my men?"

I grimace. "Because, *unlike* your men, I was pretty sure you'd ask some questions before you started shooting."

"That's quite a chance to take." His tone hasn't changed, but the darkness in his eyes intensifies. The sun has dipped below the horizon. Though the office is lit, it feels several degrees colder.

A shiver runs down my spine. I continue taking even breaths, but I have to pinch my leg to get a handle on my fear. I remain silent.

A tinkling jingle fills the air. It's familiar. McKinnan reaches into a pocket, and my stomach drops as I recognize the sound. It's my phone, the ringtone I use for unknown numbers.

He gives me a wary look. Understandable—this could be a call to trigger an explosive device, it could be to confirm a kill, it could be to bring in backup... it could be a lot of things.

He holds up the device to show me the number displayed on the little screen on the front. Once I see the area code, I know who it will be. I blink, feeling an eye twitch starting up.

"Dangerous?"

I take a deep breath. "Not for you."

He squints at me but sets the phone on the desk and lets it ring out. "So, we've established how I'll be maintaining my reputation. I'm going to go out on a limb and assume you're the reason Jacobson cut his contract short in the first place?"

I nod.

"Well, that cost us quite a bit of—"

He breaks off as the jingle starts up again.

"How about we turn off that ringer?" I grin weakly, my nerves reaching the breaking point.

He reaches over and presses the volume button on the side until the ringing stops. Almost immediately, the phone goes off again, vibrating loudly across the desk. I bend forward and rub my forehead. This is a fucking nightmare.

The vibrating stops abruptly, and I look up. McKinnan is holding my cell again. He flips it open and puts it to his ear. "Hello?"

"*Who is this? Where's my daughter?*" The angry voice of my mother rings out surprisingly clearly through the little speaker.

I wince and reach out my hand.

McKinnan raises an eyebrow at me. "Who is *this*?" he says into the phone.

"Put my daughter on the phone. Now."

He places the cell in my hand. I flash an apologetic smile and hold up a "just a sec" finger, then mouth "sorry" as I put the phone to my ear.

"Hi, Mom, now is *not* the best time. Also," I grit my teeth in frustration, "how did you get this number?"

"How *dare* you, young lady!"

My mother's voice is so loud McKinnan's eyes widen substantially. She doesn't give me a chance to respond, and instead, launches into an angry rant.

"I have been trying to get ahold of you all weekend. We did *not* raise you to be a bigot. How could you treat your brother this way? It's unacceptable. When did you decide to lose your morals?" —the irony of that one is not lost on me— "You need to call Nicky and apologize immediately!"

"*Ma!*" I shout into the phone.

McKinnan stands, walks to the bar in the corner of the room, and pours himself a glass of something from an ornately decorated bottle.

I lower my voice and cup my hand around the phone. "Mom, I can't get into this with you right now. I will call you in a few days."

I swear I can hear her signature head shake and pursed lips. "That's not good enough. You need to fix this with your brother."

"I'm very aware, Mother. I've tried him about fifty times. He won't answer me."

"Well, I'll call him next, so you just better try again. He'll pick up next time if he doesn't want to deal with an angry mother."

"Yeah, no one wants to deal with an angry you, Ma. I gotta go. I promise I'll call you in a few days."

"Sure, hon. Oh, by the way, your father was telling me about this reunion coming up. I think you should—"

"Gotta go, Ma, 'bye!"

I hang up mid-goodbye. Honestly, you say you have to go, and she launches into a *War and Peace*-length story.

I glance up at McKinnan. He stands, leaning against his bar, drink in hand, and a sardonic smile peeking out from under his mustache.

"Sorry about that," I say weakly. "Parents." I gesture vaguely.

He nods. "I understand."

"Right." I stand—the effort of which sends a sharp pain through my ribs—and join him at the bar. He goes to grab another glass, but I wave it away. "We were discussing how much your company lost because this contract was cut short."

He takes a drink. Amber liquid sloshes up against his sand-colored whiskers. "You cost us quite a bit of money."

"Give me a number. You'll get paid."

An eyebrow raises, and an incredulous smirk crosses his lips. "This is real money I'm talking about, Miss Belle. Not the kind you earn from a night with a john. Where do you plan on getting that kind of cash?"

I let out a little chuckle. "Jacobson is about as security conscious with his bank account information as he is with damning evidence of criminal activity. You can give him the option to pay you if you'd like. If he doesn't concede..." I shrug. "You can take what you want."

It's his turn to chuckle. "All right. What about you? Surely you'll be wanting a portion?"

"My income stems from a different revenue source."

He gives me a long stare. "I like the way you work. You aren't what I was expecting."

"I get that a lot."

"So, I think the last piece of business is what to do about my man."

I nod. "Lucas."

"His body wasn't in the truck."

I meet his eye. "I didn't think forcing your men to travel with a dead comrade was a good way to ensure a positive relationship. But I know where he is. We laid him out a good ways from the factory and covered his body. I can give you the location. And I'm more than happy to pay reparations and funeral costs as well as a year's salary for any family he left behind."

McKinnan turns from me again and walks to the desk. He faces the maps on the wall, silent for several minutes.

I work to keep myself quiet. My lack of patience is not a desirable trait in situations like this.

I'm curious about what is going through his mind as he stares at those old maps. They aren't decorative. They're war maps. Stained, ripped, and marked with plans for death. Is he remembering other fallen friends? Thinking about missions gone wrong? Acts of vengeance followed through?

"There was a time," he says, "when I'd have had to demand an exchange. A tit for tat. A body for a body."

My blood runs cold, and a flash of icy fury pierces my heart. I dig my nails into my palms. "Mr. McKinnan, let me make this perfectly clear." I struggle to keep my voice steady. "You're *not* getting one of my girls."

He turns to me, and something in my clenched jaw and cold eyes makes him start to take a step back. Instead, he reaches forward and opens the box on his desk. He pulls out a thick, dark cigar and clips the end.

As he lights it up, I force my fingers to unclench and smooth the uneasy look on my face. "I'd think you could consider the dead Hmong reparation enough for your man. They lost far more than you did."

The distinct scent of a Gurkha cigar fills the air. If I'm not mistaken, it's a Churchill Maduro. Expensive and pungent.

He opens his mouth, and a swirl of smoke obscures his features for a second. "My men might not find that to be enough."

"They're *your* men. If you tell them it's enough..."

He meets my eye. "If one of your girls was killed, would it be enough?"

I inhale deeply. "My girls don't run slave encampments."

"Don't pretend you're better than me, Miss Belle. Neither one of us works in what you'd call a reputable business."

"Very true." I bow my head in acknowledgment. "But we don't kill innocent people."

His eyebrow raises at the same time that I realize I've worded that poorly.

"What I mean to say, is that the situations would never be the same."

"If they were... would it be enough?"

I clench my jaw and take a long moment, thinking over my words. "If it had to be."

He puts the cigar back between his lips and gives it a pull. Silence lingers in the air with the smoke. He's thinking. I can see it in the way he holds the cigar, in the way his fingers tap along the hilt of his sword as he paces back and forth in front of those maps. Finally, he stops and turns to me. "Sounds like you've thought of everything."

"That's my job."

The silence stretches between us once more. He takes a few more puffs of the cigar, crosses to the bar, drains his glass, and looks back at me.

"Once we get paid... the slate is clear."

"Thank you." I fold my hands together. "Your men can't tell anyone about this. Jacobson *needs* to think the village has been destroyed. Or he will find someone else to go in and kill those people."

"You don't have to worry about that. My men don't blab about our operations, especially failed ones. They'll be more worried about *you* telling people what happened."

"They don't need to be."

"I can see that." He puffs on his cigar for another moment. I watch him in silence. "Well, it sounds like we've got ourselves a deal."

"And your men won't come after the village or my agency?"

"You have my word."

I nod. We take care of logistics. I give him a timeframe for getting the photos and account info. A short while later, everything is worked out and finalized. We shake hands. He gets his man in the hallway to fetch my keys.

When the oversized WWE fill-in returns and I pocket the keys, I turn to McKinnan. He has settled himself comfortably leaning against the desk, dipping the end of his cigar in the liquid that fills his crystal glass before putting it in his mouth once again. He speaks around the cigar, putting the finishing touch on sounding exactly how he looks. "I still need to hear how you managed to take the compound."

I give a half chuckle, which sends a rush of pain signals from my ribs to my brain and nod. "Next time you're in the States. We can grab a scotch and discuss it."

"I look forward to it." He gives a little nod, and I move toward the hallway.

The tense knots in my stomach loosen slightly. Then I hear his voice once more.

"Miss Belle..."

My chest tightens, throat catching as fear grips me.

I turn back to see him standing next to the desk, cigar in one hand, the other resting on the hilt of his butterfly sword. "If you ever decide on a career change, give me a call." He gives me a wink and another incline of his head.

I can't help the smallest of grins as I head to the truck. I pull out of the compound, not meeting the eye of any of the mercenaries. Their boss may be fine with our plan, but until these guys get filled in, I'm just someone who kicked the shit out of a bunch of their brothers.

And killed one.

CHAPTER THIRTY

MISS BELLE

GINGER AUSTRALIANS

Thomas is still at the diner. His plate of food is untouched.

I slide into the booth across from him. "Waiting for someone?"

His dark eyes meet mine. He glares for a moment. Then the smile breaks through, and he begins shoveling food into his mouth at an alarming rate.

A waitress appears and takes my order. I kick my feet up onto the bench, lean against the wall, and watch him eat. The relief hasn't hit me yet. I know it will. I know in an hour, maybe three or four, maybe after I sleep, I'll be okay. I'll be back to normal.

Kind of.

But at the moment, my whole body is tense. My mind buzzes. I listen for the sound of cars, men, McKinnan changing his mind and sending guys to kill me.

I eat slowly when my food comes. The diner is empty. Just us and an elderly couple at the ledge. The lights are dim even though it's so dark outside. The waitress chats with the guy in the kitchen. When the couple leaves, they put on some music.

Thomas is quiet. The waitress fills his coffee cup four times before anyone else pulls into the gravel lot.

At the sound of the tires crunching across the ground, my hand automatically goes to the gun on my belt. Thomas—mid cutting up a piece of meat—flips the knife in his hand so the blade rests along his arm. Ready to slice someone open.

I flick my gaze between the window and the door, waiting for the vehicle to come into view or a person to walk into the diner. I frown as a mildly rusted 1987 Jeep Wrangler parks under the light next to our window. A very large man with flaming red hair and a purple-tinged Hawaiian shirt jumps down.

Thomas drops the knife and stands up.

I stay where I am, my hand still on the gun.

It's only when the man comes through the door and is a few yards away that I recognize his face from the picture Thomas showed me almost two days ago. It's Ben, his Australian. I pull my hand away from my gun and let out the breath I had been holding.

To anyone else, Ben would seem like a goliath. His Hawaiian shirt must be a double XL, and it still seems to be straining to cover his biceps. He is at least six feet tall, and without the smile on his face and the purple shirt he would look downright terrifying.

But he seems small as Thomas sweeps him into a bear hug—haha, *bear* hug.

The two men embrace for a moment, then Thomas turns to me with a broad smile. "Belle, meet Ben."

I hold out my hand, but Ben waves it aside and goes to pull me into a hug.

Thankfully, Thomas puts a hand on Ben's hairy tan forearm. "Cracked ribs."

Ben gives me a pained expression, takes my hand, and kisses my bruised knuckles.

"I've heard so much about you!" Ben grins as we sit back in the booth. "The woman who saved my Thomas's life. I owe you so much." He has a thick, broad Australian accent that pulls a smile to my lips.

I chuckle. "He saved my life as many times as I saved his. And *now* I owe him for helping me out with this fiasco."

Thomas waves his hand. "I was happy to help. You know that."

"Still, I'll be transferring the usual amount for your 'consultant' work." I wink.

"Honestly, Miss Belle." Ben puts a hand on the table and gazes at me. "I feel like I owe you. Without Thomas in my life, I'd be a wreck. He told me about what happened in Zambia. Without you, I wouldn't have *him*." His hand moves to cover Thomas's slightly larger one.

I already felt more at ease with my life choices after watching the village get back together. But this is just what I needed. Ben isn't inflating my ego, he isn't complimenting my looks or my skills. He is thanking me for doing what I do. For helping people in need. No matter the methods.

Thomas catches my eye, and I know he is thinking about our earlier conversation.

"All right," I smile at Ben, "if you really want to pay me back, you guys can give me a ride to the airport. I don't much want to drive the sixteen-wheeler through Bangkok traffic."

The taxi drops me off Monday afternoon, a few doors down from the Manor. I make a mental note never to ride my motorcycle to the airport when I'm going to be involved with anything dangerous. My attempt to ride home started and ended with me leaning over the frame of my bike. I clambered back off—my body furious with me for even trying—and promptly called a cab.

Now I get to pay another few days of parking until I can go pick my baby up.

Missa opens the front door as I come up the steps. I don't know how she does it. She is always at the door when I get home. How?

Her smile falters a bit as she takes in my bruises, the bullet graze on my forehead, and the ginger way I walk toward her. Blue eyes widen, eyebrows raise, and her head tilts in a motherly sort of way. "I thought you said you were fine?"

I grunt as my feet clear the last step. "I am fine."

She squints at me but stands aside as I walk into the Manor. I toss my backpack on the hall table and make my way to the kitchen. A plate of snickerdoodles sits in the middle of the large table. I pick up three and set them on a paper towel.

"You don't look fine."

Missa followed me into the kitchen and now stands across the table from me, her arms folded over her chest.

"I'm not dead. That means I'm fine," I grumble. I pour myself a glass of milk and lean against the counter, shoving a good three-quarters of a cookie in my mouth.

"Is that another bullet wound?" She points at my forehead.

I freeze with my mouth full of cinnamon goodness. "Maybe..." I mumble through the cookie crumbs.

She shakes her head and pulls a first aid box out of a cupboard. Some part of me—the part not currently occupied with sweets—realizes I haven't changed any of my bandages since before I spoke to McKinnan. Talk about an infection waiting to happen.

I probably should have done it on the plane. But I was busy being passed out.

I let Missa dress my forehead, then I carefully remove my shirt and sit down as she cleans the slice on my back. Her fingers slide over the rest of me, gently poking and prodding, feeling for breaks, bruises, and bullet holes.

Missa was going to be a doctor. Years ago. In another life.

She finds my cracked ribs when I flinch extra hard. She disappears for a moment, then comes back with a full ACE bandage to wrap around my torso and keep me from making it worse.

"This is what... six times you've been shot?"

"It's a graze."

"We aren't having this argument again," she snaps. "A graze means you got shot. End of story."

I roll my eyes. "Okay, then yes. That's six times I've been shot. And three times for you, and we've both been shot *at* about four dozen times. All things considered, I'd say we're doing rather well."

It's her turn for an eye roll. But it's followed by a look so full of concern that I immediately feel bad for joking around. If she came home in my condition, I'd be pretty damn upset.

I put my hand on hers. "I'm okay, Missa, really."

She sighs and shakes her head. "How'd it go with McKinnan and the mercenaries? And the village. You didn't really have time to keep me updated on everything that happened."

A bloody image flashes through my mind. My breath falters, my blood turning cold as it moves through my body.

I force a smile onto my face. "I'll tell you about it later. Once we get everything sorted out with Lacey."

Missa frowns.

I keep talking to stop her from asking me anything else. "I need to call Nicky. But I don't know what good it'll do. He's still not answering me."

"He might now. They recalled the bill. It didn't pass, and it's not coming up again while that piece of shit is in office."

"Oh! That reminds me." I glare at her. "Who the *fuck* gave my parents my cell number?"

She stifles a chuckle. "It wasn't me. Or anyone in the Manor. I mean, they did call about twenty times while you were gone. I wondered why they'd stopped."

I close my eyes and exhale in frustration. "It was probably Emily. Dammit."

It was a risk giving my number to my brother and sister, but I figured as fellow children they would understand my desire to *not* give my parents my cell phone number. Nicky might be mad, but at least he didn't sink that low.

"Give her a break. You know how your mom gets."

"Yeah." I roll my neck. For *some reason,* it's incredibly sore. "I'm gonna go call Nicky." I rub my face. There's also the matter of the new girl I apparently have to deal with. Missa filled me in during a layover, and while I can't be mad at Lacey, I definitely didn't plan on dealing with a new recruit while healing from cracked ribs and a bullet graze. "I need to talk to Lacey too. How long do you think I have before I need to get to Chicago?"

"The girl's with Erin. I'd say you can wait until next week. Might not want to make any offers with your face looking like that."

I give her a squinty glare.

She smiles. "Lacey's with Doc. I'll have her come see you when she gets home."

I nod and leave the room, taking my milk and cookies with me.

I change into comfy clothes when I get to my bedroom, then I plunk myself down on the crisp blue sheets on my bed, set my cookies next to me, and pull out my phone. I close my eyes, hoping Nicky will answer the call. Then I grind my teeth together, hoping I can think of something to say to explain things to him. Without—ya know—actually explaining things to him.

The phone rings once, twice, three times before I hear the telltale click. A wave of relief floods me when I hear my baby brother's voice.

"Hey, Ana."

"Nicky! I'm so glad you picked up. I've tried calling you about a hundred times."

"I know. I've uh... I've been a little too pissed to talk to you."

"Right..."

There is silence for a moment.

"Listen, Nicky I—"

"I got a call this morning," he interrupts.

"Okay..."

"From a friend of yours. Thomas?"

I freeze, then close my eyes and pinch the bridge of my nose. What did he *do*? I pull my knees up to my chest and groan. "What did he say?" Hesitation lines my voice.

"Uh, he said a couple things. He said you had something to do with the bill getting pulled. He also said he wouldn't be able to explain why properly. And neither would you."

I lick my lips and press my palm against my forehead. "Did you believe him?"

"Well, considering that he told me about it three hours before it hit the news, yeah... I believe him. Why didn't you just tell me that in the first place?"

There's no one to give an incredulous look to, so I look incredulously at my cookies. "Maybe because you didn't let me get two words in before you hung up and ghosted me for a week."

There is a significant pause on the other end of the phone. "Okay, good point. But still... What did you have to do with the bill getting pulled? I don't see how a travel writer has that much influence with the vice president."

I can't help the grin spreading across my face. "Like my friend said, little brother, I can't tell you that."

"Fine. Be all secretive. But I'll find out eventually."

"Yeah, sure. Hey, do you know what Emily did?"

His evil little laugh comes over the line. "I do. She gave Mom your number. I honestly told her not to, but you know how Mom gets. She probably threatened to stop paying for her college."

I shake my head. "I'm still mad about it."

He chuckles again. "Why am I not surprised?"

"This is nice. I've missed you."

"You too, Sis."

"Tell me how things are going. How's Ray?"

I pick up a cookie and munch on it while my little brother fills me in on Ray, their new Corgi, the music industry in New Orleans, and their lives in general. As I listen to him, happiness sneaks in, finding a home in my chest and lighting up my smile.

Chapter Thirty-One

Lacey

Do What Your Shrink Tells You

I glance at the clock on the wall. I don't mind visiting Doc, Miss Belle's on-call psychiatrist. But I prefer to speak to her because I want to, not because Miss Belle or Missa require it.

"That's a lot of guilt you're still carrying," Doc says.

I've spent the better part of a quarter hour telling her about my dreams.

"And shame," I mumble.

She nods. "But you *know* what you're feeling. That's half the battle."

"And the other half?"

"Getting to a point where you don't *feel* guilty or ashamed about the past. A lot of it comes from reflection. But I think in your case, you'll also need to face some aspects from that time that you may not want to face." She meets my gaze for a moment before switching gears. "Do you still blame yourself?"

"What's the difference between that and guilt?"

"You can hold onto the guilt while acknowledging that you aren't to blame for the situation."

I let that sit with me for a moment before responding. "No."

Doc nods. "How about for this most recent assignment? Do you feel any animosity toward yourself for taking the job?"

A frown tugs at the edges of my mouth. "I'm not sure what you mean. I took the assignment because they needed me to. The only thing I feel bad about is trying to come home early."

"You went above and beyond what was expected of you. Even with the pressure of seeing Nathan again... Did you consider saying no when they asked you?"

"None of the other girls could have gotten as close as I did."

"That's not what I asked."

I stifle my irritated sigh. I usually have more patience, am calmer, more able to let words slide over me. But Doc gets me riled up. She has since our first meeting four years ago. It makes sense, I suppose; it is her job. "Yes. I considered saying no. But how could I?"

She tilts her head.

Her shoulder length, brown-fading-to-blonde hair is parted on the side and curled into gentle waves. Her lavender shirt is a short sleeve top and doesn't cover the intricate flower tattoos scrawled down her right arm. Her voice has an upper-class east coast lilt to it, brisk and clear.

Doc is older than me, older than Miss Belle, I'm sure. She is one of the very few people outside the Manor who knows the entire scope of what we do. She has to. Every person who works for Miss Belle talks to Doc. I had six months of sessions, three a week, during my training year. Then one every two months for the next two years.

She's converted part of a townhouse, just off 71st Street on the Upper West Side, into her office space. A bay window looks out onto the street. The furniture is antique, soft beige fabric with a dark walnut wood finish. Decorative crystal bowls sit on the coffee table and her desk; they are consistently full of treats. At the moment, dried apricots and cashews.

She is easy to talk to. Like an older sister who doesn't judge you. That's why I answer her question honestly. I did consider saying no. And I know she won't think less of me because of it, even if I think less of myself.

"How could I?" I repeat. "After all Miss Belle and Missa have done for me?"

"Is that why you said yes? Because you feel like you owe them?"

I sit in silence for a moment. Was that why? Or was it because I knew the stakes? I knew the mission parameters when they asked me to take it. I was already well aware of what Nathan was capable of. "I don't think so."

She raises an eyebrow.

"That's part of it, or maybe it's more because I'm grateful to them than feeling like I owe them. But that's not the only reason I said yes. I knew what the job was, I... I knew there was a decent chance the slave factory existed. Especially if Nathan was involved. He always liked to cut costs."

"You knew him well."

I nod. She already knows. She knows how many times a month he came to see me. She knows he was one of the few who liked to talk before, and after. One of the few who was satisfied with simple, who didn't need to hurt me to feel good.

We sit quietly for a few minutes. This is a tactic therapists use. They wait for you to fill the empty space. People end up sharing more than they usually would.

It doesn't really work on me, and Doc breaks the silence first. "Did some part of you want to see him again? Nathan?"

I bite the inside of my cheek. My nose itches; my eyes are burning, stinging as tears start to form. "I don't know. I hope not. Why would I want to see him again? After... after everything that happened..."

Doc nods and puts a hand on my arm. "Because he was kind to you. Because of all the men who paid for you, he was the only one who treated you gently. It's something men like him do. They want you to feel like you owe them. They want to be your rescuer."

I sniff and mumble, "He was the one who called Miss Belle. It's because of him I got out of that house."

She leans back in her chair and gives me a hard look. "That just isn't true. He didn't save you. He used you. You don't owe him anything."

I nod and wipe the tears away.

Doc stands up and gets us each a glass of iced tea from the table by the window, then brings mine over and offers me the glass. "What about the girl?"

I take the tea and sip. A tang of mango flows across my tongue. "Delilah."

"Delilah." She stands by the window, watching me. "You weren't supposed to take her to Chicago. You were supposed to wait until you could talk to Miss Belle."

I nod.

"You brought her anyway. You paid for two first class tickets to Chicago and escorted her to the safehouse."

"I don't like flying coach."

She chuckles. "Me neither."

Another silence fills the space. But it's more comfortable this time.

"I couldn't... I couldn't leave her. Jacobson would have told her pimp what happened." I shake my head. "She'd have been hurt. Maybe worse."

"You were able to help her, so you did."

I mull that over. "Yeah."

"Do you think, in some way, that makes up for you not being able to save someone else?"

I go cold.

Doc moves back to the couch and sits down. She sets her tea on a crocheted coaster, picks up a few dried apricots, and leans back. "Let's talk about Amanda for a moment."

Miss Belle drops me off at the airport. It's Friday; she's been home for several days, but the effects of the trip to Thailand are still painfully apparent. She limps a little as she walks me through to security. A decent-sized scab on her forehead is drying out. Missa has been slapping her hand away from picking at it all week.

There are other injuries, ones we can't see. She flinches when people touch her back, and her eyes still scan the area no matter where she is. It's normal. After something like that, the violence, the danger... it takes more than a couple days to get back into the civilian routine.

She goes through security with me, the cheapest ticket available in her hand. She's not actually going to St Louis, but she wants to wait with me.

I'm grateful not to be alone.

We sit together at a little café near my gate. Miss Belle buys us drinks. I get an Americano. The caffeine will calm me down. My fingers are shaky as I take my little ceramic cup. She gets herself an herbal tea with lemon. A smart idea, as I'm pretty sure any caffeine would send her over the edge.

We nestle into a pair of comfy armchairs in the far corner of the lounge. There is silence for a few minutes, a strange phenomenon when sitting with Miss Belle.

I begin to relax when she sets down her tea and looks at me.

"I spoke to Doc."

I nod. Regular psychiatrists have a stronger confidentiality agreement. Doc doesn't tell her everything, but she has to make recommendations as to whether we are fit for field missions and such.

"I want to clear something up."

I raise an eyebrow. "What?"

"Nathan. I don't think we ever went over what happened when he called me. You made it very clear once we had you that you didn't want to talk about your time there. At least not outside of your sessions with Doc. You didn't want to see anyone or anything to remind you of that place. And we tried to respect those wishes as much as possible. Now I think it would have been better if we had discussed a few things."

I drop my gaze to the cup of almond-colored liquid in my lap.

"But, as we can't go back in time and talk, we'll talk now. Nathan called me after his last appointment with you in

Houston. But not for the reason you think. He had a falling out with the man running the house. Prices went up with no notice, and he didn't like having to pay extra to see you." She scowls. "He called me to see if I could find a girl who looked like you."

Her voice is sharp and cold. And though I know the anger behind her words isn't for me, I can't help the shudder that runs across my shoulders.

Disappointment, followed by anger at myself for being disappointed, clenches in my stomach. Next comes another bout of anger. Frustration that I was so foolish.

Something of my emotions, usually so well guarded, must flicker across my face because Miss Belle reaches out and puts her hand on my knee.

"You don't *owe* him anything. You never have. And I..." Her jaw clenches and she shakes her head, something close to grief flashing through her eyes. "I never should have asked you to go there. To be with him again."

She lets out a heavy sigh, and I put my hand on hers. "I said yes to the mission. I could have said no. That's something you've always made clear. We can *always* say no."

She shakes her head again, an angry look on her face. "No one ever does."

"Because we know what we're doing." My voice is stronger than usual. More defiant than I mean it to be. "We know what our work does. I know how many people we helped because I saw him again. Another girl wouldn't have had the access I had. I'm not saying I enjoyed it. Seeing Nathan again..." I sigh. "It brought up a lot. But I did my job, and I did it well. And because of that, and because of *you*, a lot of innocent people are still alive."

Miss Belle chuckles. "That's exactly what Missa and Thomas said. Maybe I should start listening to you guys."

They call for boarding group one, and I stand up. My fingers twitch. My mouth is suddenly dry.

Miss Belle stands also. She picks up my bag, takes my arm, and walks me to the line of people slowly forming in front of the boarding gate. "Stay as long as you need. Call me if anything goes wrong—or if you just want to call me. Take care of yourself. Okay?"

I nod.

She gives my chin a nudge with her knuckles. "You'll be all right, kid."

I meet her smile with one of my own. Miss Belle pulls me into a tight hug. The line moves forward, and she lets me go, watching as I scan my ticket and disappear down the walkway.

The flight is short compared to going to Tokyo. I've never been to Sacramento Airport before. It's nice. The baggage claim has luggage stacked to the ceiling in two pillars. I stare at them for a few minutes, picking out the older pieces, imagining where they've been. I don't usually check luggage. But I don't know how long I'll be here.

I want to go back to the Manor. But Miss Belle bought the ticket... and it's been so long.

Mr. Johnstone is waiting in the pickup lane. I was told to look out for his silver minivan. He jumps out of the driver seat with a big grin on his face. He's tall, with brown hair, wide ears, and small glasses. He shakes my hand, asks, "Is a hug okay?" waits for my nod, hugs me, and then puts my bag in the trunk.

The drive isn't terribly long. We speed through the valley's rolling hills. Everything is green at the moment. I've heard mixed reviews about California weather, but the spring is gorgeous. Finally, we exit the highway and roll along an almond-tree-lined road. Pink and white petals are beginning to fall, reminding me of the cherry blossoms back in Japan.

We pull up to the house. It's a two-story home with full windows and a large chimney sticking out of the top. A massive garden sprawls to the right, and an array of flowers circle the vegetable patches. To the left is the start of acres of orchards.

My heart is beating faster than it should. And why wouldn't it? It's been four years.

Mr. Johnstone parks beside a small red Mini Cooper. I open the door slowly. The urge to run springs into my legs. I fight it.

As we make our way toward the front door, it opens. Beatrice Johnstone steps out, her smile as wide as her husband's. Miss Belle does take after her mother—there is a mischievous quality to both their smiles. The dogs, two big fluffy beasts, push past her and run toward me. A quick word from their dad makes them turn and tackle him instead.

And there, behind Miss Belle's mom...

She's grown so much. Her dark hair is braided to the side. She has a brush of color on her eyelids, a touch of rouge on her lips. I lose my breath when she steps out of the house.

My heart breaks at the sight of Amanda. My baby sister. Oh God, what if she hates me? What if she is ashamed of me?

What if every fear I've tucked away since we escaped that place is real?

Her sneakers pound the wood as she comes down the steps. Tears are in my eyes before she reaches the ground. I swallow and fight the flood of emotion. I am frozen in place, breathing heavily and terrified.

But she smiles. A dazzling thing, bright and full of joy. She is running now, running toward me. And she throws her arms around my neck and squeezes the fear out of me. When did she get so tall?

"*Lacey!*" She dances back for a moment, her hazel eyes locked on my face. Then she comes back again and pulls me into a hug.

"Hey," I whisper, my voice hoarse. "I've missed you."

"It's been so long. I'm so glad to *see* you. Do you want to go for a walk?" She gestures toward the orchards.

I glance at Miss Belle's parents. "I should probably bring in my things."

Mr. Johnstone gives a wave of his hand. "Don't worry about it, I'll bring everything in for you. It'll be in the spare bedroom when you get back."

Beatrice grins and nods. The wrinkles on her face crease into laugh lines. "Head back soon, though, I've got dinner in the oven."

Amanda already has my hand in hers and is dragging me toward the trees.

"Thanks, Mom!" she shouts over her shoulder. Her bright eyes focus back on me. "I can't believe you're here. Mom said I probably wouldn't see you until graduation. I'm so glad you're *here*! You look amazing. I've read every one of Miss Belle's travel books. Which ones did you work on?"

She is talking so fast I can hardly catch every word. She is excited, but I can feel her nervousness. In the tremble of her voice and the sweat of her hand, still clenching mine as we march through the even rows of towering brown, green, and pink.

"*You* look amazing." I grin at her. "You've grown up so much."

"Yeah." Her smile falters for a split second. I'd have missed it if I wasn't watching her face. "I passed my driving test last week. I can't believe Mom and Dad bought me a car for my birthday. A *car*. It's the little red Mini in the driveway. Insanely sweet of them. I'll have to take you around town tomorrow."

"Definitely."

The pace has slowed a bit now that we are deeper in the trees. The ground is pretty even other than the occasional hole a squirrel scurries down. It's odd. I've never walked through orchards before. It is like being in an overly organized forest. The grass is a vibrant green, the trees are adorned with gnarled, rough, dark-brown bark. The branches jut out, this way and that, each turn sharper than the last. Even the petals, white in this particular set of trees, are unfamiliar so close up. They flutter down around us with each breeze. The scent is overpowering but beautiful.

"I'm... I'm glad you're happy here. I wasn't sure..." I break off, unsure of what to say.

"The Johnstones are great. I think they missed having someone else in the house. They really treat me like a daughter. It's like with Gran."

My heart twangs at this. This reference to the person we lost so long ago. The unspoken reminder that between Gran and the Johnstones (or Miss Belle), our lives were a living hell. The heavy weight in my stomach seems to grow.

"Good." I swallow. "Listen, Amanda, I'm..." I stop walking.

Her hand falls from mine. When she glances back at me, her eyes wide, her smile hesitant, I take a shuddering breath and bite my lip to keep myself from sobbing.

"I'm so sorry."

"Lacey..." Her eyebrows draw together in concern, and she shakes her head.

She looks so like she did as a child, worried Santa wouldn't find us in a new house... the memory is too much for me. The tears break through. My smooth, calm self shatters. Like the stone pounded one too many times by the sea. Before I can stop myself, uncontrollable sobs wrack my body. The only break in the wails comes from my urgent apologies.

"Shh." She steps toward me and reaches out a hand. "Don't, Lacey, don't cry. It's okay."

"It's not okay." I jerk away from her. "I should have gotten you out of that house. I should have... I should have..."

She vigorously shakes her head. "I know there was nothing you could do. Nothing either of us could do. I noticed, you know... after a while. I noticed the bruises, the strange men. I just didn't know what it meant. You know what he told me? When I asked about your bruises? He said if I told anyone, he would kill you. I may have been too young then, but I..." She stops, fist clenched. Fury burns in her eyes. "I've realized it over the past couple years. I get what you did for me."

"You were so little. I couldn't—" I can't keep talking. A fresh flood of tears cascades down my cheeks.

"You kept me safe, Lacey. You didn't let him—or anyone else—hurt me. I'm sorry I didn't..." It's her turn for tears. They come so suddenly that it startles me out of my own sobs.

"Amanda, what..."

"I'm sorry I didn't tell anyone," she mumbles into her hands. "I know that's why you didn't come to see me. I'm so sorry."

"No!" Horror guts me as I realize what she means. I grab her hands away from her face and pull her into my arms. "No, no, no, Amanda, that's not why. I couldn't... I couldn't deal with being reminded about what happened. It had nothing to do with you. You didn't do *anything* wrong. I wanted you to be safe. I wanted you to have a childhood, or at least, what was left of one. When Miss Belle offered up her parents to take you in I... I figured California was nice and far away from Texas. And at least I'd know you were in good hands."

"So you're not..." She sniffs and pulls away, watching my face. "Not mad at me?"

"No. If anything, I've been worried you would be mad at me. Ashamed of me. I'm ashamed of me. I should have done more to... to get us out."

She shakes her head, the tears vanishing as quickly as they came. My own tears still fall down my cheeks, but silently now, without the wracking sobs.

"I'm so sorry I didn't come see you sooner." I look down at the dirt, my heart aching. She thought I was mad, maybe hated her, this whole time. These four long years while I couldn't get past my own issues.

"It's okay." She wraps her arms around my shoulders. "I'm glad you aren't mad," she mumbles into my neck.

We stand there in silence for a few minutes, her holding me. Eventually, I reach my arms up and wrap them around her as well. Like I did when she was little, when she had a nightmare and needed me.

When we break apart, she is smiling.

"What?" I ask.

"I've got four years of stories to tell you." She laughs and grabs my hand. "And you've got to tell me all about your adventures working with Miss Belle."

I let out a half-snort, half-chuckle and nod. I wipe my face. Mascara comes away as I drag my fingers under my eyes. Amanda watches me with an expression of concern that reminds me of Gran.

"Are you okay?"

"Yeah." I grin at her. "I am now."

The fear that's been inside me, the terror that I ruined her life, it's gone. I don't think I even realized I'd been carrying it for four long years. I didn't want anything that reminded me of what I'd been through, but I also didn't want to face Amanda.

When Miss Belle offered up her parents to raise her, right after she and Missa got us away from that house, I eagerly agreed. She'd be far away. From me, and from *him*.

Now, as Amanda tells me about the colleges she's thinking of applying for next year, about the two best friends she has, the violin recital she had a month ago, the swim team she's trying out for in a week, the life she has made here, I know without any doubt that I made the right choice.

Who knows what would have happened if I'd tried harder to get us out of that house? But she's happy. And so am I. No amount of nightmares can change that.

I close my fingers around the small globe dangling from my neck. I picked it from a variety of items on my first birthday. A dollar bill, a book, a pair of my mom's heels, and this little blue orb, all lined up by my giggling mother, trying to explain the tradition to my father. I don't think he really ever got it. But she explained it to me about a hundred times. The dollar would mean I was destined for great wealth, the book, great wisdom, the shoes, apparently something about being a fashionista. But I chose the globe. I was destined to travel, explore, and experience the world around me. Or so my mom always said.

It certainly didn't happen the way either of us could ever have imagined... but I suppose she wasn't wrong.

I link my arm around Amanda's as she leads us back toward the house. I wonder what the Johnstones are making for dinner.

Chapter Thirty-Two

Miss Belle

The Ending, or Whatever

I take the long way home after dropping Lacey off at the airport. My forehead itches. I fight the urge to scratch it. Missa will know if I've been picking at my scab.

Spring has taken over New York during the past week. Every tree is in bloom, every flower humming with the hope that bees and butterflies will land on it.

I want to focus on the flowers. I want to focus on the fresh air, the light traffic, the business-free weekend in front of me. But each time relaxation approaches, my mind drifts into nightmares. I see their faces. Blood dripping from the bullet holes I put in their heads. I imagine their families, the lives I destroyed.

I shake my head and blink rapidly. Focus. Focus on *literally* anything else. It's bad enough I haven't slept all week. I don't need to be losing it on the drive home too.

I park and walk up to the Manor. A ripple of frustration goes through me at the sight of that stupid gray van parked across the street. It's time for a chat.

"Hey!" I shout as I walk over and bang on the back door. "Enough is enough. You guys have been out here for over a week with nothing to show for it. I'm getting real tired of you taking up valuable street parking."

Nothing happens.

I wait for a moment, then bang on the door again, harder this time. "I know you're in there. The fake plumber sticker is peeling off the side of this creeper van!"

The door opens and "Detective" McKinley glares out at me, hunched over and trying to use his bulk to hide the other two—significantly smaller and younger—men in the van.

"I have every right to be here, Miss Belle. If you didn't have something to hide, you wouldn't mind us staking out the place."

I heave a sigh, bite my tongue, and plant my hands on my hips. "First of all, that is just awful logic. I don't have to be breaking the law to be annoyed by your constant surveillance. And second, I'll be heading down to the precinct Monday morning to make sure you *do* have a right to be here. And let me tell you, if I find out this hasn't been cleared by your captain, I'll have your badge."

I leave him open-mouthed, gaping like a fish as I turn and walk back to the Manor. I don't glance back as I open the front door, close it behind me, and turn the lock with a satisfying click.

Missa is standing in the hallway, her arms crossed over her chest, and an expression I've come to associate with detention or a grounding on her face.

"Don't give me that look. McKinley deserved it. I'm going to deal with all this surveillance crap first thing Monday morning." I hang my purse on one of the hooks on the wall. "Well, second thing. As soon as we get back from Chicago."

"Thomas called."

I freeze for a split second, my arm still up in the air. I blink, swallow, and recover. I turn back to look at Missa. "Oh. Is everything okay?"

"I don't know." She unfolds her arms, and her blue eyes bore into me. "Why didn't you tell me about the Thai police?"

"I was going to, as soon as Lacey was gone. I just... I wanted to give it a couple days."

She nods slowly and the look on her face changes. She looks sad, concerned, maybe even a little scared.

"Listen, I did what I had to do." Even as the words leave my lips, I can hear how defensive I sound. Against my will, fury flares up inside me. My cheeks grow hot, my hands clench into fists, my stomach knots. "I don't need you and Thomas talking behind my back."

The concern slides off her face and is replaced with a severe glare. "That's not what this is, and you know it. He's worried about you. And so am I. This kind of thing takes a toll on someone. And from what he said, you didn't even discuss it with him before you pulled the trigger."

"I discussed it enough. We didn't have a choice. If I'd let them go, it would have put the entire village in danger." My voice rises.

"You killed four men in cold blood, Ana. Don't you think that's something you should talk about with someone? Doc, maybe?"

My hands are shaking now. I can't do this. I can't talk about this with Missa, and I sure as shit can't talk about it with Doc. I shake my head. My jaw is clenched, my breath coming in shallow, angry bursts. "I don't need to talk to anyone. I *did* what *needed* to be *done*. And I'd do it again. For some reason, you and Thomas can't get that through your heads. Maybe because I'm *always* the one who does the dirty work. You two don't have to deal with the choices *I* have to make."

I've hit a nerve. I can see it in the flash of anger that darkens her eyes, the tightening of her jaw, the slight flare of her nostrils.

Somehow, she keeps a steady voice, even as my own anger reaches a dangerous peak. "We need to talk about this."

I shake my head, my lips pressed together for fear that I might say something too far over the line. I turn away from her and stride up the stairs. When I reach my room, I slam the door shut behind me.

I can barely see. My vision is blurred with the unreasonable amount of blind rage inside me. I strip and go into the bathroom.

The water is cold as I step into the shower. The bandage on my back isn't supposed to get wet. I peel it off and toss it into the trash. Blood joins the water that swirls down the drain. The cold is so sharp it stings my skin. I turn into the downpour and let the freezing droplets pelt my face. The pain helps to drown out my anger.

Missa finds me on the couch. It's late, or early—I don't know at this point. It's dark. I'm in a ball, trying to breathe. Unable to stop my muscles from clenching. Unable to stop my mind from dragging up the images of the men I killed. The men I murdered.

She sits down and pulls me to her. I lie in her lap, tears finally forcing their way from my eyes. Shuddering sobs soon join them.

She strokes my hair as I weep into her leg. She hands me a pillow, and when the screams come, I muffle them in the brown fabric. When it's done, when my throat is sore, and my eyes are dry, she reapplies the bandage on my back. Then she lets me fall back into her arms.

"I didn't have a choice," I murmur. There is a pleading in my voice. I'm begging her to accept it. To tell me I did the right thing. To tell me it's okay.

"I know." I hear the tears in her voice as well. "You never do, Ana..."

She rocks me back and forth as I finally fade into sleep.

"You never do."

Acknowledgements

Lots of people to thank for this one, so let's dive in.

Tracey, the cover. Oh my god, the cover. Thank you so much for diving into the story and theme and creating something that pushed me so hard to get this out. You're an amazing friend and a fantastic writer.

Mom and Rachel, obviously you're both on the list; you always are. This book wouldn't have happened without you both. Neither would the next several. Thanks for everything, I love you both.

Hubby, you know why you're on the list. Time and support. Thank you so much for all the time you spend to give me the time to write. I love you so much.

There's a whole ton more: my writing girls, my llama ladies, my D&D group, the folks at the Y, my old publishing company, my family, and many more. Thank you all for the support, the time, and the love.

Where to Find More...

If you enjoyed Lacey Goes to Tokyo, please consider leaving a review!

Hungry for more? Well, usually I do an "Also By" page... but it's getting too long at this point. Head to chlyn.com to find my complete collection of works, sign up for my newsletter, and find out about upcoming in-person events.

Damen Goes to Peru is out now! Keep reading for a short excerpt.

Damen Goes to Peru
Damen

Guilt, shame, and that burning frustration which comes when you've made an irreparable mistake and nothing can fix it, roil in my stomach and chest. My palms are drenched with sweat.

I expect a vehicle. But Lydia doesn't take me toward the cars. Instead, we make for the front gate. Her boots, black leather that stop just below her knees and match the vest over her cream-colored shirt, click against the freshly pressed cobblestone.

"Where are you taking me?" Information. That's what Missa always says. When you are in a hopeless situation, get as much information as you can. The more you know, the more options you have.

"I don't want the Señor getting worked up over a worm like yourself. We are leaving the villa so as to not make a fuss."

Outside the wall of the villa, the world is dark. Stars twinkle in and out of sight, hidden by the rolling clouds. She takes us up the road, toward the bridge I crossed to get here. The gentle rumble of the river is the backdrop to our steps.

Halfway down the road, I have to do something. Lydia could be taking me anywhere. For any purpose. I'm not sticking around to find out.

I close my eyes in a long blink, send up a quick prayer, and spin.

I've cooperated long enough that the change in my behavior startles her. I swoop from her loosened fingers. Grab her wrist. Pull her arm behind her back and put her between me and the guards with the guns.

"Stop," I command. My chest heaves.

Lydia jerks, slashing backward with the blade still in her other hand. I block it, knocking her wrist hard enough that she releases the knife. It clatters to the ground.

In the same movement, she kicks back at my shin. Her heel makes contact and pain flares along my leg.

I swing. My fist connects with the edge of her jaw as she reaches for the fallen knife.

She rolls to the side as a shout breaks the night.

I glance up. The guards are watching Lydia, their guns pointed at me. I heave a breath, straighten, and brush my hair back with my hand.

"No." Lydia curls her lips into a twisted grin. "Don't tell him to stop." She holds up a hand to the guards, her gaze on me. "You want to do this, Damen? You want to test yourself against me?"

She looks down at the blade in her hand and tosses it away.

I shift my feet, tensing my core.

"It's been three years, little pup. Have you improved since our last round?"

I bring up my hands, balled into fists, and give her the smallest nod.

My focus is on this moment. This fight. This chance to distract her and the guards, slip down the side of the riverbank, and let the water disguise me and carry me to safety.

Still, the back of my mind wonders what Miss Belle would say about everything that has happened tonight. Her voice flashes through my head. *Hand up. Balls of your feet. Move. Keep moving. Don't be a target.*

I inhale through my nose as Lydia brings her hands up as well. She's got fourteen years on me. Fourteen years, a full decade of mercenary work, and an unhealthy worship-like love for the man I came here to kill.

I don't need to win. I just need to get her down long enough to sprint the twenty yards to the riverbank.